Through her marriage to Reggie Kray, Roberta Kray has a unique and authentic insight into London's East End. Roberta met Reggie in early 1996 and they married the following year; they were together until Reggie's death in 2000. Roberta is the author of many previous bestsellers including *No Mercy, Exposed, Survivor* and *Stolen*.

Also by Roberta Kray

The Debt
The Pact
The Lost
Strong Women
The Villain's Daughter
Broken Home
Nothing But Trouble
Bad Girl
Streetwise
No Mercy
Dangerous Promises
Exposed
Survivor
Deceived
Stolen
Betrayed
Double Crossed
Hunted
Cheated
Traitor

Non-fiction
Reg Kray: A Man Apart

ROBERTA
KRAY
PAYBACK

SPHERE

SPHERE

First published in Great Britain in 2025 by Sphere

1 3 5 7 9 10 8 6 4 2

Copyright © 2025 by Roberta Kray

A CIP catalogue record for this book
is available from the British Library.

ISBN 978-1-4087-3006-5

Typeset in Garamond by M Rules
Printed and bound in Great Britain by Clays Ltd, Elcograf S.p.A.

Papers used by Sphere are from well-managed forests
and other responsible sources.

Sphere
An imprint of
Little, Brown Book Group
Carmelite House
50 Victoria Embankment
London EC4Y 0DZ

The authorised representative
in the EEA is
Hachette Ireland
8 Castlecourt Centre
Dublin 15, D15 XTP3, Ireland
(email: info@hbgi.ie)

An Hachette UK Company
www.hachette.co.uk

www.littlebrown.co.uk

PAYBACK

PROLOGUE

It was a surprise, and everybody likes surprises, don't they? Well, the good ones anyway. Today was her birthday and although it was only late afternoon, she was already tipsy on lager and fizzy wine. Her laughter rang out in the chill October air. She stumbled forward, eager and excited. The car ride had been a short one, a blindfolded one for the last bit, and although they weren't that far from home she couldn't say exactly where they were.

'Keep walking,' she was told, and she happily obeyed.

'Where are we? I-I can hear something. Water? Is it water? I can feel the wind. It's cold here.'

'Keep walking.'

The ground had been soft and giving beneath her stilettos but now it changed to something firm and solid like wood. Her heels tapped against it. Her arms, held out in front of her, like in a game of blind man's buff, randomly searched the air for obstacles. 'Are we . . . are we nearly there?'

'A few more steps.'

'Where are we?'

1

'Almost there.'

She'd had other plans for this afternoon, but the phone call had changed all that. *You have to come*, the caller had said. *It's a big surprise.* She giggled, imagining all sorts in her head: fairy lights strung through the trees, a rug on the ground, a surprise party with a bottle of champagne. She was happy. She was twenty-five and without a care in the world. The bad stuff was behind her, the future stretching ahead like one great adventure.

'One more step.'

She was still smiling, still laughing, when she took that next step and encountered ... nothing. Thin air. For a moment she had no idea what was happening. God, what? She was hurtling through darkness like a bird falling out of the sky. There was only confusion, fear, panic, before the ice-cold shock of the water took her breath away.

Then she was under, going down, kicking out with her legs, frantically searching for the bottom. Not there. She clawed at her eyes to rip the blindfold off. She thrashed about with her arms, beating at the black water, trying to get to the surface. She couldn't swim. She'd never learned. Who needed to swim when they lived on an inner-city estate?

She would be saved. She was sure of it. All she had to do was hold on, push up, try and stay afloat, stay calm, until she was pulled to safety. Or a rope was thrown. Or a yell for help brought other people running. An accident. That's all it was. A terrible mistake. A surprise that had gone horribly wrong. She made it to the surface, to a different kind of darkness, and gulped in oxygen. Gulped in river water too, briny and metallic. Her eyes desperately scanned the bank. There they were, standing, watching, a thin silhouette in the darkness. Not moving. Not doing *anything*.

What?

Horror rolled through her. Her head went under again, stifling her cries. The current began to carry her away. Her birthday dress swirled like seaweed. She struggled in vain as the water sucked at her, pulling her back down into its depths. She prayed to God to help her. She wanted her mum.

1

It was by pure chance that Julia bumped into him on the Strand, and she would have walked right past if he hadn't stopped, done a double take, and said, 'Julia Reeve!'

She gave a vague smile while she waited for her brain to roll through its face-recognition process and come up with a name. Although he did look familiar, she couldn't quite place him. A client? A business associate? A neighbour? A friend of a friend?

'Tom Finch,' he said, his face dropping a little.

'Of course!' she said. 'Tom. I'm so sorry. It's been such a long time.' She hadn't seen him since she was fourteen. They had been at school together and lived on the same estate in Kellston, until her mother had decided they should leave London. Tom looked the same and yet different, still tall and gangly, still with that earnest expression in his eyes, but without the spots. 'God, how are you?'

'Not too bad, considering. Still trying to come to terms with it all, to be honest.'

Julia looked at him, confused. 'Come to terms with it?'

'About Angel,' he said.

'What about her?'

Tom's hand flew up and briefly raked through his floppy brown hair. He shifted from one foot to the other, his eyes refusing to meet hers. 'Oh, shit. You don't know? You haven't heard?'

Julia felt a tremor run through her. She had a bad feeling, a terrible feeling, and wanted to cover her ears, to not hear what was coming next. Angela Glover – known to everyone as Angel – had been her best friend back in the day. They had been inseparable, devoted, sharers of each other's secrets. And now . . . 'No, I haven't heard. What is it? What's happened?'

'Angel's dead. She died a month ago.'

Julia shook her head. Even though she'd suspected what he was going to say, she still couldn't accept it. 'She can't be. How? How did it happen?'

'She drowned in the River Lea.'

'What?'

'On her birthday. It looks like it was suicide, or some kind of awful accident. They didn't find her body for three days.' Tom paused and then said, 'Sorry, I thought you'd know. I thought that was why you were here, that you'd come back for the funeral.'

'No, I work here now. I've just started a new job.' This wasn't strictly true – she'd been in London for the past nine months – but she felt guilty and ashamed for not getting in touch with Angel. Damn it! Why hadn't she? Well, she knew the answer to that but didn't want to dwell on it right at this minute. 'They're only just having the funeral?'

'Post-mortem and stuff. It's on Monday, twelve o'clock at St James's, the church by the cemetery. You should come. Renee will be pleased to see you.'

6

When Julia thought of Renee, of what she must be going through, her heart turned over. Renee had been like a second mum to her, the kind of mum she'd have preferred if she was being honest – reliable, attentive, and not forever rushing off to the next political rally or peace protest or feminist work group. 'Monday?' Only three days away. 'I'm not sure I'll be able to get the time off, but I'll try. How is Renee doing?'

'Oh, you know,' Tom said, shrugging.

There was a brief, awkward silence. Under normal circumstances they would have asked the usual questions about jobs and homes and families, but Angel's death made all that seem mundane and irrelevant.

'It must be awful for her,' Julia said eventually.

Tom nodded and started to edge away. 'Well, maybe I'll see you on Monday.'

'Yes,' Julia said. 'Of course. I'll try my best.'

They parted then, each going in different directions. As Julia headed back to the office she couldn't stop thinking about Angel. Suicide? Why would she take her own life? Especially when she had a son to take care of. And then she remembered that she hadn't even asked about Jack. He would be eight now. Poor kid. Angel had got pregnant at sixteen, had him at seventeen, and been a single parent ever since so far as she knew. Although she hadn't raised him on her own; Renee had been there to help. Renee was the sort who was always there. She *should* go to the funeral.

Julia went down Southampton Street, past the shops which for once she didn't stop to look in, through the dark blue door and up the stairs to the office. There was the usual Friday-afternoon rush with everyone trying to tie up loose ends before the weekend. People on phones, people wading through piles of paper. She walked to the far corner, went through the door, took the ham salad sandwich out of her bag, and laid it on a serviette on her desk.

She had thought when she'd got the job with Harley Jenks – a public relations company within spitting distance of Covent Garden piazza – that she'd be entering a glamorous world of endless possibilities. But nothing could have been further from the truth. She was on the lowest possible rung of the ladder and as such had been landed with all the clients that no one else wanted – the awkward ones, the stupid ones, the boring ones and the ones who were more trouble than they were worth.

She glanced over at Cressida, her immediate boss, and said, 'Do you think I could book Monday off? I've got a funeral to go to. I know it's short notice, but I've only just heard.'

'Oh, someone close?'

'An old school friend.'

'Oh,' Cressida said again. 'Sorry to hear it. Yes, I'm sure that'll be fine.'

Somehow Cressida made it sound like she wasn't very sorry at all. And no sooner were the words out of her mouth than she frowned and said, 'Haven't you got that dreadful Apostle man coming in on Monday?'

'I can reschedule.'

'Make sure you don't forget.'

Which, in translation, meant that she didn't want to get landed with him. Ivor Apostle was a new client, a businessman who owned a security firm, pubs, several wine bars and a couple of nightclubs. There were rumours that he moved in criminal circles, that he didn't always operate within the law, and it was these sorts of rumours that he preferred to keep out of the press. 'I won't forget. Is he really that dreadful?'

'Thinks he's God's gift by all accounts, but you can manage him. He likes a pretty face, so use it to your advantage. You'll be okay. Just keep him sweet and tell him whatever he wants to hear.'

Cressida Hale was what Julia's mother, Ellie, would call hard-bitten – ruthlessly ambitious and happy to play the men at their own game. She was a curvy redhead, knocking on forty, who dressed in power suits with shoulder pads, and worshipped Mrs Thatcher. Ellie wouldn't have approved of her. Ellie believed in equality, but not at the price of women behaving like men. It should be the other way round she always said, but in reality the chances of that were slim.

'Why was he taken on if he's that dreadful?' Julia asked.

Cressida rubbed the thumb and fingers of her right hand together. 'Money, hon. Harley can smell it a mile away. If Apostle's prepared to pay, then Harley's happy to take his cash.'

Except, of course, he wouldn't be the one dealing with him, Julia thought. She flicked back her long dark hair, rolled her hazel eyes and said, 'Can't wait to meet the guy. He sounds a dream.'

Cressida gave a snort. 'You can handle him. Just flatter his ego and make him feel important.'

Julia nibbled a corner of her sandwich while Cressida took out her compact, viewed her face in the mirror, adjusted her hair and put on fresh lipstick. 'Okay, I'm off,' she said, rising to her feet. 'If anyone calls, I'm in a meeting for the rest of the afternoon.'

Cressida's meetings usually took place in restaurants and bars, and always involved a lot of alcohol. She could drink any man under the table. Her monthly expense account was eye-watering, but no one ever challenged it. Cressida got results, was loved by her clients, and brought in a massive amount of business for the company.

Julia wanted to be Cressida. She wanted to be rich and successful, respected and admired. She wanted to be as confident as she was. Alone in the office, she took another bite of her sandwich. Through the plate-glass window, she could see what was left of the rest of the staff, most of them ex-public school-boys with a sense of entitlement as big as their salaries. To rise to the top in a business like this was difficult enough, but when you were a woman, it was ten times harder. The eighties were drawing to a close, and although the prime minister was female, the world was still run by men.

Angel was dead.

Julia felt the shock of it run through her again. The sandwich stuck in her throat. She drank some water, swallowing hard. Already she was dreading Monday. All the old faces reviving memories she'd rather forget. She had turned her back on the past, left it all behind, or at least she'd thought she had.

After it had happened – *it* still clung to her conscience like a bad smell – her mother had decided it was time to get out of London. A fresh start with some Suffolk country air. An old rambling house with twisting corridors, uneven floors and rooms that always smelled of damp. A new communal life with Ellie's lentil-eating, yoga-practising, mainly lesbian friends. But Julia hadn't kicked up a fuss. Anything had been better than staying here.

'I'll write,' she'd promised Angel. The Glovers didn't have a phone then. One more expense they could do without. 'You can come and see me. Or I'll come here.'

But the letters had dwindled and only one visit had ever taken place, a few months after Angel had given birth to Jack. Julia had cooed over the baby, said how lucky Angel was, but secretly she'd been horrified. She had never been maternal and couldn't imagine being tied down to a baby at seventeen, her future dictated by a red-faced howling bundle who would probably grow up to resent and dislike her. Accordingly, the little white pill went into her mouth every morning, regular as clockwork.

When she'd taken the job here, she'd always known there was a chance of bumping into someone from the past, but the more time had passed the less likely it seemed to happen. Until today. Until Tom Finch had appeared from nowhere. If she'd had any sense, she'd have stayed well clear of London. Or had she been tempting providence, pushing her luck as far as she could, seeing if karma would eventually catch up with her?

The guilt she felt was wound around her innards, always there no matter how hard she tried to ignore it. Like a parasitic worm sucking the joy out of her life. That was why she hadn't contacted Angel. That was why she'd kept her distance. Although the external scars had healed, Angel had been left with a different kind of damage: something irreversible had happened to her brain, leaving gaps in her memory, the occasional stutter when she spoke and lapses in concentration. She would repeat herself, forgetting what she'd said, and stare into the middle distance as if some entity, invisible to everyone else, was distracting her attention.

Angel was dead.

Julia wasn't responsible for that. And yet she wondered if in some way she was, that what had happened when they were fourteen had cast such a terrible shadow over Angel's life that she had always been fated to die young. Could that be true? She pulled the crust off her sandwich and grimaced. A guilty conscience was a terrible thing.

Perhaps she wouldn't go to the funeral. It would be too hard, too emotional, too upsetting. She didn't *have* to. No one was holding a gun to her head. And booking the time off didn't count as a commitment. 'I'll try my best,' is what she'd told Tom. He would just presume that work had got in the way.

But she knew that it would be cowardly not to go. Some things had to be faced up to, no matter how daunting they were. It was only an hour out of her life. She could manage that, couldn't she? And she owed it to Angel to say a final goodbye.

2

Julia had changed her mind a hundred times over the weekend, leaning one way and then the other, leaving it until the last minute on Monday morning to get dressed in a black suit, black polo-neck jumper and boots. She put her hair up and then let it down again. She stared at her reflection, seeing the gawky fourteen-year-old girl clearly visible beneath the make-up and smart clothes. When she had first come back to London, she had thought of herself as a different person, cool and mature, but none of that was evident now.

It's only an hour, she told herself for the umpteenth time.

She picked up her bag and left.

As the bus swayed through the Camden streets, she gazed out of the window at the place that had become her home over the past nine months. She liked its mixture of scruffy and smart – she lived in the scruffier part, but it didn't take that long to walk to Regent's Park where the surrounding houses were grand and imposing and carried the distinctive smell of money. She would like to own one of those in the future.

A *long* way in the future, she thought. For now, her wages barely covered her rent and bills, with whatever was left going on clothes. It was important to dress the part for her job, to always look smart and stylish, to give the impression of success even if it was only an illusion. It was easier for men – God, what wasn't easier? – who only needed a couple of suits, a decent pair of shoes and half-a-dozen shirts and ties.

Julia's mother had tried to instil in her the notion that appearances didn't matter, that it was what was inside a person that was important – kindness and compassion – but that hardly cut it in the ruthless business of PR. There it was dog eat dog, the survival of the fittest. Why was she even thinking about this stuff? Because she didn't want to think about the funeral.

The closer the bus got to the East End, the more jittery she became. She knew that she could still change her mind. She didn't *have* to get off at Kellston station; she could take the coward's way out and stay aboard or get off early and catch another bus back to Camden. But she wasn't going to do that. She was going to do the right thing, the decent thing, and see it through.

She had thought a lot about Angel over the weekend, trying to remember the good times, that easy, comfortable friendship that had started in infant school and continued into their teens. They had hardly ever argued and had only ever fallen out once in any serious way. Their lives had been intertwined and they had told each other everything. It was hard to imagine having such a friendship again. The girls she hung out with now were more drinking partners than anything else, all people she had met through work: girls she liked well enough but who she would never bare her soul to.

How had she not heard about Angel's death earlier? The truth was that she hardly ever read a newspaper, and certainly not from cover to cover. She hardly ever watched the news on

TV either, knowing that the state of mankind with all its wars and suffering and casual violence would only depress her. Had it even been reported? Perhaps, at first, Angel had simply been a missing girl, one of many who walked out of their homes every day, and by the time her body was found it had been put down as suicide or an accident. Just another statistic, just another girl who never came home.

It was twenty to twelve when she got to the station. From here it was only a five-minute walk to the church. In order to avoid the conversations she didn't want to have, she intended to get there exactly on time, and so she took the long way round, strolling slowly through the streets looking out for any changes that might have occurred in her absence. The café was still there, the pub, the florist and the newsagent. In fact, nothing much had altered in the years she'd been away. In the distance she could see the three tall towers of the Mansfield estate. Kellston remained as grey and run-down as it had always been.

Julia's heart sank as she approached St James's. It was a minute to twelve and despite her dawdling a small group was still huddled in the doorway. Among them she recognised Angel's mum, Renee, looking much thinner and older than when they'd last met. She'd been hoping that she could slip in unnoticed as the service started but that clearly wasn't going to happen now. Any chance of beating a hasty retreat was extinguished too as everyone turned to stare at her.

Julia went straight up to Renee and said, 'I'm so sorry about Angel.'

'Thank you for coming, love. It's good to see you again.'

Julia thought she seemed dazed, not quite with it, her eyes blank and dull. Perhaps the doctor had given her something. 'I still can't believe she's gone. It doesn't feel real.'

Renee turned to the others and said, 'You go in now. I'll

only be a minute.' As soon as they were out of earshot, her eyes suddenly brightened. She gripped Julia's arm and said in a fierce whisper, 'I have to talk to you. After the funeral. We're going to the Fox. You'll come, won't you?'

'Of course,' Julia said, unable to refuse. 'What do you—'

But before she could even finish asking what it was about, Renee had hurried into the church. Julia followed her, bemused by the request. What on earth did Renee want? Something she hadn't wanted the others to know about, that was for sure. It made her feel uneasy, as if demands were going to be put on her, as if Renee was about to suck her into something she had no desire to be sucked into. Or was it about the past? Maybe Renee was about to confront her about it.

Julia felt her insides clench.

The church was surprisingly full, but it was impossible to know whether that was down to Angel's popularity or the manner of her death. The story had probably been in the local paper and publicity always attracted people. Her eyes swept the congregation but most of the mourners were strangers to her. Renee went down to the front, close to where the coffin was. It gave Julia a start seeing the coffin there, covered in flowers.

Angel was dead.

It was hard to think of her body in that wooden box, her life snuffed out, her future a blank. The pungent smell of lilies filled the church.

Tom Finch beckoned from a pew three rows from the front, but Julia shook her head, preferring to squeeze in near the back. He was sitting with the old crowd, the three others who had made up their gang of six: Lindsay March, Pauline Archer and Frankie Hays. Lindsay and Frankie smiled, but not Pauline. This didn't come as any great surprise. Pauline had never liked her; she had been one of those predatory girls, always trying to get between her and Angel, to steal Julia's place as Angel's best friend.

As the funeral began, Julia found her mind drifting back to those school days. There had been the popular kids, the swots, the sporty ones, the arty ones and the geeks. So where had the six of them fitted in? They had been the odds and sods, she supposed, the leftovers, the ones who didn't belong anywhere else. But despite their disparities, they had been a solid little band, sticking together through thick and thin. Were they all still living in Kellston, or had they come back especially for the funeral?

The mourners were on their feet and halfway through 'Abide with Me' when Julia became aware of someone's eyes on her. She glanced sideways across the aisle and met the gaze of a tall, dark-haired man in his thirties. He was staring at her so intently that she wondered if she knew him. But nothing about his face was familiar. And it wasn't the sort of face you'd forget in a hurry – sharp and angular with high cheekbones and startlingly blue eyes. When he realised that she'd noticed, he quickly looked away.

The hymn came to an end and everyone sat down. She shot another quick sidelong glance at the man but now he was staring straight ahead with what seemed like a forced determination to not be caught in the act of looking at her again. It hadn't been a lascivious look but something more inquiring, as if he was trying to place her, to make sense of her connection to Angel.

Julia listened to the priest talking about how much Angel had been loved and how much she'd be missed. She found herself thinking about what Tom Finch had told her, that she had died through suicide or an accident. What was she even doing alone by the river? Would she really have killed herself? That Angel could have been so unhappy filled her with a sudden grief. She would never have thought of Angel as the type to take her own life, but then she'd had no contact with her for years. People changed; things changed them.

And what about Jack? Julia strained her neck to peer towards the front. There was no sign of a boy. Perhaps Renee had decided that it would be too upsetting for him. She had never found out who Jack's father was. Angel had refused to say. 'He's not important,' was all she'd ever got out of her. 'He's not on the scene anymore.' But that had been then, not now. Men, like bad pennies, had a habit of turning up again.

Julia had remembered Angel's birthday on 14 October, had even considered getting in touch or sending a card. But in the end, she'd done neither. Regret swept over her. If only she'd reached out, made the effort, she might have been able to make a difference. Guilt raised its ugly head again. But she knew that she was giving her own influence too much importance, that they had been too far apart by then, that the old closeness had gone and couldn't have been repaired overnight.

Her gaze returned to her erstwhile friends. Lindsay was dabbing at her eyes with a crumpled piece of tissue. Frankie put an arm around her shoulder, and she leaned in against him. Julia caught a brief glimpse of Pauline's hands gripping the pew in front, her knuckles white against the black cuffs of her jacket. Tom sat very straight, his body rigid, as if it was taking every last effort of will to maintain his composure.

Eventually the service came to an end and the coffin was carried out, placed in the hearse and taken the short distance to Kellston cemetery. Here the priest intoned the burial rites while everyone shivered. She stayed at the back, watching and listening, her head bowed partly out of respect and partly to shield her face from the chill winter wind. She noticed that the tall, dark-haired man stood back too, even further away than her, as if to distance himself from the proceedings, to not intrude perhaps where he wasn't wanted. That made her even more curious about him.

When the holy words had been said and the soil had been thrown – landing with a dull thud on the coffin – the mourners began to drift away in twos and threes, leaving Renee to spend some final moments alone. Tom broke off from the others and came over to her.

'Nice service,' he said. 'I wasn't sure if you'd make it. Are you coming to the Fox? We're going for a few drinks.'

Julia was tempted to turn down the offer, to get on a bus and go home, but she'd already promised Renee that she'd be there. 'Sure. Why not?' She paused and then added, 'Do you really think it was suicide? *Was* she depressed?'

Tom shrugged. 'Hard to say. You never really know what's going on inside someone else's head.'

'But she seemed all right?'

'As all right as Angel ever was.'

Julia took a few seconds to absorb this. 'If it was an accident, what was she even doing by the river?'

'I've no idea.'

'Did she often go there?'

'Not that I know of.'

Julia was aware of asking too many questions but couldn't stop herself. 'Had you seen her before she . . . I mean, that day. Had you seen her that day?'

'We'd arranged to meet in the pub in the evening, but she never showed up.'

'You must have been worried.'

'Not really, not right away. Angel wasn't always dependable. She'd make arrangements and then forget about them.'

'But not on her birthday, surely. You don't forget a thing like that.'

19

Tom dug a heel into the hard earth, his eyes fixed on the ground. 'I suppose we just figured she'd got waylaid somewhere. We're often in the Fox on a Saturday night, so it wasn't as if she was putting us out in any major way. It wasn't until the next day when Renee started ringing round that we knew something was wrong.'

Despite his explanation, Julia still found it odd that none of them had been concerned about her. But what did *she* know? She hadn't been here. If Angel had made a habit of being unreliable, then maybe it was understandable.

They had begun to walk along the path, and she nodded towards the tall, dark man in front of them, lowering her voice as she spoke. 'Do you know who that bloke is? He gave me a few funny looks in the church.'

'You've lost your nose,' Tom said. 'You wouldn't have had to ask ten years ago. You'd have sniffed him out from a hundred yards.'

'Huh?'

'The law,' he said softly. 'That's DI Michael Vyse. He's in charge of the investigation into Angel's death.'

It was true that she'd have clocked him as a cop back when she was a teenager. They'd known even the plain-clothes officers then, and not just from the way they'd looked and acted. It had been like a sixth sense, an instinct, and a necessary one if you'd wanted to stay out of trouble. Not that they were ever major rule breakers, but the cops had always liked throwing their weight around.

'And what has he found out in this investigation of his?'

'Not much,' Tom said.

'So why is he here?'

'To pay his respects, I suppose. And the rest.'

'The rest?'

Tom pulled a face. 'A spot of mild intimidation just in case one of us has a guilty conscience.'

'Do you think anyone has?'

Tom shot her a look, his forehead creasing into a frown. 'Why would any of us want to hurt Angel?'

'I didn't mean you,' Julia said quickly, sensing that she'd offended him. 'Or the others. I meant if there was anyone she was seeing, or someone she'd fallen out with. Did she have a boyfriend?'

'No one that she told me about, but that doesn't mean there wasn't someone.'

'She wouldn't have told you?'

Tom sighed into the cold air, his breath emerging as a wispy cloud. 'We didn't really talk about that kind of stuff. She might have told the girls, but they say she didn't mention anyone.'

Julia was staring at the back of the police inspector's head where the dark line of his hair met the creamy paleness of his neck. He was walking quickly, maybe towards the Fox. 'What's he like then, Michael Vyse?'

'A bit of a shit, to be honest. I'd steer clear if I was you. He had us all down the station for hours, going over and over what happened that Saturday. Apparently, being in the pub surrounded by a hundred other people wasn't a good enough alibi. He's the sort of cop who isn't much bothered by the actual law. I'm sure he'd love to pin it on one of us, but he's not having much luck so far.'

Julia stopped in her tracks. 'He thinks it might have been murder then?'

'Hard to know what he thinks. Maybe he just enjoys giving people a hard time.'

Julia had no idea how much truth there was in that. And if Angel had been murdered then there was still a killer on the loose. Weren't most people killed by someone they knew?

21

3

Julia had never been in the Fox before and was surprised by how warm and welcoming it was with its log fire and wood-panelled walls. She rubbed her frozen hands together trying to get the circulation back in them as she followed Tom through to the area at the back that had been set aside for the wake. There was a long trestle table there with sandwiches and sausage rolls, crisps, a few boxes of wine, some spirits, mixers and a keg of beer.

Already the pub was filling up, but the others had got there early enough to nab one of the booths. As Tom got chatting to some bloke she didn't know, Julia helped herself to a glass of red – she needed it – then went over and sat down beside Lindsay. She had the feeling that the three of them had been talking about something they didn't want her to hear because they instantly went quiet and there was an awkward silence.

Frankie was the one to break it, leaning across to pat her on the arm and say, 'Hey, good to see you again, Julia. You're looking well. What have you been up to?'

Julia gave them the same version that she'd given Tom, that

she'd just started a new job in London, rented a flat and that everything was pretty hectic. 'I wouldn't even have known about Angel if I hadn't bumped into Tom. It's all so terrible, isn't it?'

A murmur went round the table. There was a shaking of heads, a general agreement that it was all terrible.

'It must be what, ten years since you last lived here?' Frankie said. 'No, eleven. Christ, where does all the time go? One minute we're lurking behind the bicycle sheds having a sneaky fag and the next we're all grown up and holding down jobs and getting married and having kids. Crazy, isn't it?'

Of them all, Frankie had always been the most extroverted, the most voluble, not to mention the best looking, with his smooth caramel skin and chestnut eyes. He was small, slim and lithe, and had never gone through that spotty adolescent stage, but had morphed instead from pre-pubescent boy to teenager with what had seemed like effortless grace. Now, in his mid-twenties, he had the feline elegance of a dancer.

'I'm getting married,' Lindsay said, flashing her left hand which had a diamond engagement ring on the third finger. 'But not until next summer. His name's Mark, Mark Grey.'

'Congratulations,' Julia said. 'That's fantastic.'

'And Frankie's already tied the knot. He's got two kids, a boy and a girl.'

'You've been busy,' Julia said.

Frankie grinned, as proud of the achievement as if he'd given birth himself. 'Four and three. They're a handful but they're worth it. Are you with anyone, Julia? Any kids?'

Julia shook her head. She was already aware of feeling adrift from these people who had once been her friends. For them the future was all about family and parenthood, and settling down, never straying far from what they knew. Her last long-term relationship had been in Suffolk with a charming man called

Alex who had cheated on her once too often. It had been one of the reasons she'd decided to leave. 'So, are you all still living on the Mansfield?'

'What's wrong with the Mansfield?' Pauline said sharply.

'I didn't say anything was wrong with it.'

Pauline's wide, pink-cheeked face had taken on an angry look, her grey eyes narrowing into slits. 'It sounded like it to me.'

'Then you can't have been listening properly.'

'I don't even know what you're doing here. It's not as though you've had any contact with Angel for years.'

'Don't be like that,' Tom said, arriving just in time to hear the comment. 'She's got as much right to be here as any of us.'

Pauline wrinkled her nose. 'I was just saying. I'm allowed to say, aren't I?'

Tom slid in beside Julia and placed his pint on the table. 'We're all still friends, no matter how long it's been.'

'I hope so,' Julia said, without any genuine feeling. Tom had always been the peacemaker, the calm one, the one who loathed conflict. The faint waft of a lemony aftershave drifted into her nostrils. She took a gulp of wine and looked around for Renee but couldn't see her. She did, however, spot DI Vyse standing at the bar. He was keeping his distance again, but his gaze roamed over the back room, stopping every now and again to study a face or a gesture.

'Don't mind her,' Lindsay said. 'She's just upset.'

Julia turned her attention back to the table. She smiled at Lindsay, nodding to imply that she understood. But Pauline had always been the same, always looking for an opportunity to stick the knife in. If this hadn't been Angel's wake she'd have called her out on it, but it wasn't the time or the place.

'How's Jack doing?' Julia asked. 'I didn't see him at the funeral.'

'Who?' Lindsay said. 'I don't think I know a Jack. Was he at school with us?'

Julia stared at her, bemused. 'Angel's Jack. Her son. Isn't he about eight now?'

'Angel didn't have a son. She couldn't have kids.'

Everyone was looking at Julia now, like she was nuts. She took another gulp of wine. 'What? I don't understand. I came to see her a few years after I left, and she had a baby. She said he was hers. She said his name was Jack.'

'She was having you on,' Pauline said with glee in her voice. 'That must have been Larry, her cousin's boy. She used to babysit him.'

'Why would she do that? Lie about it, I mean?'

Pauline shrugged. 'For a laugh. To see your face, probably.'

'I don't get what's funny about it.'

Pauline smirked.

Julia thought back to that summer of 1981 when she had turned up unannounced at Carlton House, the block on the Mansfield where they had both grown up, to find Angel holding a baby. 'That's just weird.'

'Angel wasn't weird,' Pauline snapped. 'Don't call her that.'

'I didn't mean *she* was weird. It was just a weird thing to do. Why didn't she tell me the baby wasn't hers?'

But no one seemed to have an answer to that. Frankie shifted uncomfortably in his seat and then abruptly stood up. 'We should get some food before it all runs out. I'm starving.'

'You lot go,' Lindsay said, 'and I'll stay here with Julia, so we don't lose the table. Bring us back some sandwiches, yeah, and a couple of glasses of wine.'

Julia leaned back against the booth, watching the three of them push their way through the crowd. She felt confused, mortified by the knowledge that Angel had lied to her. And for what? Some kind of strange joke. It didn't make any sense.

As soon as the others were out of earshot Lindsay pushed back a strand of light brown hair, sighed and said, 'Angel was devastated that she couldn't have kids. Maybe she just wanted to pretend for a while. I'm sure she didn't mean anything by it.'

Julia thought back to that day, to how she'd cooed over the baby, and debated as to whether the pretence had simply gone too far, and Angel had felt unable to backtrack. But friends didn't make up stories like that. What was the point of it? To make her jealous? But Julia had never shown any interest in having children, and envy had been the last thing she'd been feeling. 'Why couldn't she have kids? Was it anything to do with . . . you know, the accident?'

'I don't think so. It might have been. I'm not sure.' Lindsay hesitated and then said, 'She used to make stuff up sometimes, about boyfriends and jobs and . . . well, all sorts of things. It was like she felt some kind of compulsion to make her life appear more interesting. So it wasn't just you. She did the same to all of us.'

And Julia remembered the letters she'd received, always full of news and gossip and the fun things Angel had been doing and wondered now if any of it had been true. Her own letters couldn't have provoked any sense of missing out, compiled as they had been of numerous complaints about the cold and the damp and living in a house full of hippy women. Julia had never mentioned new friends, although she had made some, not wanting Angel to think that she'd replaced her in any way.

'She never used to be like that,' Julia said.

Lindsay gazed into the middle distance and said, 'We should have realised how unhappy she was. We all feel bad about it.'

Julia didn't know what to say to that and so she said nothing.

26

She noticed Renee heading for the toilets and decided to get their talk over and done with. Once that was done, she could get away from here, go home and draw a line under it all. 'I need the loo. I won't be long.'

Suspecting it would be busy inside, Julia waited outside the ladies until Renee appeared again. The corridor was full of mourners going to and fro, a stream of swirling black like some strange funereal murmuration. She vaguely recognised a few faces now but none she could put a name to. She looked at her watch – five to two – and shifted impatiently from one foot to the other. Unease and worry rippled through her.

Renee came out a few minutes later, saw Julia, and quickly pulled her aside into a shallow alcove where a payphone was attached to the wall. With her fingers still gripping Julia's arm she glanced furtively along the corridor that led to the bar. There was a faint sheen of sweat on her forehead and her eyes were shining.

'What have they said?'

Julia shook her head. 'What? Who?'

'Them,' Renee hissed, so close that Julia could feel her breath on her face. 'Frankie and the others. What have they said about Angel?'

Julia, taken by surprise by the question, didn't really understand what Renee was asking. 'What do you mean?'

'You have to find out what they did. They're lying, all of them.'

'Lying about what?'

Renee shot a quick look along the corridor again. 'About my Angel, of course. She didn't kill herself. She'd never have done nothing like that. She was happy that day. Happy! I know they're not telling the truth. They're hiding something and you have to find out what.'

27

Julia was shocked but thought it was probably best to humour her. If what Tom had said was true, they had all been here that night, waiting for Angel, so they couldn't have had anything to do with her death. 'They've not said anything to me. But they wouldn't, Renee. We barely know each other anymore. It's been years since I saw any of them.'

Renee, too caught up by what she was trying to tell her, wasn't listening. Her grip tightened on Julia's arm. 'They've got their neat little alibi, but not until seven o'clock. What were they all doing before then? No one knows exactly when Angel died. Those two girls were at the flat in the afternoon, but they left at about three. Plied her with booze and then took off. Or they say they took off. And that Frankie – I wouldn't trust him as far as I could throw him. He was always sniffing round Angel. I'm telling you they're not as innocent as they're making out.'

And what about Tom Finch? Julia almost asked but decided against throwing any more fuel onto the fire. Until today she had been assuming that Renee had got Jack, a grandson, to help pull her through the grief, but now she knew that this wasn't the case, the depth of Renee's grief seemed intolerable. Gaping, dark and filled with invisible monsters.

'You'll try, won't you, Julia? Tell me you'll try. I can't trust anyone else.'

'Of course,' Julia said, gently releasing Renee's hold on her arm. 'But I can't promise anything. I'm virtually a stranger to them now. What about the police? What do they think?'

Renee's face twisted. 'The law don't care about Angel. Too busy lining their own pockets, aren't they? Bent, the whole bloody lot of them. They don't give a damn. They don't care about anyone but themselves. I've told them she didn't kill herself, she couldn't have, but they won't listen.'

'What about that inspector? Vyse, is it? He was at the service.'

Renee seemed surprised by this. She hesitated. 'Was he? I didn't see him. Well, I dare say he's just trying to look good, to cover his back in case his bungling ever comes to light. They're like that down at Cowan Road, always one step ahead, always making sure they're in control.'

Julia nodded as if police bungling was nothing new to her. Cowan Road police station was just round the corner from the Mansfield, which was handy if the crime rate on the estate was anything like it used to be. 'Look, I should go. The others . . . they're going to be wondering where I am.'

'You're a good girl, Julia. You're the best friend Angel ever had. You won't let me down, will you?'

Guilt rolled over Julia, a tsunami of regret. She hadn't always been a good friend to Angel, far from it, and the knowledge of that filled her with remorse. 'I'll try. I promise. I don't think I'll get much out of them today, but I'll see what I can do.'

4

Julia returned to the booth and slid in beside Tom. There was food on the table, paper plates with a choice of corned beef sandwiches or cheese and pickle, and fresh glasses of wine. The room was warm and noisy. Frankie was going on about the new Rover hatchback to Tom while Pauline was slagging off some girl called Shirley, bitching about how she hadn't worn black to the funeral. Julia looked at each of them in turn, curious as to why Renee suspected them. Was it just paranoia springing from the loss of her daughter or something more? She couldn't imagine why any of these people would want to harm Angel.

'You okay?' Tom asked her when there was a pause in the motor talk.

Julia played with her wine glass, running her finger along its rim. 'I still don't get it,' she said. 'How did Angel get down to the river? Did she have a car? Did she even drive?'

Her questions caused everyone to stare, as if she'd just dropped a cluster of bombs into the conversation.

There was a long pause before Tom shrugged and said, 'No, she didn't drive but there are buses. She could have caught one to Hackney and walked from there.'

'Or taken a cab,' Frankie said.

'Wouldn't the cabbie have remembered her?'

'More likely the bus,' Tom said. 'They get busy on a Saturday.'

'For God's sake, do we have to talk about this?' Pauline said irritably. She glared at Julia. 'I don't want to hear it.'

'I'm sorry,' Julia said with as much sincerity as she could muster. 'But it's all still so new to me. I've not had enough time for it to sink in. It's still really . . . really confusing. Did *anyone* see her that day? Apart from Renee, I mean.'

'We saw her,' Lindsay said. 'Me and Pauline. In the afternoon. We went round to wish her a happy birthday, took her a bottle of fizz. She seemed fine. Happy. She was going to wash her hair, do some shopping and meet us in the Fox later. There was nothing wrong, nothing that we noticed anyway.'

Julia watched her carefully but couldn't see any sign that she was lying.

Pauline placed her elbows on the table and scowled. 'We've had weeks of this, weeks of the law going over and over it. Can't we just have one day to remember her in peace?'

'I'm sorry,' Julia said again. 'Yes, of course.' She sat back, unsure of where to go from here. Conducting any further interrogation was hardly feasible in the circumstances. It was then, as she looked over her shoulder, that she noticed Vyse finishing what was left of his pint, putting the empty glass on the counter and heading for the door. She glanced at her watch, pretending to be surprised by what time it was. 'Oh, I've got to go. I've got a work thing at four. Sorry to rush off, but it's been good to see you all again.'

Pauline looked relieved.

31

'Don't be a stranger,' Frankie said, flashing her one of his wide, engaging smiles.

'We should get together again,' Lindsay said. 'Have a proper catch-up. We're usually in here on a Saturday night.'

'Hang on a sec,' Tom said, quickly scrawling his telephone number on a green serviette and passing it to her. 'Give me a ring and we'll sort something out.'

'Sure,' Julia said, standing up and putting the serviette into her pocket. 'Thanks. That would be nice.'

As she walked away, Julia looked back at them. Already their heads were down, huddled together like four conspirators, all talking at once. About her? About Angel? Renee's words swirled haphazardly around her mind, and she couldn't help speculating on whether there was any truth in the accusations. She needed to find out more.

By the time she was out on the street, Vyse was already a hundred yards in front of her. He walked with a very upright gait, like an army man on parade. She hurried to catch up with him, not an easy task in the high-heeled boots she was wearing. Fortunately, he had to wait at the traffic lights, giving her time to close the distance between them. Once she was near enough, she called out his name.

'Inspector Vyse?'

He turned and gave her a long assessing look. 'That's me,' he said.

She hurried up to him, slightly breathless. 'I'm Julia Reeve, an old friend of Angel's. Could I have a word?'

Vyse raised his eyebrows as if it was a novelty to come across someone in Kellston who actually *wanted* to talk to him. 'What's on your mind?'

The traffic lights turned red, and Julia moved to one side to allow the other pedestrians to cross over. She waited until they were out of earshot before continuing. 'It's about Angel's death. Do you think it's suspicious?'

'Do *you* think it's suspicious?'

Nothing like lobbing the ball back into her court. 'You're the police. I only found out about her death a few days ago. Suicide is what people are saying but Renee doesn't seem to think so.'

'Ah, Renee,' he said, as if those two words were an adequate response.

'You think she's wrong?'

'I haven't made my mind up yet.'

'It's been a month. You must be leaning one way or the other.'

'It's not black and white. There are . . . complications.'

'What sort of complications?'

Vyse's blue eyes left her face and travelled along the road before coming back to rest on her. 'Look, this probably isn't the best place to talk. Do you have time for a coffee?'

Julia nodded. 'Sure. Okay.' She had nowhere else to be and after her futile attempt to get information out of the old gang, she was hoping for some clarity from the inspector. Having promised Renee to try and find out what she could, this seemed as good a place to start as any.

5

The Station Café, only a few yards away, was in a post-lunch lull with just a few customers. Julia was glad it was quiet. Even though she didn't live in Kellston now, old habits die hard, and she still felt that chatting to the law was something that would be frowned upon. Vyse went directly to the back of the room, away from the window and everybody else. They had barely pulled out their chairs and sat down when the waitress came over. Two coffees were ordered.

'So, Julia,' he said, 'how long is it since you last saw Angel?'

'About eight years. When we were seventeen. But that was just a fleeting visit. I left Kellston in '78 and went to live in Suffolk. We were close before then, best friends, but I suppose we . . . well, I suppose we drifted apart. Angel's mum didn't have a phone and neither of us were great letter writers. I came back to London nine months ago.'

'You didn't get in touch with her?'

'I meant to. Eventually. But you know what it's like – new job, new flat, everything a bit manic. And then on Friday I bumped into Tom Finch, and he told me what had happened. Do *you* think it was suicide? Renee seems convinced that it wasn't.'

'Parents don't always know what their kids are thinking.'

'They had a good relationship, though. Renee was a lovely mum. The others don't really want to talk about Angel's death, which I understand, but so much of it doesn't make sense. I mean, even if she was suicidal, why would she choose to drown herself?'

'Because she couldn't swim?' Vyse suggested. 'She knew that once she was in the water, there was no changing her mind.'

The waitress came with the coffees, and they stopped talking until she left again. Julia shivered at the thought of Angel in the river, of the desperation that might have led her there. 'Do you know where she went in?'

'We know where her coat and bag were found. On the bank of the river Lea in Hackney. By then, of course, any evidence as to whether she went there alone or with someone else had been destroyed. It rained pretty hard for a few days, and the ground was sodden. All this was in the local paper,' he added, as if to make it clear that he wasn't telling her anything not already in the public domain.

Julia picked up her cup and sipped her coffee. 'I didn't see it. You said, "someone else"?'

'It can't be ruled out.'

'And you think that someone could have been one of her friends?'

'Could have been.'

'But why?'

'If I knew that, I'd have this all wrapped up already.'

'But you must have a reason for suspecting them.'

'What can I tell you? It's a cliché but something doesn't smell right.'

35

It didn't smell right to Julia, either. But she wasn't sure if that was down to Renee's suspicions, the way the others had behaved, or just her growing refusal to believe that Angel had killed herself. 'I've got a bad feeling about it too.'

'That could just be your guilty conscience.'

Julia gave a start. 'What?'

'You feel bad about not getting in touch with her and now you're secretly hoping that it was murder rather than suicide because that gets you off the hook.'

Julia's mouth fell open. Her voice, when she found it again, had a higher pitch than usual. 'What the hell kind of thing is that to say?'

'A true thing. But don't feel bad about it. It's a perfectly natural reaction. In situations like this people always stress over what they didn't do. If only you'd got in touch, if only you'd made the effort, if only you'd made a different decision. You get what I mean.'

Julia did get it but didn't like him for saying it out loud. She liked him even less because it was true, and nobody liked to hear unpleasant truths. Vyse and his bluntness were discomfiting. She clamped shut her mouth and stared at him.

'Ah, now I've pissed you off. But we may as well be straight with each other if we're going to be working together.'

'Who said anything about working together?'

Vyse gave a smug smile. 'Isn't that why you're here? To pick my brains, to find out what I know? Well, I'm happy to help but I expect something in return. A quid pro quo if you like.'

'Which is?'

'You do some delving into the stories of those mates of yours, find out what's really going on.'

'You want me to spy on my friends?'

'Don't sound so shocked. It was what you were going to do

anyway. Tell me I'm wrong.' He nodded when she didn't respond. 'I'm just asking you to share the information. Two heads are better than one, right?'

'I'm not sure if I'm comfortable with that.'

'Tough,' he said. 'That's the deal. If you've got qualms, if you can't do it, then walk away now. But if you want to find out if Angel really did kill herself or if someone shoved her into that river, then you're going to have to sweep your finer feelings aside.'

Julia could see why Renee didn't like Vyse. Recalling what she had said about all the police being bent, and listening to him now, it wasn't beyond the bounds of possibility that he *was* on the take. But where was the advantage in what he was asking her to do? It certainly wasn't financial. Unless he hoped to get a promotion out of it. Or maybe he was just the sort of guy who didn't like to lose.

She studied his lean face and cool blue eyes. The problem with attractive people, she thought, is that you often gave them the benefit of the doubt, as if their good looks entitled them to an extra helping of trust. But that could be a big mistake. If anything, you should trust them less. So used were they to getting their own way that they tended to take it for granted. And then it occurred to her that even if she did agree to his demands, she only had to tell him what she chose to tell him.

'Okay,' she said. 'As long as you don't keep stuff from me. You mentioned "complications" when I first asked you about Angel's death. What did you mean by that?'

'Gut complications,' he said.

Julia frowned at him. 'Gut?'

'Yeah, those four mates of yours. My gut tells me they're lying and my gut's rarely wrong.'

'And that's it? That's all you've got to go on?'

'It's enough. They all tell the same story and it's way too pat. And they all say Angel had been down recently, depressed, withdrawn, and yet her mother says the very opposite.'

'Lindsay told me she was fine in the afternoon.'

'Yeah, she told me that too. But quickly went on to say that it wasn't always the case, that she was very up and down, that she suffered with her mental health. Lindsay said that she wasn't surprised at what she'd done. Shocked but not surprised.'

'That could be true.'

'Could be,' he agreed. 'But none of them have got a firm alibi for late afternoon or early evening. From seven, yeah, they were in the Fox, but there was plenty of time before that. Renee was at work so she can't confirm that the two girls left when they said they did, or that they left without Angel. They say they went back to Pauline's flat, next door in Haslow House, where they had something to eat before going down the pub.'

'Were they together the whole time?'

'That's what they claim.'

'Why didn't they pick up Angel on the way to the pub?'

'She told them she had something to do first.'

'And what was that?'

'Washing her hair and then doing some shopping for her mum, although Renee says that wasn't the case. That she had any shopping to do, I mean.' Vyse pulled a face. 'So someone was lying. Anyway, Frankie Hays claims he was tinkering with an old motor he's doing up in his garage – but no witnesses. His wife, Clare, was at her mum's place with the kids. Tom Finch says he was working alone in his flat, catching up on some paperwork. So, basically, any one of them, or all of them, could have gone with Angel to the river. Frankie, Tom and Lindsay all have cars.'

'But what motive could they have in killing her?'

'You don't want to get sidetracked by motive. Love, hate, money, revenge, fear. It's usually one of them. Take your pick.'

Julia heaved out a sigh, placed her elbows on the table and rubbed her face with her palms. 'To be honest, I don't even know where to start. It's going to look suspicious if I carry on asking lots of questions. They're going to realise what I'm doing.'

'Divide and rule,' he said. 'Take them one at a time if you can. Who do you get on with best?'

'It's been years but Tom, I suppose.'

'Good. Start with Tom then. See if you can get some background, what was going on before Angel died. Just keep it casual, not too probing, and try to get a feel for how the group was interacting then. If any of them had fallen out, were sleeping together, cheating on their partners, the usual stuff.'

'Is that the usual stuff?'

'Yeah,' he said. 'In my experience.'

Julia supposed that his cynical views came with the job, or that he had a somewhat colourful set of friends. But then she remembered Renee saying that Frankie had always been 'sniffing round' Angel. They weren't fourteen-year-old kids anymore and the lives of adults could get messy. 'I can't see any way of getting Pauline on her own. She's never liked me, and the feeling's mutual.'

'Where do you work, Julia?'

'Harley Jenks,' she said, surprised by the sudden change of subject. 'It's a PR company.'

'Yeah, I know what it is. And what they do. Don't you spend most of your working life putting a spin on things, doing damage limitation, making bad things look good, making a silk purse out of a sow's ear and all that?'

'I wouldn't put it like that exactly.'

39

'What you need with Pauline is a charm offensive. Think of her as a client. I'm sure you can win her round.'

'When hell freezes over.'

Vyse grinned, reached into his jacket pocket, removed his wallet and took out a couple of business cards. 'Here,' he said, passing them over the table. 'Call me if you find out anything. And write your number on one so I can get in touch with you.'

Julia found a pen in her bag, scribbled down her name and number and gave the card back. 'That's home.'

'What about work?' he said.

'I'd rather you didn't ring me there.'

'What if it's an emergency?'

Julia frowned. 'And what would constitute an emergency?'

'I won't know until it happens. But don't worry, I can get the number from the phone book.'

Julia put the other card in her bag. 'Try and ring me at home if you have to call. There's an answer machine. You can leave a message.'

Vyse didn't make any promises. He drained his mug, rose to his feet and said, 'Well, nice meeting you, Julia. Good luck with everything.'

Julia watched him go over to the counter and pay the bill. She kept her eyes on him until he'd left the café – he didn't look back – and then she sat and wondered what she was getting herself into. Trouble was the first word that sprang to mind.

6

Tom Finch put down his pint and looked around the table. He had other friends now, friends from work, friends from the Labour party meetings he went to on a Friday night, but he couldn't shake free the ties of his school days. Most Saturdays, whether he wanted to come or not, he would be here at the Fox having the same conversations with the same people. This was different, of course, being Angel's wake, but he still had the feeling of being trapped in something he couldn't escape from.

'She won't call you,' Pauline said smugly. 'That's the last we'll ever see of her.'

'She might,' Tom said. He wasn't convinced but he said it anyway. It had been a surprise running into Julia Reeve on the Strand; he'd only gone up West to pick up a present for his mum's birthday. He'd recognised her straight away even though she was sleeker now, slimmer, a woman rather than a girl. It had been disheartening to see the confusion on her face as she tried to figure out who he was. Although, if he was putting a more positive spin on it, maybe that was a good thing. It showed that he'd changed and hopefully for the better.

Pauline carried on. 'No, she won't be back. She reckons she's too good for us now, thinks she's a cut above with her fancy job and fancy clothes. Did you see those boots she was wearing? They must have cost a bomb. No, Julia won't be darkening our door again. She only came out of curiosity, and to look down her nose at us.'

Tom, who had not got this impression, didn't bother to argue. Perhaps it would be better if Julia did stay away. Everything was too messy right now, too tangled up. If she started digging, God knows what she'd uncover. And what had Renee said to her outside the church? Renee had been weird with them ever since Angel's death, as if she had suspicions, as if she knew things she couldn't possibly know.

Tom lifted his glass again and took another swig of beer. Pauline had arrived at Kellston Secondary Modern a year later than the rest of them and had hated Julia right from the start. He'd presumed with Angel and Julia being so close that she'd pal up with Lindsay, but she'd had other ideas. Angel had been the one she'd set her sights on, wooing her as ardently as a potential suitor, whispering in her ear, taking every opportunity to be alone with her, taking her arm proprietarily whenever the six of them were walking together.

Angel had liked the attention. There was no denying that. Although she pretended otherwise to Julia. Like illicit lovers, they had sneaked around behind her back until the accident . . . but Tom didn't want to think about that. It was a depressing enough day without piling on the misery. What was past was past and there was no point dwelling on it. Nothing could be changed now.

Tom glanced across the table at Frankie, who grinned back

42

at him. He sometimes wondered what went on in Frankie's head besides motors, football and girls. Having kids hadn't changed him. He still slept around as if sex was going out of fashion – and didn't spare the details. Tom only had to mention anything faintly political and he would roll his eyes, as if to give due warning that the listening part of his brain was turning off.

They had nothing much in common now other than history, but that history was deep and dark and dangerous. It was enough to keep them bound together, reliant on each other's loyalty and silence. Perhaps one day, no longer afraid of exposure and repercussions, they would naturally drift apart, but he couldn't see that coming any time soon. If he had more courage, he'd cut the ties, but fear kept him attached. Well, that and self-preservation. He was the one who kept the group calm, who ironed out the problems and prevented disagreements from spiralling out of control. Without him things would fall apart.

Lindsay, he noticed, was on her third glass of wine. Her cheeks were flushed and she was more animated than usual. Her eyes darted around the pub, maybe searching for Renee. They were all afraid of what Renee might say publicly; ravaged by grief, she was a loose cannon, more than capable of spreading unfounded accusations. Or even well-founded ones.

Tom suspected that once Lindsay was married, she would gradually shift away from the group and spend more time with her husband's circle of friends. Already Mark was talking about buying a flat away from Kellston, somewhere affordable but more up-and-coming. Apart from Lindsay, nobody much liked Mark Grey. He was a right-wing Tory boy who had a menial job in the civil service but acted as though he was running the country.

Mark had chosen not to come to the funeral today, and Tom was glad of it. The man had never really got on with Angel. Even after he'd been told about her troubles, he had still treated her with callous condescension. How Lindsay put up with him, *why* she put up with him, was a mystery. Desperation, Pauline said. It was a worry that she might confess all to her fiancé – isn't that what couples did? – but Frankie said she wouldn't, that she'd be too afraid of losing him, that some things couldn't be forgiven.

Now Angel was gone, they were down to four. If Lindsay left, they'd be three. A trio of conspirators. A ghastly triangle.

7

It was already growing dark by the time Julia got home. She hated November with its short gloomy days, cold weather and depressing atmosphere – all those months stretching ahead before spring came around again. And now, just to make it all worse, it would be forever associated with Angel's funeral. Normally a funeral would bring things to a natural close, but not on this occasion. Instead, a whole new can of worms had been opened. Had Angel killed herself? Had somebody killed her? She had to know one way or the other.

Julia let herself into the flat, switched on the light in the living room and hurried through to the tiny galley kitchen where she put on the heating and the kettle. The one advantage to living in a shoebox was that it warmed up quickly. She was tempted to finish off the bottle of wine sitting on the counter but then thought better of it. With Ivor Apostle to deal with tomorrow she couldn't afford even the slightest of hangovers. He might be a client that no one else wanted but she still had to make a good impression.

While she waited for the kettle to boil, she searched the fridge for something to eat. It was slim pickings. She should have done a shop on the way home. One egg, half a cabbage, a bottle of milk, butter, two carrots and a can of Coke. Delia Smith might have been able to create something wonderfully inventive from what was on offer, but Julia's mind was a blank. She bunged two slices of bread in the toaster and put the egg in a pan of water.

She ate standing up in the kitchen, dipping the soldiers in the egg, eating slowly to make it last longer. There was a Chinese takeaway not that far down the road, but it was too much of an effort to go out again. Anyway, she couldn't afford to waste money on chow mein and spring rolls. Funds were low and there was still another fortnight before payday.

The phone started ringing as she was doing the washing up. Immediately she thought of Vyse. Quickly drying her hands on a tea towel, she went into the living room and snatched up the receiver.

'Hello?'

'Only me,' her mother said. 'You're home early. I was just going to leave you a message to let you know we got back safely.'

'Yes, I was . . .'

But before Julia could even finish the sentence Ellie had launched into a garrulous account of her weekend yoga retreat in Cornwall. Quite why she had to retreat to Cornwall to manoeuvre her body into impossible positions was anyone's guess, but it had clearly been a resounding success. 'We just got back. It's a fantastic place, stunningly beautiful. You should come with us next time we go. There's room in the car. It would do you good to get out of London for a while, blow those cobwebs away.'

It was another five minutes before Julia could get a word in edgeways. First there was Cornwall, then her mother's views on the ordination of women into the Church of England (positive), then the fall of the Berlin Wall which had happened the previous Thursday and was still all over the TV (exciting), and finally the fact they had added yet another cat to their household menagerie (amusing). 'He just walked right in and made himself at home.'

'I have some bad news, Mum,' Julia said.

There was a sharp intake of breath from the other end of the line. 'Oh God, you're pregnant, aren't you?'

'No, I'm not pregnant. Of course I'm not. Why would you say that?'

'Accidents happen, love. Nothing's one hundred per cent.'

'Well, no accidents have happened here. And anyway, I'm twenty-five. *You* were twenty-five when you had me.'

'So I know how tough it is raising a child on your own. He might say he's up for it, might make all the promises under the sun, but when push comes to shove – excuse the pun – and reality hits home, it's another story altogether. And you've only just started that job. You don't want to be taking time off now.'

Julia, realising she'd been sidetracked, quickly returned to the point. 'It's about Angel, what I've been trying to tell you.' She took a deep breath. 'She's dead, Mum. They think she committed suicide.'

There was another gasp from her mother. 'What? How awful! Poor girl. Poor Angel. I didn't even realise you two were back in touch.'

'We weren't, but I bumped into Tom Finch, and he told me. It was the funeral today at St James's. That's why I'm home early. I took the day off.'

As if her mother's brain was still catching up with what she'd been told, there was a short pause before she said, 'What do you mean they *think* it was suicide?'

'She drowned,' Julia said. 'Well, it could have been an accident, but no one seems to know why she was at the river in the first place.'

'God, she was so young. Why would she go and do a thing like that?'

'I don't know, Mum. She was depressed, I think. Not coping.' Julia decided not to tell her about Renee's suspicions or her conversation with Vyse. She knew her mother would advise her to stay out of it, to let the police do their job, to not get involved. 'All the others were at the funeral: Tom and Frankie, Lindsay and Pauline. It was strange seeing them again.'

'And Renee? How's that poor woman coping?'

'Oh, you know,' Julia said. 'It's hard for her.'

'Devastating, I should think.'

Julia's mum had never been especially close to Renee, the only thing they had in common being daughters who were best friends. Ellie wasn't interested in TV shows or gossip, and Renee had no time for feminism or politics. They had got along in a cheery, superficial way but that was about the sum of it.

'It's weird to think of her being gone,' Julia said. 'I don't think it's quite sunk in yet.'

'That girl was always fragile.'

'I never thought of her like that.'

'Well, sensitive then. She took things to heart.'

'I suppose so,' Julia said. 'It was her birthday. That's when it happened.'

Ellie sighed. 'Are you all right, love? Why don't you come and stay for a few days or at least the weekend. This must have been an awful shock.'

Julia shook her head even though her mother couldn't see her. She was thinking of her promise to Renee. 'Maybe later. I've got a lot on at work right now. I'd rather just get on with it.'

'The offer's always there if you change your mind. It's open house here. You can come and meet Darcy.'

'Darcy?' Julia said frowning, instantly imagining Jane Austen's hero practising his prejudice in the large gloomy rooms in Suffolk.

'The cat. That's what we've called him. He's very haughty.'

'Oh, right. Yeah. Well, I'll be home for Christmas if I don't make it before.'

Julia put down the phone after they'd said their goodbyes. It was then, suddenly, that she was assailed by the phantom smell of lilies. Funeral flowers. The air turned chill, and she shivered. The heady scent passed as quickly as it arrived, but it was as if, for a few seconds, Angel or her ghost had been right there in the room.

8

Julia dressed in her best linen suit on Tuesday morning, swept her hair up into an elegant bun and applied her make-up with extra care, all armour against what she suspected could be a trying morning appointment with Ivor Apostle. Rich, successful men were rarely forgiving, and she knew that she would have to compensate for having cancelled on him yesterday with an extra-large dose of interest and enthusiasm.

She was early into the office but already it was busy. The atmosphere was always manic with large emergencies and small ones vying for attention. Reputations were what Harley Jenks PR was here to preserve, enhance or salvage depending on the situation. There was no sign of Cressida yet, but she'd left a few press releases that needed checking for typos. Julia read through them, made some corrections and returned them to her boss's desk. Then she opened the top right-hand drawer of her own desk and pulled out the slim file on Apostle.

For the next half hour, she studied the information available. There was an unsmiling photograph clipped to the inside of the file – Apostle in a grey fedora and a smart suit – and the rest of the contents comprised a brief precis of his career to date which seemed to mainly involve security, pubs and wine bars, and a sheaf of press cuttings, some of which showed him falling out of nightclubs in the early hours with one vacuous-looking blonde or another.

Apostle was forty-one with a face – square-jawed and battered – that only a mother could love. His crooked nose looked like it had been broken more than once and a deep scar bisected his left cheek, running from just below the eye to the upper edge of his throat. He was a man, she thought, who you wouldn't want to meet down a dark alley – or anywhere, come to that.

By nine thirty when reception rang through to tell her that Apostle was here, Julia had learned as much as she was going to. She stood up, smoothed down the skirt of her suit, pushed back her shoulders, picked up a notepad and pen, and made her way to Conference Room 2. This was the smaller of the two rooms used to meet clients, less flashy with an uninspiring view, but comfortable enough. She paused for a moment outside the door, took some deep breaths and painted on a wide smile.

'Mr Apostle,' she said, as she entered. 'Julia Reeve. It's lovely to meet you.'

Apostle rose to his feet, providing her with the first big surprise of the morning. He must have been six foot four or more and loomed over her like a giant. Taking her hand, he gave it a brusque shake before sitting back down in the chair.

'Glad to see you could make it this time.' His accent was London, his expression resentful. 'I hope I'm not keeping you from anything more important.'

'I'm so sorry about yesterday,' she said. 'I had to go to a funeral. I didn't hear about it until Friday, hence the last-minute postponement.'

'A funeral, huh?' he said, as if he'd heard that excuse a thousand times before.

'Yes, an old school friend,' she explained. 'I do apologise. Can I get you a tea or a coffee? A cold drink?'

'Coffee,' he said. 'Black, no sugar.'

Julia went over to the cabinet where a tray had already been laid out with cups, saucers and a cafetière. There was a kettle too in case he wanted tea. No expense spared. She poured two coffees and handed him one.

'Whose funeral?' he said, clearly unwilling to let it go. 'I mean, what was their name?'

Julia was irked by the question. She didn't like being cross-examined, and what business was it of his? She sat down in the leather chair opposite his own. 'Angela Glover,' she said tightly. 'St James's church in Kellston at midday. You can check if you like.'

Apostle grinned as if pleased to have riled her. 'Yeah, I know Kellston. It's a dump. So you went to school there?'

'Until I was fourteen. Then we moved away.'

'Yeah, you don't sound like a Kellston girl. You don't look like one either, come to that.'

'And what do Kellston girls look like?'

Apostle stroked his chin while he stared at her. 'Not like you,' he said eventually. 'Nothing like you.'

Julia held his gaze. His eyes were a washed-out shade of grey. His hair, light brown, was slicked back from his forehead and worn collar length. She tried to stop her gaze from straying to the brutal scar that dominated his face. 'And where did you grow up?'

'North London,' he said.

'Ah,' she replied, hoping to make a connection with him. 'That's where I live now. In Camden.'

'Finsbury Park,' he said. 'That was a dump too. I cleared out as soon as I could.' A small bark of triumph erupted from his throat. 'I'm living in the Barbican now. Still, I dare say you know that already.'

Julia did know it, had read it in the file and she also knew that the flats in the block he lived in cost an arm and a leg. 'Lovely,' she said, sensing that he wanted praise for this financial achievement. 'Lucky you.'

'Luck didn't have anything to do with it. If you want the good things in life, you have to work for them.'

Julia nodded and sipped her coffee. 'I'm sure you're right.'

'You look young,' he said, as if suspecting he'd been fobbed off (which he had) with the office junior. 'Do you have much experience in PR?'

'Plenty,' she replied. 'I wouldn't be sitting here if I didn't.'

'I need someone who knows what they're doing.'

'Is there a particular problem?' she asked before he could delve too deeply into her work history. Four years at a small Ipswich PR company probably wouldn't do much to reassure him. The trick was to look confident and sound confident, and not to let him intimidate her. 'Or are you after something more general?'

Apostle reached into his jacket pocket, pulled out an envelope and threw the contents – a heap of press cuttings – onto the coffee table. 'These,' he said. 'I want you to do something about these.'

Julia recognised most of the articles from her own file. As she spread them across the table, she noticed that he'd used an orange highlighter pen to call attention to every time the word 'ex-con' had been used. It was a lot of times.

'I take it you've got contacts in the press?' he said.

'Of course.'

'So get them to stop doing that.' Apostle leaned forward and prodded at the cuttings with his forefinger. 'Ex-con, ex-con, ex-con. This sort of crap is costing me money, costing me investments. Who wants to go into business with a criminal? It's a load of bullshit. I should sue the bastards.'

'That could be costly,' Julia said.

'I've got money.'

'Although if you've never been to prison – I assume that's what you're saying – then you've got a good case.'

'I went to borstal for a year when I was fifteen. That doesn't make me an ex-con. It makes me someone who made mistakes when they were young.'

'Ah,' she said. 'I see.'

'And what the hell does "Ah" mean?'

'Well, I suppose they'd argue that you have been incarcerated even if it wasn't in an adult prison.'

Apostle glared at her. 'Whose side are you on, love?'

Julia felt her shoulders tighten. If there was one thing she loathed it was men who called her love, especially in that tone of voice. 'I'm just ... I'm on yours, naturally. But you have to pick your battles. The press can be tricky. If they know it annoys you, they'll keep on doing it to try and provoke a reaction.'

'So just grin and bear it. Is that what you're saying?'

This wasn't going well. Julia, hearing his frustration, could imagine him storming out of the room, accosting Harley and demanding that she be replaced with someone more senior. The very thought of it was mortifying. She had to come up with an idea to placate him – and fast. 'Actually, I was thinking more along the lines of approaching it from a different angle. Instead of trying to stop them from referring to your past, perhaps you should actively encourage it, embrace it and use it to your advantage. Something along the lines of bad boy made good, how you turned your life around, how you've grown and developed.

A good example to all those other kids who haven't had the best start in life.'

Apostle didn't look impressed. He stared at her as if she'd just suggested throwing himself under a bus.

Quickly she went on. 'We could find a journalist for you to do an interview with. Someone sympathetic. Maybe a magazine.'

'I don't do interviews,' he said sharply.

'That's even better. You haven't been overexposed.'

'What don't you understand about *I don't do interviews*?'

Julia was holding on to what little was left of her patience. What was with the attitude? The man was a confrontational arse. 'I'm just suggesting it as an option, that's all. If you prefer to go down the legal route that's entirely up to you, but there's no guarantee you'll win. And not only will you spend a fortune, you'll also make an enemy of the press for life. Now, I appreciate that you might not care about that, but it's always better to have them on side than against you. Keep your enemies close and all that.'

Apostle didn't say anything immediately. He picked up the cuttings and stuffed them back in his pocket.

Julia's heart sank. She'd screwed it up and he was going to make her pay. Her career was about to go into freefall. If she couldn't be trusted to keep a minor client sweet, what hope was there for any advancement? She considered some damage limitation – perhaps having a word with a few of these reporters who insisted on referring to him as an ex-con – but she knew it would be pointless, even counter-productive.

'Okay, Julie,' he said, standing up and glancing at his watch. 'I have to go.'

'Julia,' she said, rising to her feet too. 'My name's Julia.'

Apostle gave a wolfish grin, as if he'd been testing her, seeing if she'd have the nerve to correct him. 'Do you know Molly's on Floral Street, Julia? It's not far from here. It's one of my wine bars.'

'Yes, I know it.'

'Meet me there on Friday. Say one o'clock? We'll carry on this discussion then.'

Julia wasn't sure what to make of this latest development, but at least he didn't look quite as angry as he had. It felt like a reprieve although she wasn't sure if it was. 'One o'clock. I'll be there.'

'Don't bother showing me out. I know the way.' Apostle opened the door and then looked over his shoulder. 'And try to keep your friends safe until then. I don't want you blowing me out for another funeral.'

9

'Are you certain you want to let him loose on the press?' Cressida said, when Julia told her about the suggestion she'd made to Ivor Apostle. 'Especially if he's going to be aggressive. He could make everything worse.'

'Oh, I'm sure he'll be on his best behaviour.' Was she sure? Not really. But she'd had to come up with something in a hurry. 'He's not keen right now but if he decides to go down that road, I'll talk him through it, so he knows what to expect.'

Cressida gave a low laugh. 'You can try. Although from what I've heard he isn't the kind of man who appreciates good advice.'

'Or any advice.'

'Just be careful,' Cressida said. 'Don't let him take advantage of you. He's got a reputation when it comes to women.'

Julia wrinkled her nose. 'Not my type.'

'Yes, well, by the time he's poured a bottle of Chardonnay down your throat, your type might get a little blurry round the edges. Just be on your guard, that's all I'm saying. Some men view any woman as easy game.'

'I don't really get it, why any girl finds him attractive. He's not what you'd call charming. Or good looking. Or even faintly interesting.'

'But he is what you'd call rich,' Cressida said. 'It's surprising what a full wallet will do for a man's popularity.'

Julia's second surprise of the day came at lunchtime when a call was put though to her from Lindsay March. She barely had time to gather her thoughts before Lindsay's voice came tumbling down the line, a little rushed, a little breathless.

'Sorry to call you at work. I couldn't think how else to get hold of you. I remembered you saying that you worked for a PR company and Tom said he'd met you on the Strand, so I just checked the phone book and ... You don't mind me calling, do you? I know Tom gave you his number, but I wasn't sure if you'd ring him or not.'

'No, of course I don't mind. It's great to hear from you.'

'I was wondering if you'd like to meet up one day after work? Tomorrow, maybe? I can come into town. It would be nice to have a proper catch-up. We didn't really get the chance to talk properly yesterday.'

Although Julia had been planning on approaching Tom first, she wasn't going to pass up this opportunity. And the fact that Lindsay had sought her out, rather than the other way round, was to her advantage. This way it wouldn't look as if she had only wanted to meet to probe for information. 'Yes, that would be lovely. How about Covent Garden piazza, by the church at six? Would that be okay for you?'

'Yes, six, that would be fine. I'll look forward to it.'

'Me too,' Julia said.

It was only after she'd put the phone down that she began to question Lindsay's motives. Why would she want to meet her alone rather than with the others? And hadn't her voice sounded slightly flustered, strained, as if she was trying too hard to be natural? Or maybe that was just her own guilty conscience raising its head again; she could be doing that weird transference thing.

Julia had never been especially close to Lindsay, but they'd got on okay. She was probably overthinking it all. Perhaps Lindsay genuinely did want a catch-up and preferred to do it without Pauline's constant sniping. But something still niggled at the back of her mind, little warning flashes to be on her guard. The group had always been tight, and she was no longer part of it. What if she'd been seen talking to Renee in the Fox? Or to Vyse in the café? What if Lindsay was being sent out on a spying mission, as keen to find out what she knew as Julia was to find out what *they* knew?

She suppressed a groan, feeling the cogs in her brain begin to stall. The more she tried to second-guess Lindsay the less convinced she was that she knew anything at all.

10

Pauline Archer was surrounded by dead flesh, by chunks of body parts, by thighs and breasts and livers and kidneys. Small puddles of blood pooled in the trays. By now she had grown immune to the smell and to the omnipresence of death. Her father sawed and sliced and chopped, his face as gleeful as a serial killer. She hated him. She hated the shop and everyone who came into it.

Orders were being taken for Christmas turkeys, for pigs in blankets and boiled hams. It wouldn't be long before the tree and the tinsel went up, before big red Santas started appearing everywhere and the carol singers began doing the rounds. Ted Archer loved this time of year when his profits went up and the till never stopped ringing. He smiled and joked with the customers, pretending each of them was his favourite, slipping little extras into their orders. Ted Archer was a cynical bastard.

Pauline wanted something more to her life than working in the butcher's, than slicing bacon and wrapping up chops. She wanted to smell of something other than dead animal. At twenty-five she was still living at home, stuck in that dreary flat with nothing to look forward to. Her mother had walked out years ago, walked away and never glanced back. She could have taken her with her, but she hadn't; she had left her here at the mercy of Ted and his tempers and his limitless greed, and for that she could never be forgiven.

Although her father was at the top of the list, Pauline's dislikes were wide and varied. She loathed Kellston, the Mansfield estate, cops, chihuahuas, Tories, teachers, salad and rich people. And that was just for starters. Julia Reeve held a prominent position too. Seeing her at the funeral had made her blood boil. What right did she have to turn up after all these years? It should have been Angel's day, but instead she'd swanned in like the Queen and distracted everyone's attention. Bloody Tom and his invitations. If Pauline had seen her in the street, she'd have walked straight past without a second glance. Some people deserved to be ignored, consigned to the bin of oblivion for ever.

'Don't just stand there, Pauline,' Ted said. 'The devil makes work for idle hands.'

There was a lull in activity and the shop was empty. They'd been rushed off their feet all morning, but he still resented her taking a breather. Like he'd resented her taking time off yesterday to go to the funeral, insisting she put in a couple of hours' work before leaving for the church. Sometimes she dreamed about picking up one of those sharp knives and plunging it right through his chest.

Not a word of sympathy about Angel. Her *best* friend and he didn't give a damn. How are you, Pauline? How are you dealing with it all? No, none of that. Just a constant grumbling because he'd have to work on his own for a few hours. And he hadn't even had to do that. He could have paid George to come in on his day off, but he was too miserly to do it.

Pauline didn't hate George Abbott, but she didn't like him that much either. He was tall and skinny with a face the colour of parchment. Like one of those vampires that never went out in the sun. But he wasn't unkind. Boring but not mean. The worst thing was that he was always sucking up to her father like toadying was going out of fashion, laughing at his unfunny jokes and agreeing to stay late even when he had other plans.

George had asked her out for a drink, but she wasn't interested. The only person she had ever loved was Angel. The first time she'd seen her, it had been like falling off a cliff, a plunging, heart-in-her-stomach moment. Angel, with her long fair hair, blue eyes and small rosebud mouth, was the loveliest girl she'd ever seen. Not beautiful or showy, but soft and sweet and delicate.

Angel was gone.

Pauline would never see her again, never walk down to the Fox with her, never sit in her bedroom, never watch her deciding what to wear, or listen to her chattering on about something Frankie or Tom had said. All that was over. It couldn't be over. It was.

'Are you listening to a word I say, Pauline?'

'I heard you, Dad.'

'So why are you still standing there like a limp lettuce? Go and fill up those trays. We're almost out of bangers. I shouldn't have to tell you what to do when the stock gets low.'

Pauline trudged through to the back and started heaping sausages onto the cold metallic trays: pork sausages, beef sausages, chipolatas. Behind her hung rows of carcasses, the flesh pink between the ribs. A couple of rabbits, their soft fur still intact, lay ready to be skinned, their dead eyes staring at her.

No more Angel.

She wished it was Julia who was dead. That girl had been a

thorn in her side, a barrier between her and Angel for years. Always there when you didn't want her to be. The two of them with their private jokes and shared memories and secret glances. It hadn't been Angel's fault; she'd been too kind for her own good. She hadn't seen what Pauline had seen – that Julia Reeve only ever cared about herself.

And that had been proved after the accident. Hadn't they just cleared off, her and that hippy mother of hers? Julia had claimed she didn't want to go, that she didn't have a choice, but no one believed that. Just when Angel had needed her most, she'd hightailed it to Suffolk, leaving the rest of them to pick up the pieces.

Not that Pauline had been sorry she'd gone. Far from it. With Julia out of the way, Angel had finally been hers. But it hadn't been quite the same Angel. It was as if she'd been broken and put back together with some of the pieces missing.

'What are you doing in there, Pauline?'

'You know what I'm doing.'

'Well, do it faster. I haven't got all day.'

Pauline took the trays through to the shop and shoved them under the counter. Her father, she knew, was about to say something snide, but a couple of customers came in before he could do it. Immediately all his attention was transferred to them, his fleshy lips widening into a smile, the ingratiating banter spilling from his mouth. Mr Archer, the jolly butcher. What a joke! If only they realised what he was really like.

Now that Angel was dead, there was nothing keeping Pauline here. She would have followed in her mother's footsteps and walked away, gone somewhere else, anywhere else, if it hadn't been for Vyse still sniffing around. He'd take any sudden departure as proof of guilt. And anyway, there was still unfinished business: loose ends to be tied up and scores to be settled.

11

Julia had a frustrating Wednesday. With her mind not fully on the job, she misfiled the information on one of Cressida's clients and had to spend twenty minutes tracking it down. She forgot to pass on a phone message and missed a typo that went out on a press release. Her boss was not pleased. Then, when she glanced out of the window, she was sure she saw Tom Finch on Southampton Street and spent so long staring, trying to figure out if it was really him or not, that Cressida got the hump – again – and asked if there was something she'd rather be doing.

'Sorry.'

'What's the matter? You don't seem all here today.'

'Sorry,' Julia repeated. Her head was too full of Angel and Lindsay, of Renee and Vyse, to concentrate properly. 'I'm still trying to think of a suitable journalist for Ivor Apostle. Can you suggest anyone?'

'I wouldn't waste too much time on that. Didn't he say he wasn't keen on an interview?'

'He might change his mind.'

'And he might not.' Cressida shuffled some papers on her desk, lowered her voice, and said, 'Look, I probably shouldn't be telling you this, but with the current state of the economy Harley's talking about cutting costs.'

It took a few seconds for the implications to register with Julia. 'What?'

'It's no reflection on your work, but . . . well, it could be last in, first out, I'm afraid. I just thought I should warn you.'

Julia, who worked long hours, above and beyond the call of duty, was horrified. And okay, she'd made a few mistakes today, but they had been aberrations. Usually she was on the ball, one step ahead, giving it her all. She went cold at the thought of losing her job. 'He's going to fire me?'

'The phrase he prefers to use is "let you go". But nothing's been decided yet. I'm in your corner, Julia. I'm fighting to keep you. You're better than half the blokes here, but you didn't go to Eton, and Harley's all for promoting the old school tie.'

'God,' Julia said. 'Has someone made a complaint? One of my clients? Has Ivor Apostle complained?'

'No, I told you. It's purely a matter of finances.' Cressida paused and gave Julia a wary look. 'Why would Apostle complain? Is there something you didn't tell me?'

Julia shook her head. 'He's just the type, that's all. And he said I was young. I don't know. What should I do? Should I have a word with Harley?'

'Shit, no,' Cressida said. 'If he finds out I told you, he'll blow a fuse.'

Julia could feel the panic growing inside her. How long would it take to find another job? What if she couldn't? How would she survive without any money? She'd have to give up the Camden flat and go back to Suffolk with her tail between her legs. And

65

she could hardly investigate Angel's death from there. 'I have to do something. I can't just sit here waiting to be fired.'

'Just do your job and hope for the best. It'll be another month or so before he makes a final decision.'

'So, Christmas,' Julia said, 'that's going to be a festive present and a half.'

'And don't make any more silly mistakes. You've been all over the place today. It could be that the figures will be better this month, and he'll reconsider.'

'What are the chances of that?'

'It depends on new clients coming in, and not losing any that we've already got. So you'd do well to keep Apostle sweet. You don't want him cancelling five minutes after he's signed on the dotted line.'

Suddenly everything was falling apart for Julia. Her hopes for a glittering career were beginning to crumble. She felt helpless and depressed. Hopeless. Even if she did manage to hold on to Apostle, she could still be out on her ear by Christmas. The next month was going to be a nightmare: four stress-ridden weeks while she waited for Harley to make up his mind.

The afternoon passed slowly. With the threat of redundancy looming large, Julia felt like she was standing on the edge of a cliff waiting for Harley to shove her off. She knew that she had to do everything within her power to impress him, but her power didn't amount to much. Should she push herself forward more, or keep her head down? Should she attempt to acquire more clients? Perhaps she was better off trying to keep her current ones happy.

At five to six, with her thoughts still in tumult, she left the office and walked to the piazza. Despite the dark and the cold, Covent Garden was still busy, swarming with office workers and tourists. From a distance, she saw Lindsay standing by the church. She was one of those prim-looking girls, dressed neatly but unadventurously, her pale brown hair cut into a tidy bob, her body hunched as if she was hoping to make herself smaller and fade into the background.

Had Julia been forced to describe her back when they were teenagers, she would have used words like quiet, pleasant, ordinary and, if she was being completely honest, just a little bit dull. Like a familiar piece of furniture, Lindsay had simply been there, inoffensive and barely noticed. She felt bad now that she'd never made the effort to talk to her properly. Her friendship with Angel had always been a priority.

But should she feel bad? Julia pondered on this as she approached, recalling Renee's suspicions and those bent heads as she'd left the Fox. It *was* odd that she'd called, bearing in mind the casualness of their friendship. And even more odd that she should choose to meet her without the rest of the group.

As she got closer, Julia forced her mouth into a wide smile. Eventually Lindsay noticed her, gave a slight start and said, 'Hey, great to see you again.' There was one of those awkward moments where they both stepped forward – would they do that kiss-on-the-cheek thing that was so popular these days? – but indecision got in the way and neither of them was quite prepared to make the first move.

'Where would you like to go?' Julia said. 'Any preference?'

'Oh, you choose. I don't mind.'

Julia didn't want to go to any of her regular haunts in case she bumped into someone she knew and couldn't get rid of them. 'There's a pub in the basement,' she said, pointing across the piazza. 'I've never been there but I've heard it's okay.'

'Let's go there, then.'

As they set off, Julia said, 'So how have you been?'

'All right, thanks. I mean, it's still all a bit strange with what happened to Angel and everything, but I just try and take it a day at a time.'

'It must have been an awful shock.'

'It was.'

They walked across the piazza, went down the steps and into the pub. It was dimly lit with something of a dungeon feel to it. But thankfully it wasn't crowded, and it was warm. They ordered two red wines at the bar and took them to a table away from the other customers. Julia wasn't quite sure how to play it. Did Lindsay want to tell her something, find out something, or was this going to be an evening of social chit-chat? She sensed that Lindsay was on edge and moved the conversation on to safer ground.

'So, you're engaged. Tell me about Mark.'

'He's a civil servant in the Home Office,' Lindsay said, as if this was the most important thing about him. 'He wants to be an MP one day. He's very ambitious. You can't change anything, he reckons, unless you're at the centre of things.'

'And what would he like to change?'

Lindsay gave a light shrug. 'All sorts. The benefit system for a start – too many people skiving off work, he says, and living on handouts – and longer sentences for criminals. We need to clean up the streets and make them safe again. He's very keen on law and order. He's got lots of ideas.'

Julia had already formed a negative opinion of him. Mark sounded like the sort of man who had simplistic vote-winning 'solutions' to complicated problems. And *she* might be one of those so-called skivers before too long. Her heart sank once more at the prospect of losing her job. But she had to forget about the precarious state of her employment for a while and concentrate on Lindsay. 'Where did you two meet?'

'In the Fox. He was there with some friends, and we got

chatting. That was . . . oh, almost two years ago now.' Lindsay hesitated and then said, 'I don't think the others like him much. He's got strong opinions and they're not keen on that.'

'Pauline's got strong opinions.'

Lindsay laughed and took a sip of wine. 'Yeah, but not about anything important. She just sounds off about all the things that annoy her.'

'I imagine that's a long list.'

'True.'

'I suppose I'm on it too. Probably near the top.'

Lindsay's gaze slid away from Julia's face and settled somewhere over her right shoulder. She pretended to be distracted by a couple of customers at the bar while she tried to decide how to respond. Eventually her eyes met Julia's again. 'I think she was just surprised to see you, that's all. Pauline's mouth runs away with her. She can't help herself. I'm sure it wasn't anything personal.'

Julia, who was sure it *had* been personal, didn't press the point. Lindsay's defence of Pauline – or was it of Julia's feelings? – was admirable, but unnecessary. It wasn't as if she was bothered by Pauline's dislike of her. 'So are you working? I haven't even asked what you do.'

'I'm a teacher. At Oak Road Primary.'

'Are you? God, that must bring back some memories.' It was the school they had all attended apart from Pauline. 'It must be strange being back there.'

'It was at first, but I'm used to it now. The kids are all right. It's when they get older that the trouble starts.'

'You like teaching, then?'

'Love it,' Lindsay said. 'It's really rewarding. And the hours are good. What about you? PR, isn't it? I'm not really sure what that means.'

'Nor am I half the time.' Julia, thinking that she might not be there much longer, pulled a face. 'But yeah, it's okay. I'm not sure if I'll stay, though.'

'You've only just started, haven't you?'

Julia quickly reminded herself that if she was going to tell lies, they had better be consistent. She had told them all that she hadn't been back in London for long. 'Yes, but I'm still trying to figure out if it's really for me. You know what it's like when you start a new job. It takes a while to settle in.' To avoid any more difficult questions she said, 'And what's everyone else doing now?'

'Pauline's working for her dad at the butcher's, Frankie's a mechanic, and Tom has a job with the council. The housing department.'

'Kellston council?'

'Yes.'

'I wonder what he was doing here on Friday. I bumped into him on the Strand.'

'Just meeting a mate, probably. Or doing some shopping.'

It had not occurred to Julia that Tom might have mates other than the old gang, but of course there was no reason why he shouldn't. However, unless he had unusually long lunch breaks, it seemed like a long way to come for a meet-up or a snappy bit of shopping. 'I thought I saw him today as well, walking down Southampton Street.'

'Did you? Are you sure?'

'No, I'm not sure. I was up in the office. It might just have been someone who looked like him.'

Was it her imagination or did Lindsay seem relieved by her answer? It was hard to tell. She didn't know her well enough these days to be sure of what she was thinking. And why should she be thinking anything? What Tom Finch did in his lunch break was neither here nor there. But Julia couldn't help wondering if he'd been hoping to bump into her again, to contrive another meeting. He had suspected, perhaps, that she wouldn't call and decided to take matters into his own hands.

'Does Tom know about us having a drink together?'

Lindsay shook her head. 'I haven't seen him since the funeral. We meet up on a Saturday but not every week. Mark likes going to the cinema or the theatre; he's not that fussed over pubs.'

Or not that fussed over the company, Julia thought. She wanted to ask outright why Lindsay had rung, why she'd wanted to see her again, but knew that it would come across as rude. Instead, she said, 'Did Angel have a job?'

'At the nail bar on the high street. She enjoyed it there, chatting to all the customers. She used to do my nails too.' Lindsay briefly held out her right hand, fingers splayed. 'I don't make half as good a job of it as she did.'

'You must miss her.'

'We all do,' Lindsay said.

Julia waited for her to say something more, but she didn't.

12

By the time they were on their second glass of wine the conversation was starting to falter. They'd exhausted all the usual subjects – relationships, work, family, the weather – and Julia was becoming increasingly convinced that Lindsay had no ulterior motive in meeting her tonight. It was a disappointment. She had geared herself up for clues or revelations, but even when she nudged the conversation back to Angel, none were forthcoming. And then she pulled herself up short. Surely that was a good thing, wasn't it? The possibility that one of her old friends had been involved in Angel's death was too awful to contemplate. And yet, of course, she had been contemplating it, had even agreed to pool her information with Vyse.

Julia decided to finish her drink and make a move. It was still early but she was sure there was nothing more to learn. Lindsay, she decided, had only called out of some misplaced sense of nostalgia or, even worse, a feeling of obligation. Had she felt sorry for her, returning to London after all these years, alone and possibly friendless in the big city? Being on the receiving end of someone else's pity always made her feel uncomfortable.

Yes, she'd neck the wine and make her excuses. If she was going to keep her job, she'd need to have her wits about her. No hangovers. No late nights. No distractions. Well, not the sort of distractions that didn't lead anywhere. She wasn't giving up on her amateur sleuthing, but she needed to focus her attention. It was Tom who'd given her his number, and he seemed a more likely source of information.

But then, suddenly, everything changed.

Lindsay cleared her throat, shifted awkwardly in her seat and said, 'Erm ... so, did Renee ... did she say anything to you at the funeral?'

Julia's ears pricked up. 'Outside the church, you mean?'

'Or in the Fox.'

'Nothing that made much sense,' Julia said, acting ignorant. 'Except she seems convinced that Angel didn't kill herself.'

'I know. She's been weird with us ever since it happened. She went round to Pauline's and more or less accused her of ...'

Julia waited a few seconds and then prompted, 'Of?'

'Oh, you know, that we'd had something to do with it.'

'Heavens. Why would she think that?'

'Because we were the last ones to see her, I suppose. But she was fine when we left. I swear she was. And we'd never have hurt Angel. Why would we?'

Julia recognised a pleading note in her tone, but whether that was down to innocence or guilt she couldn't say. And hadn't Tom uttered something similar when they were leaving the churchyard? 'I don't really understand why Renee would make those accusations. You were mates with Angel for years. How would she come up with an idea like that?'

'Frankie says there's something wrong with her. That she's not quite right in the head.'

Julia recalled what Renee had said about Frankie always

73

'sniffing round' Angel. 'Well, she's just lost her daughter. Grief does awful things to people.'

'No, but even before that. She took against him for no reason at all.'

'Was there anything going on between the two of them, between Frankie and Angel?'

Lindsay looked shocked. Or pretended to. 'What do you mean? Frankie's with Clare. No, of course not. They're married. They've got kids and everything.'

But Julia knew that some men just couldn't help themselves. One woman was never enough. And having a couple of kids was hardly a guarantee of fidelity. 'What about before that? When they were younger, perhaps?'

Lindsay vehemently shook her head. 'No, never. We all used to hang out but there was never any boyfriend/girlfriend stuff. It wasn't like that. Just mates, that's all.' Her hands did a nervy dance on the tabletop. 'That Inspector Vyse has been listening to Renee. I'm sure he has. He keeps pulling us into the station and asking the same questions over and over. Tom says its harassment, that we should make a complaint, but I think that would just make us look guilty.'

'Didn't you say that Angel made stuff up sometimes? Maybe something she said to Renee made her think. And she told Vyse, and he . . .'

'What kind of something?' Lindsay said, a little too eagerly. She was probing, trying to find out if Renee had elaborated.

Julia shrugged. 'I've no idea.'

'But she must have given you a reason as to why she thinks it wasn't suicide.'

'No, not really. A mother's instinct?'

A scowl briefly made an appearance on Lindsay's forehead – frustration? Annoyance? – but was gone almost as soon as it had arrived. 'Maybe.' She paused for a few seconds and then said, 'So were you still in touch with Angel? Did she ever call or write to you?'

Julia hesitated, uneasy at getting caught out in a lie but certain that Lindsay was worried about something Angel might have told her. 'Not often,' she eventually said. 'Every now and again. You know what it's like. I should have made more of an effort.'

'When was the last time?'

'I'm not sure. A while ago.'

Lindsay looked like she wanted a more specific answer but wasn't sure how to go about it. Her tongue slid along her upper lip. 'Not recently then?'

'Not *that* recently.'

Relief again on Lindsay's face.

'Why do you ask?' Julia said bluntly.

'Oh, no reason. I just wondered, that's all. Angel didn't mention it.'

'She probably forgot.'

Lindsay lifted her glass and took a sip of wine. 'Yes, she was always forgetting things. And half of what she did tell you wasn't true. You had to take everything she said with a pinch of salt. Like that baby when you went to see her. Jack, yeah? Or Larry. I don't care what Pauline says, it wasn't a joke, it was just typical Angel, wanting you to believe things that weren't true.'

Julia was growing more suspicious by the minute. Lindsay's insistence that Angel couldn't be trusted had to have a purpose, and that purpose seemed to be the laying of doubt in her mind. Doubt about Angel's truthfulness, about something important Angel might have told her. Except, of course, Angel had told her nothing because they hadn't been in touch for years.

'If Angel killed herself, why didn't she leave a note? There wasn't a note, was there? I didn't hear any mention of it.'

Lindsay shook her head. 'No, no note. But people don't always, do they? Sometimes they just decide and that's that.'

But Julia couldn't imagine Angel leaving nothing for Renee, not even a few scribbled words. She had always been close to her mum. Or had something changed in the time she'd been away? 'What exactly did Renee say when she went round to Pauline's?'

'Well, I'm not sure *exactly*. I mean, I wasn't there. But Pauline said she was angry and a bit incoherent, that she was claiming we knew more than we were letting on, that because we'd seen Angel that afternoon, we must be hiding something. But we're not. I swear. Angel was fine when we left.'

'She could have gone to the river with someone or met them there. Her drowning wasn't necessarily suicide.'

Lindsay looked doubtful. 'I suppose. But who? She didn't have a boyfriend. Who would she be meeting?'

'Someone you didn't know about.'

'But she'd have told us if she had a new bloke. Why would she keep quiet about it?'

'Maybe he was married or attached.'

'And you're thinking they could have killed her?'

'It's not impossible,' Julia said, 'if they thought Angel was going to go public. Maybe she was trying to force his hand. Men have killed for less.'

Lindsay pondered on this for a while, but then shook her head again. 'Angel wasn't good at keeping quiet about things. She'd have told Pauline even if she didn't tell me.'

Julia had more she wanted to ask, but Lindsay looked at her watch, drank the rest of her wine and put the glass down firmly on the table. 'Sorry, but I'll have to make a move. I've got some lessons to prepare for tomorrow. But we should do this again. It's been nice.'

It was only twenty past seven when they departed from the pub and stepped out into the cold. They left the piazza together, striding towards the Tube. During this short walk Lindsay kept up a long stream of empty chatter, perhaps to prevent Julia from asking any more questions. They separated outside the station with cheery goodbyes and promises to stay in touch.

While she waited for the lift to take her down into the depths of the Underground, Julia replayed the evening in her head. None of it sat well with her. Lindsay, she was sure, had been on a fishing expedition; she had come with an agenda, but what was the motive behind it? To find out what Julia knew. Well, what did she know? Only that Lindsay was worried, but that was enough, more than enough, to make her want to keep on digging.

13

After changing at King's Cross, Julia got off the Tube at Camden Town and set off for home. It was only a ten-minute walk, and she spent it thinking about Angel. There was something about a childhood friend that was special, a link to the past, to a time when you were still unformed and open. Their lives had taken different directions, but the connection remained. It might be thin, a little tenuous, but it was still there. She couldn't let Angel's 'suicide' slide by without being sure that there wasn't a more sinister side to it.

The night air was cold, and she huddled down into the collar of her coat. Her breath escaped in thin wintry clouds. She knew that she was partly driven by guilt and the fear that some of Angel's depression had its roots in her own past actions. Perhaps Lindsay's motives weren't the only ones that needed examining. Be that as it may, she still felt determined to see it through.

She should talk to Renee again and see if there was anything more solid to her suspicions. Not that there was anything wrong with feelings, but the law didn't tend to take them seriously.

Well, maybe that wasn't true. Hadn't Vyse talked about his gut feeling? But then it was always one rule for the police and another for everyone else. She had no phone number for Renee but could check with directory enquiries, and if that yielded nothing she would just have to go to the Mansfield.

It started to rain as Julia trudged down the stone steps to the basement, her path clearly lit by the flat above. Their kitchen light was on, the blinds still raised. The three-storey, sub-divided house had six other tenants, all couples who occupied a floor each. Her flat had been converted from part of the former cellar and always smelled faintly of damp.

She took the key from her bag and was about to open the door when she noticed that both of her terracotta pots had been moved. Not by much but just enough to reveal some of the former outline of where they'd been sitting. That was odd. A cat? No, they were too heavy for a cat to accidentally nudge. She had no idea if they'd been in place this morning. She'd left early, in the dark, and hadn't looked down.

Then, as she put in her key, she noticed something else: clear scratches and dents in the metal panel, as if an attempt had been made to force the lock. God, someone had tried to break in! She gave a startled jump, instinctively looking over her shoulder in case the would-be intruder was still in the vicinity. There was nowhere to hide down here but they could be on the street or round the corner.

Julia quickly opened the door, slammed it shut behind her and pulled the bolts across. She flicked on the light and gazed around. There was no sign of anyone having gained entrance. *That* was a relief. Somone just trying their luck, perhaps, an opportunist seeing the flat in darkness. She was glad of the bars on the windows – not the prettiest things to look at but a good defence against burglars. A fast scout around the flat reassured her that everything was as she'd left it in the living room, bedroom, bathroom and kitchen.

Her heart was still beating at a rate of knots though. She didn't have much to steal – the TV, the stereo, some jewellery – but it was the idea of a stranger in her home, going through her personal possessions, that disturbed her. It would have been a feeling of violation, of contamination. The fact that they had got as far as the front door was bad enough – she shuddered at the thought of their greedy hands, their bad intentions – and sent up a silent prayer that on this occasion they'd been thwarted.

But what if they came back? This time armed with better tools. Maybe tomorrow or the next day. The door was solid, strong, but it wouldn't withstand brute force. And she couldn't be here keeping guard round the clock. The only deterrent she could think of, other than buying a large, noisy dog, was to pull down the blinds and leave the light on in the living room when she left in the morning.

Julia went to the kitchen, poured herself a glass of water and sipped it standing by the sink. It was then that it came to her. What if Lindsay had asked her out tonight so that one of the others could try and get into her flat? But that was ridiculous. What could they think she had that would be of such importance? No, she was just being paranoid. Or was she? It suddenly seemed like a coincidence too far.

She went into the living room, rummaged in her bag and took out a business card. Then she picked up the phone and dialled. When it was answered she took a deep breath and said, 'Is Inspector Vyse there please?'

It was another forty minutes before she heard the inspector's heavy tread on the stone steps. She jumped when she heard the bell even though she'd been expecting it. When she opened the door, he smiled at her. He was wearing a dark overcoat with the collar turned up, and his hair was damp from the rain. Vyse seemed in that moment to be a very solid and reassuring presence, and for the first time since getting home she relaxed.

'Sorry to call so late,' she said. 'You didn't have to come round.'

'I thought I might as well see the scene of the crime.'

'There's not much to see. And I'm not sure I'd call it a crime exactly.'

By the light from the hallway, Vyse bent to examine the lock on the door. 'Yeah, someone's made an attempt to get in. A pretty clumsy one at that. Not what you'd call a professional job.' He looked around the small exterior area as if searching for clues. There wasn't much to see.

'And the pots have been moved,' she said. 'I can't swear that was today, though.'

Vyse bent to examine them, lifting them up slightly to examine underneath. 'Looking for a key. You'd be surprised how many people keep their spare in places like this.'

'Not me,' she said, deciding to keep quiet about the fact that she kept hers *in* one of the pots, wrapped in cellophane and buried a long way down. She realised now that any burglar worth his salt would probably just upend the pot and empty out its contents. They would hardly be deterred by a few winter pansies. Later, after Vyse had gone, she would dig out the key and find a better hiding place.

'Let's go inside before we both get soaked,' he said. 'You can tell me about tonight.'

Julia had mentioned during the call that she and Lindsay had met up. She made two mugs of coffee and took them through to the living room where Vyse was sitting on the sofa with his long legs stretched out in front of him. With nowhere else to sit she perched on the other end. Now he was here, she wasn't sure if she'd done the right thing in calling.

'Cosy place you've got here,' he said.

'Bijou is the word you're looking for.' She had, however, made the best of the limited amount of space available, choosing her furniture judiciously, hanging a couple of paintings on the wall and introducing a riot of greenery. 'Or just plain small.'

'I like it,' he said. 'It's got character.'

As she related the events of the evening, Julia found herself fighting against the desire to exaggerate. Lindsay's responses had felt suspicious at the time but as she repeated them, she could see that they might come across as perfectly normal, mere snatches of conversation that were as innocuous as a chat about the weather. Nothing damning about them, nothing particularly dubious. She wanted him to believe her, though, to trust in her instincts. What she feared was that she might come across as one of those hysterical women who overreacted to everything, or even as some kind of attention seeker. Although why did she care what he thought of her? She quickly pushed the question aside.

Vyse only interrupted occasionally to clarify a point here or there. For the most part he kept quiet, listening intently, his eyes fixed on her.

When she came to the end, Julia sighed and said, 'I don't know. Perhaps I'm making something out of nothing. Everyone's on edge, aren't they? No one's behaving normally. But when I got home and found the lock had been messed with, it all seemed like too much of a coincidence.'

'And you're certain that those marks were made today? And the pots were also moved today?'

Julia hesitated, suddenly not that sure at all. 'I think so. I think I'd have noticed. But I can't swear to it.' Her shoulders slumped. 'And if it was one of the old gang, how did they even know where I live? I haven't given my address to any of them.'

'That's easy enough. There's the phone book or the electoral register or failing that the good old-fashioned method of just following you home from work.'

Julia didn't like the idea of having been followed and, even worse, of not having noticed. 'But why would they want to get into the flat anyway? There's nothing here connected to Angel. It doesn't make any sense.'

'Unless . . .'

'Unless what?'

'Unless you said something at the funeral that made them think.'

Julia racked her brains but didn't come up with anything. 'I can't . . . nothing comes to mind.'

'Lindsay said that Angel wasn't always truthful, didn't she? Perhaps Angel told her that you *had* been in touch. Or maybe that she'd sent you something, a letter perhaps, a letter with information that has some bearing on her death. Something she didn't want to say over the phone. They might not have believed her at the time but now, with you suddenly turning up out of the blue, they're worried that she wasn't lying.'

Julia considered this – it wasn't impossible – and then pulled a face. 'But wouldn't they have waited until Lindsay talked to me? Why risk getting caught trying to break into my flat before they even had the facts?'

'Timing,' Vyse said. 'They knew for sure you'd be out this evening and that gave them at least a couple of hours. They'd have wanted it to be dark. And even if you'd denied being in touch with Angel, which you didn't, why should they believe you? If you do have something on them, they want it back quickly before you realise how important it is and tell the police.'

83

'But I didn't even know about her death. Tom's aware of that. He was the one who broke the news. That doesn't really tally with me having contact with her.' But even while she was speaking, she could remember the relief on Lindsay's face when she'd said it had been 'a while' since she'd been in touch with Angel.

'Guilty people can get paranoid. You and Renee were talking outside the church, and then later in the Fox. They might think you're working together.'

'You were at the bar. How could you have seen that?'

Vyse grinned. 'I wasn't on my own. I was the cop in plain sight, but there was another one mingling with the crowd. She told me. Outside the ladies, yeah? She said Renee seemed quite heated.'

'She was, but she didn't tell me anything I haven't already told you. I thought I might call her. Do you have her number?'

'You'd be better doing it face to face.'

'If she knew anything for definite, she'd have told *you* about it.'

'She's wary of the law. And maybe there are things she doesn't want me to know.'

'Like what?'

Vyse shrugged. 'Personal things. Who's to say? I'm just whistling in the wind. She might open up to you.'

Julia thought about this, decided to leave the decision for another day, and moved on. 'Going back to the attempted break-in – if that's what it was – then they're going to come back, aren't they? Try again.'

'They might. You need to let them know that you're aware of it. Who's next on your list of people to see?'

'Tom Finch,' she said. 'Yes, I suppose it's Tom.'

'When you call, don't make a big deal of it. Just slip it into the conversation that someone tried to break in, and that you've alerted the neighbours. It might make them think twice about trying again.'

Julia leaned back and placed her neck against the top of the sofa. 'The more I think about all this, the less it adds up.' She stifled a yawn. 'Maybe I'm making too much of it. The stuff with Lindsay, I mean. It could have been perfectly innocent.'

'You're tired,' he said. 'Long day?'

'They're all long days. Harley Jenks likes to get his money's worth.' She felt a sudden urge to tell him about her job being on the line, of how she could be out of work by Christmas, but smartly held her tongue. He wasn't here to listen to her woes or offer sympathy. Vyse was a cop, not a friend, and she had to remember that.

'So what happened to Angel?' he said after a short pause.

'Isn't that what we're trying to find out?'

'No, I mean before this, before she drowned. Renee said she'd had an accident when she was fourteen, a fall that left her with damage.'

Julia felt a tightening in her chest as she drew in a breath. 'She did. She fell down some steps on the Mansfield.' She took a moment to steady herself. Even after eleven years, it was still hard to talk about. 'It was one afternoon after school. We'd been drinking cider at Angel's flat. Renee was at work. All of us were there and another boy called Liam. We weren't blind drunk, but I suppose we weren't exactly sober either. I was in the kitchen with Angel, and we had a stupid argument. Fourteen-year-old girls rowing over a boy. God, it all seems so ridiculous now. We both had a crush on Liam, stupid teenage crushes, and had agreed that because we both liked him neither of us would try and date him. Except that afternoon Angel had been flirting non-stop and had agreed to go with him to the youth club on Friday.'

85

Julia paused. She could see him again, a slim fair-haired boy with blue-green eyes wearing an Iron Maiden T-shirt. The temporary focus of all her teenage desires. 'I was jealous, of course. I told her she was a bad friend. She stormed out of the flat and I followed her. She was saying it wasn't a date, not a real one, just a night out with a mate. But we both knew that wasn't true.'

Julia stopped again, pushing her hair back from her face. 'We never usually argued. It was weird and awful. She kept saying it was nothing, and I kept saying it was everything. It all sounds so pathetic now. It *was* pathetic. We were outside on the external walkway near the stone steps that led downstairs. I don't know what happened. I was too busy being stroppy and resentful. One minute she was there and the next . . . She must have stumbled, I suppose, lost her balance and next thing she was rolling down the steps. I ran down to her, but she wasn't moving so I rushed back and yelled for the others and then went home – I only lived a couple of doors away – and called an ambulance.'

'How badly hurt was she?' Vyse said.

'She spent over a month in hospital with a fractured skull and spinal injuries. And even when she came out, she still had problems. Angel always said that she couldn't remember what had happened, that all she could remember was us all being in the flat together and the rest was a blank. If I could go back . . . but there's no going back, is there? She fell because we were arguing.'

'And because she'd been drinking,' Vyse said.

'But she wouldn't even have been outside if it hadn't been for me.'

'It was an accident,' Vyse said. 'They happen.'

Julia wanted to feel reassured, but she didn't. She knew where the blame lay; it was with her, and nothing was going to change that. 'That was the point when Mum decided to move to Suffolk. We left about six weeks after Angel came out of hospital. I felt bad about it, for not being there for her when she needed me, but, in a way, I was relieved too. Does that sound terrible?' She didn't wait for Vyse to respond. 'Yes, it *was* terrible. I felt so guilty about everything and just wanted to get away. And ... and I felt that they suspected me. The others. Pauline even asked me straight out if I'd pushed her.' She stopped, cleared her throat, and glanced at Vyse. 'I didn't, in case you're wondering.'

'I wasn't.'

'But I wasn't completely innocent either. That fall changed Angel's life. She was never the same after.'

Vyse drank his coffee, keeping his eyes on her. 'Guilt eats away at you. You can't let it take over. It was an accident. I'm not saying move on, get over it, but the things you can't change you have to learn to accept.'

'Wise words, I'm sure.'

'Yeah, I'm known for them.'

Julia raised a weak smile. 'Anyway, that's what happened. We kept in touch for a while, wrote letters, and then it kind of fizzled out.'

'What made you come back to London?'

'Work,' she said. 'A better job, better prospects.' Even though her prospects weren't looking too good right now, she didn't want Vyse to think she was a complete loser. 'I did intend to get in touch with Angel again but ... I don't know, I kept putting it off. I wasn't even sure she'd want to see me.'

'And this Liam – what was his surname?'

'Liam? Oh, it was Crosby. Liam Crosby.'

'Did they stay friends?'

'I don't know. She never mentioned him when she wrote, but that doesn't mean anything. She might have felt uncomfortable talking about him. You'll have to ask the others.'

'Or you could. You could ask Tom when you see him.'

'Okay, I'll do that. Does the name mean anything to you? Is he still living on the Mansfield?'

'He used to. He did a bunk a few years back, scarpered when things got too hot for him. There's still a warrant out for his arrest. He's a small-time drug dealer, petty thief, general toerag.'

Julia frowned, unable to connect this description to the cute boy she had once mooned over. 'It's sad,' she said. 'That he turned out like that, I mean.'

'Sad for the people he thieves from,' Vyse said.

'Yes, that too.'

'Well, I think we're done here,' he said, rising to his feet. 'I'll leave you in peace. Let me know how it goes with Tom. And Renee,' he added, 'if you decide to go and see her.'

'Of course. And I appreciate you coming round.'

Vyse gave a brusque nod. 'Take care of yourself.'

At the door he thanked her for the coffee, said good night and walked up the steps. Julia stood for a while, breathing in the sulphurous November air. Bonfire Night had been over a fortnight ago but the smell of it still lingered, hanging in the atmosphere, sharp and smoky and underlain by the whiff of diesel.

She heard Vyse get into his car, start the engine and drive away. And then she was alone. What now? She bent down and picked up one of the terracotta pots, took it inside and prepared to get her hands dirty.

14

Pauline had the hump with the whole bloody lot of them. Why couldn't they just leave things alone? No, instead they had to go chasing around after Julia Reeve, stirring things up when they were best left alone. Lindsay was looking pathetically smug like some witless Miss Marple sharing her thoughts on the latest village murder. Frankie was hanging on her every word. Tom was frowning as if he was hearing something that he didn't want to hear.

She slurped her lager while she looked round the pub. George was at the bar and she thought about joining him, but that would only give him the wrong idea. Once, in the shop, she had laughed at something he'd said and he'd spent the rest of the morning trying to catch her eye as if they had an understanding, a connection, as if they'd taken the first step on a walk down the aisle.

George wasn't interested in her so much as with what she came with. He fancied running her father's shop one day and marrying Ted Archer's daughter would bring him one step closer to fulfilling that ambition. Jesus, what sort of man dreamed of spending his days with his hands covered in blood? She lit a fag, wondering if she smelled of pig fat and mince. It was probably the equivalent to perfume in George's quivering nostrils.

Pauline shifted on the seat, crossing her legs at her ankles then uncrossing them. She looked at the three other people gathered round the table. Everything felt odd, as if there was no anchor, nothing holding them down – or together. The connection between the four of them was flimsy like they were just so much flotsam bobbing around, bumping into each other before separating again.

'What do you reckon, Pauline?' Tom said.

'About what?'

'About what Julia said to Lindsay.'

Pauline flicked her cigarette towards the ashtray. 'I don't think anything about it. Only that it was stupid going to see her. If she does know something, she's not going to say, and if she doesn't then you've just made her ten times more suspicious.'

Lindsay, who'd been enjoying her ten minutes in the spotlight, scowled at her. 'I didn't say anything to make her suspicious.'

'It's not what you *said*, it's the being there. Don't you think she's wondering why you rang her up, why you slogged all the way over to Covent Garden, why you suddenly felt the need to be in her company when you were never good friends to begin with?'

'We were friends,' Lindsay whined. 'We were all friends.'

Pauline rolled her eyes. 'Sure.'

'Why do you say it like that?'

'Oh, don't be so bloody sensitive. All I mean is that *I* would have thought it was weird if I was Julia. She only came to the funeral because she had to, because it would have looked bad if she hadn't. If you'd all just left well alone, she'd have been and gone, and we'd never have seen her again.'

'You don't know that,' Frankie piped up. 'Now she's back in London she might want to hang out. Not with you, of course, you were always a cow to her, but with me and Tom and Lindsay.'

'I was never a cow.'

Frankie grinned. 'No, sugar and spice and all things nice, that's you.'

Pauline swatted the comment aside. 'Yeah, yeah.' She wasn't bothered by anything Frankie said, because he never had anything useful *to* say. His only redeeming feature was that he was pretty to look at. She could see why the girls went for him, but it was all candy coating. Once you bit into it there was nothing inside. He was hollow, devoid of all but the most basic intelligence and driven purely by his desires.

Lindsay was back talking about her meeting with Julia, and Pauline switched off. She glanced around the pub again. She had always loved it in here when she was with Angel, the two of them sitting side by side, elbows touching, always laughing, getting slowly pissed on a Saturday night. Light and dark: Angel with her long fair hair, and Pauline with her black. The perfect contrast. And light and dark in other ways too. She didn't want to think about that.

Abruptly, Pauline stubbed out her cigarette, got to her feet and set off in the direction of the ladies. When she got close, she glanced over her shoulder, dug in her pocket for some change, veered into the alcove where the payphone was and picked up the receiver. While she dialled, she kept her gaze fixed on the corridor leading from the bar.

The pips went and she shoved the money in. 'Hey, it's me. I'm in the Fox.'

'What's going on?'

'Lindsay got back after her meeting with Julia.'

'And?'

'And nothing much. Just what you'd expect really. She's all full of herself, like she just did something amazing instead of downing two glasses of wine and making small talk for an hour. I can't see that she learned anything useful.'

'Did you expect her to?'

'No.'

'Well then.'

Pauline pressed the phone against her ear. 'What are you doing?'

'Watching the news.'

'And then?'

'Going to bed.'

She could hear the TV in the background, could visualise the room the TV was sitting in. She didn't want to ask but she did. 'Why don't you come to the pub? There's still time before last orders.'

'I don't feel like it.'

'Yeah, I might head home soon.'

'Is that it?'

'Yeah, I guess.'

'Okay. Got to go. Bye, Pauline.'

Pauline replaced the receiver and picked up the change that came tumbling out. She wished she hadn't called now, wished she hadn't bothered. Her pride usually kept her from doing stupid things. She had just wanted to hear another voice, one that wasn't Lindsay's or Tom's or Frankie's. And yes, if she was being honest, she'd been hoping for an invite. *Come on over if you're not doing anything else.* It had been a mistake. Loneliness could do that. Without Angel, she was all at sea, floundering.

Slowly, she walked back to the table. What she had to remember was that she had a job to do, promises to keep, retribution to dispense. Nothing else mattered. Nothing came even close.

15

In between attempting to impress Harley Jenks, worrying about her would-be burglar and trying to make sense of what had actually happened to Angel, Julia had endured a stressful Thursday. It had been a relief to get home in the evening and find the flat undisturbed. She hadn't been able to get hold of Tom yet but had left a message on his answering machine. Now it was Friday, and she had another trial to look forward to – a lunchtime meeting with Ivor Apostle.

At quarter to one she went to the bathroom, brushed her hair and put on a fresh layer of lipstick. She studied her reflection in the mirror. Did she look tired? Although she'd gone to bed early last night, she hadn't slept much, overly alert to any noises: the ticking of the cooling radiators, the rain beating against the windows and the indeterminate creaks that can't be attributed to anything other than an old house shifting and flexing in the early hours of the morning.

Julia was wearing a rose-coloured shift dress, not too short and not too long, but classy enough to show she'd made an effort. Holding on to Apostle as a client was imperative if she was going to keep her job. And so was walking that fine line between being professional on the one hand, and approachable and friendly on the other.

When she was certain that no more improvements could be made – that comment of Vyse's about making a silk purse out of a sow's ear sprang to mind – she sprayed on some Paris, pushed back her shoulders and tried to assume an air of quiet confidence. Who was she fooling? Absolutely no one. A flutter of panic rose in her chest. Just keep your cool, she told herself. You can do this.

But maintaining her cool proved difficult as she grew closer to Molly's. When she was a few yards away she could see through the plate-glass windows that the place was busy. She pushed open the door and stepped inside.

The bar was bigger, brighter and airier than she'd expected. Most wine bars were so dim and gloomy you could barely see the person sitting in front of you, but Apostle – or his designer – had gone for a less dreary approach. The walls were a pale yellow, providing a backdrop for bright modern paintings, and the tables and chairs were of warm honey-coloured wood. Most of the tables were occupied and there was a loud buzz of conversation, a chink of glasses and the scrape of cutlery on plates. A long bar occupied the far end, the mirrored shelving behind it filled with bottles.

Julia glanced around but couldn't spot the man she was supposed to be meeting. A waitress passed by, and she introduced herself and said she was here to meet Mr Apostle.

'Come this way,' the girl said.

Julia had the impression that the waitress had given her an assessing look, one of those fast up-and-down judging glances that sometimes came with lifted eyebrows. She was led to the back of the room, to a cosy corner apart but still in sight of the other customers. She chose a chair facing out so she could people-watch while she was waiting.

'I'll let him know you're here. He shouldn't be long. Would you like a drink?'

Knowing she had to keep her wits about her, Julia ordered a tonic water with ice and a slice. Then she sat back and let her eyes roam over the room. There was a mixed clientele: couples, office workers, ladies lunching and business types doing deals over large glasses of wine.

Her drink arrived and she sipped it while she read the menu. It was a mix of upmarket fast food – burgers and pizzas – with some pasta dishes and a few salads. Not exorbitantly priced but not cheap either. The kind of food that was only there to mop up the alcohol. Were they going to eat? Julia was vegetarian in Suffolk, a carnivore in London. Christmas dinner with her mum would be nut roast with all the trimmings. The house would be full to bursting with the usual residents plus some additional waifs and strays. Children too, probably. Not to mention Darcy, the cat with attitude. Opportunities for peace and quiet would be thin on the ground.

Five minutes passed, and then another five. She began to wonder if Apostle was keeping her waiting deliberately, as some kind of payback for postponing their Monday appointment. A mild impatience was gradually turning into irritation. To distract herself, Julia thought about Michael Vyse, but this only produced a different sort of tension. She was attracted to him, that was the trouble, attracted to that sharp angular face and those piercing blue eyes.

Was the feeling mutual, though? Vyse had driven over to Camden, but that didn't mean anything. He was working on a case, putting in the hours, chasing after any new clues that came his way. And even if he did like her, it wouldn't be smart to get involved. Too messy. Too complicated. Too soon after her awful break-up with Alex. (Was nine months too soon?) Thinking about that man's cheating didn't improve her mood. Not just once but ... how many times? She didn't know for sure. And anyway, once was more than enough. She should have walked away then, instead of trying to hold on to something that wasn't worth holding on to.

This was why she was frowning when Apostle finally showed up. Well, that and the fact that he was fifteen minutes late.

'Sorry,' he said, pulling out a chair and sitting opposite her. 'Bit of an emergency but it's all sorted now.' He glanced over his shoulder and then looked back at her. 'So what do you think of the place? Not bad, is it? We've been doing good business since it opened.'

Julia had already gathered from their last meeting that Apostle was a man who needed his achievements acknowledged. 'Lovely,' she said. 'Congratulations. I'm impressed. You've done a great job.'

'Yeah, I think so. It's busy in the evening too. What are you drinking?'

'I'm fine, thanks,' she said.

'We should get some champagne. Celebrate.'

Julia wasn't sure what they were supposed to be celebrating – the success of the bar, her role as his PR agent, the fact that it was Friday? – so she simply shook her head and indicated towards her glass. 'I'm fine with this.'

Apostle picked up the glass and sniffed at it. 'What is it? Tonic water?'

'Yes.'

'No, we'll have champagne.' Apostle attracted the attention of a waitress and before Julia could make any further protestations ordered a bottle of their finest. 'It's good stuff. You'll like it.'

Julia was irked by being railroaded into drinking when she didn't want to – a perfect example of his macho presumption – but she couldn't afford to offend or annoy him. Keeping Apostle on side was essential. She recalled Cressida's warning and gave herself a mental instruction to drink slowly and in moderation.

'Just a glass then,' she said to be agreeable.

'Good girl.'

Julia had to fight to keep the smile on her face. *Good girl.* What sort of a response was that? Men could be so damn patronising. 'So have you thought any more about what we talked about at our last meeting?' Making it clear, she hoped, that this was business and nothing else.

Apostle leaned forward, placing his large elbows on the table. He had an immense, almost overwhelming, presence with his massive frame and wide shoulders. 'Oh, that,' he said dismissively. 'I haven't made up my mind yet.'

Which kind of begged the question of what she was doing here. 'Was there something else you wanted to talk about?'

Before he could answer, the champagne arrived in a bucket along with two glasses. The waitress went to open it, but Apostle waved her away. 'I'll do that,' he said.

He made a show of opening the bottle with consummate ease, thus proving to his audience of one that he was a man who was used to drinking champagne. He passed her a glass and said, 'So, Julia, do you have a boyfriend?'

'Pardon?'

'A boyfriend,' he repeated.

'What do you want to know that for?'

Apostle shrugged. 'I'm just curious. If we're going to be working together, we should get to know each other.'

Do you have a girlfriend? she felt like retorting but immediately realised that this could be misinterpreted as her having a romantic interest in him. 'Yes,' she said instead, deciding to resurrect her ex. 'Alex. He's a photographer.'

'In London?'

'No, in Ipswich.'

Apostle smirked. 'Long-distance relationships never work.'

'It's hardly long distance. He's not living across the other side of the world. It only takes an hour, just over an hour, on the train. It can take longer than that to get across London. I suppose it's a matter of trust.'

'Trust!' He snorted.

Julia sipped her champagne, watching him over the rim of her glass. She only had to think of Alex for a red mist to descend, but she battled to keep her voice neutral. 'It works for us.'

'I'm not the trusting sort. I couldn't put up with that. Out of sight, out of mind. Nobody likes to be made a fool of.'

Julia had the feeling he was talking from experience. Knowing how tough it was, how humiliating it was to be cheated on, she experienced a brief pang of empathy. It didn't last.

'Not that it ever happens twice,' he continued. One strike and they're out. I don't do second chances.' Apostle picked up the menu and thrust it towards her. 'We should order some food.'

Julia considered the carbonara but then had visions of random strings of spaghetti dropping off her fork and down her nice pink dress. It wasn't a dish that could be eaten with decorum. Instead, when the waitress arrived, she opted for a small margherita pizza and a side salad. Apostle asked for a burger and fries.

'So tell me about you,' she said, picking up her glass and putting it down again. The champagne *was* good, very good, but she couldn't afford to get tipsy. 'What got you into wine bars and nightclubs and security?'

'It's business, that's all. You have to spot the opportunities and grab them, find the gaps in the market. Without ever putting all your eggs in one basket. Diversification, that's the key. You never know what's going to happen. What's popular one day is out of favour the next.'

'And what's the long-term plan?'

'Retirement at fifty,' he said. 'What's yours?'

'I haven't thought that far ahead.'

'You should. Life has a habit of passing you by if you don't keep an eye on it. Or are you just planning on marrying well, finding a rich sugar daddy and living the high life: luxury flat in town, big house in the country, fancy car, kids you never see because you pack them off to public school?'

'Oh sure,' she replied, deciding to play along rather than give him a lecture on female emancipation. 'That's the dream. Do you know anyone who'd fit the bill?'

He heard the sarcastic edge to her voice and gave a thin smile. 'I've met plenty of women like that, only out for what they can get.'

'Maybe you're mixing with the wrong women.'

'You a feminist, then, Julia?' He asked the question as if he was accusing her of something.

'Give me your definition of the word feminist and I'll tell you if I'm that or not.'

Apostle didn't rise to the bait, or maybe he couldn't think of a suitable answer. The food arrived and he used the natural pause to change the subject when he started up the conversation again. 'So what's it like working for Harley Jenks?'

'Good,' she said. 'Yes, I'm enjoying it.'

'How long have you been there?'

'Just under a year.'

'I've always found Harley a bit of a wanker. All red braces and big cigar. Does he actually do anything other than strut around playing the big I am?'

Julia chose not to answer the question, asking instead, 'If you don't like him, why did you choose to come to the company?'

'If I only did business with people I liked, I wouldn't do much business.'

Apostle bit into his burger. He ate like she expected him to – voraciously and without finesse – stuffing the food into his mouth as if it might disappear if he didn't dispose of it in double-quick time. She took a bite of pizza. It was okay, nothing special, but she nodded and murmured 'Mm' like it was a culinary treat.

'So where next?' Apostle said.

Julia frowned. 'Next?'

'Don't you career girls tend to move around, hop from one firm to another as you climb the slippery ladder to success?'

'Oh, I'm happy where I am for now.'

'That's a shame.'

'Is it?'

Apostle leaned forward, picked up the bottle of champagne and refilled her glass before she had the chance to stop him. 'I'm looking for a new assistant. My girl's leaving at Christmas, having a sprog. And it's not mine, before you ask. Anyway, she's not intending to come back so there's a vacant position and I need to fill it soon.'

Julia, beyond surprised, felt her jaw drop. This was the last thing she'd been expecting. What? The very idea of working for him made her recoil but then she thought again. With her current job on the line, she couldn't afford to be too hasty. 'Why me?'

'Why not? You seem competent.'

Which was hardly a ringing endorsement of her abilities. 'I'm not a secretary if that's what you're looking for. There are plenty of those out there.' She made a brief sweeping gesture with her right hand. 'You can walk into an agency and get one in five minutes.'

'I'm not looking for a secretary. An *assistant*. A PA. I need someone I can work with, someone smart, adaptable, calm in a crisis.'

'Are there many crises?'

'They come and go. There'll be long hours sometimes, but I'll give you time off in lieu.'

'Like I said, I'm happy in my current job.'

Apostle made a derisory sound in the back of his throat. 'Who could be happy having to work for Harley Jenks? The man's a muppet. He's got no respect for the people who work for him. His staff are disposable. He'll chew you up and spit you out.'

It appeared that Ivor Apostle knew more about Jenks than she'd expected. 'He's not so bad,' she said weakly.

'I bet he gives you all the crap clients. Don't even bother denying it. Clients like me, right?' He grinned. 'I know what he thinks of me. He spent fifteen minutes crawling up my arse while at the same time looking down his nose. Quite a balancing act. He reckons I'm working-class scum, but he still wants my money.'

It crossed Julia's mind that poaching her might be Apostle's way of getting his own back on Harley. If so, he was barking up the wrong tree. Not that Apostle needed to be made aware of that. 'I don't know anything about wine bars or security.'

'It's not rocket science. You'll soon pick it up. And I'll pay you more than you're getting now.'

'You don't know what I'm getting.'

'It doesn't matter.'

'Anyway, it's not about the money,' she said, even though the thought of a better salary was tempting. Especially when she could be on the dole by Christmas. 'You barely know me. What makes you think we can work together?'

'I know you better than some random girl who turns up from an agency. Or some girl who only tells me what she thinks I want to hear. I'm prepared to take a punt if you are.'

Julia drank some more champagne. She wasn't seriously considering it – how could she possibly work for this man? – but she wasn't about to permanently slam the door shut either. Beggars couldn't be choosers. 'And what happens if your punt doesn't come off? Where's my job security? I could leave Harley Jenks and find myself unemployed in a few months.'

'There is no job security these days. Don't you read the papers? The economy's on the rocks. It's every man for himself, sink or swim, survival of the fittest. Sometimes you have to take a risk. I'll do it if you will.'

Julia wasn't about to commit herself, far from it. Out of the frying pan and into the fire. Wasn't that the saying? And there was still a chance that she'd keep her position at Harley Jenks. She ate some lettuce and a slice of tomato. 'There's a lot to consider.'

'Think about it,' he said. 'Let me know in a week. I'll keep the job open until then.'

'I can't make any promises.'

'Sleep on it and let me know.'

'You said you'd give me a week.'

'Okay, sleep on it seven times and let me know.'

16

It was just after three o'clock when Julia got back to the office. The afternoon felt a bit surreal, like a dream she was still trying to process. Some of that could have been down to the champagne – they had finished the bottle by the time she left – but most of it was down to the surprise of being offered a job out of the blue.

'You survived,' Cressida said. 'I wasn't sure if we'd see you again today.'

'Yes. No problems. He hasn't decided yet about the press interview, but we threw a few ideas around.'

'He didn't try it on then?'

Julia wondered if she should be pleased or offended by the fact Apostle hadn't made a move on her. But then he'd had other things on his mind. 'Good as gold. Maybe he's not as bad as people say.' She threw this in, as much in the hope of persuading herself as persuading Cressida. Not that she was intending to take up his offer, but if she *had* to, if she was left with no other choice, then she hoped she could find some virtue in among the macho arrogance.

Cressida's eyebrows went up an inch. 'Don't tell me you've been charmed by him?'

'God, no, Apostle doesn't do charm. But he behaved himself, so I suppose that's something.'

'Miracles do happen. Oh, you had a couple of calls from a man called Michael Vyse. He didn't leave a message, just asked you to call back. Said it was important.' Cressida rummaged through the papers on her desk, came up with a scrawled number and passed it over to her. 'Mean anything to you?'

Julia, caught unawares, stared at the number for a while. 'Yes,' she said eventually, glad that he'd had the discretion not to use the official portion of his name. She didn't want to have to explain to Cressida about the investigation into Angel's death or her part in it all. If it got back to Harley that the police were calling her at work, he might get the wrong end of the stick. 'He's a letting agent. I've been looking for a new flat. Noisy neighbours,' she explained.

'Better call him then. He might have found something.'

Julia would have preferred to make the call in private but unless she went out again and used a phone box there was no chance of that. She picked up the phone and dialled, wondering what was so urgent that it couldn't have waited until she was at home. Had he found out something? He'd said it was important when he left the message. That sounded ominous. Her fingers tightened around the receiver. After a couple of rings, the phone was answered.

'Cowan Road police station.'

'Could you put me through to Michael Vyse please,' she said, hoping that whoever had answered the phone wasn't going to insist on her calling Vyse inspector. 'It's Julia Reeve.'

'Hold on. I'll see if he's here.'

Julia held on, tapping a biro against her notepad while she

waited. She had to be careful what she said to him with Cressida earwigging. Through the glass partition she could see Harley Jenks standing in the main office, chatting to one of his employees, sharing a joke, slapping the bloke on the shoulder. Yes, it was a men's club all right. When it came to smashing through that glass ceiling, Cressida was the exception to the rule.

It was a minute or two before Vyse's voice came down the line. 'Julia?'

'Hi, yes, what's happening?'

'There's been a development. Can you come into the station for a chat?'

'What, now? I'm at work.'

'As soon as you can. Come after work. I need to talk to you.'

Julia wanted more information and tried to think of a way of asking without revealing who she was actually speaking to. 'Can you . . . can you tell me any more about it?'

'I'll see you later,' he said, and hung up.

'Okay,' Julia replied into a dead line, frustrated by his shortness. 'Thanks. Yes, I'll see you then.' She put the phone down and smiled at Cressida. 'A flat's come in that might be suitable. I can see it later.'

'That's good. Why don't you go now in case someone else snaps it up?'

Julia glanced towards Harley, who was still mingling with the chosen few. 'It might not be a good idea. Aren't I already top of the list of people to get rid of? Leaving early will only give Harley another reason to make me redundant.'

'Don't worry about that. Wait until he goes back into his office and then scarper. I'll tell him you're meeting a client.'

'What client? What if he asks me about it on Monday?'

'He won't ask. But if he does, tell him you were delivering some paperwork to Apostle.'

Julia never usually left early. In fact, she made a point of putting in the extra hours, but she was desperate to know what Vyse had found out. This morning, unsure as to how long she would be at lunch, she had cleared her desk of everything outstanding. And really, after all the unpaid overtime she'd put in over the past nine months, she reckoned she was owed one early escape.

'I can deal with anything urgent that comes in,' Cressida said.

Julia was still dithering, eager to get over to Kellston but not at any price. Then, like a sign, Harley suddenly withdrew to his office and closed the blinds. If she went now, she could get away without being seen by him. 'Okay, I think I will.' She quickly stood up, retrieved her coat from the peg and slipped it on. 'Thanks. Have a nice weekend.'

'You too, hon.'

It was almost five by the time the bus forced its stop/start way through the Friday traffic and finally arrived at Kellston. Julia got off at the train station and walked up the high street, feeling the cold wind whisk around her legs. Darkness had fallen along with the temperature. She shivered, hunched her shoulders and turned up the collar of her coat.

It was only when she got to Cowan Road and was approaching the police station that she slowed her pace. The last time she'd been here was eleven years ago when she'd spent over two hours being questioned about Angel's accident. The memory wasn't a pleasant one. Although her mother had been with her, she'd still been frightened. She wondered if Pauline had already put the boot in by then, sharing her suspicion that Julia had pushed Angel down the steps.

The inside of the station looked much the same: bare and slightly forbidding with shabby beige lino pocked with cigarette burns, a few crime posters on the walls and a row of plastic chairs, all of which were currently empty. She went up to the desk and waited behind a middle-aged woman making a complaint about 'yobs' on the Mansfield who had broken one of her windows. The duty sergeant was taking down the details with a resigned expression on his face.

'We'll look into it, Mrs Bates.'

'That's what you said the last time. And what did you do? Sod all, that's what. Those kids think they can get away with it, and that's because they can.'

'We'll send someone round.'

'And what am I supposed to do about my window? It ain't good enough. They're running wild, those yobs; they need locking up.'

It went to and fro like this for a while with Mrs Bates frequently repeating herself before she finally finished venting her frustration and withdrew, muttering under her breath, and with a face like thunder.

'I'm here to see DI Vyse,' Julia said, smartly stepping forward in case Mrs Bates decided she had more to say. 'Julia Reeve.'

'Take a seat,' the sergeant said. 'I'll phone through.'

Julia perched on the edge of a blue plastic chair. She felt on edge, anxious and jumpy as if she'd done something wrong and was about to pay the price for it. Why had Vyse summoned her? A development. What did that mean? Perhaps they had arrested someone for Angel's murder. Or found definitive proof that it was suicide. Although quite what that proof could be, she had no idea.

For the second time that day she was left waiting. Although she could excuse Vyse on the grounds that he wouldn't have expected her to get here so soon, she wasn't so sure about Apostle's 'emergency' and still had a sneaking suspicion that he'd left her kicking her heels deliberately. Apostle was a man who liked to be in control, to be in charge. No, she couldn't work for him; it was unthinkable. He'd resent her good ideas and punish her bad ones. No second chances was what he'd said, and she was sure that applied to his employees as well as his lovers.

Julia was just checking her watch again when Vyse walked through the door that led from the interior of the station. She felt a slight lurch inside her, part attraction, part trepidation, a confusing mix that made her heart beat faster. He was dressed casually in trousers and a shirt with his sleeves rolled up.

'Sorry to keep you waiting,' he said. 'I wasn't expecting you until later. Come on through and I'll get you up to date.'

'That's all right. I haven't been waiting long.'

Julia stood up and followed him through the door and into a long corridor. It rang a bell somewhere in the back of her mind, a distant teenage memory floating up from the past, but she couldn't remember which room she'd been taken to then. There was a smell of bleach underlain by the more human smells of sweat and stale tobacco.

'Apologies for dragging you over here,' Vyse said, 'but I'll be stuck in Kellston until late.'

It was the first time she'd seen Vyse in his natural surroundings, at home in the police station, and it made her vaguely wary of him. 'That's all right. I didn't have much on this afternoon.'

Vyse turned left and opened the door to a small room with comfy chairs and a low table. 'Grab a seat. Would you like a drink?'

'No, thanks. I'm fine.'

'Probably a wise decision. Cowan Road canteen isn't renowned for anything even faintly drinkable.'

They sat down facing each other across the table. Julia had a quick look round. It was a space, she suspected, that was used to break bad news or to interview more vulnerable people. The room wasn't exactly cosy, but an attempt had been made to soften the harder edges with carpet, curtains and cushions. 'I take it something's happened?'

'You haven't heard from anyone?'

Julia shook her head. 'No, nobody. What's going on?'

Vyse arranged his features into what might have been a sympathetic expression or just a guileful one. He was watching her closely. 'I've got some bad news.'

Julia's first thought was her mother – her stomach plummeted – but she quickly dismissed the idea, realising that there would be no reason for the Suffolk police to contact Vyse. 'Tell me.'

'It's about Lindsay March. There's no pleasant way of saying this but she was found dead in her flat this morning.'

'Lindsay? Oh my God!' Julia's mouth went dry. Shock ran through her. She stared at him in disbelief. 'But how? Why?' She swallowed hard, trying to absorb the information. 'When you say dead, do you mean . . .?'

'She was murdered last night. Attacked from behind, hit over the head with a blunt instrument of some sort. A hammer, maybe. Look, are you sure you don't want that drink? A glass of water?'

'Yes, I'll have some water. Thank you.'

Vyse stood up, left the room and came back thirty seconds later with a plastic cup. Julia thanked him again, raised the cup to her mouth with a shaking hand and gulped the water greedily.

'Was it a robbery do you think?' she asked.

'There was no forced entry, no mess. And nothing missing as far as we're aware. It looks like she let the killer in, which suggests that she knew them.'

Julia's first thought was the fiancé, Mark, the man Lindsay had been so proud to talk about. 'Like . . . erm, a boyfriend?'

'Mark Grey, you mean. He's got an alibi. He was in a meeting until nine and was home by nine thirty. His flatmate, who stayed up late, claims he didn't go out again.'

Flatmates could lie, Julia thought, or fall asleep. Boyfriends could get someone else to do their dirty work for them. But then again, he could be innocent. Vyse wasn't stupid and Mark would have been top of his list of suspects. 'He must have been distraught.'

'It appeared that way.'

'You think he was putting on an act?'

'He seemed genuinely shocked.'

Julia was in shock too, still trying to make sense of it all. A headache, the legacy of the champagne she'd drunk earlier, was starting to throb in her temples. She sipped some more water. 'God, it's awful. Terrible. Poor Lindsay.'

Vyse placed his palms on his thighs and leaned forward a little. 'I hate to ask you this, Julia, but I'm afraid I have to. What were you doing last night?'

'Me?' she said, bewildered. 'You can't really think it was me. Why would I want to kill Lindsay?'

'Why would anyone?'

Which was a good question. Lindsay had been a mild-mannered, non-confrontational sort of person – not the kind of girl to provoke murderous thoughts. And yet someone *had* murdered her.

'I know it's hard not to take it personally, but it's just routine,' Vyse said. 'I have to cover all the bases. If I didn't ask, I wouldn't be doing my job.'

Julia nodded. She wasn't happy about it, but just the fact she was sitting in here, rather than in some bare bleak interview room, told her that Vyse didn't have her pegged as a serious suspect. 'I left work at about half six, got home after seven, had some dinner, had a bath, watched TV and went to bed. And no, there's no one that can corroborate that. I was on my own.'

'Did you make or receive any phone calls?'

'I called Tom at about eight o'clock, but he wasn't in. I left a message on his machine and mentioned the attempted break-in.' Julia paused, wondering suddenly if she was putting Tom in the line of fire. 'What time did it happen? What time was Lindsay killed?'

'Late evening, about ten or eleven probably.'

Julia shifted in the chair, uneasy at being a possible suspect and of providing evidence that might put Tom in a tight spot too. '*He* couldn't have killed her. Tom doesn't have a violent bone in his body.'

Vyse, ignoring the comment, said, 'Could we go over Wednesday night and your meeting with Lindsay?'

'I've already told you everything about that.'

'Tell me again.'

So Julia went over the conversation, everything she could remember about Lindsay's engagement to Mark, her job as a teacher, the probing questions as to whether she'd been in touch with Angel recently, about Renee going round to Pauline's, and all the small talk that had come in between. She paused for breath and took another sip of water. Then, in sudden realisation, she looked up from the plastic cup and said, 'You think Lindsay's murder is connected to Angel's death, don't you?'

'What do you think?'

'I've no idea,' Julia said. 'It could be, I suppose. Lindsay seemed relieved when I said I'd had no recent contact with

Angel, but I got the feeling that she wanted to know more. She was worried about something.'

'You thought they all knew more than they were letting on, all four of them. Well, three of them now.'

'I didn't say that.' Julia didn't like Vyse putting words into her mouth, even though it was true. She'd thought exactly that at the funeral wake, that something was being hidden from her, that she was being kept in the dark. But there was nothing factual about her suspicions. She didn't want to point the finger when she had nothing more to go on than Renee's wild accusations and her own possibly dubious instincts.

'Don't worry, I'm not taking anything down in evidence. I'm just interested in your take on it all.'

'Have you talked to the others?'

'Yes, of course.'

'And what do they say?'

'What I expected them to say: all neatly tucked up and fast asleep at the time their pal was being murdered. But they live close by – Pauline and Tom on the estate, Frankie just round the corner in Violet Road – so it would have been possible for any of them to pay her a visit, strike the fatal blow, and be back in bed within fifteen minutes.'

'They'd have had blood on their clothes, wouldn't they?'

'Probably, but they could have got rid of what they were wearing. The bins were emptied early this morning. We're still following that up but the chances of finding anything are slim. It'll all be in landfill by now.'

'It still begs the question why.' Julia shuddered as she thought about the brutal way Lindsay had met her end. 'Who found her?'

'One of the staff from school. When she didn't turn up for work and wasn't answering her phone, they sent someone round, late morning, to check on her. Lindsay was reliable, not the sort to take days off whenever she felt like it. The door was closed but unlocked and the woman went inside. A decision she's always going to regret. Lindsay was lying on the floor in the living room. She'd been dead for about twelve hours by then.'

'Poor woman. You wouldn't want to walk in on that.'

'No, it wasn't a pleasant sight.' Vyse shifted in his chair and sighed. 'As to the question of why, it's all just conjecture at the moment. Lindsay March doesn't seem the type to have had enemies. She was a schoolteacher leading a quiet life, and a pretty inoffensive person so far as I can gather. She certainly gave me that impression. So what made someone want to kill her? The only unusual thing that's happened recently is Angel's death.'

'You think she knew something about it, and was killed to shut her up?'

'It's a line of enquiry. Which brings me to my next point. I think you should back off from the group, stay away from them until we've got a clearer picture of what's going on. It's not safe to be asking questions right now.'

'So what do I say when Tom calls me? What if he wants to meet up again?'

'Just make an excuse. Anything. Busy with work, a family emergency, flu; you'll think of something.'

'Isn't that going to seem a bit odd?'

'It doesn't matter how it seems. Whatever's going on, *if* anything's going on, then you need to keep away from it. Don't get pulled into this, Julia. The more you find out, the more danger you could be in.'

Julia let this sink into her headachy brain. It didn't make her feel any better. 'What about Renee? What about—'

'Stay away from all of them. Yeah?' Vyse glanced at his watch. 'I'm sorry but I have to get on. I'll walk you out.'

Julia stood up and followed him into the corridor. She had more questions, a jumble of them, but it was too late now.

Vyse escorted her as far as the inner door where he placed his hand lightly on her arm. 'Take care of yourself. Remember what I said.'

17

Outside, the cold evening air hit Julia like a slap to the face. She strode down Cowan Road at a brisk pace, wanting to get home as soon as she could, needing the familiarity of her own flat before she could even begin to come to terms with what had happened to Lindsay. She kept her eyes peeled for a black cab even though she couldn't really afford it. The yearning to be away from here was more important than the price of it.

The horror of what Vyse had told her pressed down like a dead weight, provoking a whirling confusion of disbelief and a haphazard jumble of memories. She and Lindsay had never been close, but they'd had history, shared experiences as they'd been growing up. Lindsay had always been part of the tapestry. Now that tapestry was being pulled apart – first Angel, then Lindsay – and the loose threads were spilling everywhere.

Julia was almost at the high street when she walked past a dark-coloured car parked near the corner. The sudden beep of the horn made her jump, shaking her out of brooding introspection and back into the present. She turned and peered through the gloom at the man inside. It was Tom Finch. He wound down the window.

'Hey,' he said. 'How are you?'

She leaned down to talk to him. 'I've just heard about Lindsay. A bit stunned, to be honest.'

'I know. Christ, it's awful, isn't it? A bloody nightmare. I can't get my head around it. Look, do you fancy a drink? I don't know about you, but I could do with one.'

Julia hesitated, recalling what Vyse had recommended about staying away from the old gang. But she trusted Tom. He was a gentle person, calm and kind, and about as far as you could get from some hammer-wielding murderer. 'Okay, but not round here. Not the Fox. Everyone's going to be talking about it. Can we go somewhere else?'

'Jump in,' he said. 'We can go wherever you want.'

Julia walked round, opened the door and slid into the passenger seat. It was a relief to be out of the cold. The inside of the car was neat and tidy and had that artificial smell of pine air freshener. She pulled her seatbelt across and fastened it.

'It's Camden you live, isn't it?' Tom said. 'I think you mentioned it at the wake. How about we head for there. There's a nice pub near Regent's Park. The Spread Eagle?'

Julia nodded. 'Yes, that's fine if you don't mind driving that far.'

'It's not that far. To be honest, I'll be glad to get out of Kellston too.' Tom started up the engine, checked the rear-view mirror and pulled away from the kerb. 'So how did you hear about Lindsay? I was going to call you later.'

'Vyse told me about it.'

'Vyse? Why would he contact *you*? How would he even know how?'

As soon as the words had come out of her mouth, Julia had

realised how peculiar they must have sounded. So far as Tom was concerned, she had no connection to the inspector. He had no idea about her chat with Vyse in the Station Café or his visit to her flat. She gave Tom a quick sidelong glance – he was frowning – and quickly delivered what she hoped was a feasible explanation. 'I bumped into him after the wake. He must have noticed me drinking with you and the others and he asked what my connection was to Angel. I told him that we'd been friends, but I hadn't seen her since coming back to London. He still insisted on taking my number though. He said he might want to talk to me about her. When he rang today and asked me to come into Cowan Road, I presumed it was about that. He didn't tell me about Lindsay until I got here.'

'Nice of him. God, that man really is the pits.'

'He's a cop. They're all the same,' she said, feeling that this was what he wanted to hear. Even as a teenager his attitude towards the police had been one of suspicion. They were the enemy and couldn't be trusted. He had always been on the side of the underdog, the disadvantaged and disenfranchised, and he saw the law as doing nothing to protect them. 'Someone must have told him about Wednesday. Did you know that I went for a drink with her after work?'

Tom nodded. 'She dropped by the Fox on her way home. We were all there, me and Frankie and Pauline.'

So much for rushing home to prepare her lessons, Julia thought. That had been a downright lie. She wanted to ask what they had all been doing in the Fox on a Wednesday – didn't they usually meet up on Saturdays? – but couldn't think of a way of phrasing it that didn't sound accusatory. 'When did you find out what happened to her?' she said instead.

'About lunchtime. Some plods came to the office and dragged me down to Cowan Road. Then I got the third degree from

Vyse: what I was doing last night, where I was, when I last saw Lindsay, and all the rest of it.'

'You've been there all afternoon?'

'For most of it.' Tom lifted his right hand off the steering wheel and raked his fingers through his hair. 'I was just trying to get my head together when I saw you come out.'

The rain was lashing against the windscreen now and Julia was glad she wasn't standing at a bus stop. The traffic was still bad, the tail end of rush hour, and the journey was slow. 'You must be exhausted.'

'I don't know how I feel. Like it hasn't sunk in yet. It's the shock, I suppose. And with it coming so soon after Angel . . .'

'Do you think there's a connection?'

'A connection?' Tom frowned again. 'I shouldn't think so. I can't see how.'

'Two deaths in such a short period of time. People who knew each other. I got the impression – I might be wrong – that Vyse is seeing a link there.'

'Yeah, well, Vyse sees whatever he wants to see. If I was him, I'd be taking a close look at Mark Grey. I never trusted that bloke. Lindsay deserved better.'

'Is he the violent type?'

'Not that I've witnessed, but who knows what people are capable of?' Tom sighed. 'Oh, don't mind me, I'm just voicing my own prejudices. I've never liked him. He's a pompous idiot, completely up his own backside. I can't really see why he'd kill Lindsay, though.'

'Maybe they had a row, and things got out of hand.'

'Lindsay wasn't the argumentative sort. She'd always agree with him even if she didn't, if you know what I mean. Anything for a quiet life. Anything to keep him happy.'

'Perhaps she'd had enough of keeping him happy.'

'Did she say something to you on Wednesday?'

Julia shook her head, immediately contradicting herself. 'The opposite. She was almost bragging about him, about the ambition he had, about how he wanted to be an MP.'

'God save the country if *he* ever gets elected. Yeah, she always defended him, always stuck by him no matter what. I didn't get it. Pauline reckoned she was just desperate to get married, terrified of being left on the shelf.'

'She was only twenty-five, for heaven's sake. That's hardly being on the shelf.'

'Yeah, but she wasn't like you.'

'What do you mean?'

'She didn't have much confidence, and she wasn't good at being on her own. Her mum died a few years back and she's been living alone ever since. Mark was her way out, an escape from loneliness, I suppose.'

Guilt swept through Julia. Lindsay hadn't mentioned her mother's death, and she hadn't thought to ask about her. They had only briefly touched on family – Julia's – before quickly moving on to something else. She could see now that Lindsay had deliberately swerved the subject, perhaps not wanting to hear the condolences that would inevitably follow. She tried to conjure up an image of Mrs March but all she could retrieve from memory was a hazy impression of a brown-haired woman in a tweedy coat.

'That's sad,' she said. 'Her mum can't have been very old.'

'Early fifties. It was cancer.'

They were both quiet for a while, the only sound the rhythmic swooshing of the wipers on the windscreen. Julia wished that she had picked up on Lindsay's loss and maybe she would have done if she hadn't been so preoccupied by trying to find out what had happened to Angel. Now, when it was too late, she focused her mind on Lindsay. 'She wouldn't have opened the door to just anyone, would she? She was always careful, cautious. Vyse said there was no sign of a break-in and that nothing appeared to have been taken. She must have known her killer.'

'It looks that way.'

Another silence. Julia wondered if they were both thinking the same thing: there was a limited number of suspects and two of them (if she counted herself) were sitting in this car.

18

The Spread Eagle was starting to fill up with Friday-night customers drifting in from work, but it was a large pub and there were still plenty of free tables. Tom insisted on buying the drinks – a pint for himself, a red wine for her – and they chose an empty corner where they could talk in private.

Julia would have liked to probe more deeply into Lindsay's life and death but suspected that after an afternoon down the nick and then the car ride, Tom might have had his fill of answering questions about her. So instead, she asked about his job in the council's housing department and found herself rewarded with a diatribe about Mrs Thatcher's Right to Buy policy.

'It's complete crap, Julia. Unless you're building new properties to replace the ones that have been sold, there's going to be a serious shortage of social housing in the future. And are the council being allowed to build? No, of course not, because Thatcher wants to run down the social housing stock and turn the country into a bunch of property-owning Tories. But what about the people who'll never be able to afford to buy, who are unemployed or on low wages? Where the hell are they supposed to live? It's immoral, a disgrace. Just another example of the haves trampling on the have-nots.'

Julia, who was only half listening – she had heard it all before from her mother – gave the odd nod or murmur of agreement to show that she was paying attention. In fact, most of her thoughts were still with Lindsay and her brutal death. She drank some wine, hoping it would soften the edges of her headache.

'And there's hardly any money for repairs,' Tom continued. 'The Mansfield estate is falling to pieces; it's a battle just to keep the flats in a liveable condition. Every day I get residents coming into the office complaining about damp and draughts and heating that doesn't work properly.'

'It must be frustrating.'

Tom placed his elbows on the tale. 'Ignore me. I'm just sounding off. And trying to distract myself. Lindsay's murder, it's ... it's too much to properly take in. I keep thinking that if it was someone she knew, then I probably know them too.'

Julia's thoughts had been running along much the same lines – Frankie, Pauline, Mark? – but she kept her response neutral. 'Possibly, but there must be people from Oak Road school as well, teacher friends, parents, Mark's friends, even neighbours. The circle could be wider than you imagine.'

'A man, though, don't you think?'

'Women kill too,' she said.

'But the way it was ... the violence of it ... it feels more like something a man would do.'

Julia wasn't so certain. An angry woman could hit someone hard enough to kill them if she hated enough, if she was mad enough. 'Have you spoken to the others yet?'

'No, Vyse made sure we never got the chance. I think we were all pulled in around the same time.'

'Were Pauline and Lindsay close?'

'I wouldn't say close. They hung out together sometimes, but mainly it was Pauline and Angel. I think it was tough on her – Lindsay, I mean – always being the third wheel.'

'She had you and Frankie.'

'Yeah, but it's not the same, is it? Girls like to talk about . . . I don't know, girl stuff.'

'Boys and make-up?' Julia said, even though she understood what he was getting at. 'Feelings and all that sensitive stuff?'

Tom gave a wry smile. 'Well, not cars and football. Although Pauline can hold her own when it comes to Arsenal.'

Julia knew how it felt to be an outsider. She had never quite fitted in at the school in Suffolk and the friendships she had forged there had been casual affairs, fluid, with no special other person. After Angel, she had built a wall around herself, future-proofing against any further loss and pain. And then, because she didn't want to dwell on Angel and the closeness they had once had, she quickly said, 'Have you seen Renee since the funeral?'

Tom visibly tensed. 'No, have you?'

'No. What's going on with her?' Julia asked, deciding to get straight to the point rather than dance around it. 'I got the sense there was some tension there.'

'Why, what did she say to you?'

'Oh, nothing specific. It was just a feeling, that's all. And Lindsay said she'd gone round to Pauline's and made some sort of scene.'

Tom played with his pint glass, turning it around with the tips of his fingers. 'She's been strange with us ever since Angel died. Especially with Frankie. Like she thinks he might have had something to do with her death.'

'Did the two of them ever . . . was there something going on between Angel and Frankie?'

'No,' Tom said sharply, glancing up at her. 'Who told you that?'

'No one told me anything. I just wondered.'

'Nothing was going on. They were mates, that's all.'

Julia had got the same response from Lindsay. She heard the rise in his voice; it was too strident, too insistent. She gave him a long hard look. 'You're a dreadful liar, Tom. It's a good thing you're not a murderer or Vyse would have hung you out to dry by now.'

'I'm not . . .' he began, but then stopped, wondering perhaps if Lindsay had been less discreet than she should have been. 'Look, they hooked up a couple of times, that's all. It didn't mean anything. It wasn't serious. You won't tell Vyse, will you? If he finds out, he'll have Frankie well and truly in the frame.'

'I won't,' she said, and she meant it – for now. She couldn't believe Frankie had killed Angel and didn't want to cause un-necessary trouble. 'When was this?'

'Ages ago.'

'Before Clare?'

Tom looked shifty. 'About six months ago. But he and Angel . . . it was never anything . . . you know, they were just . . .'

'Just sleeping together.'

'Once or twice.'

'Does Renee know about this?'

'I hope not. No, I don't think so. She'd have told Vyse, wouldn't she?'

'I suppose so.' Julia drank some wine. Was this what it had all been about then – the whispering in the Fox, the sense that something was being hidden from her, the meeting with Lindsay – just them trying to find out if Angel had told her about Frankie? It was possible but she wasn't convinced. She could see how such a revelation would get Vyse's antennae twitching, how it would be a bombshell for Clare, but it didn't really account for the attempted break-in or Lindsay's murder. 'I thought Frankie was busy playing happy families with his wife and kids.'

'He always had a soft spot for Angel. He's a bloody fool. If Clare ever finds out . . .'

'Did everyone else know about it?'

'You mean Lindsay and Pauline? Yeah, Angel wasn't good at keeping secrets. But I don't think she told anyone else. And I shouldn't have told you.' Tom lowered his voice, looked at her earnestly. 'Frankie would never have hurt Angel. You know that, don't you? He might be a class-A idiot but he's not violent. If this comes out, he could lose everything.'

Julia almost retorted that Frankie should have thought about that before he jumped into bed with Angel, but she was in no position to pass judgement. When it came to bad decisions, she was hardly whiter than white herself. 'I said I wouldn't. You can trust me.'

'I still think it was suicide, but Vyse isn't buying it. Angel was all over the place. She was manic, impulsive, up one moment and down the next. You could never tell what mood she'd be in. I think she lived in a world of her own and sometimes that world was too much for her.'

Julia could see that Tom had convinced himself – rightly or wrongly – of Angel's suicide. But he could hardly do the same with Lindsay. Was it possible that the two deaths were unconnected? It seemed too much of a coincidence, but coincidences happen.

Tom drained his pint and put the empty glass down on the table. 'I'd better get back. I'll give you a lift home if you point me in the right direction.'

'You don't want another drink?'

'No, thanks. I should check on the others, make sure they're okay.'

'Well, I owe you one.'

When they were back in the car, heading towards her flat, Julia's head was in the past, on Angel's fall down the steps and what had led up to it. She gazed through the windscreen. It was still pouring down, the rain glittering in the headlamps. 'Whatever happened to Liam Crosby?' she said.

Tom's eyebrows shot up. 'God, that's a name I haven't heard in years. What made you think of him?'

'I don't know. He was there on the day Angel fell.'

'Oh, yeah. But he was more Frankie's friend than mine. Last time I heard he was in jail but that was years ago. I haven't seen him around for a while.'

'In jail?' she said, acting surprised. 'What did he do to end up there?'

'Thieving, I think. Or dealing. I can't remember which.'

'That's a shame. Did he and Angel ever get together? You know, after the accident?'

Tom gave her a sidelong look. 'No, he kept well clear after that.'

A minute or two later they arrived at Julia's flat, and he pulled up at the kerb, keeping the engine running. 'Will you be okay? I'm sorry to rush off.'

'It's fine. *I'm* fine.'

'We'll be in the Fox tomorrow evening if you fancy some company. Well, if Vyse hasn't locked us all up by then.' He grimaced. 'I shouldn't joke about it. I hope he finds the bastard who killed her. I still can't believe she's gone.'

'No, it's awful,' Julia said. 'Will *you* be okay?'

Tom shrugged. 'Why would anyone do that to her?'

Julia wished she had an answer, but she didn't. She got out

of the car, thanked him again for the drink and said she'd see him soon. 'Take care of yourself.'

'You too. Call me if you want to chat. Any time.'

Julia jogged down the steps to the basement, hurrying to avoid getting drenched, unlocked the door and went inside. There was post on the floor. She bent down to retrieve it, put the light on, shut and bolted the door and went through to the kitchen. She threw the envelopes on the counter, turned on the heating and the kettle and took off her coat.

After the water had boiled, she made a mug of tea and swallowed a couple of aspirins, still feeling a dull ache in her temples. She wondered if Tom was all right. He had always been the protective one of the group, the glue that held them together, but she worried that Lindsay's murder, coming so soon after Angel's death, might be too much for even him to take.

It had been a long day and her lunch with Apostle seemed an eternity ago. She warily eyed the post – two bills and a small Jiffy bag – before pushing aside the bills. She couldn't take any more unpleasant surprises. Inside the bag, she guessed, was some small gift from her mother, a souvenir from Cornwall. Ellie nearly always sent something when she went away.

Julia tore the bag across the top and peered inside. An oblong of tissue paper. She emptied it out onto the counter. It was fastened at both ends by small pieces of Sellotape. She ripped through the paper and revealed what was inside: a short lock of light brown hair tinted with red and tied at one end with a strand of pink cotton. She held it up, bewildered. At first, she didn't understand what she was seeing. Why would her mother send her ... but then realisation struck, and the full horror descended. She dropped the lock of hair and jumped back as if she'd been scalded. A scream rose in her throat. She couldn't breathe. Nausea swept over her. The hair was Lindsay's; the hair had come from a murdered woman. The killer had cut it off and delivered it to Julia.

19

It was a long thirty minutes before Vyse arrived. Julia spent them pacing the living room trying to fight off the hysteria that threatened to engulf her, her arms wrapped around her chest, her eyes deliberately avoiding the kitchen and what lay on the counter there. Why? That was the question that kept spinning round her head. Why had the killer delivered this to her? She had met up with Lindsay, had a couple of glasses of wine, and then, just over twenty-four hours later, Lindsay had been murdered. What was the message in the lock of hair? Why had it been posted through her door? A threat. A warning of some sort, but a warning about what?

Julia was no closer to reaching an answer when she heard voices and the heavy tread of boots on the steps outside. She rushed to the front door and opened it. Vyse gave her a nod, introduced her to the two men who were with him – names that slid through her mind without settling into memory – and followed her through to the kitchen. 'They'll be dusting the letterbox for prints and searching the outside space.'

'There,' she said, pointing towards the counter, as if he might fail to notice the horrifying gift that had been left for her. 'It was lying on the floor with the other post when I got home this evening. I didn't notice that there wasn't a stamp on it. Not at first.'

Vyse pulled on thin rubber gloves and studied the items in question without immediately touching them.

'It might not be Lindsay's hair,' she said, more in hope than expectation. 'Was there . . . was there any missing?'

'We're checking. There was nothing obvious at the time, but it could have been cut from underneath.' Vyse carefully and separately bagged the lock of hair and the Jiffy it had come in. 'Do you remember if it was lying over or under the other post?'

Julia tried to remember, replaying the moment in her head, trying to visualise what order the envelopes had been in as she scooped them up. 'Not a hundred per cent. I think the Jiffy was on top, but I couldn't swear to it.'

'It's all right,' he said, 'I'm just trying to get a timeline for when it was delivered – before or after the normal post. When does your post usually come?'

'I don't know. I'm usually out of the flat by eight, so some time after that.'

'We'll have a chat with the neighbours, see if they noticed anyone come down here, but I'd guess it was late this afternoon, probably after dark. Someone trying to scare you.'

'They're doing a good job.'

'What about the handwriting on the Jiffy? Anything familiar about it?'

Julia shook her head. Her name and address had been written in block capitals with blue ballpoint pen. 'It's just ordinary, isn't it? I presumed it was from my mum, so I didn't really look at it closely. I just ripped it open and . . .'

'No note or anything?'

'No.'

'What time did you get back from the station?'

Julia looked at him, knowing that he wasn't going to like what she was going to say. 'Only about ten minutes before I called you. I went for a drink with Tom Finch.'

Vyse stared at her. 'You did what?'

'Yes, I know you suggested I stay away from him, from all of them, but he offered me a lift home and it was raining so . . . I couldn't see the harm in it. Look, I've known Tom for years. He's a friend and . . .'

'He *was* a friend,' Vyse said. 'He was a friend eleven years ago when you were both kids. People change, Julia, and not always for the better. How come he offered you a lift? Where was he?'

'Down the road from the station. He was parked near the high street.'

'So he was waiting for you.'

'No, I don't think so. He was just taking a minute to get his head together – he said he'd spent most of the afternoon at Cowan Road.'

'We let him go at quarter past four,' Vyse said. 'You left at about half five. That's a lot more than a minute.'

Julia frowned, unwanted doubts creeping into her head. It *was* a long time to just be sitting in his car. 'But he couldn't have even known I was there. How could he?'

'He might have seen you go in or simply guessed that you'd show up at some point. We were bound to want to talk to you after your night out with Lindsay.'

'I could have already been and gone for all he knew.'

Vyse shrugged. 'Perhaps he was just taking a punt.'

'Or he could have been waiting for Frankie and Pauline. That

132

doesn't make him guilty of anything other than caring about his friends. Perhaps he wasn't expecting to see me at all.'

'We released them before him.'

'He might not have known that.'

'Talk me through this drink.'

Julia would have liked a stiff drink now. She was tense and anxious, her thoughts returning again and again to the psychopath who had walked down her steps and pushed his (or her) vile delivery through the letterbox. 'There's nothing much to tell. We went to the Spread Eagle up the road. He had a pint, and I had a glass of wine. He was upset, shocked, just trying to hold it together. First Angel and then Lindsay . . . losing two friends so close together is a hard thing to take. Or understand.'

'Did you talk about her? Lindsay, I mean.'

'Of course. We were both thinking the same thing: that if she let them in, she must have known them. And she didn't have a huge circle of friends. Tom's opinion of Mark Grey isn't exactly the greatest, but even he couldn't think of a reason as to why he'd want to kill her.'

'What else did you talk about?'

'Not much. Work. And Renee. How she'd gone round to Pauline's and kicked up a fuss.'

Vyse folded his arms across his chest and leaned against the counter. 'And while all this was going on, it gave someone else enough time to deliver a nice little parcel to you.'

Julia bridled at this. She couldn't believe, didn't *want* to believe, that Tom had deliberately kept her out of the way. 'I never usually get home much before seven. They'd have had time with or without his intervention.'

'It's always useful to make sure, though, isn't it? What else did you talk about?'

133

'Nothing else, unless you include a brief lecture on the evils of Mrs Thatcher's Right to Buy policy.'

Julia was not being completely honest with him, but she wasn't lying either. It was more a case of withholding information. If Vyse found out about Frankie sleeping with Angel, he wouldn't be slow in jumping to conclusions and she didn't want to be responsible for that. Anyway, she'd promised to keep it to herself, and she would until she had good reason not to.

One of the other officers put his head round the door and said, 'We're finished here, guv. A few prints on the letterbox but they're probably the postman's, and a few on the door too. We'll check who has this round. Nothing obvious outside but we'll take another look tomorrow in daylight. I've talked to the neighbours and none of them noticed anyone coming down here this afternoon or this evening.'

'You may as well get back to the station then.'

Vyse turned to Julia. 'We should get going too. We'll need your prints to eliminate them.'

'I've got to come down to Cowan Road again?'

'The sooner we have them, the sooner we can get on. It'll only take ten minutes. I'll have someone give you a lift back after.'

Julia nodded. She stared at the two plastic bags that Vyse was now holding. She took a long deep breath before speaking. 'I still don't understand why anyone would do this.'

'Like I said, to scare you. They think you know something, and they want you to keep your mouth shut.'

'But I don't,' she said. 'How could I?'

'Maybe you don't even realise you know.'

20

Julia didn't see Vyse again after they got to Cowan Road. He disappeared down the long corridor and left her to have her prints taken by an older, uniformed officer. It was a messy and uncomfortable business, uncomfortable because it made her feel like she was under suspicion. Or that she was guilty of something. After she'd cleaned her hands, wondering if this meant that her prints would be on record for ever, she was told to wait in the foyer, and someone would be found to drive her home.

It was still relatively early, but the station was already getting hectic with a steady stream of lads, most of them probably from the Mansfield, being pulled in for being drunk and disorderly. The accused, for the most part, were noisy and angry, protesting their innocence while they hurled abuse at the arresting officers.

Julia was sitting on one of the hard plastic seats and starting to think it might be easier and certainly less painful to her ears if she just left and got herself a cab, when a young woman with cropped auburn hair wearing jeans and a navy-blue sweatshirt came through the internal doors, looked around, spotted her, and came over.

'Julia Reeve?' she asked.

'That's me.'

'I'm DC Carol Forshaw, your lift for this evening.'

Julia could tell that she wasn't best pleased at being on taxi duty, her expression being one of resentful resignation. 'I can get a cab if you've got other things to do. I don't mind.'

'Oh, I just do as I'm told, and that's anything the important guys can't be arsed to do. That's "important" in inverted commas. You get what I mean?'

'With bells on,' Julia said, thinking of Harley Jenks.

'Yeah, you can always rely on men to screw you over. Come on, let's get out of here. It's Camden, isn't it?'

'Thanks, yes, just off Camden Road.'

It had stopped raining now, but the yard was still slick with water. Julia followed the DC to an old black Peugeot parked off to the side. Even in the dim light she could see that the car was scratched and pitted with dents.

'Let's see if this heap can get us there without breaking down,' Carol said, jiggling the keys.

They got into the car, fastened their seatbelts, and Carol drove slowly out of the station. 'I wouldn't mind,' she said, reverting to her earlier grievance, 'but most of them haven't got two brain cells to rub together. And if you come up with a good idea, they pretend they haven't heard and present it as their own two minutes later to a roomful of praise. It's maddening. It's like being invisible. It's like being a member of a club without really being a member.'

'It's the same where I work. Jobs for the boys, all the good stuff, and I get whatever's left over.'

'Makes you wonder why you bother sometimes.'

Julia felt a weariness descend on her. She yawned. Her eyes felt heavy and ready to close. She'd be glad to see the end of this day with all its traumatic and tumultuous events. But there was still a question she had to ask. 'How long do you think it will be before you know about the hair?'

'Jesus, yeah, that must have been a shock. DI Vyse is on his way to see the pathologist now. Are you okay? You seem to have got caught right in the middle of this.'

'It looks that way,' Julia said. A small part of her was beginning to wish she'd never bumped into Tom Finch on the Strand, but the other, larger, part refused to be cowed. So someone was trying to scare her – well, mission accomplished – but that didn't mean she was going to run for the hills. Sometimes a stubborn streak came in useful.

'You're from Kellston, then?'

'I lived here until I was fourteen. Then we moved to Suffolk.'

'Oh, nice. What made you come back?'

'A job. A better job.'

'I'm from Portsmouth originally. I suppose it must feel a bit strange seeing your old friends again. Whenever I go home, I'm not sure how much in common I have with them anymore.'

'I haven't seen much of them to be honest. And the circumstances haven't been exactly ideal.'

'Hell no, sorry, you must feel like you've walked into a nightmare.'

They were halfway to Camden before Julia caught on to the fact that she was being subtly interrogated. She wasn't sure whether to put her belated realisation down to exhaustion or to the other woman's guile. Did it matter? Not really. But she wondered if Carol was simply trying to prove a point to her male colleagues, to find out something they hadn't, or if Vyse had put her up to it.

From that point on, although she had nothing to hide – okay, she had Frankie's liaison with Angel to hide – she thought before she spoke. She couldn't see herself as a suspect for murder but perhaps the police thought she was more involved than she was letting on. Carol continued to ask questions and Julia continued to answer them albeit with an extra dose of caution.

Eventually she decided to turn the tables and see if she could glean some information of her own. 'Two girls, two friends, dead in just over a month. DI Vyse thinks there's a connection, doesn't he? He thinks it's more than a coincidence.'

'He's keeping an open mind.'

'But what do *you* think?'

Carol looked pleased to be asked, as Julia had intended her to be. 'That I wouldn't fancy being part of that friendship group right now. It's getting smaller by the minute. You should try and keep some distance, maybe even get out of London for a while.'

Wise advice, she was sure, but Julia had heard most of it before. And she wasn't prepared to skulk away and hide. By sending her the hair, the killer had singled her out as worthy of attention, had proved to her, just as Vyse had said, that she might already know more than she thought she knew.

21

Pauline placed the placatory mug of tea on the low side table beside her father. He'd had the hump all evening, acting as if it was *her* fault that Lindsay had been murdered and that the law had come into the shop and dragged his daughter off to Cowan Road to be questioned. Like a dog with a bone, he wouldn't let go of it.

'How do you think it looks for the business?' he grumbled. 'It'll be all round the neighbourhood by now. No smoke without fire they'll be saying, no smoke without bloody fire.'

'They can hardly believe that *I* did it.'

'Why not you?' he said. 'What makes you so special?'

'She was my friend, Dad. I don't go around murdering my friends.' And a bit of sympathy wouldn't go amiss, she thought, but wasn't stupid enough to say it. It was just the same as when Angel had died – zero comfort, not a kind word to be heard – and this time she didn't expect anything else.

Pauline hadn't loved Lindsay, not like she'd loved Angel. Angel had been everything to her. But if she mentioned the

L-word to her father, he would jump to his usual bigoted conclusions. Queer, he'd call her, even though she wasn't. Queer or bent or *one of those*. As if you couldn't love another woman without wanting to do unspeakable things with her.

'Then you should choose your friends a bit better,' he said.

'It wasn't *their* fault.' He talked like they'd brought it on themselves. Although in Lindsay's case that was probably true. She wouldn't miss Lindsay much. She wouldn't miss her banging on about Mark or the kids at school or what she'd eaten for her damn dinner. Lindsay had been one of the most boring people she'd ever known.

'You shouldn't worry, it'll probably give the business a boost,' Pauline said. 'They'll all be coming in to get an eyeful of the girl who's under suspicion for murder. A pound of pork sausages and a quick glimpse of Pauline Archer. I bet you take twice as much tomorrow as you did today.'

Her father scowled at her over the rim of his mug, but she could see the idea whirring around in his shitty little mind. 'I've got a reputation to uphold. I can't have the police marching through the shop every five minutes. It doesn't look good, Pauline. It doesn't look good at all.'

Pauline rolled her eyes. His *reputation*. It made her skin crawl just to listen to him. She had witnessed the way he'd treated her mother, using her as a punchbag, pushing her to the limit until she'd packed a bag and done a runner. Where was she now? Well, wherever she was it would be better than here.

'What did that Tom Finch want?' he said.

Tom had called ten minutes ago while she was making the tea, to make sure she was okay. 'What do you think? Some people are concerned about how I might be feeling. It's not a whole lot of fun being grilled by the law . . . or finding out that one of your mates has been murdered.'

'I'd be looking at that boyfriend of hers. Mark whatsisname.'

'Grey,' she said. 'Apparently he's got an alibi.'

'And have you got one?'

'What kind of a question is that?'

'A bloody sensible one unless you want to spend the next twenty years inside.'

'I was here,' she said. 'You weren't, though, so it's not much of an alibi. You were out at one of your satanic meetings.'

'*Masonic*,' he said. 'Yes, I was at the Lodge.'

'Well, at least you can account for your movements.'

'And why should I need to? I barely knew the girl.'

Pauline, who always liked to play with his head whenever she got the opportunity, raised her eyebrows. 'But you've known her for years, Dad. I went to school with her. She was often here at the flat. Yeah, I dare say the law will be sniffing round you too before long.'

Her father's face was a picture. 'Me? Me?' he blustered. 'Why would they want to talk to me?'

'You don't need to worry, not if you were at the Lodge. Although they may want to know what you were doing after you left. They might even want to search the shop. The weapon's not been found yet and that place is full of possibilities.' Pauline sat back and smiled. 'God, that'll give the customers something to gossip about.'

22

Julia had a fitful night's sleep and woke on Saturday morning to the chilling knowledge that a killer had delivered a lock of Lindsay's hair to her – had wrapped it in tissue paper, put it in a Jiffy bag and pushed it through her letterbox. Vyse had called late last night to confirm and to ask that she keep the information to herself for now.

'I'm afraid the skull was ... well, everything was a bit of a mess. That's why we didn't notice at the time. I won't gross you out with the details. Anyway, we'd rather the press didn't get hold of the story, for our sake and for yours. Some things are best kept quiet while an investigation is ongoing. We don't want copycats and I'm sure you don't need a load of reporters camped out on your doorstep.'

Julia had agreed that she most certainly didn't. She had gripped the phone, pressing it hard against her ear. 'They know where I live though. The killer, I mean.'

'I don't think you're in any immediate danger. It was sent as a warning. But I'll call the Camden boys and get them to keep an eye on the flat.'

Julia had gone to bed with that word 'immediate' still waltzing round her head. Now, drinking her morning coffee in the kitchen, she wondered if she should move out for a while. But go where? She couldn't afford a hotel. She could go back to Suffolk temporarily and commute every day but that would be expensive too, and her mother would have questions. Of the few new friends she had made in London – could she even call them friends? – none of them were the sort she could confide in. And none of them, understandably, would thank her for bringing a killer to their front door.

Julia knew that she could be followed to wherever she was staying and so, really, she might as well just stay here. But she should be prepared in case the worst happened. Some kind of weapon to protect herself. A gun would be useful. There were probably people living on the Mansfield who could get her a gun, but it wasn't the kind of thing you could just go up to anybody and ask about. A knife then. She had plenty of those in the kitchen. So, one by the bed and one secreted in the living room, in places she could reach easily if the worst came to the worst. The front door was sturdy and there were bars on the windows, so no one was going to get in quietly.

An officer had already been round to do the second check on the small space outside. So far as she was aware he'd found nothing helpful. She'd been hoping that Vyse might come but obviously he had better things to do – like chasing after clues and catching murderers. She prayed he was good at his job. Renee didn't seem convinced.

Thinking of Renee reminded her that she hadn't got back to her yet. She rang directory enquiries, asked for the number of Irene Glover living in Carlton House on the Mansfield estate in Kellston, and held her breath while she waited, hoping that Renee wasn't ex-directory. She wasn't. Thirty seconds later Julia had the number. She thanked the operator, put down the phone and stared at the digits she'd scribbled down.

She picked up the phone again, began to dial and stopped. Was this a bad idea? She'd just been sent a warning, presumably to keep her nose out of it, and here she was about to poke her nose straight in again. So yes, maybe it wasn't the smartest move, but it was still better than sitting here doing nothing. Anyway, she owed Renee the courtesy of a call even if she didn't have any new information. Their last hurried conversation had been strange, bewildering, and she wanted to get to the bottom of what Angel's mum did and didn't know.

Renee sounded half asleep when she answered, even though it was almost ten o'clock. Perhaps she'd taken a sleeping pill last night or was on Valium. Something to take the edge off. She perked up when she heard Julia's voice, her tone instantly changing from monotone to animated.

'Have you seen them? Have you talked to them?'

Julia didn't want to raise Renee's hopes only to dash them again. 'I haven't found out anything yet,' she said quickly, 'but can we meet up? I don't want to come to the Mansfield in case someone sees me. How about that café by the station? Would midday be all right for you?'

'I can do that,' Renee said. 'Did you hear about Lindsay?'

'Yes, I heard. It's shocking, terrible.'

Renee left a long pause as though she was considering whether it *was* terrible or not. 'Some people reap what they sow.'

Julia sucked in a breath. Had she really said that? It was so cold and heartless, and for a moment she wondered if Renee had been the one who'd killed Lindsay. Was that possible? But Renee was a small middle-aged woman and not strong enough, surely, to overpower someone so much younger. Although there was always the element of surprise. And the force that anger brings. 'You can't be sure she had anything to do with Angel's death.'

'I know what I know,' Renee said tightly.

Julia decided not to prolong the conversation. She said her goodbyes and hung up, still disturbed by what she'd heard. Although she understood that Renee was grieving, and that grief does crazy things to people, when it came to proof, to evidence, she'd been told nothing yet that would put Lindsay in the frame.

And why would Lindsay kill Angel? Why would anyone?

Julia was still asking these questions when she got off the bus at Kellston station and walked the short distance to the café. She doubted Vyse made a habit of frequenting the place – hopefully he had more pressing things to do – but she made a point of peering through the window before she ventured inside anyway.

It was only ten to twelve, but Renee was already there. Julia pushed open the door and went in. It had been raining again and the café smelled of damp coats. Only about half the tables were taken and Renee had chosen a spot in the far corner; she was hunched over the table gazing into a cup.

Julia pulled out a chair, sat down and said, 'Hello, Renee. How are you doing?'

Renee raised her face – cheeks sunken, eyes full of sorrow – and widened her lips into the semblance of a smile. 'Bearing up, love. It's the best I can do. Would you like a brew? I ordered a pot.'

Julia would have preferred coffee, but she nodded and said that would be great.

Renee poured the tea and pushed the cup across the table. 'You're early.'

'You're even earlier.'

'Oh, well, I don't know what to do with myself these days. When I'm not working the days seem to go on for ever. I like to get out of the flat, off the estate. Everything there reminds me of her.'

'It must be hard.'

Renee sipped her tea. 'So what about you, Julia? Are you back in London for good or just passing through?'

'I've got a new job here.' Julia was about to give her usual spiel on how busy she'd been with the flat and work, but looking at Renee, at the grief etched on her face, the excuses felt flimsy and self-serving. 'I should have got in touch with Angel. I meant to but I kept putting it off and then ... then I met Tom on the Strand, and he told me what had happened.'

'She never blamed you. For the accident, I mean. She never thought it was your fault.'

Julia gave a light shrug, embarrassed by the fact that Renee knew exactly why she'd put the reunion on the back burner. 'We shouldn't have been drinking.'

'You were kids. Kids make mistakes. She missed you when you left.'

'I missed her too.'

'Pauline was kind to her, kept her company, but it wasn't the same.'

'That was good of her,' Julia said through gritted teeth.

'I've never much liked the girl, to be honest. I've always thought she's a bit ... intense. Controlling. Do you know what I mean? She wanted to know what Angel was doing all the time, where she was going, who she was going with. It didn't seem right to me, but Angel didn't seem to mind. She said she was just being protective.'

Julia nodded, thinking it was probably best not to share her own feelings about Pauline or they'd be here all day. She'd come

146

to get information, not to get sidetracked by personal enmity. 'Can you tell me about the night Angel disappeared?'

'What have they told you?'

'Only that Pauline and Lindsay went round to see her in the afternoon and took a bottle of fizz. They stayed for an hour or so. Angel told them she had some things to do, washing her hair and shopping for you, and they agreed to meet up later in the Fox.'

'That's not true,' Renee said. 'About the shopping, I mean. I didn't ask her to do that.'

Julia had already heard this from Vyse, but she nodded again, as if she was hearing it for the first time. 'Perhaps she just wanted some time on her own – or she'd made other plans.'

Renee wrinkled her nose. 'What plans? She never told me about any plans. And what kind of so-called friends don't raise the alarm when the birthday girl doesn't show up?'

'Yes, I know, but they said she could be . . . unreliable.'

'Well, I wouldn't argue with that, but on her birthday? No, that doesn't make any sense. They could have called. Why didn't they call?'

'Perhaps they didn't want to worry you.'

'But there was good reason to be worried. When someone doesn't show up, when it's their *birthday*, any sensible person picks up the phone to find out what's happening.'

'Yes,' Julia said. 'You'd think so, wouldn't you?' But in a way she also saw Tom's point of view and understood how if Angel had made a habit of this kind of thing they wouldn't necessarily have panicked.

'I didn't start to worry until the morning,' Renee continued. 'Angel said that they would probably go on to a club and that she'd sleep over at Pauline's because it would be late when they got in and she didn't want to wake me. Pauline lives with her dad, but he's got a lady friend he stays with every Saturday night and so the girls would have had the place to themselves.'

Julia could remember Pauline's father, a large man with a gleaming bald head who talked too much and too loudly. 'Did she often stay there?'

'Every now and again. Anyway, like I said, I wasn't worried at first. But then it got to eleven o'clock and when I rang Pauline's there was no reply. I thought they might just be sleeping off a hangover, but something didn't feel right. When I rang Lindsay, she told me that they'd waited in the Fox until closing time, but that Angel hadn't shown up. Tom Finch said the same thing.' Renee's face tightened and her right hand clenched into a fist. 'How could they not have realised that something was wrong? Angel disappears into thin air and they're acting like it's all perfectly normal. I'm telling you, Julia, they know a damn sight more than they're saying.'

'But why would any of them have harmed Angel?'

'That's what we have to find out. Pauline's supposed to be her best friend and even *she* wasn't concerned when Angel didn't show. Pauline, for heaven's sake! The girl who used to follow her around like she was her shadow. I reckon they might have argued in the afternoon, had a falling out. Maybe one of them lashed out and Angel died as a result. They could have been too scared to call the police, to admit what they'd done.'

'I can't see how they'd have got her to the river, even with two of them. You can't carry a body through an estate like the Mansfield without someone noticing.' Julia winced, aware that she'd been insensitive and that talking about a 'body' was hardly appropriate when she was sitting with the victim's mother. 'I'm sorry, I didn't mean to sound callous. It just doesn't seem very feasible.'

But Renee was too wrapped up in her own theories to be

148

bothered about the niceties of language. 'They could have got help. They could have called Tom and Frankie. That's what friends are for, right?' She said it sneeringly, her contempt clear as day. 'The four of them could have managed it, got her in the lift and then into a car. Then all they had to do was drive her to the river and . . .'

'But she drowned, didn't she? Pathologists can tell if someone drowned or if they died another way.'

Renee flapped a hand as if the workings of science were a minor detail.

'But you could be right about the row,' Julia said. 'Perhaps they did have a falling out and Angel decided to make other plans for the evening. It would account for why they weren't surprised when she didn't show up.'

'So why lie about it? They said she was fine when they left in the afternoon. Not that an honest word ever comes out of their mouths. Take that Frankie, for example. I got home from work early one afternoon – this was about three months ago – and caught him coming out of the flat. Shifty, that's how he looked, like he'd just been doing something he shouldn't be doing.'

Julia knew they were getting on to dangerous ground. 'Did you ask Angel about it?'

'She said he'd just called round for a coffee. I don't think she was telling the truth, though. There was something going on between those two and I told her, I told her straight that nothing good ever came from playing around with married men. She put on the innocent act, but she didn't have me fooled for a minute. I mean, he had a motive, didn't he? Maybe Angel wanted more than he was prepared to give her. Maybe she was threatening to tell Clare.'

'Have you told Vyse all this?'

Renee gave a light shrug. 'I've mentioned that he used to drop by, but I don't know anything for sure, do I? Frankie's already denied that it was anything more and I don't have any proof. I don't want Vyse thinking that Angel was the sort of girl who slept around. They make judgements, those coppers.'

'The others wouldn't have covered for him, not if they thought he'd killed her.'

'Are you sure of that?'

Julia, of course, wasn't sure of anything. But there was a big difference between adultery and murder. 'I can't see it.' Then, because she didn't want to linger on the subject of Frankie and Angel, she said, 'I met up with Lindsay on Wednesday evening. She rang and asked me to go for a drink.'

Renee's eyebrows shot up. 'What did she say?'

'Nothing much, but I was surprised that she called. Then when we met up it all just seemed like idle chatter, catch-up stuff and the like. I was starting to think that was all it was going to be but then—'

'Then?'

Julia wasn't sure if she should be fuelling Renee's suspicions, especially when she was already so intent on pointing the finger at the old gang. 'I can't be certain, but I got the impression she was worried that I might have been in contact with Angel recently. That Angel had told me something or given me something. She was digging and looked relieved when I said we hadn't been in touch for a while.'

'Well, there you go!' Renee said triumphantly.

'But where do we go? Angel didn't send me anything. Was there anything missing from her things?'

Renee shook her head. 'Not that I've come across. There were some old diaries that Vyse took away with him, but nothing recent. She always used to keep one when she was younger, but I think she stopped.'

Julia considered this, or at least the possibility that Angel *hadn't* stopped. Was that what Lindsay had been worried about? If Angel had kept a day-to-day record, she might have written down something incriminating, decided it was too risky to keep the evidence and passed the diary on to Julia. It would account for the questions and the attempted break-in at her flat. 'Then who killed Lindsay, and why?'

'Because she was the one most likely to blab, the weakest link, the one who'd buckle under pressure.' Renee gave a sigh of frustration. 'She never had the bare-faced cheek of the others. Perhaps they began seeing her as a liability and decided to get rid.'

For Julia this all seemed too far-fetched. Covering up one murder with another? And she had never seen Tom Finch as the shameless sort. Pauline, yes. Frankie, yes. But Tom had always been the principled one, the boy with a rigid sense of right and wrong. It seemed impossible to her that the others would do anything without him knowing. 'We've still not got a reason as to why anyone would kill Angel in the first place. I mean, yes, it could have been an accident, but she was still alive at the river. How did she get there? I can't imagine her catching a bus, can you?'

'I told you: they've got cars. They could have driven her.'

'But why was she killed?'

Renee's eyes shone with unrestrained fervour. 'That's what we've got to find out, Julia.'

23

The rest of Julia's weekend had been a quiet affair: some food shopping to restock the larder and a short walk round the block on Sunday. Most of it had been spent in trying to unravel the mysteries of two murders that might or might not be connected. Now, on the bus going to work, it was all still going round in her head. Although she wasn't convinced by Renee's theory that one – or all – of the old gang had been responsible for Angel's death, she couldn't dismiss it out of hand. It seemed to her that Renee rapidly jumped from one idea to the next, barely pausing for breath, pulling one random string after another until eventually everything wound into a knot.

Yesterday, after her walk, she had dug out a notepad and pen, sat down and made a list of suspects. She had written ANGEL at the top of the page and underlined it. Underneath she had written:

Frankie (because of the relationship)
Clare (ditto)
Pauline (because of a row?)
Lindsay (?)
Tom (?)
Mark Grey (?)

It had been a far from satisfactory exercise because apart from the first two nobody had an apparent motive for murder. Vyse had said to ignore motive, but she didn't see how she could. People didn't kill for the fun of it, not unless they were psychopaths. Anyway, these couldn't be the only ones in the frame. Angel's circle must have been wider than this with people she had known from work, neighbours, ex-boyfriends (she should have asked Renee about that) and friends of friends. Did Tom have a girl-friend? Did Pauline have a boyfriend? There was, quite possibly, a much longer list of suspects, characters she wasn't aware of. Except, and this was important, Lindsay's killer had delivered the hair to her, which meant, surely, that it was someone she knew.

Vyse hadn't called and she hoped he was making better pro-gress than she was. He hadn't mentioned the diaries, and she wasn't going to tell him about Angel and Frankie. That was fair, wasn't it? They were both withholding things although maybe her omission was more important than his. No, it was only more important if it mattered, and she still wasn't convinced that it did.

There was a glimmer of sunshine and a pale blue streak run-ning across the sky. She gazed out at the London landscape, at the endless traffic and the crowds of people. Everything normal. Everyone going about their business. Except nothing *was* normal, not for her. Lives had been ended and nothing would be quite the same again.

Julia was still distracted when she walked into the office. If she'd been more on the ball, she'd have clocked the meaning of the hushed room and the averted eyes. As it was, she just put it down to Monday morning apathy. Big mistake. No sooner had she entered the inner office, before she even had time to take her coat off, Cressida looked up and said, 'Harley wants to see you.'

She stopped in her tracks. 'Damn. Is it bad news?'

'I tried,' Cressida said. 'Sorry. I thought he was going to wait a while but . . .'

Julia, who had thought things couldn't get worse, now had to face the fact that they certainly could. She looked over her shoulder towards Harley's office and scowled. The blinds were down, and she couldn't see inside the room. Why her? She might have been last in, but she wasn't the weakest member of staff. She'd worked hard, really hard, with what she'd been given, but her industry and diligence hadn't been good enough.

'Best get it over with then,' she said, resigned to her fate.

'You'll get something else,' Cressida said. 'Something better.'

Julia gave a weak smile, pushed back her shoulders, retraced her steps to Harley's office and knocked on the door. She was aware of being the focus of attention, of twenty pairs of eyes fixed on her. There but for the grace of God, they were probably thinking, although maybe they weren't; maybe they were all so sure of their position in life that redundancy never occurred to them.

'Come!' Harley called out.

Julia went inside. The next five minutes were an ordeal. Harley leaned forward, assumed a this-is-as-painful-for-me-as-it-is-for-you expression and rattled on about bad times, a shaky economy and having to make tough decisions. *Just get it over with.* Eventually he opened a brown cardboard folder, took out her P45 and a cheque and passed them over to her.

'Three months' salary,' he announced grandly, as if he was giving her the world. 'We're not obliged – you haven't been with us for long – but we want you to know how grateful we are for all your hard work.'

Julia muttered her thanks, and quickly rose to her feet. She would have liked to throw the cheque back in his face but then she'd be unemployed *and* broke.

'Cressida will take care of your clients from now on,' he said, just in case he hadn't made it clear that he expected her to leave immediately.

Back in her own office, she emptied the drawers in her desk of the few possessions she kept there: a paperback copy of *The Golden Notebook* (still unread), a swanky silver-coloured ballpoint pen that her mum had bought her, a packet of gum and a spare black T-shirt that was there in case of unfortunate spills. Not much to show for nine months but at least it could all be stuffed into her bag.

'I'm here if you need a reference,' Cressida said. 'I'll give you a good one. And stay in touch, let me know how you're getting on. I'll call if I hear of anything decent going.'

'Thanks. I appreciate it.'

Julia had to take a deep breath before she ventured out of the room again. It felt like a long way to the exit, a walk of shame past all the other desks. She kept her head up, tried to look unconcerned, tried to act as though losing her job was no big deal to her. She was glad that Cressida had given her some warning. If it had come out of the blue, she wasn't sure how she'd have reacted. With tears, probably.

'Good luck,' someone murmured.

It was a relief when she'd cleared the office and was jogging down the stairs. As if to match her mood the weather had taken a sudden turn for the worse and big black clouds were rolling across the sky. Great. All she needed now was a soaking and the morning from hell would be complete.

Julia banked her cheque, bought three newspapers – *The Times*, the *Guardian* and the *Evening Standard* – and caught the bus home. The journey back to Camden was quiet with most of the traffic going in the opposite direction. She studied the employment pages, searching for anything that might be suitable. There were positions in media, publishing, sales and a lot of secretarial stuff. Well, she could type but not at any great speed. And did she really want to spend her days churning out letters and making endless cups of tea?

There was nothing in PR apart from a couple of executive positions, way out of her league and with salaries so eye-wateringly high that she wondered what they spent it all on. Big houses and foreign holidays. Clothes. Or maybe they stashed it in offshore accounts and watched the money grow.

Still, she had no need to panic. Three months' salary was enough to keep her going while she waited for the right job to come along. But then another thought occurred to her: it wasn't going to look great being dumped by Harley Jenks after only nine months. What did that say about her to any prospective employer? Nothing good, that was for sure. She could imagine her application form going straight in the bin.

There was always Apostle. No, she couldn't work for him. But what if the right job didn't come along? What if she spent the next three months getting only rejection letters? Any job was better than no job and you always stood a better chance if you were applying from a current position rather than the dole. So maybe she should take it and look around for something else when she didn't have desperation snapping at her heels.

Apostle had given her a week, so she still had a few days to think about it. But what if he rang Harley Jenks in the meantime and found out that she'd been made redundant? That might cool his interest. He might even withdraw the offer. Nobody wanted someone's sloppy seconds. But then she didn't want to look too keen.

By the time Julia got off the bus she had come to a decision.

24

Tom Finch gazed out of the window at the high street beneath him. His dad had always said that if you wanted to find a council office anywhere in England all you had to do was look for the grandest building in the district and that would be it, some imposing edifice that had been donated by a Victorian benefactor who had made his riches off the backs of the poor and wanted to leave a legacy that could be seen every day.

This was true of the Kellston council offices, which were housed in an ostentatious four-storey grey-brick building with a flight of shallow steps and six sturdy Doric columns at the front. It was completely at odds with the rest of the street – two rows of shabby shops – and stuck out like the proverbial sore thumb. Inside was a labyrinth of corridors leading to various departments. Housing was on the third floor and there was no lift, so by the time any older or unfit tenants made it to Tom's office they were already in a bad mood.

It had taken him seven years to secure a desk by a window and although the view was hardly inspiring it was a good deal better than staring at a wall. He opened his desk drawer, took out a paper bag, removed the cheese and pickle sandwich and started to eat, savouring the peace and quiet before the doors opened again. Once he'd got satisfaction from his job, even pleasure, but now he felt increasingly frustrated by the lack of funds and inability to make a difference.

But he had other things on his mind today. Lindsay's murder. Was he a suspect? Vyse would like him to be. The inspector had despatched two uniformed officers to take him down to Cowan Road on Friday. Coming so soon after Angel's unexplained death, tongues had started to wag. His co-workers didn't know whether to be sympathetic or suspicious. Tom Finch was, clearly, dangerous to be around.

Last Wednesday evening, in the Fox, Lindsay had announced the mortifying news that Julia thought she had spotted him in Southampton Street. He should have been more patient. He should have waited to see if she'd call him but instead, in an act of recklessness, he'd gone back up West in his lunch hour to try and contrive an accidental meeting and invite her to join them on Saturday night. Maybe he had wanted to prove Pauline wrong about never seeing her again – there would be some satisfaction in that – but the bigger truth was that he had just wanted to see her.

Tom wasn't sure if he believed in fate, but there had been something fateful, surely, about bumping into Julia on the Strand just a few days before Angel's funeral. Like she'd materialised out of nowhere just when he needed her most. All those years of missing her. He'd had a bit of a crush back in the day, back when most of the boys were drooling over Angel, but he'd kept it to himself. Acne had been a good defence when it came to disguising the hot flush that swept over his face whenever she addressed him.

Julia was different, smart, going places. And she had got away from the Mansfield. He'd had a chance to leave too when he was eighteen and had been offered a place at Durham University to study history and politics. Another part of the country, a chance to find out who he really was. But his father's fatal heart attack had put a halt to that. Leaving his mother on her own had never been an option.

'Go,' she'd insisted. 'I'll be fine. You can come back and visit in the holidays.'

That was his mother all over, never thinking of herself, putting on a brave face even when her heart was breaking. By then his older sister Jenny had already flown the nest, flapping her wings all the way to Australia where she'd met a local on the Gold Coast, got married and settled into a life of babies, hope and sunshine.

Tom's father hadn't had any life insurance. Money had always been tight in the Finch household and anything spare was put into the holiday fund so that, when they were kids, they could have a week in Cromer in the summer holidays. Always the same B & B with its rooms full of knick-knacks, a worn carpet on the stairs and the lingering smell of overcooked cabbage.

He could have gone to university, could have done what his mother told him to do, but he'd known she'd be lonely and that she'd struggle to make ends meet. Her job at the Spar didn't pay much and by the time she'd forked out for the rent and the rates and all the other bills there wouldn't be much left over. Even at eighteen he'd felt a sense of responsibility. Which is how he'd ended up working for Kellston council, slowly climbing the ladder, gradually forging a career for himself. He never resented his mother for his lost opportunities – none of it was her fault – but there were times when he quietly railed against whatever deity ran the universe.

Julia hadn't mentioned the Southampton Street incident when they'd gone for a drink in the Spread Eagle, but then she'd had other things on her mind. They both had. And an afternoon down the nick didn't do much for anyone's mental faculties. He remembered, with horror, how he'd gone on about Thatcher and her housing policies, a bitter verbal attack while they should have been talking about Lindsay. But then death was a tricky subject, murder even more so.

Sometimes he would go three or four hours, even a whole afternoon, without thinking about what he'd done, but then, like a tsunami, it would roll over him in a huge, icy wave that took his breath away. Guilt was a terrible thing. He told himself that it would get better, that human beings had the ability to adapt and adjust, and that eventually the horror of it all would subside into something less nightmarish. There was, however, no sign of that happening yet.

25

Julia put the phone down. What had she done? Ivor Apostle's smug voice lingered in her head, the voice of a man who always got what he wanted and who hadn't been the slightest bit surprised when she'd called to discuss his offer of a job. She felt deflated and defeated, as if she'd bowed down at the first sign of trouble, too afraid of rejection to put herself out in the marketplace and look for a post she really wanted. You're just being sensible, she told herself. It's tough out there and you have to grab what you can. You can't afford to be picky.

She glanced at the piece of paper she'd used to write down the address of the office. Shoreditch. She'd been hoping, if she was honest, for somewhere a little more glamorous, but the upside was that it wasn't too far away. They'd agreed to meet there on Saturday morning and talk through the details.

So, that left her the rest of the working week to concentrate on other things. Like the killing of Angel. *If* she had been killed. Suicide wasn't completely out of the question. Birthdays weren't always times of celebration. Sometimes they were just an unwanted reminder that another year had passed and nothing had changed. But she didn't believe, couldn't believe, that Angel had taken her own life.

Had it not been for the gruesome delivery of that lock of Lindsay's hair, Julia might have spread her net wider, but it seemed to her that the gesture must have come from one of the old gang or someone close to them. Who else would know about her connection to Angel, or even care about it? Stay away, Vyse had said, but she'd already gone against that piece of advice by seeing Tom and Renee. Which only left Frankie and Pauline. Well, it left Mark Grey too. She'd never met him but his connection to Lindsay couldn't be ignored. And Clare, Frankie's wife, couldn't be ruled out either.

On paper, Frankie was the main suspect – a man who had a lot to lose if his relationship with Angel became public – but Clare would have motive too. A woman scorned. She was, however, more inclined towards Pauline, and she knew this was because she didn't like her. Pauline was bad-tempered, sarcastic and quick to judge. And she'd wanted to steal Angel from her. Every time Julia had turned around, Pauline had been there trying to muscle in, trying to push her aside. So, yes, she was prejudiced, she knew that, but it didn't mean that Pauline was innocent.

Julia picked up the phone, dialled directory enquiries again, and got the number for the butcher shop. Would Pauline be working today? If she worked Saturdays she might have Mondays off. There was only one way to find out. The phone was answered on the second ring.

'Archer's,' a woman's voice said in a somewhat peremptory fashion.

'Oh, hi, is that Pauline?'

'Yeah.'

'It's Julia. I was wondering if we could meet up, have a chat.'

'What for?'

Julia rolled her eyes. 'It's about Angel.'

'What about Angel?'

'I'd rather do this face to face than on the phone. Are you free this evening? We could go for a drink.'

There was a long pause, probably while she tried to think of an excuse, but eventually Pauline sighed down the line and said, 'Okay, I'll see you in the Fox at six.'

'I'd rather it wasn't the Fox. Could we meet somewhere else?'

'What's wrong with the Fox?' Pauline snapped, slipping into her usual confrontational mode.

'There's nothing wrong with it, only everyone goes there, don't they? I'd rather talk in private.'

'If by everyone you mean Frankie and Tom you don't need to worry. Frankie will be looking after the kids tonight because Clare has her evening class, and Tom doesn't go out on Mondays.'

'Oh,' Julia said.

'I'll see you at six then.'

'Okay, see you later.'

No sooner had Julia put down the phone than it rang again. She picked it up. 'Hello?'

'It's me. DI Vyse. I just wanted to see how you were doing.'

Julia wondered if he had a sixth sense for when she was going against everything he'd advised. 'I'm all right, thanks.'

'Not at work today?'

'No, I've taken some time off.' She would have to mention at some point that she and Harley Jenks had parted company but couldn't quite face it today. 'Do you have any news?'

'Sorry, nothing at the moment,' he said. 'We're following up some leads.'

'What kind of leads?'

'I can't tell you that.'

'What about Angel's diaries? Did you find anything in them?'

Vyse's voice turned sharp. 'How do you know about those?'

'Renee told me. I called her yesterday to see how she was. That's all right, isn't it? I mean, I can't ignore her. I knew her for years and she's just lost her daughter. Anyway, yeah, she told me about the diaries.'

'They're old, from years ago. There's nothing of interest in them. Just kid's stuff, teenage stuff.'

'Up until when?'

'Until she was twenty or thereabouts. And then they stop.'

'Or someone took the others.'

'Or someone took the others,' he echoed.

'Can I read them?'

'What for?'

'There might be something that you missed, something that wouldn't mean anything to you, but might to me.'

'No,' he said, 'not without Renee's permission.'

'When are you returning them?'

'Soon,' he said. 'This week, probably.'

'Okay, I'll talk to Renee.'

Vyse sighed down the line. 'I thought you were keeping out of this.'

'That's kind of difficult after what happened. I mean, someone else has already involved me, haven't they? Whoever sent the hair. Whoever killed Lindsay. And if *they* want me to stay out of it, then that's probably good reason not to.'

'Even if you're putting yourself in the line of fire? You're only doing this because you feel guilty about the accident.'

Julia wished she hadn't confided in him now. She wondered

why people felt the need to act like amateur psychologists. 'You told me that motive wasn't important.'

'Actually, what I said was not to get sidetracked by it. And anyway, I was talking about the killer's motive. Why put yourself in harm's way? Leave it to the police.'

'And how's that going? It's been a month since Angel died.'

'We still don't know if that *was* murder.'

'Well, you haven't got that problem with Lindsay. And it seems unlikely that they're not connected.'

'You can't jump to conclusions.'

'I can put two and two together.'

Vyse sighed again. 'Yeah, okay, so they *may* be connected, but that's all the more reason for you to stay out of it. Will you?'

Julia wondered what he'd say if she told him about meeting up with Pauline this evening. Nothing good, that was for sure. 'I'll try.'

'Why do I get the feeling that's a no?' Vyse didn't even wait for a reply. 'This is serious stuff, Julia. I don't want you to be the next victim I'm scraping off the floor.'

Julia, unsurprisingly, didn't want that either.

26

It was ten to six by the time the bus got to Kellston train station. Julia, dressed in jeans, a cream sweater and her warm winter coat, walked the short distance to the Fox and went inside. She had a list in her head of all the questions she wanted to ask and was running through them as she looked around the pub.

It was quiet, the combination of it being a Monday and still early, and she spotted Pauline sitting in the far corner with a half-drunk pint in front of her. Julia went over. Pauline looked up – there was nothing welcoming in her expression – and gave a brusque nod.

'Hi, it's good to see you again. Would you like another drink?' Julia asked pleasantly, thinking it was best to approach this in a friendly fashion, and that it would be no bad thing to ply her with alcohol and maybe loosen her tongue a little.

'London Pride,' Pauline said. And then, almost as an afterthought, 'Ta.'

Julia went to the bar and ordered a pint and a half of Pride. She would have to be careful how much she drank herself. If she wanted to catch Pauline out, she needed her wits about her. While she waited for her order she looked back across the room. Was it really possible that Pauline had killed Angel? It had seemed perfectly feasible when she'd written out her list of suspects, but now she found it hard to imagine. It wasn't that she thought Pauline incapable of murder – the girl had a hard edge to her – but that she found it impossible to grasp why she'd kill someone she cared about so much. But then she was back to motive again and she saw now how easily that could muddy the waters.

Julia paid for the drinks and took them over to the table. 'Quiet in here this evening.'

Pauline stared at her. 'What is it you want, Julia?'

Okay, so small talk seemed off the agenda. She might as well get straight to the point. Julia took a sip of beer and put the glass down. 'Do you think Angel killed herself?'

'No,' Pauline said. 'Why would she do a thing like that?'

'That's what I think too. It doesn't seem to add up. No note or anything, and Renee said she was happy that day. Why weren't you worried when she didn't show up here on her birthday?'

Pauline pushed a strand of long black hair behind her ear. 'Angel could be unreliable.'

It was a familiar refrain, Julia thought. Tom had said it, and Lindsay had said it too. That didn't mean it wasn't true, but it could also mean that it was something they'd all decided to use as an excuse if they were asked about it later. 'Was she annoyed at you about something? Did you have a row that afternoon?'

Pauline's eyes flashed. 'No. What's going on here? Are you working for the law now? Only it sounds like it with all these bloody questions.'

'I told you I wanted to talk about Angel.'

'Talk about her, yeah, but this sounds more like you're

accusing me of something. I didn't kill her if that's what you're getting at. Is that what you think? That I took her to the river and pushed her into it? Jesus, you've got a twisted imagination.'

'I'm not suggesting that.'

'Sounds like it to me.'

Julia kept her voice calm, not wanting the exchange to blow up into the kind of argument where everything got out of hand and nothing got resolved. 'All I'm saying is that something must have happened that afternoon to make her absence in the evening no big deal to you – or to the others.'

'I told you. She was unreliable.'

'Yeah, yeah, change the record.'

'And what the hell is that supposed to mean?'

Julia maintained eye contact, determined to show that she wasn't prepared to back down. 'It means that it doesn't add up, doesn't make sense. You all looked out for Angel. There must have been a good reason why none of you panicked when she didn't show up. Not even a phone call to the flat.'

Pauline shrugged. 'You didn't know her like we did.'

Julia bristled at the comment but ploughed on. 'Why was she trying to get rid of you and Lindsay in the afternoon? Washing her hair, doing some imaginary shopping – it sounds like she'd made plans. Was she seeing someone else, do you think? Meeting someone before she went to the Fox?'

'How would I know?' Pauline said.

'Because you were close to her. Did she have a boyfriend, a lover, someone she didn't want anyone else to find out about?'

'If she didn't want anyone to know, then how would I?'

'I'm not saying that you *knew*, only that you might have guessed. It must have seemed odd when you took over a bottle of fizz to celebrate her birthday and then she couldn't wait to get rid of you.'

'It wasn't like that.'

'So what was it like?'

For a while it seemed like Pauline wasn't going to reply. She drank some beer, lit a cigarette and gazed around the pub for thirty seconds before eventually returning her attention to Julia. 'We were there for a couple of hours. Everyone was fine. She was in a good mood, happy. It was her birthday after all. But she could have arranged to see someone later, between seeing us and meeting up at the Fox.'

'What time did you leave?'

'About three.'

'So that leaves four hours before you were due to meet again. Plenty of time to see someone else. Did you tell Vyse this?'

'Tell him what? He's got half a brain. I'm sure he's worked it out.'

'But who could it have been?'

'Anyone,' Pauline said. 'I've no idea. If you're looking for a name, I haven't got one. If I had I'd have given it to Vyse.'

That was a lie, Julia thought. Frankie was a name, and Angel had been seeing him. Perhaps her scepticism showed on her face because Pauline narrowed her eyes and glared at her.

'You think I'd let the bastard who killed Angel get away with it?'

'No, of course not,' Julia said quickly.

'You think you knew her, but you didn't, not really.' Pauline carelessly flicked her cigarette towards the ashtray. 'Angel liked attention, a lot of it. I don't mean that in a nasty way, it's just the way she was. It made her easy game for predatory men. She mixed up sex and love. She wanted the whole happy-ever-after thing, the cottage with roses round the door, a loving husband, a golden Labrador and a house full of kids. She couldn't have kids, but she talked about adopting. Every new man who came

170

along was the *one*. She'd get swept away and then she'd get let down again.'

'Are you saying that she slept around?'

'I'm saying that men took advantage of her. Once they'd got what they wanted, you didn't see them for dust.'

'So there could have been a new man on the scene?'

'Could have been.'

'But Lindsay said Angel was no good at keeping quiet about things, that she'd have told *you* about a new bloke even if she didn't tell her.'

'Lindsay talked a load of crap,' Pauline said crossly. 'I know you shouldn't speak ill of the dead, but she didn't know what she was talking about.'

It was the first time they had touched on Lindsay's murder. Both were silent for a moment. Julia was the first to speak again. 'Do you think there's a connection between their deaths? Do you think the same person was responsible?'

'Mark Grey killed Lindsay. I can't see why he'd have killed Angel though.'

'Hasn't he got an alibi for the night she was murdered?'

'Alibis can be bought.'

'Maybe Mark was seeing Angel and Lindsay found out.'

'God, no,' Pauline said, spluttering out a mouthful of beer. She wiped her mouth with the back of her hand. 'Mark and Angel? You've got to be kidding. I know she had terrible taste in men, but even *she* wouldn't go there. The man's an arse. And anyway, she'd never cross that line. He was Lindsay's fiancé. There are some rules you never break.'

Although Angel *had* been sleeping with Frankie, Julia thought. But maybe that didn't count as betrayal with Clare not being in the original friendship group. 'What did Lindsay see in him if he was such an arse?'

Pauline stubbed out her cigarette, screwing it down into the ashtray. 'A way to get off the Mansfield, I should think. She wanted a husband, and any man would do as long as they were going places. He has ambition, you can say that for him. He's not going to be stuck in this hole for the rest of his life.'

Julia heard the bitterness in her voice. 'Are you still working for your dad?'

'Unfortunately.'

When she didn't elaborate, Julia went back to her original line of enquiry. 'Does Mark live on the Mansfield?'

'God, no, he wouldn't be seen dead living in that dump. He shares a flat just round the corner from here. He says it's because it's convenient for the City, but really it's just because it's cheap.'

'Why do you think he killed Lindsay?'

'Who else?' Pauline said. 'It's usually the nearest and dearest, isn't it?'

'But why would he? They're only engaged. He could walk away at any time.'

Pauline gave another of her now familiar shrugs. 'Maybe she discovered some terrible secret about him.'

Julia wondered what could be so terrible that it would have to be concealed by murder. And anyway, it didn't add up. She didn't even know Mark, had never met him, so why would he single her out to deliver the lock of hair? But if she dismissed Mark, if she crossed him off her list, then she was back to the members of the old gang and Clare.

Pauline drained her glass and thumped it down on the table. 'Are we done here, Julia?'

'No, I've still got a few more questions.'

Pauline raised her eyes to the ceiling. 'I'd better get another round in then. Two pints. I don't order halves.'

Julia wondered if Pauline had caught on to her ploy to ply

her with booze and get her talking – and was now turning the tables. The old animosity was never far from the surface. It lay there smouldering, ready to burst back into flames. They disliked each other, always had and always would, but she couldn't afford to let it influence her. On the other hand, she couldn't completely dismiss the possibility that Pauline had killed both Angel and Lindsay.

27

While her old enemy was waiting at the bar, Julia took the opportunity to scrutinise her. As she stared, a memory was sparked of when Pauline had first appeared on the scene all those years ago, and instantly latched on to Angel. Like she was laying a claim. And the cow hadn't been the slightest bit bothered that Angel already had a best friend, that the post was already taken. It had been a shock, disturbing, when a few months down the line she'd discovered how much time the two of them were spending together – doing homework, going to the cinema, just hanging out – a fact that Pauline hadn't been slow to slip into the conversation, as if she was taunting Julia, as if it was a war she intended to win.

Julia finished her beer, feeling again the sting of teenage angst. When she'd casually mentioned it to Angel, Angel had pulled a face. 'To be honest, I don't even like her that much, but Mum says I should be nice to her, that it's lonely when you move to a new place and start a new school. Mum says I should try and make her feel welcome.'

Now, looking back, Julia wondered if that was true or if Angel had just used it as an excuse. Perhaps she'd been flattered by Pauline's attentions, had enjoyed being the centre of attention, being fought over like a juicy bone pulled to and fro by two squabbling bitches. Were teenage friendships always so fraught, so fragile, so ludicrously punishing?

Julia still resented Pauline. Even though she'd never managed to drive a wedge between her and Angel, it hadn't been for the lack of trying. No, in the end it wasn't Pauline who'd destroyed the friendship. She'd managed to do that herself when, full of cheap cider and petty jealousy, she'd confronted Angel over Liam Crosby, a row that had spilled out onto the walkway and ended in disaster.

'Thanks,' Julia said when Pauline came back with the drinks. She waited until the other girl had sat down. 'I wanted to ask you about Angel's diaries. Was she still writing one? Do you know?'

'I don't think so. Not for a while. Why?'

Julia was watching her closely but there didn't seem to be any sign of deceit or anxiety. However, Pauline could just be an excellent liar. And a confident one. 'I rang Renee yesterday to see how she was doing, and she mentioned that the police had taken some of Angel's diaries away to be examined.'

Pauline, who couldn't resist having a dig whenever the opportunity arose, said slyly 'What's the matter? You worried about what she might have said about you?'

Julia didn't rise to it. 'Actually, I was wondering why she stopped keeping one. She was always scribbling stuff down. She loved writing in those diaries.'

'I suppose she got bored of it. I mean, why do people feel the need to write about everything?'

Julia ignored the question. 'Or someone took them.'

175

'Why would they do that?'

'Because there was something in them, or one of them, about the person who killed her. Something that person didn't want anyone else to read.'

'It's a theory, I suppose.' Pauline wrinkled her nose as if she didn't think much of the idea. 'So how does it work exactly? Someone goes round to see Angel and says, "Excuse me while I just slip into your bedroom and snaffle your diaries." Doesn't sound very likely.'

'Maybe they were already in the bedroom. The two of them, I mean.'

That gave Pauline food for thought. She lit another cigarette and slowly inhaled. 'But how would he even know where her diaries were?'

'She never used to hide them. They were on the shelf behind her bed. She always used those ones with the locks on so Renee couldn't read them.' Julia thought Pauline must have already known this. 'It wouldn't have been hard to slip a few into a bag when Angel was in the loo or the kitchen.'

Pauline frowned a little but then her face suddenly grew dark. 'If you're thinking it was me or Lindsay who took them, you're way off the mark. We never went into her bedroom that afternoon. We were in the living room the whole time.'

'I didn't mean you and Lindsay. I mean someone who came to see her *after* you.'

Pauline made a huffy offended sound in the back of her throat. 'I wouldn't know about that, but it wasn't us.'

Julia was starting to wish she'd never mentioned the diaries. If Pauline had taken them, she would destroy them now or dump them in a bin somewhere. She had wanted to see her reaction but having seen it, she was none the wiser.

The pub had started to fill up since she'd first come in.

Julia glanced towards the bar and saw a tall, thin man looking at Pauline. He was in his late twenties, gangly and pale, with short brown hair. 'There's some bloke at the bar staring at you.'

Pauline turned her head, briefly raised her hand to him in a vague gesture of acknowledgement and then turned her attention back to Julia. 'That's just George. He works at the butcher's.'

'He seems very interested in you.'

'George would be interested in any girl with a pulse.'

'Not your type then?'

But Pauline wasn't in the mood for female bonding. 'Drink up. You're lagging behind.'

Julia took a swig of her pint. Was George someone she should be adding to her list? He must have known Angel. Lindsay too. She looked over again, caught his eye and quickly looked away. 'Why do you think Lindsay wanted to see me?'

The sudden change in subject matter took Pauline by surprise. She tipped back her head and blew a couple of perfect smoke rings. They hung in the air like misty haloes. 'Just being friendly, I guess.'

'She seemed worried that I knew something.'

'What kind of something?'

'Something that Angel had told me.'

Pauline grew more alert, her body tensing a little. 'I thought you hadn't been in touch with Angel for a while.'

'Off and on. The occasional phone call. I told Lindsay.'

Pauline didn't know how to respond to that. Her gaze wandered around the pub, her eyes seemingly determined not to meet Julia's. Eventually she forced a smile. 'Really? Angel never mentioned it. And Lindsay said . . .' She stopped abruptly, leaving a long pause, before continuing. 'I never listened much to what Lindsay said.'

Julia was seeing the same anxiety she'd witnessed with Lindsay. Interesting. She took a punt. 'Friends have to stick together, don't they? It's not as though I'd ever say anything. Secrets are safe with me.'

Pauline's eyes finally met hers. There was another long pause. Her tongue slid across her lips. 'I've no idea what you're talking about.'

'Loyalty's the most important thing,' Julia said, pressing on. 'It's all that matters in the end, don't you think?'

Pauline opened her mouth but whatever she was going to say remained unsaid. A young woman dressed in jeans and a grey sweatshirt was walking towards the table carrying an orange juice. Julia recognised her as the DC who'd given her a lift home after Vyse had broken the news of Lindsay's death.

Carol Forshaw stopped and smiled at them both. 'Hello, ladies. And how are you tonight?'

'All the better for seeing you,' Pauline said sarcastically. 'Shouldn't you be out catching criminals?'

'Finished for the day,' Carol said. 'Just having a well-deserved drink before I head home.'

'Orange juice,' Pauline scoffed. 'What kind of a drink is that?'

'The kind of drink that guarantees I won't have a hangover in the morning.'

'Have you arrested that Mark Grey yet?'

'Mr Grey has an alibi, Pauline. You already know that.'

'Yeah, I bet he has. Doesn't mean it's genuine, though. If you spent less time harassing innocent people and more time chasing the guilty ones, you might be making some progress.'

'I'll bear it in mind,' Carol said drily. 'Thanks for the advice.'

Julia had been sitting quietly during the exchange. It was annoying that Carol had turned up now, just as she'd reached an interesting point in her exchange with Pauline. Still, she had made it clear that she knew something and that, she hoped, might put the cat among the pigeons.

'You all right, Julia?' Carol asked, switching her attention. 'You two having a catch-up?'

'I'm fine, thanks,' Julia said, ignoring the second question.

'Glad to hear it. Oh well, I'll leave you to it. I'm sure you've got lots to talk about. Have a nice evening.'

'What was all that about?' Julia said, as Carol moved off and headed back towards the bar.

'The usual police intimidation. Her letting us know that she's watching us. She's never off duty, that one. She's always sniffing around, seeing what she can find out. You should watch out or you'll be next on the list of suspects.'

'Those interview rooms are dire, aren't they?' Julia said, even though she'd been taken to the more comfortable version. 'I'm sure people confess just to get out of them.'

Pauline had her gaze fixed on the DC at the bar. 'I should think that's the idea.'

'You must be sick of it, the constant questions and everything.'

'Yes, I'm sick of it.' Pauline dragged her eyes away from Carol Forshaw and looked at Julia. 'And now you're here doing exactly the same thing.'

'Sorry, it's been such a shock; first Angel and now Lindsay. I can't get my head round it. Vyse said I should stay away from you all. He seems to think that just being in your company puts me in some kind of danger.'

'Jesus, did he? That's funny. He's so bloody stupid.' Then Pauline grinned and said, 'Maybe you should take his advice.'

Julia frowned. 'I don't like people telling me what to do.' When Pauline didn't respond she said, 'What's Clare like? I haven't met her yet.'

179

'Small, blonde, pretty. Frankie's usual type. He never had much imagination when it came to women.'

'Will she be here on Saturday?'

'Probably. She won't want to miss the latest gossip on Lindsay.'

And Julia didn't want to miss the opportunity to meet her. 'I might join you if you don't mind.'

'Do what you like. It's no skin off my nose.'

Julia sensed that she'd reached the end of the line when it came to fishing for information. Already Pauline was staring at Carol Forshaw again, anger pinching the corners of her mouth. Occasionally Carol looked back, a smile playing on her lips, more amused than bothered, a woman who knew she'd got the upper hand.

28

On Tuesday morning Julia sat down in the living room with a mug of coffee and her notebook. It was odd having no work to go to, every day empty until Saturday when she'd meet up with Apostle. She had to do something useful with the time. Losing her job had been devastating, an axe-like blow to her self-esteem and confidence. She'd been so sure that she was going places, that she was on the ladder to success, and now all her hopes and dreams had been shattered into a thousand jagged pieces. How had this happened? How was she going to repair it? Everything felt so impossible.

She pulled herself up short. Here she was drowning in self-pity, inwardly whingeing about how rubbish her life was, when Angel and Lindsay were dead, wiped off the face of the earth for ever. It put things into perspective. Her pride had been dented, but she'd recover. She'd lost her job, but it was hardly the end of the world. She might not *want* to work for Apostle, but it would mean a wage coming in.

Julia, having given herself a good talking to, returned her

attention to the notebook. What had she learned from last night? That Pauline, like Lindsay, had got jumpy when she thought Julia might have talked to Angel more recently than expected; that Pauline had Mark Grey firmly in the frame for Lindsay's murder; that Pauline didn't think Angel had killed herself; that Angel had bad taste in men. Julia pondered on the latter. She understood what it meant to make poor decisions, to trust the wrong man, to always be ignoring the hazard signs. It saddened her to think of Angel having to go through that over and over again. You could kiss as many frogs as you liked but that didn't mean you'd ever find a prince.

Julia scribbled most of this down, then added a few lines about the missing diaries. Missing or unwritten? If you'd always kept one, would you suddenly stop? Was it a habit you could break? She had kept a diary for six months when she was thirteen but the fear of it being read by her mother was greater than her desire to record all the daily upheavals, the joys and disappointments and the turmoil of being a teenager. That her innermost thoughts might be read without her permission filled her with such dread that she'd ripped all the pages out, screwed them up and pushed them into the bottom of the kitchen bin under the used tea bags and dinner leftovers.

The only member of the old gang who she hadn't talked one-to-one with now was Frankie. He would probably be in the Fox on Saturday night, but it could be tricky separating him from the others, and especially his wife. He must have been on tenterhooks since Angel's death, wondering if his relationship with her would come to light.

Julia tried him out for size as the number-one suspect. He had all the credentials – opportunity, an illicit affair, a lot to lose if the truth came out – but it still didn't sit well. Even if Angel had threatened to tell Clare, she couldn't imagine him killing her. It was too risky. A lifetime in prison, or twenty years at least, if he was caught. Frankie wasn't the sharpest knife in the drawer, but he could still have worked out that being divorced from Clare was preferable to being locked up in a cell for the best years of his life. Unless it had been a crime of passion, a moment of madness, but that didn't really tally with him taking her to the river and pushing her in. That kind of thing involved planning, premeditation.

Although Julia sensed that they were all hiding something, she wasn't convinced that it was murder. More likely it was just the Angel/Frankie liaison they were trying to cover up. Which meant that Angel had been killed by someone outside the group. Her latest boyfriend? An angry ex? Maybe a man she'd only recently met, a man who had taken her for a drive, a man who had taken her to a place she would never return from alive. But why? Was she talking about a psychopath, someone who killed purely for the pleasure of it? If that was the case, then she was out of her depth.

It was hard to dismiss the idea that Lindsay's death was in some way connected to Angel's. Which brought her back to the lock of hair and why it had been left for her. The thought of it being clipped from the murdered girl's head made her stomach turn over. If Pauline was right and Mark Grey had killed Angel, then how had he found out where Julia lived and why did he think she was such a threat?

Julia sipped her coffee while all this went round in her head. She wondered how she could get to meet Mark Grey. With his fiancée recently murdered he probably wasn't at work or doing much socialising. He'd have to play the grieving partner whether he was grieving or not. Pauline knew where he lived. She should have asked. Would it be all right, she wondered, if

183

she just dropped by to express her condolences? Maybe not, seeing as he didn't know her from Adam, but she wanted to meet him face to face, ask a few subtle questions and try to read his body language.

Julia was about to call Pauline when she heard footsteps outside, the distinctive sound of someone descending to the basement. Not the postman; he'd already been to deliver another unwelcome bill and a reminder about a dental appointment. Instinctively she held her breath, afraid that her would-be burglar had returned to try again. The bell went. Two long rings. Did burglars ring bells? Well, they probably did, just to make sure there was no one at home.

Slowly she rose to her feet, undecided as to whether to answer or not. For a moment she stood very still. But then, her mind made up, she hurried towards the door, eager to see who was on the other side. If it was Tom or Frankie or Pauline – all of whom must have believed she was at work – then they'd have no good reason for being here and could, accordingly, be bumped up her list of suspects.

Julia must have girded herself because when she opened the door and saw who was standing there her shoulders instantly relaxed and her mouth broke into a smile.

DI Vyse smiled back. 'I'm not disturbing you, am I? Sorry to drop by unannounced but you said you were off work for a few days.' He held aloft a Tesco carrier bag. 'I've got something for you.'

For a moment, she was confused. Was Vyse doing her shopping for her now? She stood back to let him in. 'What sort of something?'

'Angel's diaries,' he said, making his way into the living room. He placed the bag on the coffee table. 'I had a word with Renee, and she was fine about you seeing them. Carol's already been

through them – DC Forshaw, I mean – but she didn't find anything relevant. Another pair of eyes might be useful.'

'Thanks,' Julia said. 'Would you like a coffee?'

'No, ta. I can't stay long. I just wanted to make sure you're
okay. No other big surprises? No more attempted break-ins?'

'No, nothing,' Julia said. Her eyes strayed towards the bag.
'When do the diaries stop?'

'1984, when Angel was twenty.'

'So there could be five missing.'

'Could be,' he agreed.

'Whoever killed her must have taken them.'

'Might have done,' Vyse said. 'If she didn't just stop keeping
them. So how did it go with Pauline last night?'

Julia's gaze quickly rose to his face. 'Do you have me under
surveillance?' she said, only half-jokingly.

'Carol was in the Fox. She mentioned that she saw you there.'

Julia nodded. 'Oh, yes, of course. She came over to say hello.'

'Did you find out anything interesting?'

'Not really,' she said, unwilling to share her own hazy suspicions. But, in exchange for the diaries, she felt obliged to give
him something in return. 'Only that she's convinced Mark Grey
killed Lindsay.'

'Yeah, she has mentioned it . . . once or twice.'

'But he's got an alibi, right?'

'He's got an alibi.'

'He could have paid someone else to do it.'

'That's not as easy as you think. You need friends in low
places to organise a hit. And lots of cash. Unless you're going to
go down the non-professional route, in which case you're taking
the chance of employing someone who could screw it up and
then sing like a canary when they're caught.'

They were both still standing up, which made the room,

small as it was, feel even smaller. 'You don't think it was him,' she said, phrasing it more as a statement than a question. 'You think Pauline's wrong.'

'She doesn't like him; therefore, he has to be guilty.'

'Sounds like Pauline. What's he like? I've never met him.'

'What have the others told you?'

'That he's an arse. Well, that's Tom's and Pauline's take on him. Lindsay seemed to think he was something special. I guess she wouldn't have been marrying him otherwise. What's your opinion of him?'

'That he's an arrogant dick, but that doesn't make him guilty. He was lawyered up fifteen minutes after we took him down the station. Refused to say a word until his hotshot brief showed up. That's his right, of course, but I got the feeling he was more shocked than distraught.'

'If he's not guilty then why would he need a pricey brief?'

'Yeah, well, I suppose when your fiancée's just been murdered, the duty solicitor doesn't seem like the smartest option. And Grey's got a law degree, so he knows how the system works and knows that he's going to be up there on the shortlist of suspects.' Vyse put his hands in his jacket pockets and then took them out. 'Anything else crop up last night?'

Julia shook her head again. She could have told him about what she'd said, about how she'd suggested to Pauline that there were things she knew, things she'd keep quiet about, but suspected this wouldn't go down well with the inspector. That's just asking for trouble, he'd say, and he'd be right. 'She doesn't trust me, but I'm working on it.'

'Good luck with that.' Vyse nodded towards the bag. 'Okay, give me a bell if you come across anything. I won't be holding my breath, but there could be something that we've overlooked.'

'I suspect we're missing the important ones. It's the recent stuff we need to know, isn't it? The people she was seeing, the places she was going. It's interesting though that they took the last five. Doesn't that suggest some history, an acquaintance that goes back a few years? Whoever took them was worried about their name cropping up.'

'Maybe,' Vyse said, but she could see he wasn't convinced.

Julia followed him to the front door and thanked him again for the diaries. 'So no new leads?' she asked as he prepared to leave.

'On Angel or Lindsay?'

'Both. Either.'

'We're working on it.' Vyse gave her a long interrogative look, his blue eyes gazing straight into hers. 'Nothing you're not telling me?'

'Of course not,' she said, acting innocent. 'Why would I not tell you things? I want this man caught, and the sooner the better.'

'Or woman,' he said.

'Do you think it could be?'

'I'm just going down the equality route.' Vyse reached out and touched her arm. 'Be careful, Julia. I know I've said it before, but your friends might not be quite as innocent as you think.'

'I'm treading carefully.'

'Are you? It's easy to get caught up in old loyalties.'

'My loyalty lies with Angel, not them.'

Vyse nodded. 'You know where I am. Call me if you need anything.'

Julia stood by the door as he climbed the steps. She still felt the touch of his hand on her arm. The inspector was full of contradictions: telling her to stay away from the old gang, bringing her the diaries, wanting her to stay out of the investigation and simultaneously pulling her in. He hadn't asked why she'd taken time off work. He had referred to DC Forshaw as Carol and she wondered if there was more to their relationship than work. What did that have to do with anything? She shut the door and went inside.

29

Pauline put down the phone and went through to the public part of the butcher's. Her father, full of smiles and bonhomie, was passing over some change to the only customer. The minute the old lady had passed through the door, the smile dropped from his face, and he turned to glare at his daughter.

'What have I told you about making private calls at work?'

'We're not exactly rushed off our feet. What difference does it make?'

'It's unprofessional. Make your calls on your own time, not mine. What's so important it can't wait until lunch?'

'I needed to catch someone *before* they went to lunch,' she said. 'Otherwise, they wouldn't be there.'

'You should have thought about that last night.'

Pauline didn't try to argue. Her head was still hammering from a hangover that two paracetamols had done little to relieve. She'd got home too late and too drunk to ring Tom last night, but she really needed to talk to him about what Julia had said. They'd arranged to meet in the Station Café at ten past one and already she was clock-watching – an hour to go – desperate to share her information.

She wiped down the counter and glanced at George who rewarded her with an unwelcome wink. While her father was busy serving one of his regulars, George sidled over and said softly, 'Hair of the dog is what you need, love. I'll stand you a pint in the Fox at lunchtime.'

'Sorry, I've got other plans.'

'This evening then.'

Pauline wondered why the stupid bloke never took the hint. He had a hide as thick as an armadillo. 'Busy,' she said, even though she wasn't. Her plans for the evening included nothing more exciting than a long hot bath and a few hours of telly, but that was none of his business. No matter how hard he tried, George Abbott wasn't getting in her pants.

'Well, the offer's open,' he said.

Pauline forced a smile. She had no other allies in the shop and so it probably wasn't sensible to offend him. 'Ta,' she said grimly.

The hour passed slowly, time dragging like it always does when you want it to speed by. She did her share of serving and cleaning and replenishing supplies while her father continued to grumble under his breath. He was never happy unless he was making her unhappy. Paternal encouragement was beyond him. As was empathy, sympathy and love. *You're just like your mother*, he'd say when he had the hump with her. To which she could have replied that if she was anything like her, she'd have packed her bags and done a runner long ago. It was only the hope of inheriting his money that kept her here.

Ted Archer ate too much and drank too much and should, if there was any justice, drop dead of a heart attack before he was sixty. Although knowing her luck he'd do something perverse like leaving the business to George or his blowsy lady friend. Pauline rarely referred to her by name. Nancy Whitmore was a well-off widow with a large house, a full figure, a wardrobe full of mutton-dressed-as-lamb clothes and an irritating high-pitched voice. Ted wined and dined her and frequently proposed, although to date she hadn't accepted. Maybe she was smarter than she looked.

At precisely one o'clock Pauline went into the back, grabbed her coat and made a hasty exit. 'Don't be late back,' she heard her father yell as the door closed behind her. It was cold outside with an icy wind whipping down the high street, but she was still glad to be away from the shop. She strode up to the junction traffic lights, crossed over and made her way to the café.

It was busy inside – the lunchtime rush – but Tom had already nabbed a table. She pulled out a chair, sat down opposite and said, 'Thanks for coming.'

'You said it was urgent.'

'It is.' Pauline thought he looked tired. Worn out. There were bags under his eyes as if he hadn't been sleeping. But then, who had? Without any further preamble she took a deep breath and said, 'I think she knows.'

'Who? Who knows what?'

'Julia,' she hissed, leaning forward so the customers at the surrounding tables wouldn't hear. 'She rang and asked me to meet her in the Fox last night. I told you on the phone.'

Tom looked at her through sceptical eyes. 'I don't see how she could know anything.'

'She was banging on about loyalty and friendship and how she wasn't going to tell anyone. She said we could trust her to keep her mouth shut.'

'In relation to what?'

'What the hell do you think?'

'Well, I don't know. It all sounds a bit vague. Didn't she tell you what she was talking about?'

Pauline spoke through gritted teeth. 'She wasn't going to spell it out, was she? God, I wish you'd never clapped eyes on that woman again. I knew she'd be trouble. What are we going to do now?'

The waitress arrived before Tom had a chance to reply. He ordered the soup of the day and a roll. Pauline, who couldn't be bothered to check the menu, ordered the same. 'And a brew,' she said. 'Do you want one, Tom?'

'I'll have a coffee, please.'

After the waitress had gone Tom placed his elbows on the table and sighed. 'Was she talking about Frankie and Angel?'

There was something about the way he said it, the way he suddenly looked all shifty, that set off alarm bells in Pauline's head. 'God, you told her, didn't you? You told her about the two of them?'

'She won't say anything.'

Pauline barked out a laugh. 'What were you thinking? Why would you do that?'

'We went for a drink. I bumped into her outside Cowan Road.' Tom shrugged. 'I dunno. I was in shock, I suppose, after all the Lindsay business. She knew I wasn't telling her something so . . .'

'So you felt obliged to drop Frankie in the shit?' Pauline could barely believe what she was hearing. 'He's your mate, for God's sake. How could you do that?'

'She won't say anything,' he repeated stubbornly.

'Well, you can remind yourself of that when they cart him off to jail.'

'It won't come to that. We can trust her. If she says she won't tell, she won't. Frankie's her friend too. She won't want to get him in trouble.'

'You might trust her, but I don't. Are you going to let Frankie know?'

Tom shook his head. 'What for?'

'So he can be prepared when the law come calling.'

'They won't.'

The soup arrived and they both fell silent while the bowls, bread rolls and mugs were placed in front of them. Pauline was seething. How could he have been so stupid? He hadn't seen Julia Reeve for eleven years and already he was telling her stuff that she had no business knowing. She ripped apart the roll and spread some butter on it. She wasn't very hungry, but the food might help her hangover. What was the soup? Vegetable? Chicken and vegetable? It was hard to tell even after she'd taken a mouthful.

'What else did you tell her?'

Tom's head jerked up and he stared at her. 'Nothing.'

'Jesus, Tom, you'd better be telling me the truth.'

'Why would I lie to you?'

'Who knows? Why do you tell a woman who is, let's face it, a virtual stranger that Frankie was sleeping with Angel?'

'She's not a stranger, not even a virtual one.'

Pauline shook some salt on the soup and tried to keep her temper. 'She spent all last night digging, trying to prise information out of me. She's trouble, Tom. I wouldn't believe a word she says. I reckon she's got some idea in her head about riding in on a white horse and finding out who killed Angel. The triumphant heroine of her own stupid story. It's probably because she feels so guilty about taking off after the accident. *If* it was an accident.'

'She didn't have much choice in the matter, did she? It was her mum's decision to move to Suffolk, not hers. And I'm sure it *was* an accident. Julia would never have deliberately hurt her.'

'The problem with you, Tom, is that you always see the best in people.'

'Is that a bad thing?'

Pauline slurped some soup, looked at him and raised her eyebrows. 'It is when it blinds you to what someone's really like. You know Renee's convinced we had something to do with Angel's death, and Julia's been talking to her. The two of them are plotting, I'm sure of it. They've got it in for us.'

'Don't be so paranoid.'

'I'm not being paranoid. I'm being realistic while you just put your head in the sand and pretend it's not happening. She was going on about the diaries. She's convinced they've been stolen.'

'I dare say Vyse has taken them for some bedtime reading.'

'I don't mean the old ones,' Pauline said. 'I mean the ones she might have been writing for the last five years.'

Tom frowned. 'I thought you said she'd stopped keeping a diary.'

'That's what she told me but maybe she was lying. You know what she was like. Sometimes she'd just say whatever it was she thought you wanted to hear. They weren't on the shelf above her bed, but that doesn't mean they weren't somewhere else.'

Tom laid his spoon down, raked his fingers through his hair and gave a groan. 'If that's the case, then we're all in the shit.'

30

The diaries were in chronological order, dating from 1976, when Angel was twelve, to 1984 when she was twenty. Julia piled them up on the coffee table and stared at them. She knew where she wanted to start but was trying to resist the temptation. 1978 was the year Angel had fallen down the steps and that was the diary that drew her eye. How had Angel really felt about that day? Had she blamed her? How had she felt after Julia had moved away? She reached out her hand but then withdrew it again.

No, she should start at the beginning and work her way through. That was the sensible way to approach the task. The diaries were in different colours and all the locks had been broken. She wondered what Angel had done with the tiny keys – clearly kept them somewhere so safe that even the police hadn't been able to find them. Renee would probably come across them one day.

Julia took a sip of coffee, swallowed, sucked in a breath, picked up the diary on top of the pile and opened it. She felt a curious mix of pleasure and despair at seeing Angel's small, neat handwriting again. New Year 1976. But no sooner had she begun to read than she felt a qualm of conscience. It felt wrong, intrusive, to be reading Angel's innermost thoughts. Renee may have given her permission but that didn't make it right.

However, as she read on, she realised that Angel's entries weren't that personal, more an itinerary of where she'd been and what she'd done. She quickly skipped through the pages. There were mentions of her, of Tom and Frankie, of school, of visits to the Wimpy, her aunt's and, in the summer, days out to Southend and Clacton. Ice creams on the beach, pennies in the slot machines.

Julia began to see why the police hadn't been very interested. The diary for 1977 ran along much the same lines. It wasn't until 1978 that Angel began to put more of herself onto the pages. Some of this was about boys, and she mentioned Liam Crosby more than once. *Does he like me?* she asked. *Does he fancy me?* Julia was transported back to that long-ago summer when they had both mooned over the same boy.

There were numerous mentions of Pauline too. Pauline says this and Pauline says that, as if she was some kind of oracle. What about what Julia had said? She obviously hadn't said anything worthy of note. She felt a sudden stab of jealousy, of remembered teenage angst, and had to remind herself that this was all in the past, that Angel was dead and none of it mattered anymore.

As spring passed into summer many of the diary entries were taken up with Angel's crush on Liam: the way he'd looked at her, what he'd said to her, how she longed for him to kiss her. Julia cringed at this point, embarrassed for Angel and for herself. The two of them had spent countless hours fantasising over a lad they barely knew, dreaming of the perfect boy who would sweep them off their feet. Too many hormones rushing through their

196

bodies, too much romantic fervour, too much misplaced 'love'. It was easy, looking back, to see how ridiculous, how sad, it all was, but back then it had felt like the most important thing in the world.

Finally, she came to July and to the entry before the date she'd been dreading. *Last day of school tomorrow!* Angel wrote. *Mum's going to be at work until seven so everyone's coming back to my place. Frankie says he'll bring cider – and Liam!!*

Julia read it and re-read it, knowing what had come next and wishing she could stop time, turn back the clock, have the day never happen in the way it had. What if Frankie hadn't brought the cider? What if Liam had decided not to come? What if she had never argued with Angel in the kitchen? But what ifs couldn't change anything.

When she turned over the page, Julia knew what she would see – nothing. A blank page. Empty and accusing. And then there were more blank pages, months of them. Even after Angel had come out of hospital, she hadn't written anything. No entries about her injuries, about what had happened, about how she felt about it. When Julia had left for Suffolk, there wasn't a word. As if she'd not had the strength to put pen to paper. And yet she had still replied to Julia's letters.

The entries resumed in October: a birthday meal with Renee at a new Chinese restaurant; a trip to the West End to spend her birthday money; a Sunday get-together on the green with Pauline, Tom, Lindsay and Frankie. The green was a piece of land off the high street, a small park-like area the size of a football pitch, with a few benches, some trees and shrubs. It was mainly used by dog walkers, or it had been back in the day. A few kids off the estate used to hang out there too, drinking cheap booze or smoking dope. She wondered if that's what the quintet had been doing and could imagine them lying supine on the grass, chatting and laughing, passing round a bottle while they wiled away the afternoon.

Julia continued reading until she reached the end of December when she closed the diary and put it down on the coffee table. A faint tremor ran through her. Pauline hadn't been entirely off the mark when she'd suggested that Julia wanted to know what Angel had written about her. Had Angel blamed her for the accident? Had she hated her for it? Had she felt her life ruined by one fateful moment? There were no answers to these questions. In a way the absence of any comment was as disturbing as what she might have written. Perhaps she had just not had the words to express how she felt. Perhaps her enmity had been so vast, so all encompassing, that mere words could not begin to cover it.

Julia stood up, went through to the kitchen and made herself another coffee. Then she returned to the living room, picked up the next diary and resumed her reading. Two hours later, she had finished them all. She leaned back against the sofa and sighed. The diaries had covered Angel leaving school at sixteen, her first job at a hairdresser's, a course she had taken to become a nail technician, a boy called Gary Ross who appeared to be her first steady boyfriend – a relationship that had lasted six months – many mentions of Pauline, a few of Tom, Frankie and Lindsay. No more references to Liam, who had clearly cut his losses after the accident.

The diaries ended in 1984, when Angel was twenty. By this time, she'd had numerous boyfriends, none of them lasting long and most of them causing her some kind of heartbreak. For Angel the search for true love had been a grim one. Were there any clues to who her murderer was? If there were, Julia couldn't spot them. She was, unfortunately, no further along than when she'd started.

31

On Wednesday morning, Julia put the diaries in the carrier bag, caught a bus to Kellston and then walked up the high street. She had called last night and arranged to see Renee. Hopefully the others would be at work. Although she couldn't see anything wrong with dropping by to visit Angel's mother, she knew it might look suspicious. As if the two of them were scheming. And that wasn't without an element of truth.

The moment she set foot on the Mansfield estate she was transported back to the past, to her childhood, to the part of her life she had lived here. Except the place seemed greyer, dirtier and more hostile than she remembered. There was an air of menace about it, an ominous atmosphere. She clung tightly to her handbag as she advanced on Carlton House.

As she neared the tower, Julia raised her gaze to the seventh floor, almost expecting to see a younger version of herself leaning over the rusting balcony. And beside her, a smaller girl with long fair hair. Both of them laughing. They'd laughed a lot in those days. Something shifted inside her; a sense of loss mingled with nostalgia and regret. It had all gone so wrong and there was no repairing it.

Suddenly she had the weird feeling she was being watched: a prickling sensation on the back of her neck, goosebumps on her arms. Her eyes scanned across to Renee's flat but there was no one at the window. She looked over her shoulder – nobody there – and then quickly pushed through the door and went inside. The lobby was quiet, the floor littered with fag ends and tin cans. Had it always been this filthy? Perhaps she just hadn't noticed.

Julia went up in a stinking lift – no change there – and walked along the corridor, passing her old flat on the way. The door was a different colour now, blue instead of green. She rang Renee's bell and waited. It didn't take long for her to answer the door.

'Come in, love,' Renee said, beckoning her inside. 'I'll put the kettle on.'

Julia followed her through to the kitchen where she placed the carrier bag on the counter. 'I thought you'd want these back as soon as possible. Thanks for letting me borrow them.'

'Did you find anything useful?'

Julia shook her head.

Renee stared at the bag. 'I'm not sure if I can bring myself to read them. Do I want to?'

'Oh, there's nothing bad. I mean, it's mostly just day-to-day stuff.' Julia paused, recalling the details of the failed relationships and the subsequent heartbreak. 'Well, some boy trouble, but we've all been there.'

'She never had much luck with boys. I always wanted her to find a nice young man but it's easier said than done, isn't it?'

'Was Gary Ross a nice young man?'

Renee was making tea the old-fashioned way, with a pot and

loose tea leaves. She poured on the hot water and left it to steep. 'That's a name from the past. They were just kids then. Sixteen, seventeen? He was a quiet boy, never said much. I wonder what happened to him.'

'He doesn't live round here?'

'He used to. I think he went away to college. They split up anyway. Pauline reckoned she saw him out with another girl, said he was all over her, and persuaded Angel to finish with him.'

'Do you think she was telling the truth?'

'I'm not convinced that anything she says is the truth. I don't think she liked Angel having a boyfriend. Jealousy, I suppose, because she didn't have one of her own. I told Angel that she should make up her own mind about things, that she shouldn't listen to other people, but I might as well have been talking to the wall.'

Julia leaned against the counter, nodding. Pauline's influence had obviously played a big part in Angel's decision-making. Would it have been different if she'd been here, if she hadn't moved away? There was no way of knowing. Once Pauline had got her claws into Angel, that had been that.

Renee put the teapot on a tray along with a couple of mugs, a jug of milk and a sugar bowl, and took them through to the living room. They sat side by side on the sofa. Julia looked around. The room hadn't changed much. A different sofa and some new cushions but the rest remained much the same. There were two framed photographs of Angel on the sideboard: one of her as a child playing on a beach, another taken in her late teens.

How many times had she sat in here with Angel, after school or at weekends, gossiping and flicking through magazines, reading aloud the problem page from *Jackie* and listening to Radio 1? Later, when they were older, they'd spend more time in Angel's bedroom, and she wondered if that looked different, if Angel had altered the curtains or the rug or bought new pictures to put on the wall.

Renee strained the tea and passed a mug to Julia. 'Help yourself to milk and sugar.'

'Thanks. It's the later diaries, if there are any, that would be most useful. Are you sure she stopped keeping one?'

'Four or five years back. I used to buy her a diary every Christmas, the ones with the little locks on, but that year she said she didn't want one, that I shouldn't waste my money.'

'Did you ask her why?'

'She just said that she wasn't keeping a diary anymore.'

'But she could have changed her mind, bought one for herself later on.'

'She could have.'

'That was when she was about twenty?'

'Yes,' Renee said. 'I think so. I don't remember exactly.'

Julia wondered if something had happened that year, something that had silenced her as in the months after the accident. 'It's strange to keep a diary for so long and then just stop.'

Renee gave a light shrug of her shoulders. 'Was it hard reading them?'

'It was nice in a way, you know, kind of hearing her voice again. But sad too. God, she was so young.' Julia wished she could provide some more comforting words, but she didn't know how. It hadn't been that long since Angel's death and for Renee the loss of her daughter must still be raw.

'I'll wait awhile, I think. I don't feel up to it yet. Have you found out anything from the others?'

'I met Pauline for a drink. She seems convinced that Mark Grey killed Lindsay.'

Renee's mouth tightened at the corners. 'Well, that's what she would say.'

Julia already knew that she suspected the others of not just killing Angel but of killing Lindsay too. 'He lives round here, doesn't he?'

'In those modern flats. Round the corner from the station. That ugly grey block with the red doors. Well, I say modern, they've been there for years.'

'I'd like to get his take on things, but now probably isn't the best time. You must have met him. What's he like?'

'Only a couple of times. Lindsay brought him round once – it must have been a year or so ago – smiling fit to bust and showing him off like he was Prince Charles. I can't say I was that impressed. He seemed pretty ordinary to me, nothing special, but love is blind and all that. I got the feeling he was looking down his nose at us, that he didn't think much of people who lived on council estates.'

'But Lindsay lived here.'

'Perhaps she was the exception. Angel didn't like him either, but she was always polite for Lindsay's sake.'

Julia thought that this must have created friction in the group. 'You said you met him a couple of times.'

'Oh, yes, he came round again a few months later looking for Lindsay. I wondered then if he was one of those jealous, controlling types, always needing to know where his girlfriend was. He didn't strike me as a kind man. She could have done better.'

Lindsay's opportunities for doing better had, sadly, been eliminated by her violent and untimely death. 'What does he look like?'

'Ordinary,' Renee repeated. 'Not ugly but no great beauty either. Slim, brown hair, dark eyes, thin lips. Tallish but not as tall as Tom Finch.' Renee's forehead wrinkled into a frown. 'Like I said, I only met him a couple of times. I'd know him if I saw him again, but nothing really stood out about him. Not in the looks department anyway. He had a way of speaking that sounded posh and fake at the same time, like he was putting it on.'

'Trying to be someone he wasn't?'

'That's about the sum of it.' Renee glanced at Julia. 'Don't go wasting your time on him though. It's the others you need to be concentrating on.'

'I won't,' Julia said, mentally crossing her fingers. If she was going to get at the truth, she felt the need to talk to everyone involved. No exceptions. 'Have you heard anything from DI Vyse?'

'Only about the diaries. And now he's going to be tied up with all this Lindsay business. He won't have time for Angel.'

'It might help if the two deaths are connected. If he finds Lindsay's killer, he might find Angel's too.'

'I wouldn't trust him to find a dog in a kennel. I've told him where to look, but they're all still out there, walking the streets, acting like they never put a foot wrong in their lives. They should be locked up, the whole bloody lot of them.'

'He needs evidence,' Julia said. 'I'm sure he'll get it in the end.'

'Then you've got more faith than me, love. I wouldn't trust that man as far as I can throw him.'

It crossed Julia's mind, not for the first time, that Renee might have taken matters into her own hands, but the thought of the older woman wielding a hammer and bringing it down on Lindsay's skull seemed so far beyond possible as to be almost laughable. And why pick on Lindsay? Frankie seemed a more obvious target.

Julia left shortly after, thanking Renee for the tea and promising to stay in touch. She was glad, in all honesty, to be out of the flat. This was no reflection on Renee, who was coping with the dreadful loss of her daughter to the best of her ability, but more to do with Angel's absence. There was an awful unfillable gap in the rooms, a black void, the sense of a space that could never be filled. And if it was hard for her to be where Angel had once talked and laughed, eaten, drank, sat on the sofa and watched TV, God alone knew how heart-wrenching it was for Renee.

She hurried through the estate and out through the gate. Only then did she stop and look back. Her gaze roamed from Haslow House to Carlton and then to the more distant Temple Tower. She understood Lindsay's desire to get away. There was a grey hopelessness about the place, a sense of despair. She was still looking when a voice came from behind her.

'Grim, isn't it?'

Julia turned to find DC Carol Forshaw at her shoulder.

32

'Grim,' Julia repeated. 'I suppose it is. I never used to think so when I was a kid. I never minded it here.'

Carol put her hands in her pockets and rocked back on the heels of her trainers. She was wearing faded jeans and a red sweatshirt with a fur-lined jacket over the top. 'You been to see Renee?'

Julia wondered if Carol's had been the eyes she'd felt on her when she'd first arrived. Was she being followed by the police? Except she couldn't figure out any reason why she should be. 'I came to give her back the diaries. You've read them, haven't you? DI Vyse said you had.'

'Nothing in them. Nothing I could find at least. It's all kid's stuff. Adolescent anguish and teenage turmoil.'

'Did you check out the former boyfriend, Gary Ross? I know it's unlikely, but he might have come back on the scene.'

'Yeah, I wondered that, but he's been living in the US for the past three years. No trips home so I think we can rule him out. Are you heading down the high street?'

Julia nodded.

'I'm going that way too. Do you mind if I walk with you?'

Julia could hardly say no, and anyway she was curious as to what Carol might have to say. 'Of course not.'

They set off along Mansfield Road. Carol was the first to speak again. 'So how's Renee doing?'

'As you'd expect. She's trying to keep it all together, but Angel was her only child. It's not natural, is it, for kids to die before their parents.'

'No, it must be tough for her. I worry, though, that she's getting a bit obsessed with the idea that Angel was killed by her friends.'

'Have you ruled it out?'

'Not ruled it out exactly but there isn't any evidence that they *were* involved. What do you think?'

Julia wondered how much Vyse had told her about their conversations. Did she know that the two of them had an informal arrangement to pool their information? Perhaps he suspected that she was holding out on him and had sent in Carol to talk to her woman to woman. Or maybe Carol was just on her own fishing expedition. 'The five of them were close. I can't see why they'd kill her.'

'Not even Pauline?' Carol said mischievously.

Julia gave her a sidelong glance. 'We might not be the best of mates, but I don't think she's capable of murder.' Julia wasn't actually sure of this but wanted to come across as a fair-minded person.

'What is it between you two? You've known each other for years.'

'Not really,' Julia said. 'Only a couple before I moved away. I haven't seen her since I was fourteen.' Julia wasn't prepared to go into the whole fighting-over-Angel business. 'Let's just call it a personality clash.'

'Pauline clashes with a lot of people.'

'I can imagine she does.'

'Frankie, on the other hand, is more easy-going, isn't he?'

Julia wondered where she was going with this. 'I suppose so.'

'And Tom. Where does he fit into it all? The clever one, the sensible one? And Lindsay was the quiet one. Not the sort to push herself forward. Which one were you, back in the day?'

'I've no idea,' Julia said. 'We weren't the Famous Five, you know. Or should that be Famous Six?'

Carol laughed. 'The witty one, of course.'

Julia knew that Carol was trying to flatter her. But to what end? To win her confidence, to make her relax, to catch her off guard in the hope that she'd inadvertently let something slip? Perhaps Vyse had guessed that she knew things she wasn't telling. Frankie and Angel. But her lips were tightly sealed on that one.

They were on the high street now, almost adjacent to the butcher's on the other side of the road. Julia glanced across and saw Pauline in her blue-and-white-striped apron serving a customer. She wanted to believe that her old friends were innocent – even the dreadful Pauline – but she couldn't be a hundred per cent sure. Although it was likely that their suspicious behaviour, their whisperings and conspiratorial huddles, were only down to trying to cover up Frankie's relationship with Angel, what if they were actually trying to cover up something much worse? What if Frankie *had* killed Angel?

'What are you thinking?' Carol said.

Julia shook her head. 'None of it makes any sense.'

'Welcome to the world of policing. But don't worry, we'll get there in the end. It might take a little longer than we'd hoped, but the truth usually comes out eventually.'

Usually, Julia thought. What if it never did? What if Renee had to spend the rest of her life not knowing who had killed her daughter or seeing them punished for it? 'DI Vyse told me not to think too much about motive, but surely that's the crux of it all.'

'DI Vyse is full of useless advice. Although I'd rather you didn't quote me on that.'

Julia smiled. Despite her distrust of Carol, she still rather liked her. The woman had gumption and a mind of her own. Making your way in a man's world was never easy, but she got the impression that Carol would be more than a match for any of her male colleagues. 'What made you want to become a cop?'

'A desire for justice? The triumph of good over evil? Or was it the opportunity to boss people around?' Carol said, grinning. 'I can't rightly recall. It seemed like a good idea at the time.'

'And now? Any regrets?'

'God yes, every day, but they're not serious enough to make me want to throw in the towel. The police aren't perfect – far from it – but what's the alternative? Someone has to be there to pick up the pieces when things go wrong.'

'Even when that someone isn't whiter than white themselves? I don't mean you,' Julia added quickly, 'I just mean in general.'

'There have always been bent cops and stupid cops and lazy cops. You have to hope that the good outweigh the bad. Anyway, what about you? You're in PR, aren't you?'

Julia decided she might as well tell the truth. It wasn't as if it was any great secret, more a matter of pride, and Vyse would find out anyway if he tried to call her at Harley Jenks. 'I was, but I've just got a new job. I'm taking a break before I start.'

'Oh, congratulations,' Carol said. 'Where are you moving to?'

Congratulations hardly seemed in order considering Julia had been made redundant, panicked and taken the first job opportunity that had come her way, but she wasn't about to share any of that. 'It's more of a PA sort of position, but the money's better so . . .' Julia shrugged. 'Well, here's hoping it works out.'

'What company is it?' Carol asked.

'Apostle's,' Julia said.

Carol stopped dead in her tracks. '*Ivor* Apostle?'

Julia stared at her. 'What's wrong with Ivor Apostle?'

'Nothing. I mean, nothing if you fancy a spell on the dark side.'

Julia's uneasiness was rapidly turning to anxiety. 'What are you saying? Is there something illegal about the business? Something about him? I know he's not the most amenable man, or the politest, but he told me the only time he'd been in trouble was when he was kid. Was he lying? I really need to know if I'm going to be working for him.'

'I'm not sure if I should tell you this . . .' Carol paused, shifting from one foot to the other while she thought about it. 'It was when I was working at West End Central a few years back.' She frowned but then her forehead cleared. 'Well, you'll probably find out anyway. He was questioned over the death of an ex-girlfriend. A heroin overdose. Alice something, her name was. I don't remember her surname. There was a rumour he'd supplied the smack. He wasn't charged, but it left a bad smell, if you know what I mean.'

'So there was no actual proof?'

'No,' Carol said. 'He's too smart for that. It's not the only thing though. When you've got a crew of bouncers working the doors of half the nightclubs in London, it's not that big a step to having them supply the customers with drugs too. Last year two of his staff were arrested for selling ecstasy after a tip-off. Apostle swore he had nothing to do with it, that they were working solo, and there wasn't enough evidence to pursue it. He's like a cat with nine lives that one, but everyone's luck runs out eventually.'

'He could have been telling the truth,' Julia said, but what she was suddenly wondering was where he got all his money to invest in fancy restaurants and bars.

Carol looked sceptical. 'He could, or he could be up to his neck in all kinds of shit. I'm only telling you this so you know. You don't want to get dragged into someone else's mess. Or get dragged down by them. Just keep your wits about you.'

Julia didn't know what to say. None of this had been in Apostle's file but then none of it appeared to have gone any further than interviews down the police station. Innocent until proven guilty. Except it wasn't that difficult to imagine Ivor Apostle as guilty. Perhaps all his anger about how he was portrayed in the press was just a smokescreen to hide what he was really up to.

Carol briefly put a hand on her arm. 'Sorry. I feel like I've just gone and rained on your parade.'

'No, I'd rather know. Thanks for telling me.'

'Okay, well I'm going down here.' Carol gestured towards a side street. 'You take care of yourself, yeah?'

Julia carried on walking towards the bus stop. What to do? She hadn't officially accepted Apostle's job offer, hadn't signed anything, so there was still time to change her mind. She could ring him and say that it wasn't for her. But now she thought about it, hadn't there been something faintly triumphant in Carol Forshaw's eyes? Perhaps the cop had an agenda of her own. A settling of old scores. Perhaps she shouldn't be too hasty.

33

Julia saw it as providence when the first bus that turned up was going to Shoreditch. With nothing else planned for the day, she decided to go over to Apostle's office and see what she could find out. She could say that she was just passing and had dropped by on the off chance he'd be around. She could say ... God, what else could she say? A cop has just told me that you were questioned over the death of a girl? Is it true that your bouncers sell drugs? Are you even worse than I thought you were?

It was only a short journey and fifteen minutes later she was getting off the bus and looking around to get her bearings. She knew Shoreditch of old, but it had changed since she'd last been here. It was cleaner than she remembered, and brighter – once it had been as dismal as Kellston – with a smattering of art galleries, health-food outlets and trendy cafés. An area on the up. She had heard that the thirty-somethings were flocking here where property was still relatively cheap and there was easy access to the City.

Julia set off along the main street, stopping frequently to

look in the shop windows. With Christmas on the horizon some of the displays had a festive air with fairy lights, fake snow and sprigs of holly. Despite her dawdling it only took seven minutes to reach Apostle's office, which occupied the ground floor of a converted Georgian house. According to the brass plaques by the front door, there was an accountant on the first floor and a financial advisor on the second. It was an impressive, attractive building with tall windows and smart paintwork, and had probably, long ago, been the home of a prosperous family.

Julia tried to sneak a peek through the front window, but the inside was obscured by slatted white blinds. Now she was here she was having second thoughts about speaking to Apostle. Perhaps it would be better to leave it until Saturday. After what Carol had said, she was no longer sure that she wanted the job. Or was she just being cowardly? Of course she was. She took a deep breath, stepped forward and pressed the buzzer.

A woman's voice floated through the small metal grille. 'Hello?'

'It's Julia Reeve,' she said. 'I'm here to see Mr Apostle.'

'Come in.'

A click heralded the opening of the door. Julia stepped inside and found herself in a rather grand hallway with red-carpeted stairs leading to the upper floors. To her left was a slim table positioned against the wall on which stood a vase of white chrysanthemums and a few items of mail. To her right was a closed door with another plaque saying IVOR APOSTLE. RECEPTION.

Julia gave a light knock and went in. The room was bright and airy with a desk set at right angles to the window, and behind the desk sat a pretty, dark-haired, heavily pregnant woman who smiled broadly at her.

'Hi Julia, I'm Una. It's nice to meet you. I'm afraid Ivor's out right now. We weren't expecting you until Saturday.'

'No, sorry. I was in the area, so I thought I'd just pop in on the off chance.'

'That's okay. Would you like a tea or a coffee?'

Una began to lumber to her feet, but Julia waved her back down. 'I'm fine, thanks.'

'Well grab a seat and we can have a chat. I'm so pleased you took the job.' Una patted her stomach. 'It's such a relief. I was starting to think I'd still be here in the New Year dangling the baby on my knee.'

Julia sat down, feeling guilty. 'Oh ... erm ... well, I haven't actually accepted it yet.'

Una's face fell. 'But you will, won't you? Ivor's great to work for. I mean, he can be a grumpy sod on occasion but as far as bosses go, he's one of the best. I wouldn't have stayed here for eight years if he wasn't.'

'But he can easily find someone else. There are lots of agencies out there or he could put an ad in the paper.'

'You'd think so but he's fussy who he works with. He's been looking for my replacement for the past two months. Not that I'm anything brilliant. He's just got used to me and doesn't like change.'

Julia couldn't imagine why Apostle had decided to offer her the post. She'd only met him twice and one of those occasions hadn't gone particularly well. 'So what does the job entail exactly?'

'There's the usual typing, filing and general admin but not too much. We provide bouncers for a lot of the London clubs and bars, so the roster needs to be done a week in advance showing who's going to be working where. Usually, I put the same guys in the same place – they get to know the clientele and who's likely to cause trouble – but sometimes someone goes off sick or has a family thing and then you have to switch it around. It's not that complicated once you get the hang of it.' Una gestured towards a bank of index cards on her desk. 'All the guys' details are in there. They're divided into reliable, not so reliable and only use if you're desperate categories.'

Julia smiled and nodded. 'Okay.'

'The guys all fill out time sheets. They go upstairs to Mr Harrold on the first floor, and he sorts out the wages. Anyway, I'll be here until Christmas so I can show you the ropes if you do decide to take the job.'

'Okay,' Julia said again.

'And then there's the fun side,' Una said. 'Once a week we do a tour of his other businesses – he likes a second pair of eyes – and check that everything's running smoothly. And he's always looking for new investments, so we visit those places too and see if they're worth considering. It means you get out of the office, get a change of scene, although sometimes it means working evenings. Would that be a problem?'

Julia shook her head. While Una was talking, she was trying to think of how to frame the question that she wanted to ask. She wasn't sure if there was a subtle way of doing it. She wasn't sure if she should be doing it at all.

'Oh dear,' Una said. 'You don't look impressed. I'm not selling it to you, am I?'

'No, it's not that. It's just . . . I'm not sure how to put this. It's a bit delicate.'

'I can do delicate. Ask me whatever you want.'

Julia hesitated. Once it was said it couldn't be unsaid and it was more than likely that Apostle would get to hear about it. 'I'm sure it's just idle gossip but . . . but someone told me that Mr Apostle had been investigated over the death of a girl. A few years ago. Alice, was it? Alice something.'

'Alice Irwin,' Una said, her expression growing serious. 'And

Ivor wasn't investigated. He was interviewed by the police but only because she used to be his girlfriend. By the time she died he hadn't even seen her for months. Poor girl. Ivor did everything he could to help – even paid for her to go into rehab twice – but she just couldn't kick the habit. It's a shame, but some people, once they go down that road, can never find a way back.'

'I suppose not.' Julia said.

'When you work in security like Ivor does, the police can be a bit heavy-handed. Don't ask me why. He keeps to the rules, but they always find a way to hassle him if they can. Anyway, he had *nothing* to do with Alice's death, nothing at all, so I hope that puts your mind at rest.'

This left Julia with the option of believing either Una or DC Carol Forshaw. As she didn't know either of them well, it was an impossible choice. 'Well, that's good to know. Thanks.'

'He's a decent bloke. You could work for a lot worse. Well, I have worked for a lot worse.'

As there didn't seem much to say to that, Julia asked instead, 'When's the baby due?'

'Not for another four weeks. I'm hoping he or she doesn't come on Christmas Day. Can you imagine that? Sitting down to dinner and the next thing you're in the car heading for the hospital. That would be just my luck. I hope you don't mind me asking this, but you're not planning on becoming a mum any time soon, are you? I know it's none of my business, but I don't think Ivor could cope with another pregnant employee.'

'No worries on that score,' Julia said. 'I'm not even sure if I want kids.'

'Well, you've got plenty of time to figure it out. How old are you? Twenty-three, twenty-four?'

'Twenty-five,' Julia said.

'I'm thirty-two next year so I figured if I want more than one,

I'd better get on with it. Anyway, can I ask you something else? Do you like the job you're currently doing?'

Julia, surprised by the question, didn't want to admit that she'd been made redundant. She shrugged. 'It's all right. I wouldn't say I love it.'

'There you go! What you need is a job that you don't mind getting out of bed for in the morning.'

'And you think this is it?'

'Nice office, decent boss, good wages, job satisfaction – what more could you want?'

'Not that you're biased in any way.'

Una laughed. 'God, yes, biased up to my eyeballs, but that doesn't mean it isn't true. Ivor isn't one of those bosses who lords it over you. Yes, he's kind of driven, which can be wearing at times, but he listens too. And you can learn a lot. I think you should give it a shot.'

'I'll think about it,' Julia said. She had to admit that Una was persuasive, but her characterisation of Apostle didn't bear much resemblance to the man she'd met. And Una had an agenda: she clearly wanted to get the position filled as soon as possible. 'I'll let you know on Saturday.'

'I won't be here, but I'll be keeping my fingers crossed.'

'Okay, well thanks for talking me through it.' Julia was about to stand up, say her goodbyes and leave when she heard the front door open and close. Next moment Apostle had swept into the room, bringing with him an air of boundless energy and brash confidence.

'Hey, Una, have you heard about . . .' He stopped when he saw Julia, his eyebrows shifting up. 'Ah, Ms Reeve. To what do we owe the pleasure?'

34

Two minutes later Julia was sitting in Apostle's office – far less tidy than Una's – and being pressed to make a decision. He wasn't the patient sort and got straight to the point. 'So I take it Una's given you the lowdown. What do you think? Ready to take the plunge?'

'I thought I had until Saturday to decide.'

'Well, you're here now. There doesn't seem much point in putting it off.'

Julia's eyes roamed over his desk, which was covered in papers and files, newspapers and magazines, two empty cans of Coke and a sandwich wrapper.

'It's organised chaos,' he said, watching her. 'I know where everything is.'

'I wasn't judging.'

'Are you sure?'

Julia had made the decision to take the job before Carol Forshaw had filled her head with a fresh set of doubts. Did she really need trouble with the police on top of everything else that was currently going on? And despite Una's best efforts she wasn't convinced that she could work with him. He would be overbearing and demanding, always wanting things done yesterday, always right, always stubborn and unyielding. Una said he listened, but she hadn't seen much evidence of it.

'You've changed your mind,' he said.

'I didn't tell you that I'd made up my mind. I said I'd come and talk to you on Saturday.'

'You gave the impression it was a done deal on the phone.'

'Did I? Then I apologise.' Julia decided to take a different tack. If part of Apostle's desire to have her work for him was tied up, in one way or another, with the wish to get one over on Harley Jenks, then she could easily put an end to that. Perhaps he wouldn't be so keen to employ her without this added triumph. 'Look, there's something I need to tell you. I think you should know that I was made redundant on Monday. Last in, first out,' she hastily added, her pride not allowing her to let him believe that it was down to incompetence or some other unpleasant reflection on her character.

'So what's the problem? You need a job and I need a PA. It's ... what do they call it? Fate or whatever.'

'Oh,' she said, realising that her ploy had backfired. He hadn't even hesitated. But she still wasn't sure that she wanted her fate intertwined with his.

'How about this: you work with Una up until Christmas and then if you decide it's not for you, we'll call it quits, no hard feelings. I can't say fairer than that.'

It *was* fair, Julia thought. Annoyingly so. Why wasn't she capable of making a decision and sticking to it? She was like a tree swaying in the wind, blown this way and that, never choosing a direction and standing firm.

'And I'll pay you twenty per cent more than you were earning with Harley.'

Julia felt the last of her reservations start to slip away. God, she could put up with him until Christmas, couldn't she? A job was a job, and the extra money would be useful. If he proved unbearable, she'd be free to go her own way in the New Year.

Apostle leaned forward and put out his hand. 'Deal?'

Julia was aware that she could still say no. She was under no obligation. She could just stand up and walk away. But she already knew she wasn't going to. She took his hand in hers, shook it and nodded. 'It's a deal.'

'You won't regret it,' he said.

But Julia knew that she might.

35

Pauline had been waiting over an hour for DC Carol Forshaw to appear again. She'd seen her pass by on the other side of the road, walking – she could hardly believe it – with Julia bloody Reeve. The two of them chatting away like they were best buddies. What was Julia even doing in Kellston? Why wasn't she at work? What was she up to? What was Carol up to? All these questions and more had been going round in her head while she doled out the endless sausages, the bacon and the lamb chops.

Yesterday she'd met Tom for lunch – and was still reeling from the discovery that he'd told Julia about Frankie and Angel. Why he'd do something so stupid was completely beyond her. And now, perhaps, it would be coming back to haunt him. Haunt *all* of them. What if Julia had already spilled the beans? She had wanted to run across the road and end the conversation the two women were having, to drag them apart, to tell Julia to shut her big stupid mouth.

Pauline, already on edge, could feel George's eyes on her. He was always doing that, peering at her from under his pale lashes as if he was making a study, as if he was trying to figure out what made her tick and how he could worm his way into her affections. No chance. His scrutiny made her uncomfortable. It made her bad mood even worse.

Every few seconds Pauline glanced up from whatever she was doing in the hope of seeing Carol Forshaw: she would have to walk past again if she was going back to the nick. But maybe she wasn't. Or not any time soon. Maybe she and Julia were holed up in the caff, heads bent together, having a long conversation about Frankie, laughing about how stupid Tom was to have confided in his old friend.

Well, Tom was stupid. She couldn't argue with that. And she still thought that he should let Frankie know that his secret was out. It was better to be prepared than have the law turn up out of the blue with 'new' information. Not that anything could be proved. Tom could deny saying it. Frankie could deny the whole thing too, front it out, but then she and Tom would have to back him up: nonsense, never, Angel wasn't interested in him that way.

Except she had been. That was the part of Angel Pauline had never understood. So convinced that a man, a lover, was the key to happiness. Even a man like Frankie who Angel had known so well, known for instance that he would never leave his wife and kids, known that they would only ever have snatched moments, known deep down that it wasn't going anywhere. But Angel wouldn't listen. She'd always believed in happy-ever-afters, even when all the evidence pointed in the other direction.

Pauline had just finished serving a customer – four rashers of lean bacon and half-a-dozen eggs – when she finally saw Carol again. There was still a short queue but taking advantage of her father being out the back, she whipped off her apron, said 'Two minutes' to George, and hurried out of the shop. She zigzagged across the road, dodging the traffic and quickly caught up with the DC.

'What was all that about?' Pauline said angrily.

Carol Forshaw stopped walking and stared back at her. 'All what?'

'You and *her*. Julia Reeve. What are you up to?'

'Bloody hell, Pauline. Who rattled your cage?'

'What's she been telling you? She's a liar, that one. She lies about everything. She's had it in for us ever since she came back. If you believe anything she says, you're a fool. She was talking about us, wasn't she?'

'You're getting paranoid, Pauline. She didn't even mention you.'

'So what were you doing with her?'

Carol gave a small impatient shake of her head. 'I'm sorry, am I reporting to you now? I don't think I got that memo.'

'I'm entitled to know when someone's slagging me off behind my back.'

'Actually, you're not.' Carol hunched her shoulders against the cold and put her hands in her jacket pockets. 'You're not entitled at all. And I just told you that your name never crossed her lips so if I were you, I'd go back to work, and we'll pretend this conversation never happened.'

Pauline glanced across the road and could see her father watching her. Great. Now she'd have him on her back all afternoon, moaning on and on about leaving the shop when there were customers in it, claiming dereliction of duty as if they were on a wartime front line and she'd run off to fraternise with the enemy. 'I think Julia's coming to the Fox on Saturday night,' she said in a slightly more conciliatory tone. 'I dare say she'll be digging for some dirt.'

'If there isn't any dirt, you don't need to worry, do you?'

'Yeah, yeah,' Pauline said. 'But that's not the point. She's pretending to be something she's not.'

'And what would that be?'

'A friend.'

'So what do you want me to do about it? Arrest her?'

Pauline sniggered. 'A night in the cells would do her good. Teach her to mind her own business.'

Carol sighed and glanced at her watch. 'Well, if there's nothing else.'

Pauline shrugged, turned away, found a gap in the traffic and strode back across the road. She didn't say goodbye. She didn't look back. Carol Forshaw got on her nerves; she was almost as bad as Julia. And she hadn't got a straight answer from her. She still didn't know what the two of them had been talking about.

Back in the shop Julia saw her father's face, pink with rage. But she knew she was safe while there were customers there. He wouldn't kick up a fuss while there were witnesses. She put her apron on and served the next person in the queue. It was ten minutes before the shop was empty again, when he placed his overlarge hands on his overlarge hips and snarled, 'An explanation would be nice. What the hell were you playing at, walking out like that? It's not the bloody playground. You can't come and go when you feel like it.'

George scurried to the rear of the shop, pretending to look busy, not wanting to get caught in the crossfire.

Pauline, who'd had a little time to concoct a story, smiled sweetly back at him. 'Actually, I was doing you a favour. I saw that cop, DC Forshaw, heading in this direction so I thought I'd cut her off. It's not good for business, is it, having the law popping in every other day?'

'They wouldn't be popping in if it wasn't for you.'

224

'Don't start that again. You can't blame me for what's happened. None of it's my fault.'

Her father snorted as if everything bad that went on *was* her
fault. 'So what did DC Forshaw want?'

'Just some info on Lindsay. Nothing you'd be interested in.'

'I'll be the judge of that.'

'Fine,' Pauline said. 'She wanted to know if Lindsay had any
relatives I knew of. Her mum's dead so . . . and she never had
any contact with her dad. They're looking for aunts and uncles,
cousins and the like. I couldn't help – she never mentioned
anyone to me – so that was that.'

He stared at her through suspicious eyes. 'And why couldn't
they have asked you that over the phone or when you were down
Cowan Road?'

'Quite,' Pauline said. 'But you know what the law are like,
always out to cause maximum inconvenience. Look, I kept
her out of the shop and out of sight of the customers so that's
something. You should be pleased. Think of all those wagging
tongues if she had come in here.'

'It's no excuse for walking out without a word.'

'Okay, next time I won't bother.'

'Why should there be a next time?'

Pauline shrugged. 'Because they like harassing innocent
people. It makes them feel like they're doing something.'

'You'd better not be lying to me, Pauline. If I find out . . .'

'I'm not,' she said firmly, looking him straight in the eye.
'What on earth would I have to lie about?'

36

DI Vyse turned up out of the blue early in the evening. Julia had just eaten dinner and was about to wash up when the doorbell went. It occurred to her as she showed him into the living room that he had visited more times than anyone else had in the past nine months. He sat down on the sofa, stretched out his legs and yawned.

'Sorry,' he said, putting a hand over his mouth. 'Long day. I don't suppose I could bother you for a coffee?'

'Of course. I was just about to make one anyway.'

Julia wasn't sure what he was doing here, which made her faintly nervous. Good news? Bad? He hadn't given any hint, only apologised for calling by unannounced and asked if she had ten minutes to spare. When she came back from the kitchen his eyes were closed. She placed the mug carefully on the coffee table, but he wasn't asleep. Instantly his eyes blinked open again and he sat forward, splaying his hands on his thighs.

'What is it I'm not getting? Two murders, two friends, no

useful forensics. I feel like I'm working in the dark, staggering around with a blindfold on.'

Julia sat down even though the sofa felt too small for the two of them. 'If you've come to me for clues, you've come to the wrong person.'

'But what's your instinct, what does your gut tell you? You know these people better than anyone.'

'Except I don't,' Julia said. 'I knew them years ago when they were kids, teenagers. People change. But I'm not giving up. I'm seeing them again on Saturday night.'

'At the Fox?'

Julia nodded. 'I haven't talked to Frankie yet. Not properly. Or Clare. What do you make of her?'

Vyse's face tightened. He looked like he might be on the verge of giving her another warning about staying away from the old gang but then sighed and gave a half shrug. 'I get the feeling she's on the outside of the group, not really part of it. Hard to say if that makes her more of a suspect or less of one. I'm not sure if she liked Angel much.'

'What makes you say that?'

'Just an impression I got. She called her a bit of a flirt which, roughly translated, means a *lot* of a flirt. Was Angel like that when you knew her?'

'She was fourteen.'

'What, and fourteen-year-old girls don't flirt?'

Julia was instantly taken back to the day of the accident when Angel had been pursuing Liam Crosby, teasing him, laughing at all his bad jokes, laying her hand lightly on his arm. She wondered if, more recently, she'd openly flirted with Frankie too. A dangerous game bearing in mind what was going on behind closed doors. She didn't reply to Vyse but said instead, 'I think you should be looking for the missing diaries. Angel stopped writing before, after she'd been in hospital, but she started again a few months later.'

'Yeah, Carol said you hadn't found anything in them.'

Julia's response was out of her mouth before she could stop it. 'What else did Carol say?'

'Just that she'd bumped into you in Kellston, that you'd been to see Renee.'

'And that I've changed jobs,' Julia said, suddenly suspecting that this was the real reason he was here. She had no good reason for thinking it, other than a sixth sense, one of those gut instincts Vyse was so keen on.

'Oh yeah, she might have mentioned that. Ivor Apostle. Interesting choice.'

'Is it?'

Vyse drank some coffee, put the mug down and looked at her. 'Do you think he had something to do with Angel's death?'

The question came as such a surprise that Julia jumped and felt her heart miss a beat. The breath caught in her throat. 'What? What do you mean? Of course not. Why are you saying that? God, do *you* think he had something to do with it?'

Vyse raised a hand as if to prevent her from travelling any further down that road. 'No, no I didn't mean that. Sorry. It just crossed my mind that you might have heard a whisper, that's all, and decided to go off and investigate on your own. I didn't mean he was a suspect. It just struck me as odd that you'd give up a perfectly good job to go and work for someone like him.'

'I'd have to be a pretty single-minded person to do something like that.'

'Are you saying you're not?'

Julia could hear the playfulness in his voice, but she was still too shocked to react in kind. 'Why would you think I'd heard a whisper? Why would you even think I'd suspect him?'

'He's got form.'

'For murder?'

'No, not for murder. There was some iffy business about a girlfriend, though. A drugs overdose. There were rumours that—'

'I know about that. Alice Irwin, right? And she wasn't a girlfriend; she was an ex. And he was only ever interviewed, wasn't he? There was no suggestion that he supplied the drugs.'

'Oh, there were plenty of suggestions,' Vyse said nonchalantly. 'Just nothing that could be proved. And the only reason I jumped to that conclusion – you know, about you trying to do some freelance investigating – is because of that, because he's been connected to the death of a young girl before.'

'Do you think he knew Angel?'

'No,' Vyse said. 'Like I said, I was just jumping to conclusions, mistaken ones by the look of it. But you have got history when it comes to taking advice. Or rather not taking it. Apostle knows his way round the East End. He even drinks in the Fox from time to time. It's not beyond the realms of possibility that he could have met Angel.'

Julia shook her head. 'But if I did suspect him, which I don't, I'd have to be mad to go and work for him.'

'People do crazy things all the time. So how did your paths cross? You and Apostle.'

'He was my client at Harley Jenks. Things weren't looking too rosy there – economic crisis and all the rest of it – and he offered me a job, so I took it. That's all there is to it.' Julia was still trying to recover herself, to recall what Una had told her, to try and keep things in perspective. 'Are you saying he's a villain?'

'A villain? No, I wouldn't call him that exactly, not in the bank robbing, twenty-years-in-the-slammer sense of the word. But is he whiter that white? I wouldn't say that either. He's a man on a mission, Ivor Apostle, and I pity anyone who tries to stop him.'

'And what mission would that be?'

'To claw his way to the top by whatever means possible. He might not be breaking the law – well, nothing we've been able to prove – but he sails pretty close to the wind on occasion. He's got a chip on his shoulder too, always thinking people are looking down on him. It's one of those weird working-class things.'

Julia was starting to calm down now. So Apostle was ambitious, so he bent the rules and rubbed people up the wrong way. None of that was undue cause for alarm. It was only the suggestion about Angel that had thrown her and which she wouldn't be able to dismiss in a hurry. But Vyse had only said that because he'd jumped to conclusions.

'I still don't get how you thought I'd be so reckless as to go and work for a guy who I suspected was a murderer.'

'Because *I* didn't get why you'd leave a perfectly respectable job to go and work for someone like Apostle. I thought there had to be more to it. You see what this case is doing to me? Both these cases. I'm beginning to see meaning, clues, even in things that are perfectly innocent.'

'If I'd heard something about Apostle, I'd have told you. I wouldn't keep it to myself.'

'Would you though?' he said doubtfully.

'Of course. I'm not some sort of . . . I don't know . . . vigilante.'

'But you'd have known I wouldn't have agreed with it, would have tried to stop you.'

'Well, it's all beside the point because my taking this job has nothing, I swear, to do with Angel's death.'

'I'm glad to hear it.'

They exchanged glances. There were a few seconds of silence. Julia shifted on the sofa and said, 'It's the hair that gets me. It has to mean something, doesn't it? Even if that something is only *stay away* or *keep out of it* or some other such warning. That's why it's hard to believe that a stranger killed Lindsay. Because if they did, how would they even know about me or where I live or that I was asking questions about Angel?'

'But then at the same time it would seem a stupid thing to do for precisely that reason. It limits the list of suspects, doesn't it?'

Julia nodded. Her notebook was still lying open on the table with her neat list of six names, one of which was now redundant. Mentally she placed a black line through it. 'Unless it's a kind of double bluff. Maybe that's what they want us to believe. Someone could have followed me home and found out my address that way. Lindsay was killed the night after we met up. Do you think that means anything?'

'It depends on whether the two deaths are connected.'

'They have to be. Surely. Don't you reckon?'

Vyse rubbed his face with his hands. 'I imagine so, probably, possibly, but it wouldn't be smart to make too many assumptions.'

'Renee's worried that with Lindsay's murder, you're going to stop investigating Angel's.'

'Do you think that too?'

'I hope you're not. But if one's linked to the other then I suppose you just have to follow the best leads.'

'Even if it means looking closely at your friends?'

Julia raised her eyebrows. 'Aren't you already doing that? Haven't we already talked about it? I don't want it to be one of them, of course I don't, but it's more important to me to find out what happened to Angel and why.'

Vyse nodded, stood up, thanked her for the coffee and walked to the front door. He opened it, stepped outside, hesitated and then said, 'Perhaps when this is all over, we could go for a drink.' He met her eyes, smiled and added, 'No obligation.'

Julia knew that she would like to, but she didn't want to appear too keen. She pretended to think about it for a few seconds. No woman, no sensible one, made it too easy for a man to get what he wanted. 'Why not?' she eventually said in what she hoped was a suitably casual tone. 'Yes, that would be nice.'

'Good,' he said. 'You know where I am if you need anything, or if you just want a chat.'

They said their goodbyes and Julia closed the door. She leaned against it for a while, glad that he had asked her, more than glad, but feeling guilty too. It didn't feel right to be thinking of romance at a time like this. Well, it was hardly romance, no point in getting ahead of herself, but even the thought of a future date gave her butterflies in her stomach. But she had to keep her mind on what was important and not be distracted by a lean body, an angular face and the bluest eyes she'd ever seen. Just for a moment there had been something fizzing between them, a chemical reaction giving off heat and making sparks fly. No, she wasn't going there, not right now. Angel was her priority, the one she had to think about, and no man was going to get in the way of that.

37

Julia spent Thursday and Friday at Apostle's office being trained up by a patient Una. The security rosters, the trickiest part of the job, were what they concentrated on, going over the available pool of staff (most of them men), deciding who was the best to place where, who couldn't – or wouldn't – work with someone else, who had to be replaced due to illness or family problems or holidays, which club needed more security, which less, and how to deal with unexplained absences.

At first, Julia hadn't been able to get her head around what seemed to be a perpetual juggling act. Even as Una was explaining everything the phone kept ringing with staff wanting to swap shifts or book nights off. What had started as a tidy list rapidly became covered in insertions and crossings out. The rosters were usually completed on a Monday and copies put out on the hall table on Tuesday morning so the guys could come and help themselves.

'I keep the front door unlocked on Tuesdays and Wednesdays,' Una said. 'That way they can just nip in and pick up their sheets without disturbing me. Although, to be honest, some of them pop in here anyway, just to say hello or have a quick brew. You'll soon get to know them. They're a good bunch on the whole.'

'That's a lot of people trooping in and out,' Julia said.

'Oh, they don't all come. One of them will pick up half-a-dozen sheets and pass them on to the others. They work it out among themselves.'

Apostle's pubs, wine bars and nightclubs all had managers who kept things running smoothly and who didn't bother the office unless the matter was important and could only be dealt with by the boss himself. This meant that, apart from some typing, the majority of the work was connected to the security side.

Julia didn't see much of her employer during these two days. He was either out or in his own office making phone calls or answering them. From time to time, he would come in and place a small cassette on Una's desk, on which were his dictated letters to various councils regarding liquor licences or opening hours or responses to noise complaints. His correspondence, at least in the small sample she witnessed, was reassuringly short and to the point. His presence, however, always made her flinch a little because she couldn't quite shift Vyse's notion as to why she'd gone to work for him.

There was no truth in it. So why did it keep niggling away at her?

At lunchtime on Friday, over sandwiches and bottled water, Julia asked Una about the origins of the business. She was still curious as to how Apostle had made his money, still suspicious, if she was being honest, that it hadn't been made legitimately.

'Ivor started off working the doors,' Una said, 'but the firms who employed him were always messing him about, you know, not paying him on time, changing his hours or not giving him any at all. So he figured he could do a better job of it himself. He started small and gradually built it up. The guys like working for him because he treats them decently and doesn't rip them off. There was a lot of trouble at first because he poached all the best staff, but it's pretty much settled down now.'

'Pretty much?'

'We get the odd bit of aggro from some chancer trying to muscle in, to nick clients from us, but even if some clubs do go with them for a while they always come back to us eventually. We're reliable, you see, and that's essential for this business.' Una took a bite of her sandwich, chewed and swallowed. 'So that's how it began. Ivor used the money he made from security to invest in other businesses, and that's where we are today.'

Julia unscrewed the cap on her water and took a swig. 'Do you get much bother from the press?'

'Only when Ivor's been out on the town,' Una said, grinning. 'They always seem to catch him falling out of some club or another, usually with a blonde on his arm. Work hard, play hard is his mantra. He pretends to be annoyed when his picture appears in the papers or magazines, but he's pleased really. It makes him feel . . .' Una paused. 'I was going to say important but that's not really what I mean. Just *someone* perhaps, not a nobody.'

Julia remembered the press cuttings in the folder kept by Harley Jenks. 'Unless they're calling him an ex-con. He doesn't seem too happy then.'

'Oh, you know about that? Yeah, it always gives him the hump. Although I can't say I blame him. It's not fair to keep bringing it up after all these years. He doesn't like the press, can't stand them. If they ever ring up here – and they do from time to time – I just take their name and number, tell them Ivor's out of the office and that he'll call them back later. He never does, of course.'

Julia wondered if her PR credentials were what had prompted Apostle to offer her the job. Did he expect her to smooth out his problems with the press? This, she suspected, would be as tricky as the security rosters. She wanted to know more about him but was careful not to pump Una for too much information in one go. Softly, softly.

Una sighed and said, 'What Ivor needs is a good woman in his life.'

'He doesn't seem short of those.'

'No, a *good* woman, not one of those. He needs someone smart, someone who isn't intimidated by him ... or just after his money.' They were sitting side by side behind the desk and Una gave her a sidelong glance. 'Do you have a boyfriend?'

'Yes,' Julia said promptly. 'Don't even go there. And I never mix business with pleasure. It causes all sorts of complications.'

'Oh well, you're probably not his type anyway.'

'What, not blonde enough?'

'Or dumb enough,' Una said grinning. 'But you could do worse, you know.'

Julia wasn't sure if she could. Apostle was arrogant, opinionated and probably a misogynist to boot. Vyse had backtracked on labelling him a possible suspect when it came to Angel's death, but now she was starting to wonder. What if Ivor Apostle had another reason for wanting to employ her? What if he was playing some dark game of cat and mouse, keeping her close in case she knew too much ...

38

It was Saturday evening. Julia dressed casually in jeans and a sweater, put her hair up and then took it down again, applied some red lipstick and then wiped it off. What she needed, she decided, was a more natural look, something non-threatening, a girl-next-door type of vibe. Clare, Frankie's wife, was top of her list for a grilling tonight – that's if she was there – and she didn't want to alienate her with expensive clothes or fancy make-up. A dab of perfume was okay though. She chose Chanel Coco from the bottles on display, an impulse purchase from a few months ago, back when she allowed herself little treats, back when she'd thought her job would last for ever.

The two days at Apostle's hadn't gone too badly although it would take a few weeks for her to feel she was really beginning to get to grips with it. It was always like that when you started somewhere new, learning the ropes, trying not to make any stupid mistakes. Her interaction with Apostle had been minimal, polite enough but distant. She hadn't changed her opinion of him and suspected that Una saw her boss through rose-tinted glasses, an almost maternal, protective view. Perhaps that's what happened when you got pregnant.

She took a last look in the mirror, trying to concentrate on what lay ahead, glad that she hadn't had to work today. Apostle employed a woman to come in on Saturdays, to answer the phone and sort out any last-minute hitches. Occasionally, if she wasn't available, the job would fall to Una. Julia didn't mind doing the odd Saturday shift but was relieved she'd had the day free to catch up on some food shopping and do her laundry.

The air outside smelled damp. It had been raining for most of the afternoon and the street was still slick with water. Julia had a fold-up umbrella in her bag and had the feeling she would need it. She stood at the bus stop, hoping she wouldn't have to wait too long. There was a chill in the air, a cold wind whipping along Camden Road. It was dark and the streetlamps cast an eerie orangey glow.

As she waited, Julia couldn't help praying that Pauline wouldn't show up tonight, that she'd have something else on, but suspected that she wouldn't leave her alone with the others. Pauline was wary of her, untrusting; she'd want to keep an eye on things, to steer the conversation away from Angel, to put a stop to any awkward questions. Would Clare take her lead from Pauline? That could be a problem.

Julia had questions to ask Frankie too. Would he know that she knew about him and Angel? Would Tom have told him? Maybe not. And if that was the case, she didn't want to break Tom's confidence. But even if he was still in the dark, Frankie must be feeling the strain, on edge, worried to death that his secret would come out. She would have to tread carefully if she wanted to discover anything.

Eventually the bus came and she climbed on board, making her way up to the top deck from where she had a better view of the city. There were plenty of seats and she chose one by a window. Although she looked out at the houses, the people, the wet litter-strewn streets, she was too preoccupied to take much of it in. Half of her mind was running through her tactics for the night ahead, the other half thinking about Apostle and how she would deal with him once Una was gone. That's if she decided to stay in the job. And then, inevitably, her thoughts leapt to Michael Vyse.

Julia was in Kellston by quarter to seven, earlier than she'd expected. Would anyone be at the pub yet? It had started to rain again so she strode the short distance from the bus stop to the Fox and went inside. It was already getting busy, a short queue forming at the bar, and a quick look round failed to find anyone she knew. There was only one familiar face and that was the skinny man who worked with Pauline. George, was it? He was standing by the counter, a pint in his hand, and his eyes followed her as she walked through to the back to check that none of the old gang was there. There was something weird about the bloke, something watchful. He must have known Angel, at least by sight, and she wondered if the police had talked to him.

Once she'd established that she was the first to arrive, Julia wasn't sure what to do next. Buy a drink, grab a booth or a table and wait? And then she had a sudden worry that they wouldn't show up at all. Pauline could have told them that she was snooping around, asking endless questions and generally making trouble. It was not beyond the bounds of possibility that they'd all decided to stay home or meet up somewhere else. She could be sitting here for hours on her own. But would Tom do that to her? She didn't think so.

Still, it was no fun being alone in a pub and she decided on impulse to head for Mark Grey's flat and see if he was in. That would kill twenty minutes, and if he wasn't there or wouldn't see her, she could always walk around the block. By the time she got back someone might have turned up. As she went out through the door, she could feel George's creepy eyes on her, his gaze boring into the back of her neck.

Julia wasn't exactly sure where the block was, but Renee had said round the corner from the train station so, after putting up her umbrella, she walked to the junction and turned left. This area was classed as south Kellston, a cut above its northern counterpart, and further along, if they hadn't all been knocked down by now, she remembered there were rows of grand ivy-clad Victorian houses with wide windows, slated roofs, fancy stained-glass fanlights and generous gardens.

Sometimes, when they were kids, she and Angel had wandered there, peering up the paths and round the high hedges, choosing their favourites and deciding which one they would move into when they were older. As if there was no world outside Kellston, nowhere else they could possibly live. But those houses were a ten-minute walk away, distanced from the scruffy high street and the dirt and the noise. At this end the properties were more modest and less salubrious, practical if uninspiring.

She found the block of flats without any trouble: an unprepossessing two-storey oblong with an ash-coloured exterior, red doors and red window trim, and crossed the car parking area to examine the rows of bells under the intercom. Her luck was in. There were name labels, most of them filled in, and she found Grey/Hepworth on the first floor. She double-checked to make sure there were no other Greys – it was a common enough name – and pressed the bell.

It was only then that she wondered what she was going to say. Having a total stranger turn up on his doorstep shortly after his fiancée had been murdered wasn't likely to be a welcome intrusion. A charm offensive then. *Come on, Julia. Get your act together. This could be your only opportunity to talk to him.*

A crackly voice came over the intercom. 'Hello?'

'Is that Mark?'

'Who is it?'

She could hear the wariness in his voice, sharp and defensive. 'My name's Julia, Julia Reeve. I was a friend of Lindsay's. I don't know if she told you, but we met up the day before—'

'Wait there,' he said brusquely.

Julia waited. Perhaps it was understandable that he wasn't just going to buzz her in, but she was still slightly miffed. She didn't want to have a conversation with him on the doorstep. That would be awkward and probably unproductive. Although if he *had* murdered Lindsay, it wasn't the best idea to be alone with him in his flat either. But Vyse had said that he had an alibi, that it had been checked out, so theoretically she didn't need to worry.

There was a light on in the lobby illuminating a clean space with a tiled floor and a flight of stone steps. Julia gazed into its emptiness. A minute passed. And then another. Just as she was starting to wonder if he wasn't going to answer the door at all, a pair of ankles appeared on the steps, the feet clad in brown tasselled loafers, then the legs – fawn trousers – shortly followed by the rest of Mark Grey.

He approached the door with a scowl on his face. Julia arranged her own features in what she hoped was a suitable combination of sympathy and affability. Immediately she saw what Renee had meant by his ordinariness. He was neither ugly nor attractive. His features were small, his hair short and brown, the rest of his clothes – a cream shirt with a beige cardigan – those of a man twenty years older.

Mark Grey stared at her through the glass before unlocking

the door. Julia smiled and said, 'I'm so sorry to just drop by like this but I didn't have a phone number for you. Renee told me where you lived.'

Mark didn't smile back. 'How do I know you're who you say you are? You could be anyone. The press have been sniffing around for days.'

'Oh,' Julia said, not expecting this. 'Hang on.' She rummaged in her bag, found her driving licence and passed it over to him.

He looked at it for what felt like a long time, glancing between her and the photo, comparing the two. 'Okay,' he eventually said, handing it back and seeming almost disappointed to discover that she hadn't been lying. 'How can I help?'

'Would you mind if I came in?'

Mark hesitated as if he was trying to think of a good reason to refuse the request, but clearly nothing came to mind because he gave an audible sigh, stood back and waved her in with a perfunctory flap of his hand.

'I hope this won't take long,' he said as they climbed the stairs. 'As you can imagine, I've got a lot on my plate at the moment.'

'Yes, I'm sorry to intrude. And I'm so sorry for your loss. It must be a terrible time for you.'

Mark didn't respond to this although she thought his shoulders tightened a little. They reached the top of the stairs and walked a short way along the corridor where he stopped and opened the door to his flat. Julia felt an odd sensation as she stepped inside, a sudden apprehension, a flutter of alarm. She realised that if something bad happened, no one knew where she was or where to look for her.

39

The flat was surprisingly clean and tidy for a place being shared by two young men. The living room, painted in the usual land-lord magnolia, was square and bland with no plants and no pictures on the walls. The carpet was brown and the furniture utilitarian: an oatmeal-coloured sofa, two matching armchairs, a lamp, a table and a bookcase full of books on politics and economics. Not a novel to be seen.

'I won't keep you,' she said. 'I'm meeting Tom and the others in a bit.' Making it clear that she'd be missed if she didn't show up.

'Oh, that lot,' he said with clear derision.

'You don't like them?'

'It's not a case of liking or disliking. I'm simply not interested in those people. They're not very interesting. God knows why Lindsay hung out with them.'

Julia could see why Tom despised him. He was one of those people who would claim to be a straight talker, to say it how it was, when all he was really doing was wrapping up his rudeness in a cold and brutal honesty. 'Old friends, I suppose. People she felt comfortable with.'

Mark's lip curled. 'Friends,' he said sneeringly.

Julia sat down on the sofa and cleared her throat. She was aware of being on borrowed time, that he didn't want her here and would get rid of her as soon as he could. She needed to catch his attention and hold it. 'I felt I should come and see you. I know we haven't met before, but we used to be friends – me and Lindsay, I mean. When we met up, I got the feeling she was worried about something.'

Mark perched on the edge of an armchair as if he didn't want to make himself too comfortable, as if he'd soon be standing up again to see her out. 'What sort of something?'

'I'm not sure. To do with Angel, I think.'

Mark's eyes narrowed. 'Angel?'

'Did she say anything to you?'

'Not really. She was shocked by Angel's death, of course she was, but . . . I'm not sure what you mean when you say she was worried.'

'I'm wondering now if she had suspicions about what happened to her.'

That caught his attention. He breathed in sharply. 'What? If she did, she never mentioned it to me. No, I don't think that's right. She'd have told me. We told each other everything.'

Julia thought this was unlikely. Couples often spared each other the truth, sometimes because it would be hurtful, sometimes because it was to their advantage not to. Little white lies. Or big black ones. 'Well, something was on her mind. She was desperate to know if I'd been in touch with Angel, if Angel had spoken to me recently.'

'And had she?'

But Julia wasn't going to give him a straight answer to that

ore secrets to come out – worse even than
tween the sheets with Angel – then she
s close to her chest. 'We stayed in touch

he police about all this?'
e they took me seriously. Feelings don't
rder investigation.' Julia knew that she
nnection between them, to bridge the
his guard. 'Did they give you a hard
there for hours going over and over
s. Those places make you feel guilty
them.'
g to feel guilty about.'
wanted to retort, but naturally she
uld afford a fancy lawyer the more
erviewed by the police didn't apply.
ays count for much. In the end you
'

he was killed,' he said. 'And so was

closely, scrutinising every gesture,
s nothing to indicate a guilty con-
on was a general irritation at being
rer then he was a cool-headed one,
reat but more of an inconvenience.
e said. 'Poor Lindsay. How could

ll find that out.'
ll at ease. There was something cold,
he was devastated by Lindsay's loss he
then shock did strange things to people
dn't be too quick to judge. Perhaps he

wasn't the sort of person to wear his hear[t]
the bottled-up, stiff-upper-lip type.

She decided to take a different tack a[nd]
by surprise. 'I hope you don't mind me [won]
dering if you were at Angel's birthday b[ash]
everyone supposed to meet up in the [

Mark frowned at this new line of e[nquiry]
and then immediately shifted forward[. His]
settled into a tight line. 'No. Like I sa[id]
sort of people. Besides, I had somet[hing]

She thought he had taken a beat [as if he'd]
been considering the right respon[se. It came]
naturally. 'Okay.'

'Why are you asking about Ang[el?']

'The two deaths, so close toget[her, I thought]
might be a connection?'

'But Angel killed herself,' he sa[id. 'How con]
nected to Lindsay's murder?'

Julia couldn't figure out if he wa[s
'I don't think she killed herself. I [don't think]
that she'd do.'

'But you've been away, haven't y[ou? For]
a long time. That's what Lindsay s[aid.
Angel was always . . .' He paused[.
'Unstable. Is that the right descrip[tion? I wouldn't]
call a balanced sort of person. S[he was]
always looking for attention.'

Manipulative. Julia rolled the wo[rd
a strong word, emotive. 'You didn't [

'I think we've already covered that. I[
'What do you mean?'
'Exactly what I'm saying. They took[

one. If there were m
Frankie's slipping be
had to keep her card
off and on.'

'And have you told t

'Yes, but I'm not sur
count for much in a mu
had to try and create a c
gap, to make him lower
time at the station? I was
everything. It was relentle
the minute you step inside

'Not really. I had nothin

Well, good for you, she
didn't. Perhaps when you c
normal reactions to being in

'Being innocent doesn't alw
even start to doubt yourself

'I was here on the night s
Darren, my flatmate.'

Julia was watching him
every reaction, but there w
science. All she could pick u
disturbed. If he was a murde
seeing her presence not as a t

'God, it's all so awful,' sh
anyone do that to her?'

'Hopefully, the police w

Julia was still feeling
fish-like about him. If
wasn't showing it. But
and maybe she shoul

on his sleeve, more

nd try and catch him
sking but I was won-
ash in October? Wasn't
ox?'

nquiry, sat back a little
again. His small mouth
id, they weren't really my
ing else on that night.'
too long to reply, as if he'd
se rather than answering

el's birthday?'
her: don't you think there

id. 'How can that be con-

s being deliberately obtuse.
don't think it's something

ou? You hadn't seen her in
id anyway. People change.
while he thought about it.
tion? She wasn't what you'd
he was odd, manipulative,

rd over her tongue. It was
like her.'
Lindsay deserved better.'

her for granted, all of

them. She was the quiet one who never kicked up a fuss. She just went along with things. She was just good old Lindsay.'

Julia thought there was some truth in that. 'Did she tell you why she wanted to meet up with me?'

'I thought you were friends,' he said. 'Did she need a reason?'

'Friends when we were kids, but I hadn't seen her for years. Apart from Angel's wake. I was surprised when she called.'

'Lindsay was a good person,' he said. 'She always made the effort.'

Julia got what Renee had said about his accent, which was oddly clipped, an imitation of an upper-class voice rather than the real thing. She took a deep breath and went for the direct approach. 'Do you think one of them killed her?'

He barked out a laugh. 'Who else?'

'But why?' Julia was surprised by the certainty in his reply.

'To preserve one of their dirty little secrets, I should think.'

'Like what?'

Mark's lip curled at the corner. 'If I knew what it was, I'd have told the police. But if you want my opinion?' He didn't wait for her to respond. 'Lindsay found out something and they killed her so she couldn't talk.'

Julia stared at him.

'I don't know what you're looking so shocked about,' he said. 'You think exactly the same thing, or you wouldn't be here.'

'I don't know what to think.'

Mark tapped his heel against the floor. 'Unless you think it's me. Is that what you're doing here? Hoping I'll drop to my knees and make a confession? Sorry to disappoint. I may be a lot of things but I'm not a murderer.'

'No,' she lied. 'I never thought it was you. The police said you had an alibi, and I presume they've checked it out. I just can't imagine what secret would be so important that someone would kill to keep it hidden.'

'People have killed for less. Half the people on that estate would kill to get their next fix or because you looked at them the wrong way. She was moving out, you know. We were going to get our own place next summer. With two salaries coming in we could have got a mortgage and lived somewhere decent. No chance of that now.'

Julia thought he seemed more upset about the loss of his foot on the property ladder than the death of his fiancée. 'If you think it's one of them, why aren't you doing something about it?'

'Like what?'

'Asking questions, digging into it all.'

'Is that what you're doing?'

'I'm trying.'

'And how's that going?' Mark gave a smirk as if he knew it was going nowhere. 'I'd leave it to the police if I were you.'

Julia didn't understand him. If her fiancé had been murdered, she'd be moving heaven and earth to find out who'd done it and bring them to justice. Leaving it to the police would never have been an option. Especially when they didn't seem to be getting anywhere. Vyse could pull in Tom and the others as often as he liked, but without any solid evidence no one was going to be charged.

Mark looked at his watch and then stood up. 'Well, if we're done here. Thanks for dropping by.'

Julia, with little other choice, rose to her feet too. 'Thank you for seeing me. And I'm sorry about Lindsay, I truly am.'

But he'd already turned his back and was walking towards the door. Julia followed him, disappointed that she hadn't found out more. Was he guilty? Innocent? She still had no idea. She knew she didn't like him though, that he was arrogant and superior and probably thought he could get away with anything – even murder.

40

Back on the street, Julia put up her umbrella and breathed in the damp night air. She was relieved to be out of the flat and away from Mark Grey. As she headed towards the Fox, she went over the conversation in her head, trying to see if she could root out anything new, anything that hadn't registered with her at the time. She wondered why he'd been so unemotional. She wondered why he'd hesitated when she'd asked about Angel's birthday. She wondered how he'd been able to afford a fancy lawyer when he obviously wasn't that well off, not able to afford a mortgage on his own, or at least not for a property somewhere more upmarket.

Then she remembered that Vyse had said Mark had a law degree. Perhaps he'd pulled in a favour from a lawyer mate. Or used some of his savings. And was any of this even worth thinking about? She was no closer to dismissing him from her list of suspects or from moving him into a more prominent position. But at least she had met him. That was something. And had the chance to form her own opinion. Although that didn't differ really from Tom's or Renee's or Pauline's.

That phrase he'd used, *dirty little secrets*, had lodged in her mind. What had he meant by that? What had Lindsay told him? Because he couldn't know they had secrets unless someone had divulged the information. Or was she just back to Frankie again? Frankie and Angel sleeping together. But if Lindsay had told him that then he'd have told Vyse, and Vyse clearly didn't know about it.

Julia turned the corner and upped her pace to get out of the rain. She sloshed through the puddles that had formed on the uneven pavement. If no one was there when she got to the pub, she would call it a night and go home. She wasn't going to sit around waiting for people who might never show up.

But when she pushed open the door, she immediately spotted Tom standing at the bar, waiting to be served. She paused, trying to see him as a stranger might, to sweep aside the knowledge that she'd more or less grown up with him, the belief that he could be trusted, that he was a friend. Only that was easier said than done. He *seemed* honest, *seemed* decent, but what if it was all a façade? People change, as everyone kept telling her.

She went over to join him, touching his elbow to get his attention. 'Hi.'

Tom, who'd been intent on catching the eye of one of the barmaids, turned and said, 'Hey, good to see you. Glad you could make it. Pauline said you might come.'

'Yes, she was overjoyed about it.'

Tom grinned. 'What are you drinking? I'm getting a round in. Or trying to.'

The Fox had filled up since her earlier visit and there was now a line of customers leaning against the counter and vying for the attention of the two barmaids. 'I'll have a red wine, thanks. How are things going?'

'Not too bad. A day at a time, I suppose.'

'Is everyone else here?'

'In the back,' he said.

Tom finally got to order the drinks – three pints of Pride, a white wine and a red – from which Julia deduced that Clare had turned up too. That was good. 'No news from the police, then? Nothing new about Lindsay?'

'Nothing. You?'

'No,' she said. 'Not that they'd tell me anyway. I shouldn't think I'm very high on their list of people to keep informed.' Keeping quiet about Vyse, not wanting Tom to guess how often they talked or what game they were playing. A dangerous game if one of the old gang had killed Lindsay – or Angel. *Leave it to the police.* Except Vyse didn't have the advantage of knowing them, of being able to drink with them, of studying them up close when one of them might, for a moment, let their mask slip.

But not Tom. Surely not Tom.

'It's all a bit much, isn't it?' he said. 'Sometimes I wake up in the morning and think it's just a bad dream.'

'I know.'

'I hope they catch whoever did it soon.'

The drinks arrived and Tom passed a five-pound note over the counter. He waited for his change and then picked up the three pints. She took the other two glasses. As they walked towards the rear Julia noticed George again, his eyes on the two of them. Watching. And perhaps he wasn't the only one. Did Vyse have one of his colleagues here too? Carol Forshaw maybe. She scanned the crowd but didn't recognise anyone else.

In the booth at the back, Frankie and Clare were sitting next to each other with Pauline on the other side. Clare was a pretty, petite girl, blue-eyed and fair-haired, not dissimilar to Angel. She welcomed Julia with a wide smile, which was more than could be said for Pauline.

'It's lovely to meet you at last,' said Clare, who looked relieved to have some female company other than what was currently on offer.

'Oh, Julia wouldn't have missed it for the world,' Pauline commented. 'She wants to know what's going on. She has us all down as murderers and needs to find a way to prove it.'

Julia pulled a face. 'I wouldn't be here if I thought that.'

'Course you wouldn't,' Tom said. 'God, Pauline, can't you give it a rest for one night?'

Pauline shrugged and reached for her pint. 'Just warning you.'

'Well, here's to Lindsay,' Frankie said, raising his glass once Tom and Julia were seated. 'May she rest in peace.'

Pauline gave a snort. 'Not much chance of that, is there? Victims don't rest easy when they've been murdered. She'll be haunting the corridors of the Mansfield until Mark Grey gets his just deserts.'

But they all raised their glasses anyway.

'It's not the same without her,' Tom said.

Pauline lit a cigarette, inhaled and blew out the smoke in a long thin stream. 'It hasn't been the same since Angel.'

Julia glanced at Frankie, but his face gave nothing away. She wondered what it was like for him to hear her name, especially in the presence of Clare. Had he cared about her? Had it been a casual affair or something more? She suspected it hadn't been the first time he'd strayed. Good-looking men like Frankie got a lot of attention from women. Even when they were at school, he'd had his admirers and plenty of dates, a different girl every week.

She pondered on how the ones who were left were coping with having lost two friends in such a short period of time. She didn't know if the group had met up last Saturday, but had the feeling that they hadn't, that this was the first occasion they'd all got together since Lindsay's murder. With the police sniffing round, they'd stayed away perhaps, the murder too fresh and too shocking for them even to think about going out.

'They kept me for hours at Cowan Road,' Tom said. 'I was at home all evening, so I reckon they thought I was well in the frame. Just a quick trip up in the lift and away you go. Except Mum was in too so that scuppered that theory. Vyse even gave *her* the third degree, and a lecture on perverting the course of justice.'

Julia had sat down next to Clare in the hope they might get a chance to talk at some point. But with Pauline having put the boot in, she wondered if the girl would be wary of her. She needn't have worried. Clare turned out to be the chatty sort and didn't seem the least bit inhibited by Pauline's warning.

'Yeah, it was awful,' Clare said. 'Even worse than when Angel died. It was like they were trying to catch me out all the time. I mean, I didn't even know Lindsay that well. I'm hardly ever here on a Saturday so ... And Frankie and me were out on the night she died. Mum was looking after the kids, so we went to that new Indian on the high street. It was all right as it happens, not too pricey and the food was good. We don't get much time on our own these days, not much peace and quiet, so it was nice to have a night off.' She paused to take a sip of her wine. 'Anyway, the cops kept asking me what time we'd got home, the *exact* time, as if we always make a note of it the second we walk through the door.'

'It was about ten,' Frankie said.

'I know. I told them that. And that neither of us went out again. But they kept looking at me like I was lying to them. Glaring at me as if they could make me change my story if they stared hard enough.'

'It's intimidation,' Tom said.

'But what's the point when we're innocent?' Clare gave a visible shudder. 'Ugh, as if either of us would do something like that. We're not monsters. It makes me feel sick just thinking about it.'

Pauline took another drag on her cigarette. 'I'm surprised the law aren't more interested in you, Julia. I mean, this bad stuff only started happening since you came back.'

'She wasn't even in London when Angel died,' Tom said, 'so that theory doesn't hold much water.'

Julia, knowing that she'd given this false impression, didn't contradict him. If it ever came out that she'd been here for over nine months she'd have some explaining to do, but for now she would just go along with it and keep her mouth shut on the subject. 'I've spent my fair share of time down Cowan Road. If I never see another interview room again, it'll be too soon.'

'Oh God, yes,' Clare said. 'Me too. You saw Lindsay the night before she died, didn't you?'

'We went for a drink in Covent Garden.'

'I asked her if she wanted to meet for a coffee once, but she said she was too busy with work. That was ages ago. Was she okay when you saw her?'

'It was just a catch-up really, although she did seem on edge, worried about something. It was to do with Angel, I think.'

'What about Angel?' Clare said.

Julia could feel the tension round the table – or maybe it was only her imagination. 'I'm not sure. She didn't come right out and ask anything other than if I'd been in touch with her recently. She was worried that I had been. Or that's what it felt like.'

'Here we go,' Pauline said. 'Didn't I tell you? She's digging already.'

'Clare asked me so I'm answering. And what's the problem

anyway? Of course I want to know what happened to Angel. Don't you all?'

'Angel committed suicide,' Tom said.

'Pauline doesn't think that. And I think it's unlikely. What if she didn't?'

The question hung in the air, unanswered. Even Pauline, for once, had nothing to say.

Later in the evening when a few more drinks had been taken, Tom and Frankie drifted off to talk to a bloke at the bar. Pauline went to the loo, and Julia grabbed her chance to talk to Clare alone.

'Were you and Angel close?' Julia asked.

'No, not really. It was always her and Pauline, like they were joined at the hip, you know. I mean, we got on okay, but we weren't best buddies. She was ...' Clare stopped abruptly, as if she'd changed her mind about what to say next. 'We didn't really have much in common.'

'No, I suppose they're more Frankie's mates than yours. It must have felt a bit strange at the beginning, being the outsider. All that history they have together.'

Clare nodded. 'That's why I just leave him to it most of the time. I only come down here every now and again. I always feel like an outsider, like I don't really belong. Not that they're mean or anything, but they've known each other for so long, it's hard to fit in.'

'I get that,' Julia said. 'It feels weird for me too, coming back after all these years. I still think of them like they were when they were fourteen. But they're different now. Not completely different but well, you know what I mean. They're grown up, adults.'

'Do you really think someone killed Angel?'

Julia shrugged. 'It's possible.'

'It wasn't any of them. I'm sure of it. I was here that night and everything was normal. Nobody could behave normally after they'd done something like that, could they? And Angel was forever not turning up when she said she would. The police thought it was strange, that we hadn't panicked, raised the alarm, but they didn't know her like we did. We just thought she'd got a better offer or that she'd show up later.'

'She could have gone to the river with someone else. Perhaps it was just an accident. She fell in and . . .'

'They just left her?' Clare gave a shudder. 'That's terrible. Just the thought of it makes me feel sick.'

'What do you think of Mark Grey?' That phrase was rolling round her head again. *Dirty little secrets.*

Clare wrinkled her nose. 'I only met him a couple of times. He's very . . . in your face. Very superior. As if *he's* anything to write home about. He was always bigging himself up and putting the rest of us down, especially Angel.'

'Why Angel in particular?'

'I dunno. He didn't like her, I suppose.'

Or liked her too much, Julia thought. Isn't that what some men did when they fancied a girl? A kind of denial. But that was playground stuff, like boys pulling pigtails. Although he could be the kind of man who always wanted what he couldn't have. Could he be a double killer? But Vyse didn't think so. And it felt like a long shot.

'He didn't like any of us,' Clare continued. 'He was constantly making digs, snide comments, and he wasn't very keen on putting his hand in his pocket either. A real tight sod if you ask me. Lindsay could have done better.'

Except Lindsay had seemed pretty pleased with what she'd got. Proud of him, happy to be getting married. 'How did he treat her?'

Clare thought about it. 'All right, I suppose,' she said reluctantly. 'He saved most of his sarcasm for us. But he never acted like ... like he was madly in love with her or anything. He always seemed a bit cool. Although I suppose some men are just like that, not good at showing their feelings.'

Pauline came back, sat down and immediately looked around as if to search out better company. 'Where are the boys?'

'By the bar,' Clare said. 'Would you like another drink?'

'A pint of Pride if you're buying.'

'I'll come with you,' Julia said. 'Help you to carry them.'

They were almost there when she looked over her shoulder and spotted DC Carol Forshaw slipping into the seat she had just vacated.

41

Pauline wasn't drunk yet, or at least not as drunk as she wanted, and she still had most of her wits about her. She leaned back and stared at her visitor. 'What is it with you cops? Can't you leave me alone for five minutes?'

'Oh, come on, you know you love me really. You'd miss me if I wasn't here.'

'Believe me, I wouldn't. What do you want?'

'I just thought I'd swing by and find out how things are. I see the fragrant Julia has joined you this evening. How's that going? Has she got any of you to confess yet?'

'You do know this is harassment, don't you? I could report you.'

'You could but you won't.'

Pauline lit a cigarette and shrugged. 'Haven't you got anything better to do with your Saturday night?'

'Haven't you?'

Truth be told, Pauline hadn't. This was where she always was on a Saturday, regular as clockwork, making sure that nothing happened she didn't know about, biding her time, watching and waiting and listening. Of course it wasn't the same with Angel gone, but what else was she going to do?

Carol flipped a beer mat off the edge of the table and caught it in her fingers. 'Did you know Julia went to see Mark Grey this evening?'

Pauline's eyes widened in surprise. 'What? No, she didn't say. What's she playing at?'

'I thought you could tell me that.'

'Well, I can't. She didn't mention it.'

'Are you two up to something?'

Pauline gave a snort. 'Like what? I can't stand the woman. You know that.'

'And yet you were in here drinking together the other night. Very cosy. Are you sure there's not something you want to tell me?'

'I don't *want* to tell you anything. Surely, you've gathered that by now.'

'Sometimes you're your own worst enemy, Pauline.'

Pauline didn't dispute this. She took another drag on her cigarette and deliberately expelled the smoke in Carol's direction. 'Are you following her then? Are you following Julia?'

'It was just chance. A stroke of luck. I was on my way here when I saw her come out of the pub and walk round the corner. I was curious so ... I kind of guessed where she might be going but I thought I'd make sure.'

'How long did she spend with him?'

'Not long. Ten minutes at the most.'

'She's asking for trouble,' Pauline said. 'She'll be his next victim if she doesn't watch out. I don't suppose he'll take too kindly to her poking her nose into his business. If he can get rid of his fiancée, he won't think twice about getting shot of her.'

'You come out with these things, Pauline, but sometimes I wonder if you really believe them.'

'Of course I bloody believe them. Are you telling me you think he's innocent?'

'Until proven guilty.'

'Oh, don't give me all that crap. Just because you can't find the evidence, doesn't mean he's in the clear. All it *does* mean is that he's going to get away with it.'

'He was at home when Lindsay was killed.'

'Yeah, right, and I'm the fairy on top of the Christmas tree.' Carol smirked.

Pauline was trying to work out what this all meant: Julia stirring things up with Mark Grey, DC Carol Forshaw stirring things up with her, a web of other people's actions and intentions that could cause all kinds of trouble. She had her own agenda and didn't need even more complications.

Carol balanced the beer mat on the edge of the table again, flicked it up and caught it. 'Don't say I never tell you anything.'

'You only tell me stuff because you think it's going to help yourself.'

'You're getting very cynical in your old age.'

'You should sod off now before everyone starts to think I'm a grass.'

'Since when did you ever care about what people think?'

'Since now.'

Carol rose to her feet, grinning. 'See you soon, sweetheart. Take care of yourself.'

Tom was sticking close to Frankie, even though it meant enduring endless chat with him and his mechanic pal about football and football and even more damn football. He sensed that Julia was circling round, looking for a chance to get Frankie on his own, and he couldn't allow that to happen. What if she asked him about Angel? What if she told him that she knew? Frankie might go into a panic or say something stupid and then Clare might start to suspect and before the evening was over everything would begin to unravel. No, it was better to avoid the situation altogether. If he kept the two of them apart, nothing bad could happen.

The minute Julia and Clare had left the booth, DC Carol Forshaw had descended on Pauline like a hawk swooping down on its prey. But he wasn't concerned about that. Pauline could take care of herself. While he stood talking, he kept tabs on Julia. She was at the bar, and she kept looking over. It was Frankie she was studying, and a small frown had appeared between her eyes. What was she thinking? What was going on in her head?

Come to that, what was going on in *his* head. Julia wouldn't betray him, or at least the old Julia, the one he'd grown up with, wouldn't. But he wasn't sure if she was the same girl. And her loyalty, ultimately, would lie with Angel – even though she was dead and gone. He could feel his palms beginning to sweat and, moving his pint from one hand to the other, surreptitiously wiped them down the side of his jeans.

He needed to have a word, to be certain, or he'd go mad. He often felt one step away from madness these days, as if he was teetering on the edge of a cliff and one small push would be all it took to send him plummeting into oblivion. And the truly insane thing was that if he hadn't stopped her on the Strand, if he'd just walked on past, then she wouldn't even be here. And he wondered if it was some kind of self-destructive thing, that deep down he wanted to be found out, wanted to be punished.

No, that was just the drink talking. Too much beer swilling around in his bloodstream. He was overreacting. He had to keep the faith. And he had to remember that this wasn't just about him. There were the others to consider, to protect. They were in this together, sink or swim – God, that was a tasteless thought – and he couldn't afford to go to pieces.

Julia dropped off the drinks at the booth and then went to the loo. She had a pee, washed her hands and ran a comb through her hair. It was getting on for ten o'clock and although she'd had a productive evening – chats with Clare and Mark Grey – she had yet to pin down Frankie. Other than following him to the gents when his bladder eventually forced him to make a visit, she couldn't think of any way of getting him on his own.

When she returned to the table, everyone was there. She slid in opposite Tom. He looked drawn, she thought, pale and tired. There were dark shadows under his eyes. And yet those same eyes were bright and alert, his gaze jumping from face to face, as if intent on harvesting every moment, every word spoken, and every gesture made. Interested or afraid? She just couldn't tell.

They were talking about the omnipresent DC Carol Forshaw. Pauline shrugged and lit another cigarette. She didn't care, she said, the woman could harass her until she was blue in the face, but she wasn't going to admit to something she hadn't done.

'Why does she always pick on you?' Frankie said.

'God knows.' Pauline leaned back and smiled, a slow sly smile. 'She did tell me something interesting, though. She said that Julia had been to see Mark Grey tonight.'

It came out of the blue and suddenly all the attention was on Julia, every face turning to look at her. She inwardly swore. *Bloody Carol Forshaw.* 'Oh yeah,' she said, as casually as she could. 'I was curious. I just wanted to know what he was like, so I went round to his flat before I came here.'

'And he let you in?' Tom said.

263

'No reason why he shouldn't, although now you mention it, I don't think he was overly keen. No red carpet or anything. Anyway, I was only there ten minutes. I told him I'd just dropped by to offer my condolences.'

'I'm sure he was very grateful,' Pauline said dryly.

'Not so you'd notice.' Julia was rapidly calculating how much she should tell them and decided as little as possible. It would come as no big surprise that he thought them responsible for Lindsay's death, but she decided not to share the information. 'I didn't take to him. He's rather arrogant, isn't he? I mean, he was just about polite, but I could tell it was an effort – and that he couldn't wait to get rid of me.'

'You never mentioned that you'd been to see him,' Clare said, frowning, as if she'd just recalled their earlier conversation. 'When we were talking, you never mentioned it.'

'Sorry,' Julia said. 'It was a bit of a non-event really. There was nothing much to say about it.'

Pauline stuck the knife in again. 'Julia likes to keep things to herself. Isn't that right, Julia?'

'I wouldn't say that exactly.'

Tom was watching her closely, his expression tight and serious. 'You shouldn't have gone there on your own. What if he did kill Lindsay? He could have—'

'There's no *what* about it,' Pauline said. 'Of course he did. He's a piece of work, that one.'

Julia thought that Pauline wouldn't have minded much if he'd brought a hammer down on her head too. 'But he had no reason to hurt me, did he? So far as he was concerned, I was only there because I'm an old friend of Lindsay's and wanted to say how sorry I was.'

'I shouldn't think he believed you,' Pauline said. 'Not for a minute. He'd have realised you were snooping the moment you turned up on his doorstep. You've got one of those faces. You're a terrible liar.'

Julia wondered if that was true – she hoped not – but she knew that what she'd done was reckless and stupid, that she should have let someone know where she was. Well, it was too late for regrets now. And anyway, nothing terrible had happened. She'd be more careful in future.

'Make sure you lock your door tonight,' Pauline continued gleefully. 'If Mark's happy to murder his fiancée, he won't think twice about you.'

'Christ, Pauline,' Tom said. 'Don't say things like that.'

'Why not? It's just a piece of friendly advice.' Pauline looked at Julia. 'I'd sleep with one eye open from now on. Mark's going to think you're on to him. He's going to be wondering what Lindsay said when you met up.'

'She didn't say anything. Well, nothing much.'

'But he doesn't know that, does he? He could be planning how to get rid of you right now. You need to watch your back. That bastard's capable of anything.'

42

By Monday morning, Julia had pretty much shoved Pauline's warning to the back of her mind. The girl had an agenda – to worry the hell out of her – and everything she said had to be taken with a pinch of salt. But she couldn't completely dismiss it. What if she was right? What if Mark Grey had killed Lindsay? *Why* he might have done it was another matter altogether, and the whole thing with the hair didn't make any sense unless he saw her as a threat. But no matter how many times she went over it, their brief conversation didn't produce any clues.

The bus rumbled slowly through the streets, stopping and starting, the passengers squashed in and still sleepy. Julia yawned. The start of a new week working at Apostle's. Another week in paradise. She leaned her cheek against the window and quickly moved it away again, aware of the thin film of grime that covered the glass. Be grateful to have a job, she admonished herself. There were thousands who didn't, hundreds of thousands. It didn't matter if she liked him or not. All that mattered was that she didn't need to worry about paying the rent.

As the bus trundled towards Shoreditch her thoughts turned back to the evening in the Fox. She hadn't got a chance to talk to Frankie alone, but doubted she would have learned much anyway. He would have been on his guard after it came out about her visiting Mark and not telling anyone. It had been a mistake to try and conceal it, but how was she to know that DC Carol Forshaw had been snooping on her? She'd keep her eyes peeled in future.

Julia had got the impression that Clare had not been entirely enamoured of Angel, that there had been things left unspoken, a holding back. Could she have suspected what was going on between Angel and Frankie? Could she drive? Was she capable of murder? There were women who would kill to keep their man, but she had no idea if Clare was one of them. Julia certainly wasn't. She was of the opinion that a cheating man wasn't worth having, never mind serving a life sentence for. And even if you did get away with it. even if you eliminated the competition, there would always be another woman on the horizon, and another and another.

Julia was so lost in thought that she almost missed her stop and had to jump up suddenly, squeeze past the passenger sitting beside her and rush down the aisle to get off before the bus moved on again. It was a miserable grey day with a sky full of rain-laden clouds, the sort of day that would never get truly light but hover instead in that strange twilight state before it grew dark again. The cold had lessened, however – something to be thankful for – and she could walk down the road without shivering.

When she reached the office, she jabbed in the code for the door and went inside. In reception, she took off her coat and hung it on a peg. No sign of Una's coat. She looked along the corridor towards the kitchen but couldn't see or hear anything.

Running a bit late perhaps. It couldn't be much fun travelling on the Tube when you were over eight months pregnant. She sat down at the desk, opened the top drawer and took out the roster. She might as well make a start. It would need to be completed today and put out in the hall tomorrow.

She was just making some adjustments when she heard the door to Apostle's office open, and seconds later he strode into the room. She was still faintly surprised every time she saw him, as if she hadn't quite accepted that she was working for him now. He was smartly dressed in a dark suit and tie, his shoes shining and his hair neatly combed. A man who had business to attend to and who wanted to look his best.

'Ah, Julia,' he said. 'I have some news.'

'Good, I hope.'

'Good for Una,' he said. 'Maybe not so good for you. She went into labour on Saturday and had the baby yesterday, a premature arrival but they're both okay.'

'Oh,' Julia said, immediately wondering how she was going to cope on her own. And then aware of the selfishness of the thought, quickly added, 'Wonderful! Is it a boy or a girl?'

'A boy.'

'Has she got a name yet?'

'Ivor, of course,' he said. 'What else?'

Julia stared up at him, startled.

He laughed. 'There's about as much chance of that as there is of Una being at her desk tomorrow morning. No, I don't think they've decided. We should send some flowers. I've got an account with a florist – it's in the address book – so could you organise that? You decide what to send. Say it's from everyone, "Congratulations. From all the crew at Apostle's" or something like that.'

'What hospital is it?'

'St Mary's, Paddington. She'll be in for a few days. They want to keep an eye on them both with the baby being early.' Apostle took a key from his pocket and put it on the desk. 'This is for the front door. Try not to lose it. You probably won't need it – I'm here most mornings – but if you're the first to arrive, you won't be able to get in with just the code. And you'll need to turn off the alarm. Four, four, eight, zero. It's the white box on the wall just inside the door.'

'Okay.'

Apostle gave a sigh. 'No more Una, then. Do you think you'll be able to manage on your own? It's not ideal but I suppose we'll muddle through. Just give me a shout if you need anything. The rosters should be put out tomorrow morning.'

'Yes, I'm working on them now.'

'Good.' Apostle looked around the office and sighed again. 'Yeah, I guess we'll manage.' He seemed about to say something else but then changed his mind and left the room, leaving behind him a whiff of regret.

Before she forgot it, Julia wrote down the number of the alarm on a slip of paper and put it in her purse. Then she linked the front-door key to her flat key ring. She opened the drawer, took out an address book that Una kept there and quickly flicked through the pages until she found the florist. It was then that she realised she didn't even know Una's surname and so had to waste ten minutes searching through files until she found it. Baxter. She could have asked Apostle but felt a reluctance to do so; it would show, she felt, a lack of initiative.

Julia ordered the flowers, wondering what kind of man had an account with a florist. The kind of man who sent a lot of flowers. To say sorry? Yes, he probably had plenty of apologies to make. Or maybe just to woo whichever poor woman currently had the pleasure of sleeping with him. Or who he wanted to sleep with. Red roses in all likelihood. Men didn't have much imagination when it came to expressing their affection florally.

She returned to the roster. Ten minutes later, the phone started ringing. One of the security team who wouldn't be able to make it in tomorrow and wanted to check what club he was working at the weekend. Julia had to explain who she was and how Una's baby had come early and that he'd be dealing with her from now on and that, yes, mother and baby were both doing well, and she'd be sure to pass on his good wishes, and all the time running her finger down the roster searching for his name. Eventually she found it and passed on the information.

When she put down the phone, she looked up to see Apostle standing by the open door. 'They're not supposed to do that,' he said. 'They're supposed to come here and pick up their sheets.'

'It's no trouble,' she said.

'Sure, it's no trouble if it's one or two of them but there's over eighty blokes on the books. What happens if they all ring up, wanting to know where they're working?' And before she had a chance to reply he continued, 'You'll be on the phone all day, that's what, with no time to do anything else. And all because they can't be bothered to drop by. Believe me, it's the tip of the iceberg. Let one of them get away with it and they'll all be at it.'

'Okay, point taken. I won't do it again.'

'I'm not being difficult,' he said, as if she had accused him of it, 'just trying to prevent you from making a rod for your own back. Taking advantage is what some people are good at. You need to have a firm hand, lay down the rules and stick to them.'

'I get it,' she said.

Apostle nodded. 'By the way, did you ever find out what happened to that friend of yours? Angel, was it? The one who died.'

The sudden change of subject caught Julia off guard. 'She drowned.'

'Yes, but was it an accident or what?'

'The police are still looking into it. Why?'

'No reason,' Apostle said. 'I was just curious. Okay, I've got to go out for an hour or two. Anything you need before I go?'

'No, nothing, I'm fine.'

'See you later, then.'

Julia waited until the front door had closed and she heard his heavy footsteps going past the window, before she allowed herself to even begin to process what he had said. Her jaw instantly clenched, her fingers curling into two tight fists. Why was he asking about Angel? How did he even know that she'd been called Angel? Angela Glover was the name she'd given when, at their first meeting, he had rudely demanded to know whose funeral she'd attended. She was sure of it. Her heart began to race.

Calm down, she ordered herself, there could be a perfectly rational explanation: the story would have been in the papers and perhaps they had referred to her as Angel there. But Vyse had said that Apostle sometimes drank in the Fox, had even hinted that he might have had something to do with her death. Although he'd quickly backtracked, it had sown a seed and now it was growing.

Julia had taken this job because she needed it, needed an income, but now she was questioning Apostle's motive in employing her. What if he – someone who hadn't even made it to her shortlist of suspects – was actually the one who had killed Angel? Perhaps Ivor Apostle thought she might be a threat. But how? Because Angel had told her about a new man in her life? Or because Angel had sent her the missing diaries for safekeeping? But if any of that had happened, she would have told the police by now and handed over the diaries too.

Julia couldn't make any sense of it. But she would be wary, even more wary, of Apostle from this point on. Safety first. She would keep her eyes and ears open, and eventually, if he *was* guilty, he would make a mistake. She only had to wait, to bide her time and then . . . and then what? She was playing a risky game and, if she wasn't careful, she'd end up down the morgue on the same cold slab as Angel and Lindsay. It didn't bear thinking about, but she could think of little else.

43

Tuning out her father's grumbles – not enough customers, the weather, the inability of his daughter to ever do as she was told – Pauline concentrated instead on the Julia Reeve problem. It was annoying to have the bitch sniffing around, her nose in the air like one of those well-trained dogs the law sometimes brought onto the Mansfield. Why couldn't she just clear off and leave them alone? She didn't belong here. She wasn't one of them. She was only out to cause trouble.

Pauline grinned, remembering Julia's shocked expression when it all came out about her visit to see Mark Grey. Who keeps quiet about a thing like that? Only someone who thinks they can get away with it. But her grin gradually faded. What if the two of them were up to something, working together, plotting? Two fuckwits conspiring. But then again, what did it matter? Maybe Grey would do them all a favour and despatch Julia in the same way he'd got rid of Lindsay. This time he might even leave some useful evidence behind.

Pauline took her break at eleven and went through to the

storeroom where she could open the back door and have a sneaky fag. She leaned against the door jamb and stared out at the backyard, cluttered with bins, damp cardboard boxes, a broken chest freezer and other detritus that had accumulated through the years. A tip. Just a pile of rubbish like her life.

The sky was low and grey, full of rain. She reached into her back pocket for the pack of Marlboro, pulled one out and lit it. She looked at her watch. Eleven o'clock, she'd said, and it was already five past. Her thoughts began to skitter, running off in all directions, crashing and colliding, breaking off mid-flow to jump to something else, someone else – Angel, Julia, Carol Forshaw, Renee, her own mother.

Pauline tried not to think about her mother too often. Mum hadn't wanted to come here, to leave the northern town she'd grown up in, but Ted Archer had always made the decisions and when Ted said jump everyone did exactly that. Pauline still considered that town her home, even though she'd lived in Kellston longer than she'd lived there. It had been a teenage fantasy of hers to get on a train – well, two trains in fact – and travel back to the family house where she would find her mother waiting with open arms. It was all bullshit, of course, because the house had been sold long ago, and the town was the last place Mum would go because it was the first place her shitty husband would look for her.

Pauline's eyes shifted back to the old chest freezer, rusting at the corners and padlocked in case kids climbed over the wall and got themselves trapped inside. At least that was what her father said. Maybe her mother hadn't left at all. Maybe he'd killed her and put her body in the freezer. She shuddered, sure that he was more than capable, sure that he wouldn't feel a jot of remorse. And it was a more acceptable explanation for her disappearing act than wilful abandonment. It still hurt, like a stab to the heart, that she had been left behind.

It was ten past eleven before she heard the light tread of Frankie's trainers. Quickly she walked to the gate, pulled the bolt across and stepped out into the alley.

'You're late,' she said.

'I couldn't get away.'

Pauline glanced to the left and right, making sure the coast was clear. 'I need to tell you something, but you have to promise to keep calm and not go off on one.'

'Shit, what's happened?'

'Julia knows about you and Angel.'

Frankie's chestnut eyes widened in alarm. 'What? How did she—'

'Tom told her. The idiot went for a drink with her after Lindsay died. He said she already suspected something was wrong and it just came out.'

'What if she tells Clare?' Frankie raked his fingers through his short wiry hair. 'For God's sake! Why would he do that? What was he thinking?'

'He says she won't tell, that she's promised to keep her mouth shut. He reckons we can trust her.'

'Can we?'

Pauline shrugged. 'Who's to say? She's playing her own game. I just thought you ought to know. It might be a good idea to keep her away from Clare for a while, though. Just in case.'

'What else has he told her?'

'Nothing. He swears.'

'Damn it!' Frankie said. 'I wish she'd never come back.'

'You and me both, mate. But don't get all stressed about it. She could have told Clare on Saturday, but she didn't, so maybe you'll be okay.'

'Should I talk to her? Julia, I mean. Do you think I should?'

'Your decision,' Pauline said. 'Sometimes it's better to let sleeping dogs lie.'

'Not if they're about to jump up and bite you.'

'Well, she hasn't told the law, so I suppose that's something. If she had, you'd have known about it by now.'

Frankie couldn't stand still. He paced a short way along the alley, turned and came back. 'I can't decide. I don't know what to do.'

'Well, you can stop acting so bloody guilty for starters. Clare's going to guess something is wrong if you're behaving like a man with a guilty conscience.'

'Plenty of things *are* wrong. Angel and Lindsay are dead, the law doesn't believe a word we say, and now Julia's got the dirt on me. How much worse can it get?'

Much worse, Pauline could have said, but she knew better than to kick a man when he was down. 'And don't do anything stupid like buying Clare flowers. That's going to make her instantly suspicious.'

Her father's voice boomed from the shop. 'Pauline! Pauline! Get your fat arse back in here. Your break was over five minutes ago.'

Pauline rolled her eyes and said, 'I've got to go.' She laid a hand on Frankie's arm. 'Just don't panic, okay? Try and stay calm.'

She gave the freezer one last dubious look before she went back inside.

44

Julia's first full week was a hectic one. Apostle was interested in purchasing two new businesses – a wine bar in Islington and a small nightclub in Soho – and letters were flying between him and the sellers, him and his solicitor, him and his surveyor, in an almost constant stream of communication. Some of the questions he was asking seemed so routine, so banal, she wondered why he didn't just pick up the phone and save himself the cost of a stamp. When she enquired about this in what she hoped was a tactful and discreet way, he told her that people lied on the blower, that people said anything to keep you sweet, that what was on paper couldn't be denied.

'I've learned my lessons the hard way. Now I get everything in writing.'

And Julia got to spend more time than she liked with her fingers flying across the keyboard. She'd had some basic training in computers but sometimes the machine seemed to have a mind of its own. If this was the future, she wasn't sure she liked it.

She watched the screen, constantly afraid that what she'd typed would disappear into the ether, never to be seen again.

A long line of security guys trooped into the hall on Tuesday and Wednesday, most of them picking up the roster and then leaving, a few putting their heads round the reception door to say hello to Una. And with Una not being there, Julia had to break off from her typing to explain about the baby, tell them that mother and child were doing well, introduce herself and try to remember their names. She gave up on the latter, five or six blokes in, as their faces started to merge, and her memory bank filled up.

Apostle was in and out of the office, always going somewhere, always meeting someone, like a hurricane blowing through. In his wake he left a whiff of Aramis and a long list of things to do.

But Julia coped. She made herself cope, concentrating on the job and refusing to let it get the better of her. In a way, it was a welcome distraction from the jumble of stuff that was always in her head: murder, old friendships, DI Vyse and, of course, the disturbing question of whether Ivor Apostle knew more about Angel's death than he was letting on.

She found herself with an opportunity to discover more when Apostle asked her to accompany him on Friday evening to the Soho club he was interested in buying. 'Another pair of eyes,' he'd said. 'I'd be interested to get your take on it.'

Julia didn't have much experience of nightclubs – they weren't really her thing – but she readily agreed, seeing a chance to dig deeper into his interest in Angel. Away from the frantic atmosphere of the office, they would have more time to talk. And after a few drinks he might drop his guard and let something slip.

Apostle picked her up from her flat at precisely nine o'clock. Not sure of what to wear, Julia had tried on various outfits before finally settling on a safe but stylish black cocktail dress. Matched with high heels, sheer tights and a fine silver chain round her neck, she thought she could blend into most London nightspots.

She slid into the back of the cab and nodded at Apostle. 'Right on time.'

'Naturally,' he said. 'It's rude to be late and arriving early doesn't go down too well with the fairer sex. It's a sad truth but you women hold grudges.'

Julia still couldn't work out when he was being serious or when he was joking so she just smiled thinly and said, 'Tell me about this club.'

The cab moved off. Apostle stretched out his legs and withdrew them again. There was plenty of room in the back for two normal-sized people but, like a giraffe in a Mini, he seemed to occupy more than his fair share. 'It's no big deal but I think it might have prospects. Hard to say right now. It's a lesbian club. Does that bother you?'

'Why should it?'

'Some people don't like queers.'

'I'm not some people, and haven't you left it a bit late to ask?'

'Not really. We're not there yet. If it offends you in any way, you've still got the chance to change your mind.'

'It doesn't.'

'Good,' he said. 'It's all about the pink pound, isn't it? They reckon it's the next big thing. Punters with plenty of disposable income. No kids to drain the bank account, and lots of free cash to go out and party.'

'Plenty of gay women have kids,' she said, thinking of her mother's friends.

Apostle ignored her. 'The club's called Gigi's and it's open from Thursday to Saturday. It's been going for a while. It's established. Regular clientele, decent income. No trouble so far as I know. I don't need trouble.'

'So why is it being sold?'

'That's something to find out tonight.'

'When you say trouble,' she said, returning to his earlier comment, 'do you mean the punters or the police?'

'Both.'

When he didn't elaborate Julia decided to take the opportunity to segue into slightly different territory. 'Do you know a cop called Vyse? DI Michael Vyse.'

'Sure. I know Vyse. Why?'

'He's the one investigating Angel's death. Her mum, Renee, doesn't think much of him. She's worried that he isn't doing enough to find out what happened to her.'

'What do you think happened?'

'I don't know. My friends, most of them anyway, think she killed herself, but something doesn't feel right about it.'

'And what does Vyse think?'

'Who's to say? He's not committing himself. Do you know the Fox in Kellston? Have you ever drunk in there?' Julia already knew the answer but wanted to see how he'd react.

'Occasionally,' he said. 'Not for a while.'

'You might have seen Angel in there. She was small, blonde, very pretty. They used to meet up on a Saturday night. There were five of them, two blokes and three girls. We all went to school together.'

'There are lots of blonde girls in the world.'

It wasn't really an answer, but Julia wasn't sure if he was being evasive or just wasn't interested. She decided to drop it for now in case he got suspicious about her reasons for asking. She glanced at him – he seemed unconcerned – and tried to suppress the thought that she could be sitting in a confined space with a murderer. They lapsed into silence with him looking out of one side of the cab and her looking out of the other.

The cab dropped them off in Brewer Street, and as it was still early they decided to have a short walk before going to the club. Soho had a buzz to it, a fizzing kind of electricity. It was sordid but sassy, a peculiar mix of strip joints, cocktail bars, theatres, pubs and restaurants. Beneath it all was that rolling undercurrent of sex. Down every side street were neon signs advertising peep shows, dirty films and dubious bookstores. Surly-looking pimps and bored-looking girls hung around doorways waiting for trade.

Because Julia still had Michael Vyse on her mind, she couldn't resist returning to the subject. 'What do *you* think of Vyse then?'

'Not much.'

'You don't like him.'

'He's a cop, hon. Liking doesn't come into it.'

Julia would have preferred some detail but could see that she wasn't going to get it.

'What?' he said when she didn't respond.

Not wanting to betray her feelings for Vyse, Julia searched her brain for something innocuous to say. 'Oh, I was just thinking you'll need to employ some women if you buy this club. I don't suppose the female punters will appreciate all those hulking great blokes watching over them.'

'That could be a problem.'

'Why? Do you not think women can do the job?'

Apostle stared down at her from his great height. 'It's not because I'm some sexist pig,' he said, thin-skinned as always, overreacting to any hint of criticism. 'It's just hard to find women who *want* to do it. I mean, they can't rely on sheer size or brute strength to break up a fight.'

'No, they have to calm things down a different way. I'm sure there are plenty of women out there who'd fit the bill. You could put an ad in the paper.'

Apostle shrugged. 'We'll cross that bridge when we come to it.' He veered down an alley and stopped outside a red door. 'Here we are.'

45

There was only one person in the lobby, a stocky thirty-something woman with cropped white-blonde hair and an inch-long silver bar bisecting her left eyebrow. She was dressed in black trousers and a white T-shirt, with a tag above her right breast reading SECURITY. Her gaze lifted to Apostle's face and a frown settled on her forehead.

'Members only,' she said sternly.

'We're here to see Andrea Harrow. My name's Ivor Apostle and this is Julia Reeve. We're expected.'

The woman had a walkie-talkie in her hand, but she didn't use it. Instead, she gave him a long hard look, said 'Wait here,' and disappeared through a door marked STAFF ONLY.

From beyond another door, presumably leading to the bar, they could hear the muffled beat of music mingled with the sound of voices.

'Sounds busy enough,' Julia said.

Apostle was examining the lobby, his gaze taking in every inch. The floor was varnished wood, the walls painted a pale mauve and hung with black-and-white photographs of trail-blazing women – suffragettes, politicians and writers. There was a desk with a guest book open on it, and a chair behind.

'It's a good location,' he said. 'Not sure about the decor.'

'What would *you* do with it?' Julia asked.

But before he could answer, the door opened again and the security woman returned with an older female. Julia put Andrea Harrow in her late fifties, a slim, elegant lady with eyes so dark they were almost black. Silver-streaked hair was scraped back from a fine-boned face with strong cheekbones. Her red lips widened into a smile when she saw Apostle.

'Ah, Ivor, good to see you again. Welcome to our little club.'

'Good to be here,' he said, leaning down to brush her cheek with his lips. 'And this is Julia, my new PA.'

Andrea raised her thin eyebrows a fraction. 'A thankless task, I'm sure.' She held out her hand and Julia shook it. 'Shona will take you through so you can get a feel for the place.' She turned her attention back to Apostle. 'You won't be able to go in, Ivor, not during opening hours, but come back to my office and we'll have a drink. There are cameras in the bar; you'll be able to see it on the screens.'

Apostle departed with Andrea, leaving Julia alone with Shona, who didn't look overjoyed at the prospect of her hosting duties.

'I'll be fine on my own if you've got other things to do,' Julia said.

'I wouldn't count on it,' Shona said. 'Some of those dykes eat straight girls like you for breakfast.'

'You reckon?' Julia retorted, resenting the presumption that she couldn't look after herself.

Shona grinned and headed for the door. 'Just stick by me, babe. I'll take care of you.'

It was warm inside, dimly lit and noisy. 'West End Girls' was blaring out from the speakers. The main room contained the bar, around which an untidy crowd was gathered in groups of three or four. All eyes turned to look at her and Shona as they walked in.

'Fresh meat,' Shona muttered almost gleefully. 'They're always curious when a new girl shows up. Do you want a drink?'

'Just a Coke, please.'

Shona yelled across the heads of the other customers to the barmaid, 'Two Cokes, when you've got a minute, Cass. Put them on Andrea's account.'

The drinks arrived twenty seconds later, and they went to sit at one of the tables. Julia took off her coat and placed it over the back of the chair. She had a quick look round, taking care not to meet anyone's eye, noticing the second room that led off from the back. There was a dance floor there with a dozen girls swaying to the Pet Shop Boys.

'Have you worked here long?' Julia said.

'Over three years. I can't believe Andrea's selling up. The place won't be the same without her. That's if it even stays as Gigi's. The new owner could do anything with it.'

Which gave Julia the chance to ask the obvious question. 'Why *is* she selling?'

'Pastures new,' Shona said, taking a swig from her bottle. 'She's had enough of London. Sick of London, sick of life: that's what I told her, but she's made her mind up. Is your boss serious about buying it then?'

'He's considering it.'

'There aren't many places where women can meet, even in London. It's a safe space. Do you know what I mean? It'll be crap if it closes. Do you know what his plans are?'

'He hasn't made any decisions yet.'

Shona took another swig of Coke and put the bottle down on the table. 'Hell, I'm probably going to be out of a job in a few months. That's a depressing thought. He'll want his own staff in.'

'Not necessarily. You could be okay. He'll still need someone on the door. Might as well be you as anyone else.'

This seemed to cheer Shona up a bit. 'I hope so. I mean, I've got the experience, haven't I? And no one knows these girls like I do.'

Julia looked around again, trying to gather information to relay to Apostle – the atmosphere, the clientele, the feel of the place – but he was probably watching everything anyway so she wasn't sure how much more she could bring to the party. The first thing she'd been aware of after they'd sat down was that even in her simple black frock, she was overdressed. This was more of a casual clothing destination: jeans and T-shirts, leather jackets and trainers. There were a few girls in skirts or dresses, but even these had a more informal look.

'It's pretty busy,' Julia said. 'Is it always like this?'

'Fridays and Saturdays. It's quieter on a Thursday.'

The women at the bar were laughing and joking, bantering with each other. A chance to unwind after the working week. And to be themselves. Despite Shona's fresh-meat comment, no one was paying them any attention now. There was a friendly, easy-going ambience and for the first time since entering the club she relaxed.

'They're a good crowd,' Shona said. 'On the whole.'

'Not much work for you to do then.'

But Shona, perhaps under the misapprehension that Julia had more influence with Apostle than she actually had, said quickly, 'That's because I make sure everything runs smoothly. I don't let the troublemakers in, and I nip any rows in the bud – you

286

know, the ones that might get out of hand. And I keep an eye out for anyone who's had too much to drink. People think I just stand around all night but there's more to it than that.'

'Of course there is.'

Julia peered into the other room where, apart from the dancers, there were a few couples sitting on sofas. It was a moment before her eyes focused on one particular pair. They were in the corner, deep in conversation, their faces only just visible. She drew in a breath. What? No, it couldn't be. She looked again. It was. She noticed Pauline first, with her distinctive long black hair, and then DC Carol Forshaw. Carol had a proprietary hand on Pauline's knee.

Julia stared for as long as she dared. Her heart had started to race. What did it mean? Well, for starters it meant they were both liars, pretending to dislike each other, playing out a charade in the Fox while they were really a couple. But what else? Did this have a bearing on Angel's death? It might, it might not. But Carol Forshaw was involved with a suspect, and that couldn't be right. Did Vyse know? Should she tell him? But she baulked at the thought of it. People's personal lives were none of her business – or his. Unless the two women were conspiring to cover up a crime.

Worried that she might be recognised, Julia shifted her chair so her back was to them. Her mind was still racing. She had to get away before she was noticed.

Shona had seen her staring, had observed the sudden movement of her chair. She grinned and said slyly, 'What's the matter? Seen something you like?'

'Not exactly.' Julia glanced over her shoulder again, saw Pauline and Carol kissing, and decided that now was as good a time as any to make herself scarce. Quickly she rose to her feet and grabbed her coat. 'Sorry, but I've got to go.'

46

Once she was in the lobby, Julia wasn't sure what to do next. Flustered, she paced the floor, knowing that Apostle would not be happy at her abandoning her mission. Only one thing to do – just look around, get a feel for the club – and she'd failed miserably. But she was even more concerned at the prospect of Pauline and Carol deciding to leave and the three of them coming face to face in this small space. Should she wait outside? She didn't fancy that either. Lurking in a Soho alley wasn't the smartest thing to do at this time of night.

Shona followed her out, carrying the two bottles of Coke. 'Everything okay?'

'Sorry,' Julia said, flapping a hand in front of her face. 'It's warm in there. I was feeling a bit faint.'

'You should sit down, have a drink.'

Julia stopped pacing and leaned back against the desk. She took a bottle off Shona and gulped down some Coke. 'Thanks.' She was aware of a trickle of perspiration on the back of her neck. Her head was still spinning, full of too many unanswered questions. Perhaps Tom and Frankie knew that Pauline was gay. Perhaps there wasn't any secret about it. But they sure as hell didn't know that she was seeing Carol Forshaw.

'You do look pale,' Shona said. 'Are you sure you won't sit down?'

'I'll be fine in a minute.'

Apostle must have witnessed her hasty departure from the bar because he emerged from the office with Andrea Harrow behind him.

'She's feeling faint,' Shona said.

'You need to go outside, breathe some fresh air,' Apostle said. 'In fact, we may as well make a move and get you home.'

Julia pulled on her coat. 'You don't need to leave on my account. If you've still got things to discuss . . .'

'No, I think we're all done here.' Apostle patted Andrea on the shoulder. 'Thanks for that. I'll be in touch.'

And before she knew it, Julia was out on the street, grateful to have escaped Gigi's without being seen by Pauline and Carol, grateful that she seemed to have got away with her feeling faint excuse, grateful even for the rain that was falling. She briefly raised her face to the sky, hoping the cool rain would help to clear her mind.

'You all right?' Apostle said.

Julia nodded, walking quickly now to put some distance between her and the club. 'I'm okay. It was just hot in there.'

'What happened?'

'Nothing. Like I said, I just—'

'Something happened. One minute you were staring into the back room, the next you couldn't wait to get away.'

It made Julia feel uncomfortable knowing that he'd been watching, but not half as uncomfortable as she would have felt if Pauline or Carol had noticed her. She hesitated, undecided as to how much to tell him. Her trust was spread pretty thinly these days, and she still had no idea of where he lay – if anywhere – in the scheme of things. But she had to give him a better explanation. He clearly wasn't buying the feeling-faint line.

'Okay,' she said. 'I saw someone I recognised, an old friend, and I didn't want her to see me.'

'Why not?'

'Because she's never told me she's gay and so I presume she doesn't want me to know.'

'I thought these things didn't matter anymore.'

Julia pushed her hands into her pockets. 'In a perfect world, but it isn't, is it? There's still a lot of prejudice. And people have a right to a private life. I didn't want her to feel awkward.' She glanced up at him. 'So, sorry about ducking out like that. How did it go with Andrea?'

'The club makes a profit but nothing life changing. I'm not sure it's for me.'

'Shona says there aren't that many places where women can meet up. Be a shame to see it close.'

'I think she could find a better buyer, someone who'll manage it themselves.'

'And if she can't?'

Apostle shrugged. 'Not my problem.'

'But if it makes a profit, then it has to be a good investment, doesn't it?'

'Not necessarily. It's like buying a painting. You can buy it because you like it or because one day it's going to increase in value and make you lots of money.'

'What don't you like about it?'

'I don't dislike it. I didn't say that. But I'm not sure if I understand the gay scene well enough to make good decisions about the club.'

'So get a manager in who does understand.'

Apostle barked out a laugh. 'For someone who couldn't wait to get out of the place, you seem pretty keen on my buying it.'

Julia was aware that she was only arguing for the purchase because he seemed against it, trying to exert her will because she had no control over anything else. But even with this insight, she persisted. 'Gay women need somewhere to go, and Gigi's fits the bill.'

'So it's my social duty to buy it?'

'Well, it's not going to *lose* you money, is it?'

Apostle spotted the light of a cab, stepped out into the road and raised his hand. 'Camden Road,' he instructed the driver, 'and then the Barbican.'

They climbed into the back, settling as before at opposite ends of the seat. Apostle leaned forward and drew across the window that separated them from the driver so they could talk in private. 'So did it make you feel awkward being there? I mean, before you noticed your friend.'

'Not really.' Julia frowned. 'Okay, maybe a bit. But no more than being in a straight bar and having men stare at you.'

'I thought women liked being looked at,' Apostle said. Then when he clocked the expression on her face, he grinned and said, 'Just trying to lighten the mood. Was it a close friend you saw in there?'

'Not especially. Someone I knew when I was younger.'

'So what's the problem?'

Julia wished he'd stop asking questions. She wanted some quiet time to think through the implications of seeing Pauline with Carol Forshaw. But she could hardly tell him to shut up. 'It's complicated.'

'Is this something to do with Angel?'

And again, she felt that sudden jolt of alarm. 'Why would it be?'

'Because Angel was a friend from your past, this girl is someone from your past, and so . . .'

'And so what?' Julia could hear the sharpness in her voice, the defensiveness, and tried, without much success, to rein it in. 'What does that have to do with anything?'

'You tell me.'

But Julia had no intention of going there. She wondered if he knew about Lindsay's murder – it must have been in the papers – and if he'd read about the connection between Lindsay and Angel. Old friends. Both dead.

'Okay,' he said, when all he was met with was silence. He leaned back, averted his face and gazed out of the side window.

Julia wondered if she'd offended him. Probably. Did she care? Well, they still had to work together so perhaps she'd better try for a more conciliatory tone. 'Sorry, I'm just on edge. I didn't mean to snap. It was a shock seeing her there, that's all. Not because she's gay but . . .' She sighed, not wanting to explain about Carol Forshaw. 'Everything's different to how it used to be. It's confusing.'

Apostle turned his head to look at her. 'You feel like people are keeping things from you.'

'They *are* keeping things from me.'

'You feel you can't trust anyone.'

Julia wished Apostle would stop telling her what she felt. Even if he was right. It made her more uneasy than she already was. No, she couldn't trust anyone, and that included him.

47

Pauline didn't like Gigi's, didn't like being surrounded by a crowd of smooching lesbians. But that was why Carol brought her here, to take her out of her comfort zone, to put her on the back foot, to push and provoke and challenge. She didn't see why they couldn't go to a normal pub with normal people.

'You're safe here. No one's going to judge,' Carol said.

Except Pauline was judging, judging herself. She didn't want that label of gay, couldn't comfortably accept it, didn't want to be defined by it.

'You can claim you're not queer until you're blue in the face,' Carol said, 'but you still prefer kissing girls to boys. Doesn't that tell you something?'

But all it told her was that Carol didn't know her at all. Whenever they were together, she felt there was a secret battle raging between them, a war of words, of intent, a thrusting and withdrawing that simultaneously dismayed and thrilled her. She only hung out with the girl because she was lonely, because she missed Angel so much. Well, that wasn't completely true because she'd met Carol almost two years ago, but she could stay away from her for weeks at a time until, usually after she'd had a few drinks, she would pick up the phone and call. In these, the darkest times, Carol didn't fill the void, but she made it less overwhelming.

Pauline had never kissed Angel, at least nothing more than a peck on the cheek. She had shared a bed with her, though, lain beside her and watched her sleep. No funny business, mind. All completely innocent. The two of them in Pauline's double bed when they'd drunk too much, and Angel hadn't wanted to go home. A sleepover, that was all. Her skin had smelled of vanilla, her hair of Wella shampoo.

The first time she'd met Carol Forshaw, Pauline had been in the Fox with Angel. It had been, coincidentally, the night that Mark Grey had entered their lives too. A Saturday, of course. At the bar Mark had homed in on Angel like a lustful dog. He couldn't have been more obvious if his tongue had been hanging out.

Angel had let him buy her a drink, lots of drinks, expensive ones too. She'd laughed at his jokes, made small talk, acted like he stood a chance, even though he never had. Mark wasn't her type, but he had money in his wallet. The men Angel preferred were the good-looking ones, the cocky ones, the ones with the banter, the flashy watches and the fashionable clothes. This guy hadn't come close.

Pauline, sidelined by the usurper, had retreated to the other end of the bar. She would have minded less if the bloke *had* stood a chance, but being dumped for a no-hoper was adding insult to injury. Sometimes, back then, she had questioned if she even liked Angel; that desperate need for attention pushed her patience to its limits. But liking wasn't the same as loving. You loved someone despite all their shitty behaviour.

A tall girl with cropped auburn hair had been queuing to buy a drink. She'd glanced over at Angel, grinned at Pauline and said, 'Why are men so dumb?'

'There's no explaining it.'

'Anyone can see he's punching above his weight.'

'Delusional,' Pauline had said. 'But he'll find that out eventually.'

'I'm Carol by the way. I've just been transferred to Kellston so I thought I'd try out the local pub.' She looked at the almost empty glass in Pauline's hand and said, 'Would you like another beer?'

'Ta. I'll have a pint of Pride, please.'

'A pint coming up. That's if you don't mind drinking with an off-duty cop.'

Under normal circumstances Pauline would have minded – relations between the law and the residents of the Mansfield had never been what could be called cordial – but there had been something about Carol that appealed to her. Tom, Frankie and Lindsay were at the table talking to George Abbott and Angel had abandoned her, so it made a change to have someone new to chat to. And, if truth be told, she was faintly flattered that this stranger had singled her out. Of course, she hadn't realised then that Carol was gay. It hadn't even crossed her mind.

They'd chatted for over an hour, an easy to and fro, a joint running commentary on life, love, the pub and its customers. They'd exchanged phone numbers before Carol left, although Pauline wasn't sure if she'd ever hear from her again. What she'd liked about Carol was that she was tough, sarcastic and funny. Everything really that Angel wasn't. But that was why Angel had needed protecting, needed someone to look out for her.

Angel had found it hard to shake off her admirer and he had followed her back to the table. She was clearly bored of him, but he wasn't getting the message. *Your own fault*, Pauline would have said to her if she'd thought a dose of honesty would have made the slightest difference. Angel was oblivious to the concept of cause and effect. This, mixed with a low boredom threshold, often got her into trouble, especially with men like Mark Grey who she picked up and dropped without a second thought. It was an irony that she treated them exactly how she hated to be treated herself.

Eventually Angel had gone to the loo, bumped into a more interesting proposition on her way back and swiftly abandoned Mark. Pauline would have been more sympathetic if he hadn't been such a crashing bore. He was a Thacher acolyte, which got Tom's back up right from the start, and tended to preach. As if they were stupid, as if they were fools, as if they should all be grateful for mass unemployment and a hopeless future.

Mark hadn't been best pleased when Angel's desertion had become obvious to him. Pauline had seen him glaring at her across the pub, probably adding up everything he'd spent and feeling short-changed. Lindsay, however, had spotted an opening and slipped right into it. A little flattery can go a long way, and she wasn't too proud to take Angel's leftovers.

So, that's how it started, and Pauline knew how it had finished. Mark Grey had never forgiven Angel, had taken every opportunity to put her down, to mock and belittle her. He was a man, she suspected, who preferred his revenge served up cold. A man who had been prepared to wait. Well, she could wait too. She had the patience of a saint.

Tonight, there were rumours rippling through Gigi's, news that a potential buyer had been to see the place. Rumours too that the club might be closing. Pauline hoped this was true although she pretended otherwise to Carol. Sometimes all you could do was lie.

48

It was after ten by the time Tom left the Labour meeting. Usually, he would go for a drink with his compatriots but not tonight. He wasn't in the mood. It had felt like the walls were closing in on him, the words tumbling into a complicated jumble that made no sense. And worst of all, he had felt that it was all pointless. They could talk, discuss, argue, plan, but nothing was ever going to change. He was suffering from lack of faith, a crisis of confidence, a pessimism that had settled on him and refused to budge.

It was a twenty-minute walk back to the Mansfield. The rain was lashing down, and he wished he'd brought the car, but he never did on these Friday evenings. Normally he'd have a couple of pints in the Black Lion, and he always worried about being over the limit. With the law on his case, he couldn't afford to take any chances.

Tom turned up the collar on his coat and strode quickly down the street as if he could outwalk the soaking qualities of the rain. He could already feel the water seeping into his shoes.

It wasn't the meeting that was preying on his mind now but all the other stuff: Angel, Lindsay and the return of Julia. Pauline had been on his case about Frankie, about letting him know that he'd blabbed about him and Angel. But Julia wouldn't tell so what was the point? Perhaps Pauline had gone ahead and done it anyway. Frankie would be pissed off, but he'd get over it.

A cab drove by close to the kerb, its tyres spraying up a wave of water and drenching the bottom half of Tom's jeans. 'Bastard,' he muttered, but his heart wasn't in it. He was getting used to bad things happening, almost expected them, and this was just one more demoralising incident in a sea of disasters.

At least Renee had given up calling, which was a relief. There were only so many times he could repeat himself. She had a mother's nose for when she was being lied to, for when things didn't add up. But would the truth make her any happier? He didn't think so. Happiness was hardly a state either of them would aspire to again.

Tom wondered how he would survive prison, because a part of him knew that was where he was heading. A different four walls. A different kind of life, laced with anxiety and fear. And his mum would come and visit and gaze at him sadly across a table in a room that was full of people gazing sadly at each other. Why did you do it, Tom? And what answer was there to that? It had seemed like the right thing to do at the time.

He reckoned that Julia would understand. If he sat her down and told her everything, explained, said it all in a calm and collected way. She would see how and why it had happened. It would be good, he thought, to let it out, to lay the truth at her feet, to let her judge him. But unfair too. Like shifting the burden. A problem shared is a problem halved is what his mum always said, but he wasn't sure if that was true.

Lights were on in the houses, a few Christmas trees already

on display in the windows. It would be nice to be a kid again, to feel that excitement, the butterflies in his stomach. They'd never had much when he was growing up, but there were always presents on the big day. He knew now how much his parents must have scrimped and saved so he and his sister would have something decent to open.

And here is your reward, Mum, he thought grimly, for all that self-sacrifice. A son who although he was taught right from wrong, took the wrong road and can't find the way back. He slowed down, pushed his hands deep into his pockets, hunched his shoulders and tried to make himself small. Not easy when you were over six foot tall.

He missed Angel with her crazy stories and easy laugh. Despite her faults and foibles – and didn't they all have plenty of those? – she had left a hole in their lives. Poor Angel would never see another Christmas. He grimaced, knowing he was getting maudlin. And what about Lindsay? The quiet one who kept her feelings wrapped up. He missed her too. Their friend-ship group, already waning before their deaths, had dwindled to three. Four if he included Julia. Could he include her? No, she was outside looking in. She had sacrificed her place, and she was the lucky one.

It would be sensible, he thought, if they scattered and ran for the hills. Go abroad, start a new life somewhere else. Except none of them would. They would sit it out and hope for the best. He was finding it tricky at the moment to figure out ex-actly what the best would be but supposed it was something to do with staying out of jail. What were the odds? Not good. Despair rolled over him, a cold dark wave. He shivered. Secrets were rarely kept secret for ever. Disturb the surface and horrors lie beneath.

49

It was too late for tea or coffee unless she wanted to be awake half the night, so Julia heated some milk and made hot chocolate instead. She took the mug through to the living room where she hunkered down on the sofa, turned on the TV and tried to figure out the implications of what she'd found out. Pauline and DC Carol Forshaw. What did it mean? Well, it meant Carol was having a relationship with a suspect in a case – not good – and that the two of them were sneaking around behind everyone's back. But was that the sum of it? What if Carol was protecting Pauline, feeding her information, using her position to keep her girlfriend one step ahead?

Julia wasn't sure how involved Carol was in either investigation, but she was close enough to have heard about the lock of Lindsay's hair being pushed through her door. Something Vyse had wanted kept quiet. Although maybe that didn't apply to his colleagues at the station. And now she knew that Carol might have an agenda she had to question what she'd said about Ivor Apostle. Had she just been throwing dust in her eyes, trying to obscure the truth, trying to shift suspicion off Pauline and on to someone else?

Apostle would not have been overly impressed by this evening's events. Her doing a runner from the bar at Gigi's must have gone down like a ton of bricks. It didn't bode well for their future working relationship. Not that she was intending to stay beyond Christmas, but she still preferred to show *some* professionalism in her job as his PA. Perhaps he was already starting to regret employing a woman who seemed overly preoccupied with things that had nothing to do with his business.

But God, no, she wasn't going to berate herself for not living up to his expectations. That was his problem, not hers. She had more important stuff to worry about. And she didn't like the way he'd been asking about Angel. Simple curiosity or something more? She didn't know. How could she know? The more she thought about the night, the more confusing it became.

Julia flipped open her notebook and stared at the list of names. Should she add Carol Forshaw to it? She could have murdered Angel out of jealousy, wanting Pauline all to herself. Except the idea of that felt ridiculous. Love could do crazy things to people, but she could not imagine the police officer being so in thrall to Pauline that she would drown the competition. No, that wasn't a suitable motive. More likely that Carol was using Pauline to try and get to the truth. Or maybe it was the other way round. Maybe Pauline was using Carol.

Julia was mulling this over, along with other possibilities, when the doorbell rang. She started. It was late for visitors. Her first thought was Vyse. Maybe something important had come up, something he preferred not to discuss over the phone. She turned off the TV, closed the notebook and placed it under a magazine, stood up and went through to the hall.

She had a moment's hesitation before opening the door – anyone could be on the other side – but the thought it could be Michael Vyse outweighed the fear of who else it might be. She quickly slid back the bolt.

Her smile faltered when she saw who it was, surprise replacing anticipation. Frankie Hays was standing in front of her, looking awkward, looking like he really didn't want to be there.

'Sorry,' he said. 'I was passing, and I saw your light was still on. I need to talk to you. Is that okay? Can I come in?'

Julia felt a flutter of alarm. She'd been sure that he hadn't killed Angel but now she had a moment of doubt. How did he even know where she lived? But then she realised that Tom must have told him, must have come clean about spilling the secret about Angel too. Which was why he was here. 'Sure,' she said, standing back.

'I've been on a call-out, a breakdown in Chalk Farm, and seeing as you were just down the road . . .'

'Yes, it's no problem. Grab a seat,' she said as they went into the living room. 'Would you like a drink, tea or coffee?'

'No, ta.' Frankie was wearing his dark blue mechanic's overalls spattered with old oil stains. Somehow, he managed to look elegant even in his work clothes. He sat down on the sofa but then immediately stood up again. He was too anxious, too impatient to stay still. He paced a few steps, turned and looked at her. 'You okay? How have you been?'

'I'm fine.' That was what people said even when they weren't. It was just automatic. 'You know, under the circumstances and all that. How about you?'

'Yeah,' Frankie said.

'You don't look it.'

'Don't I? I suppose . . . I don't know . . . I'm kind of stressed about it all.'

'About what Tom told me. Is that what you mean?'

Frankie nodded, put his hands in his pockets and took them out again. 'Pauline said you told Tom you'd keep quiet about it, that you wouldn't tell the law ... or Clare. Probably.'

Ah, Pauline. Never slow to stir things up. 'But you're worried that I will tell. You don't need to be. I mean it. I don't see how it would help anything. I don't think you killed Angel so there isn't any point.'

'Angel killed herself,' he said.

'No one knows that for sure. Renee doesn't think so, and nor does Pauline.'

'They just don't want to believe it. I don't want to believe it. It makes us feel bad knowing how desperate she must have been. We should have seen it, shouldn't we? We should have been able to stop her.'

Julia was still standing because Frankie was. She wrapped her arms around her chest, not sure what to say. He had a look of devastation on his face, his eyes full of tears.

'I know what everyone thinks,' he continued. 'They think it was just a casual thing between me and Angel, but it was more than that. We had a connection. We cared about each other.' He took a deep breath and said in small, wavering voice, 'I loved her. I really did.'

'So why would she kill herself? Love's a pretty good reason to keep on going, no matter how tough things are.'

'Not when it isn't going anywhere. She knew I wouldn't leave Clare and the kids.'

Julia nodded although she couldn't help wondering if he was overestimating his importance in Angel's life. Had she really loved him so much that she'd rather die than face a future where she was forever the other woman? But then, as everyone kept telling her, Angel didn't always think straight, wasn't always rational or predictable.

'Did you see her that day?' she asked.

'No, but I gave her a bell in the morning to wish her a happy birthday. She said she'd see me later.' As if his legs had given way beneath him, Frankie collapsed on to the sofa and fleetingly put his head in his hands. 'That was the last time I spoke to her. I should have ...' He was quiet for a moment. 'It wasn't just sex, you know. We had a laugh together. We talked. I could tell her anything.'

'So why weren't you worried when she didn't show up at the Fox?'

'I just thought she was miffed because Clare was going to be there. I mean, I couldn't tell her *not* to come, could I? She'd have thought it was odd. Anyway, I reckoned Angel had decided to go somewhere else or stay home with Renee. And I wasn't the only one. Nobody was surprised. It wasn't the first time she'd blown us out. Even Pauline wasn't worried, although she wasn't best pleased. We were all used to her changing her mind at the last minute.'

Julia sat down beside him and lightly touched his arm. 'We're friends, aren't we, Frankie? At least we used to be all those years ago. Believe me when I say that I won't tell anyone about you and Angel. You don't have to worry about that. But Renee suspects something was going on between the two of you. Has she spoken to you about it?'

Frankie nodded. 'She came round to the garage. I panicked and swore blind we were just mates. I'm not sure if she believed me, but she hasn't told the law. At least I don't think so. They haven't said anything.'

'Well, that's good.'

Frankie turned his pleading eyes on her. 'I'd never have hurt Angel. Never. This is all driving me crazy.'

'I believe you. It's a nightmare. And with what happened to Lindsay ... Do *you* think Mark Grey killed her?'

'Pauline's convinced of it.'

'But are you?'

'I don't know. I suppose he was the one closest to her, but Vyse says he has an alibi. It could have been some toerag from the estate, a robbery that went wrong. I can't think who else would do something so awful.'

'But nothing was taken, and she wasn't ... it wasn't a rape.' Julia knew that something had been taken – a lock of Lindsay's hair – but she couldn't share that information with him. 'She wouldn't have opened the door to someone she didn't know, not at that time of night.'

'I suppose not,' he said.

A silence fell between them.

Julia could tell from the pensive expression on his face that he'd already gone back to thinking about Angel, that this was all that was currently occupying his thoughts. And she recalled what Vyse had said at their first meeting about how she'd prefer it to be murder rather than suicide because that got her off the hook. Frankie seemed to have made the opposite decision, convinced it was suicide and weighing up his share of the blame. Or, if she put her cynical hat on, he was just scared rigid of the truth coming out and the subsequent consequences. A bit of both, perhaps.

Frankie stood up and said, 'I'd better get going or Clare will start to worry.'

'Okay. You take care of yourself, yeah?'

On the doorstep he stopped and gave her a nod. 'Thanks, Julia. I appreciate it.'

'It's nothing you wouldn't do for me.'

'You know what I can't figure out? Why so many bad things happened to Angel. Why her? She didn't deserve any of it.'

305

Julia immediately thought of the accident all those years ago and felt a flush rise into her cheeks. 'It's not fair, is it? You know, all I'm trying to do is to find out what happened to her. Pauline thinks I'm out to make trouble for you all, but I'm not. I'd just like some answers.'

'Sometimes there aren't any. At least not the ones you want.'

'I suppose not.'

'I guess Angel told you stuff, didn't she?'

Julia shrugged. 'Nothing I'd ever repeat.'

Frankie leaned forward, gave her a quick hug and then jogged up the steps. Julia closed the door and went back inside. Barely a minute later the doorbell rang again.

50

Presuming that Frankie had forgotten to ask her something or realised belatedly that he needed a pee, Julia retraced her steps, slid back the bolt and opened the door again. But it wasn't Frankie on her doorstep. It was DI Vyse standing in front of her.

'Oh,' she said, surprised. 'It's you.'

Vyse grinned. 'Well, not the best welcome I've ever had but—'

'Sorry,' she said quickly, 'I thought you were someone else.'

'Frankie Hays, you mean.'

Julia narrowed her eyes. 'Are you spying on *me*? Or are you following *him*?'

'I prefer to think of it as keeping you safe. I worry about you. There's a murderer on the loose in case you hadn't heard.'

Julia couldn't recall the last person, other than her mother, who'd been concerned for her welfare. It made her feel . . . well, she didn't want to examine that feeling too closely. 'Bit risky leaving me alone with Frankie, then,' she joked, stepping aside to let him in. 'If he is a murderer, I could be lying dead by now and you'd have to explain to your superiors why you were sitting outside "keeping me safe".'

'He was looking more nervous than murderous, so I thought I'd take the risk. Any chance of a coffee? I need some caffeine. I've been on the go for hours.'

Julia went into the kitchen, turned the kettle on and returned to the doorway to the living room. 'So have you found out anything interesting?'

'I was hoping to ask you that,' Vyse said as he settled on the sofa. 'What was Frankie after?'

Julia held his gaze, knowing she was about to lie and feeling uncomfortable about it. 'He had a call out nearby, Chalk Farm, so he just dropped by to see how I was doing.'

'At this time of night?'

'To be honest, I think he just needed the loo. Anyway, I didn't mind. It gave us the chance to have a chat.'

'Didn't you have one of those last Saturday at the Fox?'

Julia shook her head. 'You know what it's like when you've got a group of people in a busy place. It's hard to get anyone on their own. There are always others listening in or interrupting. Anyway, I'm convinced he thinks that Angel committed suicide. He blames himself for not realising how depressed she was, for not going to look for her on her birthday. It's all stressing him out.'

'Stress or a guilty conscience?'

Julia was saved from answering by the kettle switching off with a puff of steam and a convenient click. 'Black or white?' she said.

'Black, ta. No sugar.'

While she busied herself with the coffee, Julia tried to get her story straight. She could see how odd it looked, Frankie coming here tonight and at this late hour. She took the mug through to the living room, placed it on the low table and sat down beside him. 'I don't think he'd ever have hurt Angel. Why would he? He's just upset about it all. First Angel, then Lindsay. It's tough to deal with.'

'But why come to you rather than speak to his wife or his friends? His other friends, I mean, the ones he hangs out with all the time.'

And inadvertently, Vyse gave her the perfect excuse for Frankie's visit. 'But that's just it, isn't it? Sometimes it's hard to talk to the people you're closest to. It's easier to unburden yourself to a stranger – or at least someone who isn't part of your everyday life. He trusts me, we've got history, but I'm not part of that group anymore. Some men see it as weakness to talk about their feelings – they need to be strong for their other half, their kids, even for their mates – and that can be hard to negotiate.'

Vyse sipped his coffee, first blowing over the surface to cool it down. 'So you're crossing him off the list of suspects.' It was a statement rather than a question.

'I'm not crossing anyone off. It just doesn't seem . . . I don't know, *right* somehow. It doesn't fit.'

'He's managed to persuade you.'

Julia picked up her own mug. What was left of the hot chocolate was barely lukewarm, but she sipped it anyway, glad of the excuse to look away for a moment. It was hard to hold her nerve when she was in such close proximity to him. 'He wasn't trying to persuade me of anything. Honestly, it wasn't like that.'

'Okay, well that leaves Tom and Pauline. Who's your money on?'

Julia heard the caustic edge to his voice and shrugged. If she had to choose, Pauline was the one she'd go for, but Pauline had an alibi. However, she could tell Vyse about her relationship with DC Forshaw. Except Carol was the one she'd really be throwing under the bus, and the woman might well lose her job if the truth came out. Consorting with a suspect probably wasn't the smartest career move. No, she didn't want to be responsible for that, not if their relationship had no bearing at all on what had happened to Angel. 'Maybe we need to look outside the immediate group. Are we focusing too much on them?'

Vyse put down his mug, leaned back and placed his hands behind his head. 'You've lost heart,' he said. 'You're starting to wonder if Angel *did* kill herself, if you're just chasing after phantoms.'

'Am I? I don't know. Maybe.'

'So what about the hair? Why did Lindsay's killer post that sweet little keepsake through your door? Because they wanted to scare you, right? They wanted you to back off.'

'But if they knew me at all, they'd know that would have the completely opposite effect.'

Vyse lowered his hands, placing them on his thighs instead. 'But they don't know you, do they, Julia? Not anymore. Your old friends, I mean. The last time they did was when you were fourteen. That's how they remember you. That's how they perceive you. What were you like back then?'

'Not very different,' Julia said, although she immediately wondered if that was true. She had returned to London a more confident and independent person, more certain of her place in the world, although that had taken a knock when Harley Jenks had 'let her go'. 'It's hard to be objective, isn't it? I wasn't very sure of myself. I suppose I was more of a follower than a leader, just tending to go along with things. Whatever other people wanted to do.'

'Whatever Angel wanted to do?'

'Not just Angel, but yeah, I guess.' Julia's position back then had been as Angel's best friend, a post that encompassed always backing her up, rarely disagreeing, being happy to just go with the flow. 'Perhaps I was more easy-going in those days, less likely to kick up a fuss about anything.' Until that terrible day, she thought, when she *had* kicked up a fuss, when everything had changed for ever.

'So there you are. And then you turn up asking all these questions and they think, if they're guilty that is, that it wouldn't take much to scare you off.'

'Except that theory only works if the two deaths are connected. What if Angel *did* commit suicide and Lindsay was killed by . . . I don't know, Mark Grey perhaps. He could have been worried that Lindsay told me something when we met up, something dangerous to him. Maybe *he* left the hair.'

'Does Mark Grey know where you live?'

'It wouldn't have been hard for him to find out . . . for anyone to find out. All they had to do was follow me home from work.'

'And for that they had to know where you were working.'

Julia shifted on the sofa, knowing that most roads led back to her old friends but still reluctant to believe it. 'Lindsay knew where I was working. She could have told him.'

Vyse was quiet for a while. He drank his coffee, lost in thought. Eventually he sighed. 'Don't give up now,' he said. 'We're getting close. I'm sure we are.'

'You just don't want your gut to be wrong.'

'My gut isn't wrong. It's never wrong.'

Julia raised her eyebrows, smiling. 'There's such a thing as overconfidence, you know.'

'You reckon?'

But Julia's smile quickly faded. This was nothing to joke about. The thought of Pauline and Carol leapt into her head again. What if Carol had killed Angel while Pauline was with Lindsay? The temptation to tell Vyse about them hovered on the tip of her tongue.

'So did you have a good time tonight? Get up to anything you can share with me?'

Julia flinched, disguising the movement by quickly crossing her legs. It was as if he was reading her mind, as if he was seeing Carol and Pauline sitting in Gigi's, their lips touching, as if he already knew and was waiting to see if she'd tell him. 'So you *have* been following me?'

'No, I'm just assuming that you don't usually slip on a little black dress and a pair of heels to sit and watch telly on a Friday night.'

Relief rolled through her. 'Oh, it was only work, a new club that Ivor Apostle is thinking of buying. We didn't stay for long. I don't think he's that interested.'

'Not in the club, maybe.'

Julia laughed. Was that a hint of jealousy? 'Purely business, I assure you. Anyway, have you made any progress since we last talked. Anything new to report?'

'I'd have told you if there was.' Vyse sighed, glanced at her, glanced down at the floor and then back up at her. 'One dead end after another, if you'll excuse the pun.'

'It's so frustrating.'

'Don't give up. I can't do this without you,' he said.

'You don't have to.'

Their eyes met and what happened next had a curious inevitability about it. Who had made the first move? When she looked back, she wouldn't be able to say for sure. Perhaps they had moved together, both knowing what they wanted, neither of them able to resist any longer. Deep kisses, hands caressing, a groping urgency that had led them stumbling to the bedroom and on to the bed. And if for one moment Julia had thought that what they were doing was wrong or at the very least ill-judged, it had slipped in and out of her mind before it had even registered.

51

It was still dark, early on Saturday morning, when Julia was woken by the sounds of movement in the room. She half-opened her eyes and watched as the blur that was Michael Vyse quietly collected his clothes and slipped out into the living room. A few minutes later she heard the front door close. She released her breath, barely aware that she'd been holding it.

Although she wasn't sorry for what they'd done, she knew that it complicated the situation. It was a good thing, and a bad thing, all tangled up in a web of lust and longing. Reaching out a hand, she touched the warm space where he'd been lying. *Michael Vyse.* She could still taste him on her lips, still feel the imprint of his body on hers. The circumstances that had brought them together were terrible and yet that togetherness still felt right, fateful, as if it had been meant to be.

Or was she just being fanciful? Swept away in a rosy glow of post-coital satisfaction. She stretched and yawned like a contented cat. It was a one-off, perhaps, something that would never happen again, a release of tension, a spark that had flared into a fire and could as easily die away again. She hoped not. She hoped it was a beginning and not an end, a comma rather than a full stop. They had felt right together, their bodies tailored, their desire and their pleasure perfectly in tune.

Tom would call it sleeping with the enemy. But then, of course, she wasn't the only one doing that. Pauline was intimately involved with the law too. Which could give her some leverage. Blackmail was a nasty word, but not as nasty as murder. She had to stop dancing around her old friends and get to the truth. Subtlety hadn't achieved much. Perhaps it was time to start playing hardball.

Julia turned her head and squinted at the luminous hands of the alarm clock. Ten to five. She was assailed by a sudden sense of urgency. With her status as friend – or at least former friend – she had unique access to what was left of the old gang. And yet the truth continued to elude her. One of them was lying to her, perhaps all of them. Her earlier doubts had vanished, wiped away by certainty. Angel was dead and she had to find out why.

She knew she wouldn't sleep again and so she got out of bed, took a shower and dressed. In the kitchen she made tea and toast, taking her breakfast through to the living room to eat. There was a note on the coffee table from Michael Vyse: *Call you later.* She picked it up and examined the writing, neat and sloping. It was a short message, to the point, that gave little away but was still welcome as a sign that last night had meant *something* to him.

Julia didn't want to expect too much. Expectations had a habit of crashing down around her ears. She thought of Alex and frowned. What if Michael was cut from the same cloth? There was no way she was going down that road again. And what did she really know about him, other than he was a cop, that he was smart and attractive and that he pressed all the right buttons.

She wasn't sure if those buttons of hers were reliable when it came to judging men.

Julia nibbled her toast and wondered how to spend her Saturday. She didn't fancy going to the Fox again tonight. What would it achieve? The three of them – Tom, Frankie and Pauline – had each other's backs and weren't going to tell her any more than they already had. Well, maybe that wasn't true of Tom. If there was a weak link it was him. He'd already come clean about Frankie and Angel so who knows what else he'd reveal if she put a little pressure on.

She felt bad about this as soon as the thought entered her mind. Tom trusted her. Was she willing to betray that trust? The end didn't always justify the means. But she was running out of options. And what if Tom wasn't as honest as she believed? What if his revelation about Angel and Frankie had been a diversionary tactic, something to explain away the group's furtive behaviour and throw her off the scent? Of them all, he was the cleverest and maybe he was using that intelligence to lead her down blind alleys. It was time, she decided, for another chat.

Julia finished her breakfast, rinsed her plate and mug and left them on the drainer to dry. She went through to the bedroom where she stripped the bed – her thoughts lingering for a moment on the pleasures that had been enjoyed last night – put the sheet and duvet cover in the washing machine, sorted out fresh linen, remade the bed, opened the window to let in some crisp chill air and then returned to the living room where she slumped down onto the sofa again and wondered what to do next.

With hours still to go before it would be a respectable time to call Tom, she slipped her notepad out from under the magazine and updated it with what she had learned about Pauline and Carol Forshaw. More information, but it didn't make anything clearer. Who would want Angel dead? It was a simple question. A shame the answer wasn't so easy.

An unpleasant notion snaked its way into her head. Michael Vyse was counting on her to use her connections, her familiarity with the old gang, to ferret out the truth. Was that part of the reason for what had happened between them? Pulling her close so her loyalty would rest with him and him alone? She frowned, knowing her relationship with Alex had made her cynical. But no one likes to be used, and she promised herself to tread carefully, to not get carried away by the reckless passion that had reared its head last night.

At half past nine, after cleaning the flat from top to toe, Julia picked up the phone and dialled.

'Hello?'

'Hi Tom, it's Julia. Look, I was wondering if you could do me a huge favour.'

'Of course,' he said.

'You haven't heard what it is yet. Feel free to say no if you just can't bear the thought of it.'

52

It was twenty past ten when Julia heard the car pull up outside. By then she had closed the bedroom window, put on her coat, armed herself with an umbrella and gone over everything she intended to ask. Tom had sounded shocked by the request she'd made but, after a short hesitation, had agreed. She felt faintly guilty for putting him through the ordeal.

The morning was grey and overcast, and the air had a filmy quality, like she was seeing everything through a misted lens. It was starting to drizzle as she scooted up the steps and got into the car.

'Hi, how are you? Thanks so much for doing this. I'm really sorry to ask. I just . . . I need to see where it happened.'

'That's okay,' Tom said, although his face looked grim. 'I'm not sure of the exact spot but we can go and take a look, see if we can find it.'

'Are you sure you don't mind?'

Tom shook his head as he pulled the car away from the kerb. 'I wasn't doing anything else.'

'Do you think it's weird, macabre even?'

'Only if you're doing it for kicks which I know you're not. If it helps you come to terms with it, then ...' He lifted his shoulders in a shallow shrug. 'But like I said, I'm not sure of the exact spot.'

Julia wondered if he was repeating that to stress his innocence, to impress on her that he'd never been there before. Another way of saying, *I didn't kill her.* She was trying to look at Tom like a stranger might, or a cop, but she still couldn't imagine him as a murderer.

It only took twenty minutes to reach the river Lea. The roads were quiet, the rain coming down harder now. Tom peered through the windscreen as if everything was new to him, as if he wasn't sure where he was going. Real or pretence? The uncertainty created an uneasiness in her. She made nervous small talk, a mindless chatter, while he turned right and then left, slowing down as they passed a pub.

'It's near here,' he said. 'It's not far from that pub. That's what it said in the papers.'

'But nobody saw her? None of the customers?'

'It didn't open until six. By then it would have been dark, or nearly dark, and no one would have been sitting outside. It was a cold day, windy.'

'And she could have got here well before that. How did she even know about this place?'

'I've no idea.'

Tom pulled up close to a path that led down to the river. There was a wooden signpost there, old and weathered. He switched off the engine and they both stared along the path that disappeared into a clump of trees and bushes as it curved towards the water.

'I think there's a jetty down there. That's where she ... they found her coat and bag nearby.'

Julia girded herself. 'You don't need to come with me if you don't want to.'

But Tom was already taking off his seatbelt. 'No, it's okay.'

They got out of the car and Julia put up her umbrella. There was no one else around and the only sounds were their own soft breath and the patter of the rain on her brolly. She could understand now how Angel had gone unseen that Saturday night. Despite the pub not being that far away, this was a lonely place.

The path was overgrown, and wet foliage brushed against their legs. Julia held the brolly over the two of them as they rounded the bend, and the jetty came into view. It was old and worn with an uneven, rickety look. She could smell the water now as well as see it: a musty, earthy aroma.

'God, why would she come here?'

'Maybe it meant something to her,' Tom said. 'Maybe she came here once with someone. I mean, she must have done, I suppose. To the pub, perhaps, and then a stroll down to the river. It could have stuck in her mind.'

'As what? A suitable place to die? It's so . . . cold and desolate.'

There was nothing attractive about the grey swirling water or the muddy bank. Old gnarled tree roots poked out of the ground, a trip hazard if ever there was one. Angel could have stumbled, lost her balance and fallen into the water. An accident. Well, if it hadn't been for her coat and bag left behind. That suggested suicide or a staged suicide.

They arrived at the jetty and paused. Julia went to step on the planks, but Tom grabbed hold of her arm. 'I wouldn't. It doesn't look safe.'

So they stood together on the bank and gazed out over the water. Julia shivered. It was awful to think of Angel here, alone and desperate. And just as awful to think of her with someone else, a murderous someone who would push her into the water and leave her to drown. What kind of a person could do that to another human being?

The wind whispered through the trees: an eerie sound like the murmur of voices. Julia glanced over her shoulder. She had a feeling they were not alone. She would have been afraid if it hadn't been for Tom standing beside her. But what if Tom was the one she needed to be afraid of? One hard shove and she'd be in the water. It looked deep and dangerous, full of tangled weed, and although she could swim it would be difficult to clamber back onto the slippery bank – especially if someone was trying to stop her.

'Are you all right?' Tom asked.

Julia fought against the impulse to move away from him. 'Who could have hated her so much?' she murmured. 'Who'd bring her here on her birthday and leave her to die?'

Tom sighed. 'Perhaps the person who hated Angel most was Angel herself.'

Julia felt a spurt of irritation. 'She wouldn't have killed herself, Tom. What is it we're not seeing?' What she wanted to say was, *What is it you're not telling me?* but she couldn't quite force the words out of her mouth. They felt too accusatory, too confrontational.

'We'll never know what she was thinking.'

Julia wasn't sure if she wanted to know. Fear or despair. Probably both. Her eyes focused on the water as if the answer to Angel's mysterious death lay hidden in its icy sucking depths. 'Frankie came to see me. He's scared I'll tell the law about him and Angel.'

Tom quickly turned his head to look at her. 'But you won't, will you?'

'Of course not. Do you think Clare suspects?'

'I don't think so.' And then, as the implication of what she was asking sank in, he rapidly continued, 'You can't think she had anything to do with it. She was there in the evening. You couldn't kill someone and then go to the pub and ... I mean, how could you?'

Which was more or less what Clare had said. But she only had their word for it that they were all behaving normally that night. And what constituted 'normal' anyway? It wasn't normal to push someone into a river and leave them to drown. If they could do that, they could do anything. Her gaze was still focused on the water, on the rain pocking the surface and producing a myriad of tiny whirlpools. 'It's weird to think of her being here.'

'It's disturbing.'

Julia wasn't sure what she'd expected to achieve by doing this. Some kind of clarity perhaps. As if she might discern just from standing in this spot exactly what had happened to Angel. It had been foolish, a conceit, to imagine she might possess such powers of perception, and yet she wasn't sorry for trying. If nothing else, it was strengthening her resolve to get to the truth.

Tom cleared his throat. 'It's a shame the two of you didn't get to spend some time together. Did she, er ... did she know you were back in London?'

'No.'

'So when was the last time you heard from her?'

Julia, reminded of the very same line of questioning from Lindsay, instinctively stiffened, and then quickly rubbed her arms to try and disguise the reflex. 'None of it matters now.'

'I didn't even know you were still in touch. It's odd that she didn't say anything.'

'Do you know what is odd? How everyone seems so interested in when I last talked to her. Anyone would think you all had something to hide.'

'We did have,' he said, looking glum. 'But you know about Frankie and Angel now.'

'You're still worried about something, though. Something else.'

'I'm always worried. It's my default state of mind. I'm always waiting for the next bad thing to come along.'

'That's a depressing way to live.'

'Yeah, I know.'

Julia kept looking at the water, feeling he might say more if her eyes weren't on him. 'Are you okay, Tom?'

He didn't speak for a while. Ten seconds, twenty. Then he said, 'Shall we go?'

'In a minute.' Julia did want to go and yet she felt fixed to the ground, her feet rooted. The past, Angel's past, swam through her head – their childhood, their teenage years, the accident – events wrapping around each other, becoming twisted and jumbled, merging in a messy reminiscence that ended right here with no resolution.

Something Frankie had said last night came back to her, creating a new stream of thought and jolting her out of introspection. *Why so many bad things had happened to Angel.* Things, in the plural. Not just the accident then. She was about to ask Tom about it, then changed her mind. Some inner instinct cautioned her to keep quiet. For the moment it was safer to keep her suspicions to herself.

They walked slowly back to the car. There was no sign of what had happened here, no old police tape flapping in the wind or any other signs of disturbance. The weeks had passed and with it the physical evidence of tragedy. Julia looked around her again and listened. She still had that prickling sense that they were being watched, that from somewhere hidden in the trees malevolent eyes were on them.

She wondered if Renee had been here. Perhaps she couldn't bear to visit. The last place her daughter had been alive. And again she felt the certainty that Angel would never have left her mother, left her for ever, without even writing a note.

'I'll come back with you to the Mansfield, if that's okay. I want to drop in on Renee and see how she's doing.'

They were both quiet on the drive back, both lost in thought, but as they approached Kellston Julia remembered all the questions she'd wanted to ask. Where to start? In the end she settled on a simple one. 'Do you know a guy called Ivor something?' She didn't want to give his surname. 'He's a big guy, very tall. You wouldn't miss him in a crowd. Apparently, he drinks in the Fox sometimes.'

Tom shook his head. 'I can't say it rings any bells. Why? Who is he, this bloke?'

'He's just someone who seems interested in Angel's death. I dare say it's nothing. Only curiosity. Some people are overly fascinated, aren't they? Like those drivers who slow down on the motorway to gawp at accidents. He says he never met her, but I just wanted to check in case you'd ever seen them together.' She was faintly reassured by Tom's failure to recognise her description of Apostle, but aware too that it only brought her suspicions back to what was left of the old gang.

'Have you told the law about him?'

'God, no. You won't say anything, will you? He'll know it was me if Vyse goes sniffing around.'

'Why are you so convinced it wasn't suicide?'

'Why are you so convinced it was?'

Tom's sigh filled the car. 'Because I can't think of any reason why someone would *want* to kill her. This is Angel we're talking about. She could be impulsive, scatty, utterly unreliable, but she was funny and kind too.'

'And you don't think nice people get murdered?'

'I didn't mean that. Only that victims usually know their killers, don't they? I don't see how anyone could have forced her to go to the river.'

Which was exactly the point, Julia thought. She had gone with someone she knew, someone she trusted, and that made the list of suspects pretty small. She wasn't sure if Tom was aware of this and being deliberately obtuse or if he was in some kind of denial. By sticking to his belief that it was suicide, he didn't have to think too hard about the alternative.

'Are you coming to the Fox later?' he asked.

'Sorry, I can't. Not tonight. I've got something on. Maybe next week.'

Tom's tone was jokey but there was something wistful in his expression. 'You sick of us already?'

'Of course not,' she said.

'I wouldn't blame you. You can outgrow people without even realising it. When the comfort and familiarity isn't enough, you know? When you've not really got much in common anymore.'

Julia wasn't surprised by the admission. 'But you go on seeing them anyway because it's what you've always done.'

'Yeah, I guess. Habit.'

Julia could guess too that Tom's interests had long ago diverged from those of his old friends. She suspected that if he'd gone to university, if he had never come back here to live, then things would have been very different. He had made sacrifices in order to take care of his mother, and those sacrifices had trapped him.

'People drift apart,' she said. Like she and Angel had. Except it wasn't quite the same. Julia's guilt had created a barrier between them, an obstacle they could never overcome. What they had been left with was something thin and flimsy, irreparably damaged, a friendship that had eventually fizzled out and died.

'I suppose,' he said. 'So what are you up to tonight? Anything nice?'

Julia, who should have anticipated the question but hadn't, quickly improvised. 'I'm going back to Suffolk, just until tomorrow afternoon. It's only a fleeting visit. I haven't seen Mum for a while.'

'How is she?'

'Oh, same as ever.'

'I always liked her. She was different to the other mums.'

'Tell me about it. While your mum was ironing your school uniform or popping a Victoria sponge in the oven, mine was making Greenpeace placards and marching for animal rights. All good causes, I'm not saying they're not, but occasionally I'd have liked a little of her attention.'

Tom gave her a sidelong glance and smiled. 'Yeah, I guess that's the downside to having a mum with principles. Still, it can't have done you too much damage. You seem pretty balanced to me.'

'You should see my therapy bills.'

Tom's eyebrows went up.

'Only kidding,' she said. 'I can't afford therapy.'

Tom drove onto the Mansfield estate and then down into the cavernous and dimly lit basement car park. Despite being instructed to never play here as children, they often had, hiding behind the concrete pillars, watching people come and go, pretending to be spies or cops and robbers.

'I see they haven't smartened this place up,' Julia said as she got out of the car and breathed in the musty cellar smell and the odour of petrol fumes. 'It hasn't changed a bit since we were kids.'

Tom smiled. 'Not much you can do with a space like this.'

'Improve the lighting? Put some whitewash on the walls?'

'Other priorities,' Tom said, 'but I'll be sure to pass on your suggestions to the council.'

'The phrase "Don't waste your breath" springs to mind.'

They walked together to the lift, Julia's eyes searching the gloom, her body alert to any unwelcome company. The entire Mansfield estate had always been a mugger's paradise with its dark corners, rat-runs and connecting passageways. It hadn't bothered them when they were kids – they'd had nothing to nick – but now she clutched her bag closer to her side and steeled herself for battle should the need arise.

She was relieved when, after a short wait, they were finally able to step into the lift. Tom pressed the buttons, one for his floor, one for Renee's, and they ascended in silence. He shifted from one foot to another and cleared his throat. Julia had the feeling that he was gearing himself up to say something important, that it was on the tip of his tongue, but the words never came out.

She got off before him and he kept the doors open while he told her to keep in touch and to call him if she ever needed anything. She felt an urge to leap back into the lift, to confront him and demand that he told her the truth. What wasn't he telling her? What she did instead was thank him for taking her to Hackney and made a promise to call.

'Damn it,' she muttered after the doors had closed, certain that an opportunity had slipped through her fingers.

53

Julia, still feeling frustrated, rang Renee's bell and waited. There was no response. She rang again. Maybe Renee was at work or out shopping. Maybe she just didn't fancy talking to anyone right now. They were the obvious explanations but there was always the possibility, the terrible possibility, that she had simply decided that she couldn't go on. Her stomach began to churn.

She kneeled down, opened the letterbox and called out, 'Renee? Renee, it's Julia. Are you there?'

Nothing.

She peered through the slit at the small empty hallway. She listened. Silence. Her heart was beating faster now, her pulse starting to race. The carpet in the hall was a flecked beige, council issue, and was immaculately clean. Renee always had been houseproud. Beyond that the door was open to the living room, but all she could see was the back of the sofa.

'Renee!' she called out again, even though she sensed it was pointless.

Julia rose to her feet, went to the flat next door and rang the bell. It was answered promptly – so promptly they must have been standing right behind it – by an elderly lady with cropped silver hair and inquisitive eyes. Julia vaguely recalled the old neighbour but couldn't put a name to the face. Mrs Cowley, Crowley, something like that.

'Sorry to bother you but I'm looking for Renee. Have you seen her today?'

The old woman looked her up and down as if assessing her trustworthiness. Eventually she said, 'She's at work, love. She works every other Saturday. She won't be back before six.'

'Oh, okay, thanks.'

'Was it urgent?'

Julia shook her head, relieved that there was nothing to worry about. Now she thought about it, she realised that Renee would never take her own life while the investigation into Angel's death was ongoing and while there were still so many unanswered questions. 'I just dropped by to see how she was. I'll try another time.'

'Heartbroken is how she is, and I don't suppose that'll be changing anytime soon. That poor girl. I still can't believe she's gone.'

'No,' Julia agreed, not wanting to get into a long conversation. She began to edge away. 'Well, thanks for letting me know.'

'You're Ellie Reeve's girl, aren't you? You've grown a bit, but I never forget a face. Jackie, right?'

'Julia.'

The old woman frowned as if she didn't like being corrected or didn't like being reminded that her memory wasn't as sharp as it used to be. 'I remember you and Angel when you were nippers, always running up and down these corridors like crazy things.'

'Sorry,' Julia said. 'That must have been annoying. It all feels like a long time ago.'

'And now she's gone. May she rest in peace. Makes you realise that you can't take anything for granted. Here one day and gone the next. Did you come back for the funeral, then?'

'I'm living in London now. But yes, I went to the funeral.'

'It was a nice send-off. Well, the best that could be expected in the circumstances. I've had the cops round, of course, wanting to talk about the day she disappeared. I heard those other girls come round and I heard them leave too.'

Julia's ears pricked up at this. 'Did you?'

'Couldn't fail to, love. That Pauline Archer thinks doors are made for slamming. And I could hear her voice. I don't think she's ever done anything quietly in her life. They left about three o'clock.'

'And Angel didn't leave with them?'

'That's what they asked – the cops, I mean – but I've no idea. I can't see through walls, can I?' Then, unwilling to relinquish a captive audience, she quickly added, 'But I could still hear the music so I don't think she could have.'

'Did anyone else call round after?'

'Not that I noticed. I'd have told the cops if I had.'

Julia was aware that she must be starting to sound like a cop herself, but she continued regardless. 'And did you hear Angel leave later?'

'No, but I heard the music stop. That was about an hour or so after the others left. If I'd have known ... but how could I? It still turns my stomach knowing what she did next. She was a young woman with her whole life ahead of her. Why would she go and do a thing like that?'

'You think it was suicide, then?'

'Oh, I know what Renee says, but you shouldn't take account

of that. She's not thinking right, which is understandable. No one killed poor Angel. She left her things on the riverbank, didn't she? It's clear what her intentions were.'

Or how someone wanted them to appear, thought Julia.

'She's got this bee in her bonnet about it, about those pals of hers, but I keep saying why would any of them want to kill Angel? She was a sweet girl even if she wasn't quite right in the head. She never did no harm.'

Julia had other questions she wanted to ask, but she held back, suspecting that the old woman had told her everything she knew and that anything further would be pure embellishment.

'Okay. Thanks, I'd better get going.'

'Do you want me to give Renee a message?'

'No need,' Julia said, as she retreated along the corridor. 'I'll give her a ring tonight.'

The neighbour's door didn't close until Julia was almost at the lift. She was aware of being watched, of eyes following her, although she was in the dark as to what the observation was for. Perhaps she was just prolonging the break from the usual Saturday monotony. It was presumptuous, of course, to think the old lady's life was lonely or boring, but there had been a glow on her face when she'd been talking to Julia, a controlled excitement as if the opportunity for gossip didn't come along that often.

Not quite right in the head. Those words came back to her as she descended to the lobby, along with a familiar stab of guilt. Two teenage girls bickering over a boy. A spat that would have blown over, would have been forgotten, if Angel hadn't taken that one step back. But after that everything had been irrevocably changed.

Julia was walking across the lobby when she saw Pauline pass by on the path leading to the main exit. She held back to give her time to get a short distance ahead. It was too late for her to be going to work, midday already. Perhaps she was going to the pub for a lunchtime drink. Or meeting up with DC Carol Forshaw. Well, it wouldn't do any harm to find out.

54

Although the rain had eased off, reduced now to barely a drizzle, Julia still put up her umbrella and angled it forward so that her face was obscured. She didn't want to be spotted. Pauline was wearing a bright red anorak which meant that even on the busy high street she was still visible from a distance.

The market was in full swing, and the smell of fried onions wafted in the air. Reggae music thumped out a beat. Julia would have been tempted to cross the road, stroll up the side street and browse the stalls if she hadn't been on a mission. Anyway, she would only end up buying things she didn't need: knock-off perfume, flimsy jewellery or a sweater that shrank in the wash.

Pauline walked at a steady pace, not even glancing at the butcher's as she drew parallel. When Julia reached the same spot she saw Ted Archer inside, laughing with a customer, his fleshy fingers passing a parcel over the counter. She wasn't sure if it was the man she didn't like or the unpleasantness of his job, maybe a combination of both, but she knew that made her a hypocrite because she never turned up her nose at a bacon sandwich or bangers and mash.

Julia had a vague memory of a Mrs Archer being around when Pauline had first come to Kellston. But not for long. Leaving Pauline alone with her father. Died or gone away? She had barely known the girl then, and certainly not well enough to ask the question that, whatever the answer, was bound to cause awkwardness and embarrassment. Perhaps her mother's absence was what had made Pauline latch on to Angel with such intensity – a new focus for all her love and attention.

Still, that didn't excuse her elbowing her way into their lives. Julia's close friendship with Angel had been so long-standing that she'd taken it for granted and having a third person suddenly insert themselves had been less than welcome. She had felt threatened, that was the truth of it, and with good reason as it turned out.

Julia could feel herself getting tense, her left hand curling into a tight fist in her pocket. She tried to relax. What did any of it matter now? It was all old news, irrelevant – and yet it still had the power to hurt. Although Angel had never abandoned her, she had slowly begun to divide her affections, to spend more and more time with Pauline. She blamed Pauline for that, but it took two to tango. Angel had been complicit.

Friendships, like relationships, came and went. That was a fact of life. But a hard fact to learn when you were young. Perhaps it would have been easier if Pauline hadn't been so triumphant, so gloating, taking every opportunity to rub her nose in it. Julia could still feel the humiliation of having to share her best friend. She also knew that this stupid postmortem of the past was stirring up all sorts of unwanted emotions.

They were almost at the junction now. Instead of turning left, as Julia had expected, Pauline crossed the road and carried straight on up the south end of the high street. Then she crossed the road again and halted by a bus stop. Julia was still at the junction – she hadn't wanted to get too close – when she saw the bus coming. Destination Bethnal Green. Damn. There was a short queue waiting. If she ran for it, Pauline would see her. If she didn't, she'd lose her.

Julia decided to take the safer option and stay put. Why was she following her anyway? It wasn't going to achieve anything. She already knew about Carol Forshaw so unless Pauline had some other secret, the surveillance was unlikely to be useful. She would call it a day and go home to Camden.

But when the bus moved off, Julia was surprised to see that Pauline was still there. It was one of those bus stops with a shelter and a row of plastic seats. Pauline had sat down and was now staring straight ahead. The Bethnal Green bus was the only one that came down this way so why hadn't she got on? Her curiosity was piqued. It was puzzling. Unless she was waiting for someone to get *off* the bus.

Julia walked up to the bus stop and sat down at the other end of the seats. Pauline, oblivious, didn't even glance at her. And then the light gradually dawned: Pauline was watching the block of flats across the street. She had her eyes firmly fixed on the first floor where Lindsay's fiancé lived.

So, Julia was spying on Pauline, and Pauline was spying on Mark Grey.

'What are you doing?' Julia said.

Pauline turned her head, saw who it was and rolled her eyes. 'What does it look like? I'm waiting for a bloody train.'

'The bus has just been and gone.'

'What do you want, Julia?'

'I'm just curious as to why you're watching Mark Grey's flat.'

Pauline didn't deny it. 'Why not? I've got nothing else to do.'

'He might not even be in.'

Pauline ignored the comment. 'He thinks he's got away with it, but he'll make a mistake one day.'

'I thought he had an alibi.' It surprised Julia that Pauline was so intent on nailing Grey. She had always given the impression of being if not hostile to Lindsay then certainly contemptuous of her. And yet here she was staking out Grey's flat, spending time trying to bring him to justice. A guilty conscience perhaps for all those years of disdain.

'He's smart, but not half as smart as he thinks.' Pauline took a pack of cigarettes from her pocket and lit one. Her gaze slid between the windows of the flat and the front door. 'You shouldn't have gone to see him. He's going to get wary if people start sniffing around.'

'I should think he's pretty wary already. He must have been top of the list when it came to suspects, even with his alibi. Do you think he got someone else to do it for him?'

Pauline puffed on her cigarette, short impatient tugs that produced small clouds of smoke. 'He's a creep.'

Julia was still trying to make sense of what Pauline was doing. Waiting for Grey to show his face. What did she hope to achieve? What could she possibly find out even if she followed him around all day? She had the feeling that this wasn't the first time Pauline had staked out the flat, that this bus stop was probably a regular haunt for her.

'I still don't get it. Not really. It seems like a waste of time to me.' Julia said it to provoke her, to get a reaction, to try and get to the bottom of what was really going on.

'He'll make a mistake. They all do eventually.'

'What kind of mistake?'

But Pauline didn't reply.

Julia's brain was ticking over. Something about this didn't

add up. Perhaps Pauline was transferring her grief over Angel into a vendetta against the man who may or may not have killed Lindsay. Except that didn't make much sense. The rain pattered down on the roof of the shelter, a soft drumming that merged with the sound of the cars going past. Her thoughts shifted again, sliding off in another direction. She wondered, randomly, who decided which bus stops got shelters and which didn't. Probably some council planning committee. Tom would know.

They say when you stop concentrating on one thing and think about something else, the answer to your original problem can suddenly become clear. And that was what happened to Julia. The truth slid under and around the bus shelter conundrum and came to rest with a jolt in the forefront of her mind.

'Oh God, you think Mark Grey killed Angel!'

Pauline glared at her. 'Shout it out, why don't you? Maybe someone in France didn't hear.'

Julia shifted along the row of seats until she was sitting next to her and kept her voice low. 'But why? Why do you think he did it?'

'Why don't you just sod off home, Julia. This has nothing to do with you.'

'I'm not going anywhere.'

'Suit yourself.' Pauline dropped what was left of the cigarette, ground in the butt with her heel, stood up and started walking quickly back towards the junction.

Julia followed her. 'You must have a reason. You know something, don't you? Why haven't you told the police?'

'The law,' Pauline said sneeringly. 'They're a bloody waste of space. They don't even believe Angel was murdered.'

'But I do. I've never thought she killed herself. So why won't you tell me? Come on, Pauline. If you know something about Grey, then share it with me.'

'Leave me alone. Just clear off and get on with your own life.'

'I can't do that.'

'Yes, you can. And I'm telling you nothing so you might as well give up now.'

Julia kept pace with her, trying to decide what to do next. They crossed at the junction and went on up the high street towards the Mansfield. The three tall towers of the estate loomed over them, dominating an already dreary landscape. She felt like she was on the edge of a breakthrough and wasn't going to just walk away. 'If that man killed Angel, I want to know what proof you've got. You can trust me. I won't go shooting my mouth off to anyone else.'

Pauline gave a snort.

Something snapped in Julia. She was sick of all the evasions, the secrets and lies. She had stood on the riverbank this morning and seen the cold, dark water. She had breathed in the air that Angel had breathed. No, she wasn't going to give up now. Frustrated, she stepped in front of Pauline, barring her way and forcing her to stop.

'I know how to keep quiet about things, about Frankie, about . . .' Julia took a quick breath before she let it out. 'About you and Carol Forshaw.'

Shock drained the colour from Pauline's face. Her mouth fell open. It took her a moment to recover herself. She gave a weird tinny laugh. 'What are you talking about?'

'Don't play games. Who you date is your own business, except there could be something of a conflict of interest here, don't you think? Does Vyse know about the two of you? About your relationship? Has Carol been open about it?' And here she was being the prize hypocrite again. Whose arms had she been in last night? Whose lips had pressed against hers?

But she carried on regardless. It wasn't the same, she told herself. She wasn't involved in the investigation in the same way as Pauline.

'I don't know who you've been talking to but there's nothing going on between me and Forshaw.' Pauline was trying to brazen it out. 'I can't stand the woman. And I'm not a bloody lesbian. That's just laughable!'

'I'm not laughing.'

'You're nuts. You've got a screw loose.'

'I saw you together at Gigi's.'

Pauline flinched as if she'd been slapped. Then she sidestepped around Julia and began striding away. Julia hurried to catch up. They were almost at the butcher's now and she was worried that she would duck inside and escape into the back. But she needn't have worried. Pauline wasn't going to take the risk of being followed in, of this exchange being made public or her father asking any awkward questions.

'Look, I don't care about any of that, about you and Carol. For God's sake, just tell me about Grey. That's all I'm asking.'

Pauline carried on walking past the shop. Was she even listening?

The rain was coming down harder now and Julia could feel it sliding under the collar of her coat. She put up her umbrella. 'We can go to Connolly's,' she said, looking at the café across the road. It was where they'd gone when they were teenagers, the closest haunt to the estate to hang out, to gossip and drink Coke. She made her voice firm as if she'd brook no refusal. Playing hardball. 'Come on, I'll buy you a coffee.'

Pauline must have recognised the change in tone. She stopped again, hesitating, torn between the desire to get away and the fear of her relationship being exposed. The latter won out and they crossed the road together, dodging the cars and buses. Julia could feel her heart banging in her chest. So this was it. She was finally going to find out what Pauline knew. She pushed open the door to the café and went inside.

55

Connolly's was busier than Julia expected, full of Saturday shoppers and kids and people escaping from the rain. It was warm and smelled of fried food and damp raincoats. She had a moment of doubt wondering if this was the right place to talk, but hopefully the general chatter, the sound of the radio and the hiss of the coffee machine would drown out anything they didn't want to be overheard.

'I'll have a can of Lilt,' Pauline said.

Julia bought two cans at the counter, and they took them to one of the few empty tables. Pauline sat down and glared at her, making it clear from her expression that anything she said was being uttered under duress. Julia felt sorry for her but not sorry enough to let her off the hook.

'So?' Julia pressed.

Pauline looked left and right, making sure that nobody was listening in. She took a swig from the can and placed it on the table. Then she leaned forward and said, 'He had a thing for Angel.'

'A thing?'

'You know what I mean. He had the hots for her, but she wasn't interested.'

'Is this before or after he started dating Lindsay?'

'Both. He met Angel in the Fox, bought her a few drinks, thought his luck was in, but then she dumped him before he even got to first base. He wasn't happy about that. Lindsay stepped in as first reserve. That girl never did have any pride. Anyway, the long and the short of it is, he started going out with Lindsay but didn't stop chasing after Angel. He used to buy her stuff – perfume, jewellery and the like – even though she told him that she wasn't going to change her mind.'

'And she accepted all these gifts?'

Pauline shrugged. 'More fool him, she said. It was stupid of her, but she did stupid things sometimes. And I think she liked the attention, being fancied and all that. It was an ego boost even though he was an arse.'

'And even though he was seeing Lindsay? Didn't that bother her at all?'

'A bit. I dunno. None of us thought it would last between the two of them, between Lindsay and Mark, I mean. It was a surprise when they got engaged. Maybe it shouldn't have been. She was good wife material, and he's got ambition. He plans to be an MP one day and needs to have a respectable missus. What's more respectable than a primary school teacher?'

Julia popped the tab and drank some of her Lilt. 'Do you think Lindsay could have found out that he was still chasing Angel?'

'What, and decided to eliminate the competition?' Pauline gave her another of her trademark snorts. 'Not really her style. She was never what you'd call the murderous sort. Anyway, she was with me that afternoon so it couldn't have been her.

No, it was him, I'm telling you. He knew he couldn't have her for himself and decided that no one else was going to have her either.'

'Have you told the police about this?'

'I told them that he didn't like Angel, that he was always having a dig at her whenever we met up in the Fox.'

'And the rest? What about the gifts, the chasing, the fact he had the hots for her? Jesus, Pauline, why didn't you tell them about all that?'

Pauline averted her face and glanced around the café. She turned the can between her fingers. It was a while before she looked back at Julia. 'I wasn't sure back then if it was him or not. I mean at the beginning, right after Angel died. I didn't know for sure. Everyone seemed so certain that she'd killed herself. If I'd accused him, it would have all come out about the two of them. She would have looked a right cow. And it wasn't like that. Not really. And Lindsay would have found out about it all. It was only after he killed her that I knew he must have killed Angel too.'

'So tell them now,' Julia said. 'What's to stop you?'

'They're not going to believe me. There's no proof, is there? He's only going to deny it. They'll think I'm making it up. And Mark Grey's going to know that I'm on to him.'

Julia wasn't sure how much of this she was buying. It sounded feasible but that didn't mean it was true. Pauline had given her an entirely different story in the Fox. Yet she could see how Grey could have murdered Lindsay if she'd found out that he'd been responsible for Angel's death, and she could see too, in a way, how Pauline might have been reluctant to come clean about Angel leading Grey on, taking his gifts and giving nothing in return, but what was that compared to the harsh brutality of murder?

'You could talk to Carol, couldn't you? She'll believe you.'

'This has nothing to do with Carol.'

'She's a cop.'

'Exactly. I don't want her dragged into this.'

'But you've got new evidence.'

'For God's sake, that's the point. I haven't got *any* actual evidence.' Pauline almost growled with frustration. 'All I've got is what I know and that won't count for anything when it comes to the law.'

'Renee said that Mark Grey came round to the flat once, claiming he was looking for Lindsay. That might help back up your version of things.'

'Once isn't enough.'

'Maybe one of the neighbours saw him more often.'

Pauline shook her head. 'He'll have been careful. And the law have talked to all the neighbours. I think Angel usually met him away from the Mansfield, just for coffee or a quick drink. Away from here. It wasn't like a date or anything.'

'Grey might not have seen it like that.'

'Yeah, well, I told her he'd get the wrong idea, but she never listened.'

'So what's the plan?' Julia said. 'You hang around his flat often enough and he's going to notice you eventually. You'll end up getting arrested for harassment or stalking or whatever else he can pin on you.'

'I don't care.'

And Julia didn't think she did. There was something single-minded about her, something determined. Anything she could do to make Mark Grey's life uncomfortable, to push him into doing something stupid, was worth whatever price she'd have to pay for it. 'I still think you should tell Vyse. Grey's got a motive for killing Angel. It's important.'

'If you tell Vyse, I'll deny I ever said it,' Pauline hissed. 'I'm going to do this my way.'

'Well, don't do anything stupid. He's not worth going to prison for.'

Pauline gave her a scornful look. 'Play it safe, huh?' She finished her Lilt and crushed the can between her fingers. 'That might be your way, but it isn't mine. Some of us don't run away at the first sign of trouble.'

Julia caught the dig – she was doubtless referring to how she'd moved to Suffolk after Angel's accident – and felt a flush rise to her cheeks. 'I'm here, aren't I? I'm not running anywhere.'

'Only because you can't resist poking your nose in.'

Julia raised her eyebrows but refrained from a counterattack. *Stay calm. Don't rise to the bait.*

Pauline's mouth turned sulky. An uneasy silence fell across the table. The sounds of the café – a scraping chair, the clatter of cutlery, a sudden laugh – flowed over and around them. Then, unable to resist, Pauline said, 'What were you doing at Gigi's anyway?'

Perhaps Pauline was hoping that Julia had secrets of her own. If so, she was about to be sorely disappointed. 'Oh, I've got a friend who's thinking of buying the place. We just went to take a look.'

'I didn't see you.'

'We weren't there for long.'

'I'm not queer,' Pauline said. 'Carol's just a mate. And if I find out you've been saying that I am—'

'I don't care what you are,' Julia interrupted. 'It doesn't interest me. And I'm not a gossip so you don't need to worry. What are you going to do next? About Grey, I mean.'

'Keep an eye on him.'

'Why? What do you expect him to do?'

'God, Julia, you're just an endless list of pointless questions.' Pauline glanced at her watch. 'I've got to go. I'm working this afternoon. George has something on, and I promised I'd cover for him.'

'One last thing. Did Frankie know about Angel and Mark Grey?'

Pauline pushed back her chair, stood up and then leaned down to speak to her. 'Frankie didn't kill Angel. Get that into your thick skull. Or do you want one of us to be guilty? Is that what this is all about?'

'It was a simple question.'

'And I answered it.'

'No, you didn't.'

Pauline gave an irritated shake of her head. 'There was nothing for him to know, okay? She wasn't sleeping with Grey. He had nothing to feel jealous about.' And with that she walked out of the café before Julia could ask her anything else.

Julia sat back and sipped what was left of her Lilt. How would Frankie have felt if he'd found out? He would have had no right to be angry – he was cheating on his own wife – but reactions weren't always rational when it came to love and lust and all the complications of infidelity. But she'd believed him when he'd come to see her, and she still wasn't inclined to change her mind.

She mentally moved Mark Grey to the top of her list of suspects. *Dirty little secrets.* That was what he'd said to her. So maybe he'd found out about Angel and Frankie, and it had tipped him over the edge. Then Lindsay had suspected, started asking awkward questions, and he'd had to get rid of her too. His alibi was a bother, but it didn't mean he was innocent.

Lunch was being served and Julia realised how hungry she was. Time to go home and get something to eat. She picked up the two empty cans and dropped them into the bin on her way

346

out. The rain was tipping down now and as she stopped to put up her umbrella, she noticed someone standing on the other side of the street. Their eyes met and she instantly froze. Mark Grey was staring straight at her and making no pretence about it.

Julia waited for him to nod or smile or raise a hand in acknowledgement, but none of these were forthcoming. Instead, his eyes continued to bore into her. Like he was accusing, like he was sending her a message. Had he seen her with Pauline outside his flat? Had he followed them down here? She thought of the lock of hair cut from Lindsay's scalp and a shiver ran through her.

A few seconds later, he moved on, but the sense of menace remained. There had been something threatening in that stare, something forbidding.

56

Tom was glad his mother was out. The way she fussed over him, making endless cups of tea, was wearing. The hot, sweet brews were her maternal response to all the recent horrors, a way of showing love and sympathy, but instead they served as a constant reminder of everything bad that had happened. He was still feeling unnerved by the trip to Hackney. He wished now that he'd made an excuse, said he was busy, but it was too late for regrets. Although he didn't believe in ghosts, he had felt some kind of presence there, as if the river had memory, as if Angel's final flailing moments had been absorbed into the water.

What had Julia been thinking as she stood beside him? He shouldn't trust her too much. He knew that she was on a mission, that she had something to prove. Everything she did was tinged with guilt, but she couldn't bring Angel back. No one could do that. All she could hope to achieve was some kind of justice for Renee.

Renee had cut him dead yesterday, walked right past as if he wasn't there. All those years of knowing her counting for nothing. It had made him feel sick. He could tell her the truth, try to salve his conscience, but would that make him – or her – feel any better? Although he harboured no religious beliefs, he sometimes wished he was Catholic so that he could safely confess his sins. Although he wasn't sure if it still worked like that. Perhaps priests snitched as much as anyone else these days.

Another night in the Fox. Just the three of them this evening. The Holy Trinity. Or should that be unholy? He didn't think Clare would come. She had only turned up last week because she was curious about Julia. That feeling of pointlessness was rolling through him again. He could just stay home, stay away, but then there would be questions. Frankie, who was already spooked, would only call him from the pub and ask him why he wasn't there.

Tom felt like his life wasn't his anymore, as if it had been hijacked by events he'd had no control over. But then that had been true for years. He had responsibilities he'd never asked for, never wanted. And worse. The inside of his head was scrambled, a writhing mass of lies and secrets, a snake pit of deceit. And yet he still kept going, one foot in front of the other, a day at a time, his body making decisions without him. Breathe, eat, pee, shit.

He stood up, went over to the window and looked down on the estate. A few kids were kicking a ball about despite the big sign that said NO BALL GAMES and the pouring rain. You didn't feel the cold at that age. Boredom was your constant companion, and the feeling that all the good stuff was going on someplace else without you. Which of course it was because nothing good ever happened on the Mansfield.

He wondered what Julia and Renee were talking about. Pauline reckoned the two of them were in cahoots, plotting, trying to find a way to lay Angel's death at their door. He could believe it of Renee – she needed someone to blame – but surely

349

Julia wasn't going down that road? She trusted him, didn't she? It was a trust that was misplaced, but he didn't want to think about that right now.

And anyway, Pauline was hardly whiter than white. She was up to something too. Sneaking around. Furtive. Although he hated to admit it, he was a tiny bit scared of her. Pauline ploughed her own furrow. She was a good person to have on side – tough, fearless, outspoken – but he wouldn't like to cross her.

Everyone had secrets. That was the trouble. Who would fold under the pressure? Vyse hadn't had much luck to date, but that didn't mean he wouldn't keep trying.

57

Julia was still feeling unnerved when she let herself into her flat, bolted the door behind her and gave a sigh of relief to be safely home. The weird encounter with Grey had shaken her. If she'd originally had her doubts, she was more inclined now to agree with Pauline that he was responsible for Angel's death. And Lindsay's too. A double murderer still free to walk the streets.

Her eyes flew immediately to the answer machine, hoping to see a flashing light. But Michael Vyse hadn't called, or if he had he hadn't left a message. She felt a twinge of disappointment. But he was a busy man with a lot to deal with: murders didn't solve themselves. The fact that he had taken the trouble to write the note, and hadn't just slunk off into the dawn, gave her hope that last night hadn't been a one-off.

Julia made some macaroni cheese – her mother would be proud, no meat in sight – and ate it sitting on the sofa. She thought back to the morning, to the river, to the last place Angel had been alive. Had she gone willingly or had someone forced her to go there? There was little doubt that she'd had plans for the afternoon, plans she hadn't wanted to share with Pauline and Lindsay. It was possible, even likely, that she'd arranged to meet Mark Grey to receive what she'd hope would be a generous birthday gift.

She shovelled the food into her mouth, barely tasting it. Angel had been playing a risky game, toying with Grey, taking without giving, offering hope only to snatch it away again. Had he snapped, decided enough was enough, and pushed her into the water? It might not have been planned, he might not even have known that she couldn't swim, but the end result was still Angel's death. And from there, if Lindsay had suspected, it was only one small step to killing her too.

Well, not a *small* step but maybe a necessary one in his twisted mind. But there had been anger, rage, involved in the brutal murder of Lindsay. Or had it been done that way to disguise his true motive and to make it look like the work of a random madman? Perhaps he was a madman. She couldn't deny the coldness she'd felt in his company or the lack of emotion at the death of his fiancée. She couldn't forget the way he'd stared at her today.

Julia went back to the big question: Why had Angel been messing about with Grey behind Lindsay's back in the first place? She might not have been sleeping with him, but she'd still been leading him on. It broke the girl code, broke all the friendship rules. Bad enough that she'd been having an affair with Frankie, but to mess about with Grey too seemed unfathomable – as if she was deliberately dicing with danger or trying to prove a point. And what was that point? That despite her accident, despite the damage it had done, she was still attractive to men? Or had it all just been a strange kind of game to her?

Julia didn't understand. This wasn't the Angel she remembered. But then that Angel had maybe changed for ever on the day she went tumbling down the steps. One tiny moment, one bad mistake and life could be irrevocably altered. It was scary to think like that, to think that in a few seconds everything could come crashing down like a house of cards.

She took her bowl and fork through to the kitchen, washed them along with the saucepans and left it all to dry on the drainer. Then she made coffee and returned with it to the living room. She glanced at the phone, willing it to ring, but the machine stayed stubbornly silent. The heavy, slanting rain made the windowpanes rattle and obscured the glass. Not that there was much to see from the basement – only the brick wall – but she didn't like even this limited view being obscured. It made her feel closed in, like she was in prison.

Although it was only mid-afternoon the day was already growing dark. She switched on the lamp and sat down on the sofa. She was restless and agitated. As soon as she'd sat down, she got up again, unable to stay still, wishing there was someone she could ring to share her suspicions with. Well, there was someone – Michael Vyse – but that was one phone call she wasn't going to make in a hurry. She knew nothing for sure and didn't want to come across as desperate.

Julia sipped her coffee while she paced the room, up and down, back and forth, like a caged animal. She went through to the bedroom and stood by the barred window that provided a view of another brick wall and beyond that the small back garden that went with the ground-floor flat. November was hardly the month for glorious floral displays and there was little here to grab her imagination: just a mean square of scruffy lawn, some soggy leaves and the brown-twigged remains of a couple of rose bushes.

She would have gone for a walk, maybe down to Regent's Park, if the weather hadn't been so awful. Clearing her head was the main priority. She had to get her ideas straight, put her thoughts in order. Was Pauline right about Mark Grey? She couldn't forget that look he'd given her, that stare of pure animosity. And now he'd think she was watching him too. At least he didn't know where she lived – or she hoped he didn't. If he came round to confront her, she'd be hard put to explain why she'd been sitting at a bus stop with her gaze fixed firmly on his flat.

The doorbell went, making Julia jump. Because she had Mark Grey on her mind, her first thought was that it was him. What would she say? An outright denial seemed the best way forward. *I've no idea what you're talking about.* But she didn't need to answer the door at all. She could just stay where she was until her visitor gave up and went away.

The bell rang again.

What if it was Michael Vyse? That put a different slant on things. She hurried back through the living room, hoping that it was him. And not just because she wanted to see him again – she did, of course – but because she wanted a chance to pick his brains about Mark Grey. She slid the bolt back, unlocked the door and opened it. The expectant expression on her face quickly turned to disappointment. Instead of Vyse, Carol Forshaw was standing in front of her.

'Hi, Julia. Glad you're keeping the place secure. How are you? The DI asked me to drop by, make sure you're okay.'

Julia wasn't sure how to take this unsolicited visit. Should she be pleased that Vyse was showing concern for her or alarmed that he hadn't come himself? 'I'm fine, thanks. Do you want to come in?'

'If you're not too busy.'

Julia stood aside and then followed her into the living room. 'Would you like a coffee?'

'Oh, no ta. I can't stay long. No trouble, then? No more attempted break-ins or anything else suspicious?' Carol put her hands on her hips and scrutinised the room as if there might be an intruder hiding behind the sofa.

'All quiet.'

'That's good.'

Julia suddenly had a new idea as to why Carol had turned up. 'Did Pauline call you?'

'Why would Pauline call me?'

'I bumped into her this morning. I went to see Renee, but she wasn't in.'

'Oh, okay. Is there a problem? With Pauline, I mean.'

Julia could have replied that there was always a problem with Pauline but bearing in mind what she now knew about the two women had the sense to bite her tongue. 'No, I just thought . . . Oh, I don't know what I thought. It doesn't matter.'

'How's the new job? How's it going with Apostle?'

'Early days but yeah, it's all right. Is there any news on Angel's death, or Lindsay's?'

'Sorry, there's nothing new.'

'What's your opinion of Mark Grey?'

Carol grinned. 'Has Pauline been bending your ear? She's got him well and truly in the frame.'

'You don't think there's a chance she's right?'

'That he killed Lindsay? God, yeah, there's always a chance, but not much in the way of evidence. And when I say not much, I mean absolutely sod all.'

'I saw him today when I was coming out of Connolly's. He gave me one hell of a stare.'

'You should have said earlier. I'll go and arrest him straight away.'

Julia gave a wry smile. 'Maybe that's not such a bad idea.'

'Look, I don't much like the guy either, but he has got an alibi, and I don't think his flatmate is lying.'

Julia wanted to ask if he had an alibi for Angel's death too, but then she'd have to reveal what she'd been told about Grey's obsession, and it wouldn't take long for Pauline to hear about it. No, she had to keep her mouth shut for now. If it got back to the others that she'd been blabbing to the police, none of them would ever trust her again.

'Okay,' Carol said, 'I'll love you and leave you. I need to get home and grab some sleep; I'm covering a night shift later. You know where we are if anything crops up.'

But still Carol didn't leave. Her eyes scanned the bookshelves, the plants, the mock-Persian rug under the coffee table, before saying too casually, 'Oh, did I see you in Gigi's last night?'

And now Julia knew why the DC was really here. Pauline *had* called her, and Carol wanted to know if she was going to broadcast the information about having seen the two women together. To save her own skin, or protect Pauline? Both, perhaps.

'Well, I saw you. I didn't realise you'd seen me.'

'I wasn't sure,' Carol said. 'It was only a fleeting glance.'

Julia didn't believe her. She was pretty certain she'd got out of there before either of them had noticed her presence. 'I was with Apostle. He's thinking of buying the club.'

Carol wrinkled her nose. 'I wouldn't have thought it was his kind of place.'

'Any place that makes money is his kind of place. But I wouldn't worry; I don't think he's that keen.'

'No point in owning a club where you can't even drink at the bar. Or chat up the women. Yeah, I can't see him jumping at the opportunity. He should stick to what he knows.'

Julia decided to be blunt. 'So how long have you and Pauline been together?'

'Oh, God, we're not together,' Carol said, laughing as if the very idea was ludicrous. 'Not in the way you mean, not in a relationship. We're just mates. We hang out together sometimes.'

Mates who kiss, Julia could have said, but didn't. 'So you'd rather people didn't know that you're gay? I understand that. It's no one's business but your own. I can see how it might be tricky at work. Don't worry, I won't say anything.'

Carol grinned at her. 'Christ, everyone knows that *I'm* a lesbian. Out and proud and all the rest of it. I made that clear from the minute I got to Cowan Road. It saves any misunderstandings, and being groped by every shitty man who thinks it's an obligation to come on to you without the least encouragement.' She crossed her arms, uncrossed them and sighed. 'No, it's not me I'm worried about. I can take care of myself. But it's different for Pauline. Her father's such a bloody bigot. If it even crossed his mind that she was gay, he'd probably disown her.'

'But she is?'

'God, I don't think even Pauline knows the answer to that one. Let's call it "undecided". She doesn't want to be, but we don't choose what nature throws our way.' Carol sighed again. 'And I know what you're thinking – that I should have let Vyse know that me and Pauline had history as soon as the investigation into Angel's death started, conflict of interest and the rest, but I didn't want to get dumped from the team. It's hard to be taken seriously when you're a woman in this job; any excuse to sideline you and they'll take it. Anyway, I knew that Pauline had nothing to do with it – she was with Lindsay all afternoon – so I just kept my mouth shut. But then when Lindsay got murdered . . . well, it was a bit late to come clean so . . .'

'So you didn't.'

'No.' Carol's voice became a little more tentative. 'Are you going to tell Vyse?'

Julia knew all about being sidelined by men, and how tough it was to climb that career ladder. She could understand why the DC had decided to be somewhat economical with the truth. 'What for? I can't see that it has any bearing on Angel's death, or Lindsay's.'

Carol's shoulders relaxed. 'Ta. I appreciate it.'

'But what are you going to do if you're asked to interview Pauline and—'

'Won't ever happen,' Carol interrupted sharply. 'I promise. I'll make sure of it. If I hear that Pauline's being pulled in again, I'll make myself scarce, get as far from Cowan Road as possible. Failing that, I'll fake food poisoning or something. Don't worry, I won't do anything to jeopardise the investigation.'

'Okay.'

'Thanks, Julia,' Carol said, moving towards the hall. 'And if there's anything you ever need, you know where I am.'

Julia was on the doorstep watching Carol climb the steps when the DC suddenly stopped, turned and said, 'I probably don't need to tell you this, but watch out for Vyse. He's got a bit of a reputation at the station.'

'What sort of reputation?'

'For the ladies,' Carol said. 'Especially the good-looking ones. I'm sure you won't fall for his dubious charm, but forewarned is forearmed and all that.'

Julia's stomach lurched. Her face paled – she could feel the blood rushing out of it – but at least the light had faded enough for Carol not to notice. 'Thanks for the warning,' she managed to splutter. Did her voice sound croaky? 'I'll bear it in mind.'

'Pity his poor wife didn't,' Carol said, before giving her a cheery wave and bounding up the last few steps.

58

Julia stood rooted to the spot. *His wife?* What? Her jaw was clenched, and her mouth had gone dry. Her heart pounded in her chest. *Married.* God, what a fool she'd been! She felt horrified, mortified, disgusted. Having thought he was something special, she had now discovered he was just another cheating bastard.

She was starting to shiver, partly from the cold but mainly from shock. Carol's car started up, and she heard her drive away. Loathing for Michael Vyse swept over her, followed by a wave of self-reproach. She had let her guard down, let passion override good sense, and now it had all come back to kick her in the teeth. She went inside and slammed the door behind her.

In the living room Julia slumped onto the sofa and covered her face with her hands. She had made assumptions, that was the problem, assumed that Vyse was decent and caring when all the time he was nothing but a no-good philanderer. Was she blind? Was she stupid? Yes was the answer to both of those questions. She hadn't even thought to ask him if he was single, if he was free. She'd just assumed – there was that damn word again – that he wouldn't be going to bed with her if he wasn't.

She stood up, went to the kitchen, retrieved a bottle of Chablis from the fridge and opened it. This wasn't the time for sobriety. 'Fool,' she muttered under her breath. 'What's the matter with you? Idiot, moron.' She took the bottle and a glass back to the living room, sat down on the sofa again and poured out a generous measure. Greedily she gulped down the wine, trying to dull her anger and shame. *You* don't need to feel bad, she told herself: he kept you in the dark, he lied by omission, he didn't tell you he was married. But she hadn't bothered to check, and that made her guilty too.

Julia was on her second glass when it occurred to her that Carol Forshaw could have been lying or had got her facts wrong. What were the odds? Not that good, she decided. She had no reason to lie as far as she could see, and police stations were probably a hotbed of gossip with everyone knowing what everyone else was up to. *Stop trying to make excuses for him. Stop trying to save face.* But that 'pity his wife didn't' could be interpreted in another way – that they were separated, perhaps, that the woman had been warned but hadn't listened. But that didn't change the fact that he had a reputation, that she was just one more notch on the bedpost.

With nothing else to do, she flipped open her notebook and stared at it. Then she picked up a pen and put a hard line under the name Mark Grey. She had wanted to talk to Vyse about him, but now she wasn't inclined to talk to Vyse at all. Carol seemed convinced that Grey was out of the picture, but she wasn't so sure. There was something weird about the man, something off-kilter.

Julia continued to study the names as if by sheer persistence she could make the truth jump out at her. Perhaps she shouldn't have been so hasty in dismissing Tom's invitation to the Fox tonight. The more pressure she put on, the more questions she asked, the more likely it was that someone might slip up. But hadn't she already got Grey in the frame? If he was responsible, she was wasting her time trying to get anything out of the others.

None of this helped take her mind off Michael Vyse. Another unpleasant thought raised its ugly head: what if Vyse had only been using her to get information on Tom and the others? With the police investigation into two deaths making little progress, he might have seen her as an easy route into the inner circle. Granted they'd had a deal about pooling what they found out, but she couldn't see that he'd contributed much. Had he guessed that she was withholding information too and decided a little romance might oil the wheels?

A shudder of disgust shook her body. These thoughts weren't making her feel any better. She refilled her glass, stared at the wall, stared at the rug, stared at her notes. *Oh, for God's sake, stop being so pathetic.* Another lesson learned. Don't trust cops. Move on. It wasn't the end of the world. It could have been worse. She could have found out much further down the line when she was in too deep and getting out would have been ten times harder.

The phone rang at five thirty and again at six. She didn't answer it. After the second call the light on the answer machine went on and began to flash. She waited another ten minutes before standing up, walking across the room and pressing *Play*. Vyse's voice floated out of the speaker.

'Hey, only me. I'm at work so give me a ring if you get this and fancy going for a drink later. Okay. Speak to you soon.'

'Fat chance,' Julia said to the empty room.

She switched on the TV, flicked through the channels, found nothing of interest and switched it off again. Resisting the temptation to put on some music – she wasn't in the mood for anything upbeat, and anything sad would reduce her to tears – she embraced the silence. In the distance, above the sound of the rain, she could hear the faint hum of traffic on Camden Road.

Julia went back to her notes, studied the names, moved them around and doodled on the page. She wondered how closely the police had looked at Grey's flatmate, Darren, provider of the useful alibi. Maybe Pauline should be following *him*. She wished she had someone to talk to, someone to share her ideas with, but with Vyse out of the picture that post was currently vacant.

Exasperated by her inability to shed any useful light on the murders, she hissed out a breath. More wine. As if that was going to help. But she still reached for the bottle. She hoped Vyse wouldn't call round later on the off chance of finding her in. No, he wouldn't do that; he'd presume she was out for the evening, probably down the Fox trying to do his work for him. She glared at the notebook, angry and frustrated.

Julia found herself thinking about the diaries. Five of them missing if Angel had continued to keep them. But maybe she was grasping at straws. It was perfectly possible that she'd just stopped writing about her life. She had stopped before, after the accident, but then started again. Something was niggling at the back of her mind.

It was hard to focus. She had that feeling, like glimpsing something out of the corner of her eye and turning to find nothing there. Like groping through fog, touching something only for it to slip though her fingers. Infuriating. Frustrating. And if she was so convinced of Mark Grey's guilt, why was she even doing this?

The wine was blurring her ability to think straight. She kept jumping from one idea to another without concentrating on any one of them. It felt like a long time since she'd stood by the river and looked out over the water. What had happened to Angel that day? Was everyone lying to her, even Tom? Perhaps this would be like that Agatha Christie novel where all the suspects had done it. Some kind of crazy collaboration.

The phone went again at ten past eight. She ignored it. Whoever it was didn't leave a message. By now it was dark outside, and the room, lit only by a single lamp, was full of shadows. Worried again that Vyse might turn up unannounced, see the light and refuse to leave until she'd answered the door, Julia stood up carefully and took the almost empty bottle of wine through to the kitchen. She poured herself a large glass of water, switched off the lights in the kitchen and living room, picked up her handbag and retired to the bedroom at the back.

Knowing that she had drunk too much and would pay for it tomorrow, she rooted in her bag for the packet of aspirin she kept there, took two and washed them down with some of the water. It was too early for bed, but she turned on the radio, kicked off her trainers, lay down on the covers and started listening to a phone-in. Ten minutes later she was asleep.

59

Julia woke up, disorientated, in the early hours of the morning. Her mouth was parched, her head throbbing. There was a burning sensation in the back of her throat. The light was still on, and she could see the glass of water on the bedside table but only dimly, as if she was looking at it through mist. Her brain was sluggish, hampered by a hangover, and she thought at first there was something wrong with her eyes. Then gradually sounds came to her, sounds that she shouldn't be hearing: a weird crackling, a series of thumps, a splintering.

It came to her in a sudden rush of terror. Christ, the flat was on fire! She leapt from the bed and only then did she see the thin ribbons of smoke seeping under the bedroom door. She rushed over, reached for the handle and stopped. *Don't open it,* her inner voice ordered. If the smoke had got this far, the flames wouldn't be far behind.

Instead, she grabbed the duvet off the bed, rolled it up as fast as she could and laid it against the foot of the door. Buying herself some time. She could feel the smoke scratching at her throat, impeding her airways, making her cough and splutter. Quickly she shoved her feet in her trainers, rushed over to the window, put her hands through the bars, opened it and took a few fast gulps of fresh air. That had been the easy bit. Now she just had to find the key to unlock the set of bars and swing them back.

Her eyes scanned the ledge, but it wasn't there. What? Where had she put it? She couldn't remember the last time she'd unlocked them. Probably just after she'd moved in. There had never been a need until now. Damn, God, where was the key? She tried the dressing table, opening all the drawers in quick succession. Nothing. The bedside table. Nothing. Fear was scorching through her body. She was imprisoned with no way out.

Her panic was increasing by the second. How long before the flames devoured the door? She threw what was left of the glass of water over the duvet. Then she put her face against the bars and yelled. 'Help! Fire! Help me!' Everyone would be fast asleep, their double-glazed windows closed against the winter chill. She yanked desperately at the bars – locked firm – and then carried on shouting, hoping her cries would penetrate before it was too late.

Julia dropped to her knees and started scrabbling on the floor, hoping the key might have fallen off the ledge at some point. While she searched, she carried on shouting. Her chest was starting to ache, her lungs heaving. Was this it? Was this how she was going to die? The fire was getting closer, the heat filling the room, the smoke swirling as it met the coldness of the outside air. 'Help me!'

She stood up again and stared out into the darkness of the garden, the place of safety if only she could reach it. Turning, she looked back at the door. Should she try and make a run for it through the flat? But she knew that was hopeless. The flames would devour her before she got more than a few feet. She could hear their roar now, could feel the heat penetrating the walls.

'Help! Help me!'

Julia was starting to despair. Terror coursed through her veins. She grabbed the iron bars again and pulled and pulled. She yelled. Tears were running down her face. It was hopeless. The bars wouldn't shift. Desperately her eyes searched the room, looking for anything she could use. There was the kitchen knife she'd stashed under the bed in case of an intruder. But what use was that? You couldn't stab a fire. You couldn't keep the flames at bay with a finely honed blade. She grabbed it anyway and used the handle to hammer on the bars.

And then – was she imagining it? – she thought she heard a different noise, the sound of a door opening not so far away, a voice. Footsteps. An auditory hallucination perhaps. The last thing she might ever hear. But then the voice was made real, attached to a body, to a man in a pale dressing gown – middle-aged, wide-eyed – emerging from the dark to stand in front of her like some ghostly apparition.

'We've called the fire brigade. They're on their way. Don't worry, they'll be here soon.'

'I can't get out,' Julia croaked. 'The bars are locked. I can't find the key.'

'Are you on your own?'

'Yes, yes it's only me.'

'Wait there,' he said, as if there was somewhere else she might go.

And, like a child, she wanted to cry out, *Don't leave me. Don't leave me alone.* But already he was gone, rushing back to his flat. The fire was licking around the base of the door, the smoke swirling through the room. Soon she wouldn't even be able to breathe through the window. Where was the man from upstairs? Would he ever come back? Perhaps she had just imagined him.

It felt like an eternity before she heard footsteps again. By now she was coughing badly, spluttering in the smoke. The man was carrying what looked like a heavy mallet.

'Move away from the window,' he said.

Julia stepped to the side, placing her palms against the wall to keep her upright. She could feel herself growing weaker, each smoky breath she took becoming more of an effort. The mallet struck once, twice, three times, but still the bars remained in place. And all the time the fire was growing closer, catching on the duvet and licking up the inside of the door. She could hear the heavy grunts of the man, his frustrated exhalation as each attempt met with failure.

And then, suddenly, he hit the sweet spot and the bars swung open. She heard a heavy thud as he dropped the mallet on the ground. His hands pulled back the edge of the window. 'Can you climb out? Can you manage?'

Julia grabbed her bag, passed it to him, used the last of her strength to quickly clamber on to the ledge, wriggled through the space, launched herself out and landed in an ungainly heap on the ground. The cold night air washed through her lungs. Before she could even begin to appreciate it, the man grabbed her elbow, yanked her to her feet and half pulled, half dragged her along the path and up some steps.

The next thing she knew they were hurrying through his kitchen, through the living room, to the hall and the front door. She could barely believe she was free. 'Thank you, thank you,' she kept saying. This man had saved her life and there were no adequate words. His wife was waiting, white-faced and anxious. She took the bag from her husband, put an arm around Julia and led her away.

Back outside it was a hive of activity. There was noise and bustle. The fire engines had arrived and a couple of police cars. The sirens must have woken the neighbours because there was a gathering in the street, a small crowd in a motley assortment of nightwear. The stink of fire hung in the air. It had begun to rain again.

Time seemed to move in fits and starts, moments of clarity interspersed with elongated minutes of vagueness. She felt like she was watching an old jerky film with scenes passing before her eyes, a spectator rather than a member of the cast. Her chest hurt when she breathed, but gradually it was getting better. She was sitting in the back of the ambulance, coughing and retching. An oxygen mask was placed over her face.

Julia still couldn't fully take in what had happened. Like a nightmare made real. How had the fire started? Had she left something on? The cooker? An electrical fault? Where had she put the key to open the bars? The questions leapt inside her head like jumping beans. Someone put a blanket around her shoulders. A police officer came to talk to her. When he'd gone, she couldn't remember what he'd said, or what she had said back.

Breathe in slowly. Breathe out. She was alive. She had survived. She hoped the blaze wouldn't spread to her rescuer's flat. She peered around the ambulanceman, wondering if the fire was out yet, if anything could be retrieved from her home. No, it was impossible. But some clothes maybe if they'd got the hoses in there quickly enough. Hell, what did clothes matter when she could have been burned to a cinder? Just be thankful you're safe. Just be thankful you're still alive.

She clutched her handbag to her stomach, relieved, even amazed that she'd had the nous to bring it with her. At least she still had her bank cards and a few quid in her purse. One less thing to sort out. Voices travelled over and around her. The rain pattered on the pavement. The lights revolved on top of the police cars, and the streetlamps cast an eerie glow over the street. She felt removed, distant, as if she was watching everything from far away. After a while she became aware of someone standing in front of her.

'Julia? How are you doing? You okay?'

Julia blinked, her eyes still sore and watery from the fire. It took her a moment to focus. DC Carol Forshaw leaned down, her expression solemn, her gaze full of concern.

'I'm all right. Better now. What are you doing here?'

'The local cops rang Cowan Road when the call about the fire came in. You remember, we asked them to keep an eye on the place. Fine bloody job they did of that. So I thought I'd head over. The ambulance will take you to hospital. I'll come with you.'

'I don't need to go to hospital.'

'You've inhaled smoke. They'll be able to give you a proper check-up there, maybe keep you in until the morning.'

'What time is it?'

Carol glanced at her watch. 'Well, it is morning. Ten past two.'

'I'm all right, really I am.' Julia looked at one of the ambulancemen. 'It's not necessary, is it?'

'Always best to be on the safe side.'

But Julia had made up her mind. Tonight had been dreadful enough without spending the next few hours in some hectic hospital ward. 'No, I feel okay now.'

'Not sure you look it,' Carol said.

'I just want to get away from here. What's going to happen with the flat?'

'It'll be secured. Once they're certain it's safe, you'll be able to go in and see if there's anything salvageable. Some time next week, probably.'

'Will they know how it started by then?'

'I should think so.'

It hurt Julia's throat to talk so she just nodded.

'Any headaches or vomiting or shortness of breath, go straight to A & E,' the ambulanceman said.

Julia nodded again.

'Okay,' Carol said, 'give me two minutes and we'll get out of here.'

Julia stood up. She did have a headache but that could be as much down to the wine she'd drunk last night as the effects of the smoke. She tested out her legs – still working apparently – and took a few steps forward and back. Now that the fire was out and the excitement was over, the crowd had started to drift away. The awful burning smell, however, still clung to the night air.

Her jeans and white T-shirt were covered in black smuts as if someone had sent her up a chimney. She made a clumsy attempt to wipe herself down, but only succeeded in spreading the mess. Still, at least she was dressed and not in her winter pyjamas. She might smell like she'd just smoked a hundred cigarettes, but that was a small price to pay for still being alive.

Carol came back and said, 'Come on then, let's get you in the car before you freeze to death.'

Julia saw the frown between the woman's eyes. 'What's up? What's the matter?'

'Nothing.'

'Tell me.'

Carol gave a sigh and glanced towards the burnt-out shell of the flat. 'More bad news, I'm afraid. I was talking to the fire officer in charge. He reckons it was deliberate, says the hallway stinks of petrol.'

'What?'

'Yeah, some bastard just tried to kill you.'

60

Julia got in the car and put on her seatbelt. Her heart was drumming out a fierce beat. *Deliberate.* The word ricocheted around the inside of her head. Someone had tried to kill her. She trembled, still struggling to process it. 'Are you sure?'

Carol pulled away from the kerb. 'Sure enough, unless you've taken to storing petrol in your flat. The officer said the place stank of it. The arsonist probably put some soaked rags through the letterbox and then dropped a match on them. Sorry, I'm sure this is the last thing you need to hear. Where do you want to go? Is there a friend you can stay with, or shall I take you to a hotel?'

Julia, who was still trying to absorb the shocking news of her attempted murder, ran through the options of where she could go. It was a short list. Renee? Tom? But that would mean dragging them out of bed, waking them up in the middle of the night, and then having to deal with all the questions they would have. And she didn't really want to have to pay out for a hotel. Having lost all her possessions, she'd need every penny she had just to replace the essentials. Then she had an idea.

'Shoreditch,' she said. 'If you drive to the high street, I'll direct you from there.'

'Is that a friend's place?'

Julia was about to reply when she started coughing again.

'There's some water in the glove compartment,' Carol said. 'Shit, Julia, are you sure you don't want to go to hospital?'

Julia waved the suggestion away but accepted the offer of water. Her throat felt like sandpaper. She unscrewed the bottle lid and took a few gulps. 'I'm okay.'

'You keep saying that, but you sound like you should be in A & E.'

'It's only when I talk,' Julia croaked.

'Okay, I get the message. I'll shut up now and give you some peace.'

It didn't take long to get to Shoreditch. The streets were quiet, almost empty, and in less than fifteen minutes they were pulling up outside the office. Julia spent most of the journey checking the side mirror in case they were being followed. And why not? She had every right to be paranoid. Not that it *was* paranoia: when you knew someone had tried to burn you alive, it was wise to take precautions.

Carol was frowning again as she peered through the windscreen at the dark windows. 'Is this Apostle's office? What are we doing here?'

'It's somewhere to stay until I decide where to go. It's too late to be dragging people out of bed.'

'But it's empty, isn't it? I mean, there's no one there to look after you.'

'I'll be fine,' Julia said. 'It's only for a few hours. I'll get some sleep, and if I feel ill I'll go to hospital. I promise.'

'I don't like leaving you here on your own.'

But Julia was already rummaging through her bag for her keys. 'Thanks for the lift. I appreciate it.'

'Well, let me know where you end up. We'll have a proper talk when you're feeling a bit better. And take care of yourself, yeah?'

'Sure,' Julia said, getting out of the car. 'Thanks again.' She quickly shut the door before Carol could make any more protests, strode across the pavement and turned to give a wave. She unlocked the office door, stepped inside and put on the light. Immediately she heard the soft beep of the alarm. God, she'd forgotten all about that! What was the number? And now she was scrabbling in her bag for her purse and the scrap of paper she'd written it on. Carol was still waiting, making sure that everything was all right before she left. Eventually Julia found the code and rapidly keyed in the four numbers. She waved again through the glass and went through to the office.

Julia sat down at her desk, listening as Carol's car pulled away. Now she wasn't so sure about the decision she'd made. Was it really such a good idea to be here on her own? What if her would-be killer guessed where she was and decided to try and finish the job? She stood up, closed the blinds and sat down again. It was cold in the room, and she rubbed her hands together trying to warm them up.

She didn't want to think about what could have happened tonight but could think of little else. Had Mark Grey tried to kill her? But why? Because he thought Lindsay had told her something? Or Angel? And what if it hadn't been Grey? She remembered telling Tom that she was going to Suffolk to see her mum. She remembered the phone calls she hadn't answered. Maybe two of those calls hadn't been Vyse at all, but someone else checking that she was or wasn't there.

It was possible, she decided, that the flat or rather what might be in it – letters from Angel, the missing diaries – had been the target of the fire rather than herself. This was a slightly more reassuring thought than being the target for murder, although it wasn't going to bring any of her possessions back. Tom was the only person she'd talked to about going away, but he could have passed on the information to the others.

Julia began to shiver. She should put the heat on and make herself a hot drink. Then maybe try and get a few hours' sleep. And then? No, she was too tired to think about that. A wave of exhaustion rolled over her. All she wanted was oblivion, to close her scratchy eyes and make everything go away for a while. She had just put her arms on the desk, just laid her head down on them, when she heard it: a distinct creak from along the corridor, a sound that didn't belong in an empty office building. She started upright, her heart banging against her ribs. Then footsteps, soft on the carpet, a furtive tread. A pause. Then slowly, carefully, the door began to open. Julia's nerves, already stretched beyond endurance, were at breaking point. She was about to scream when the man's face loomed into view.

Ivor Apostle stared down at her. 'Jesus, what the hell happened to you?'

61

It took Julia longer than expected to provide a reason for her presence, the explanation being interrupted by several coughing fits. Apostle fetched her water, told her to take her time, and listened as she related her story. She didn't go into too much detail but perhaps told him more than she intended to. It was a relief to have someone to talk to, even if that someone was Ivor Apostle.

'And here was me thinking that I led an interesting life,' he said. 'You seem to have got on the wrong side of someone.'

'Yeah, it looks that way.'

'Okay, well you'd better come back to my place. You can get cleaned up there, have a shower and grab some sleep.'

'I can't do that.'

'Why not?'

'I don't want to put you out. I'll book into a hotel or a B & B.'

'Don't be daft. It's only down the road. And you'll be safe there.'

It was the safety comment that swung it for Julia. She didn't want to impose on Apostle, but she was terrified of being tracked down by the arsonist. At least she could rest easy at his flat, secure in the knowledge that no one with any sense would try and get past him. 'Are you sure?'

'I wouldn't ask if I wasn't.'

It was only when they were in his car, a sleek dark blue Jag, that some of her old fears came back to haunt her. What if she'd just walked straight into a trap? While the rest of the country was sleeping, Apostle was still up and about. Why was that? It suddenly seemed horribly suspicious. She took a couple of deep breaths and tried to steady herself. Apostle, surely, had only ever been on the periphery of her circle of suspects, an outside bet, and only then because he had shown a slight interest in Angel's death. He had no reason to cause her harm, but her nerves were so frayed that she could barely think straight. 'Why were you at the office?' she blurted out before she could stop herself.

Apostle gave her a sidelong glance. 'I was doing some work, and it got late. I couldn't be bothered going home so I set the alarm and stretched out on the couch. It gave me a bloody shock when I heard the front door opening. I thought we'd got burglars, although I couldn't figure out why the alarm wasn't going off.'

'Sorry, I couldn't think of where else to go.'

'Don't worry about it. No harm done.'

It was a perfectly reasonable explanation, but Julia couldn't quite shake her anxiety. He could have driven to Camden, set the fire and returned to Shoreditch. Even now he could be planning to put a pillow over her face while she slept. She surreptitiously sniffed the air, wondering if she might get a whiff of petrol, but all she could smell was her own ashy clothes. 'DC Forshaw gave me a lift to the office. Do you know her?' All said just to inform him that the police were aware of the last place she'd been seen alive.

'I don't think I've had the pleasure.'

'She's working with Vyse on Angel's case.'

'Ah, Vyse.'

There was an edge to his voice that Julia was quick to pick up on. 'Why do you say it like that? Have you had trouble with him?'

'Not for a while.'

'But once upon a time?'

'He used to work out of West End Central before he got shifted to Kellston. I shouldn't think he was happy about that. The pickings aren't so rich in the East End.'

'Pickings?'

Apostle grinned as if amused by her ignorance. 'Backhanders, freebies, money paid to look the other way.'

Julia was glad that he wasn't looking at her. Her opinion of Michael Vyse had already been on a severe downward trajectory and now it had reached rock bottom. 'So Renee was right. He is bent.'

'Lots of them are in one way or another. It's the nature of the beast. They start off filled with righteous indignation, with a desire to bring down the bad boys, but slowly they get disillusioned, realise that whatever they do, nothing changes and so decide they might as well have a piece of the pie. From there it's only one short step to corruption. Or they start telling themselves that the end justifies the means and before you know it, they're as crooked as the villains they're trying to put away.'

Julia's hands twisted in her lap. Yesterday she wouldn't have believed this of Vyse. Despite Renee's warnings, she'd built up a different picture in her head, of a man who had morals, who had principles, who might bend the rules a little but was fundamentally good. Now she had no such qualms about seeing him for who he really was. Not just an adulterer but a bent copper to boot. 'Hardly the best person to be leading the investigation then.'

Apostle raised and dropped his massive shoulders. 'Depends if there's anything in it for him.'

Julia wondered if she had been the 'anything', his reward for putting in the hours. It made her feel stupid and used. She was glad that Carol had been the one on night shift, that she hadn't had to deal with Vyse on top of everything else.

They arrived at the Barbican Estate, eerily quiet at this time of the morning. The Jag was parked, the lift taken up to the top floor, a short stroll along the concrete walkway and then they were there. He unlocked the door and they went inside. Julia's first impression was that the place looked like a show home, immaculately decorated in soft shades of grey with matching darker furniture. It was slick, modern and spotless, so spotless in fact that she wondered if he employed someone to come in and clean. If the state of his office was anything to go by, he certainly wasn't tidy by nature.

The flat was actually a maisonette with wooden stairs lead-ing up to two bedrooms and a bathroom. Apostle showed her the room she would be sleeping in – small but pretty – and on seeing the bed she longed to lie down and curl up under the duvet.

'There's towels in the bathroom cupboard,' he said. 'And a spare toothbrush in the cabinet. I'll find you a dressing gown. Leave your clothes outside the door and I'll put them through the machine.'

Julia didn't really fancy Apostle manhandling her smalls but seeing as she could hardly wear them again before they were washed, she didn't have much choice. 'Thanks,' she said.

'And don't bother coming downstairs after you've showered. Just get yourself to bed and try and get some sleep.'

Julia was grateful for that. All she craved now was oblivion. No more words. No more questions. After he'd gone, she stripped off in the bathroom and left her clothes, as requested, in a pile outside the door. Then she stepped into the shower and let the powerful hot jets slough off the evidence of the evening. She washed her hair twice, scrubbed every inch of her ashy skin and felt the tension drain slowly from her body.

By the time she'd finished, over twenty minutes later, she felt squeaky clean if not entirely renewed. She wrapped herself in a fluffy towel, investigated the bathroom cabinet and found a row of brand-new toothbrushes still in their wrappers. She smiled wryly, thinking that these were probably for the women he brought home. A man who was always prepared. Still, she was grateful for his forward thinking. Her mouth tasted vile, and she brushed her teeth with vigour.

When she opened the bathroom door, her clothes were gone and in their place was a white towelling dressing gown neatly folded. She picked it up and took it through to the bedroom. He had left a navy-blue T-shirt on the pillow, and a tall glass of water on the bedside cabinet. She gulped some of the water, gave her hair a rub, pulled on the T-shirt, turned out the light and crawled into bed.

At first, she thought she wouldn't sleep – there was too much going on in her head – but gradually her brain switched off and she drifted down into a place where nothing could disturb her.

62

Tom woke early on Sunday morning, made a brew and sat by the living-room window looking down on the estate. From here he had a view of the main gate and of everyone who was arriving or leaving. Not that there was much activity at this time of day, only a few poor buggers trudging home after a night shift. The drunks and the dealers had evaporated. Even the homeless would be curled up under their cardboard bedding, finding some relief from the cold and the rain in the shelter of the dim rat-runs that criss-crossed the Mansfield.

It had been a dreary evening in the Fox, and he had left way before closing time, feeling judged. Although he couldn't see what was wrong with taking Julia to the river, Frankie had got sniffy about it, and Pauline had said he was just asking for trouble. Not that Pauline ever said anything much different these days; he only had to mention Julia and her face would turn sour.

Maybe he should have refused to take her, but he couldn't see the harm. Well, if there was any it was only to himself. It had stirred everything up inside him and made his guts churn.

Standing by that riverside he'd been tempted to tell her the truth, to let it all flood out, but the consequences would have been too immense. Once said, it could never be taken back. And it hadn't been to do with not trusting her, more with the knowledge that he would be trying to offload his guilt, to spill his secrets in the hope of lifting the burden he carried.

Julia, of course, knew all about guilt. The accident was seared on her memory. There was no point in telling her it wasn't her fault. She would always feel responsible whatever comforting words were thrown in her direction. Things happened and you had to deal with them the best you could. Was that what he was doing? If this was his best, then he dreaded to think what the worst might be.

Really, everything began and ended with Angel. That was how it had always been since they were kids. She had never been the sweet, fragile girl others claimed her to be. She had always been self-centred, an attention seeker, using guile and her prettiness to get what she wanted. After the accident it had been easier to be more forgiving, but there had been intimations of her true character earlier on, in the way she played Julia and Pauline off against each other, in the way she only ever thought about herself, in the way she manipulated people. Renee had spoiled her, doted on her, giving her everything she possibly could, and the end result was a young woman with an inflated sense of her own importance and unrealistic expectations.

There had been the business with Larry too. She'd been babysitting, put him in the bath and left him alone when the phone rang. Only for a few seconds, she swore, but the poor kid had almost drowned. He didn't know all the ins and outs, but it had caused a massive rift between Angel and her cousin, a rift that had never healed. Angel's life, it seemed, had been plagued with 'accidents', things she held no responsibility for. Forever the victim.

He stared down at the grey expanse of concrete. Was it wrong for him to be thinking these things? But there was no point in looking at the dead through rose-tinted glasses. She had been who she was, flawed, far from perfect and selfish to the core. But they'd been friends and that still counted for something.

He had told the others about what Julia had asked on the evening they'd gone for a drink after Lindsay's murder. Perhaps he shouldn't have. They were already teetering on a precipice, and it wouldn't take much to push them over the edge. It made him wonder if she knew, or at least suspected. That was the trouble with a guilty conscience – it made even the most innocent questions seem laden with menace.

His mum came into the living room wearing her dressing gown. She was only fifty-two but already her short brown hair was laced with silver. 'You're up early, Tom. I thought you'd be having a lie-in this morning. It was late when you got in.'

He might have known that his attempt to sneak in quietly would have been thwarted by his mother's inability to sleep until she knew he was safely home. 'I didn't wake you, did I? I wasn't tired, so I went for a drive. There's tea in the pot. I've only just made it.'

'A drive? I thought you were going to the Fox.'

'After the Fox,' he said. 'And don't worry, I only had a couple of pints.'

'Where did you go?'

'Oh, nowhere special. I just drove around.'

63

It was after eleven when Julia woke up. For a moment, disorientated, she had no idea where she was, but gradually it came back to her. She shivered at the memory of last night's events. A slice of silvery light crept through the gap in the curtains where she hadn't pulled them together properly. She yawned, then slowly got out of bed. Her body ached, especially her right arm with which she'd been frantically banging on the bars.

She padded barefoot across the deep-pile carpet and put her ear to the door. Nothing. She opened it a crack and peered out. From downstairs came the low sound of a radio. At her feet lay her clothes, all clean and freshly pressed. She bent down and picked them up, instantly raising them to her nose to see if any whiff remained of the fire. All they smelled of was fabric conditioner. Apostle, it appeared, was more domesticated than she'd given him credit for.

In the bathroom she had a pee and brushed her teeth. Back in the bedroom, while she dressed, she made a mental list of everything she had to buy. She thought of all the beautiful clothes that had gone up in smoke, and a thin sigh escaped from her lips. What chance of any of them surviving? Slim, she decided. But there was no point moaning or mourning; they were just clothes after all, not flesh and blood. She had no insurance, of course, having believed it was an unnecessary expense on top of all her other monthly outgoings. A bad decision. There was a lot to replace.

Julia dragged a comb through her tangled hair, staring in the mirror at a pair of red-rimmed eyes and a face that was too pale. By concentrating on what she'd lost, she was avoiding the real horror of last night. *Had someone tried to kill her?* She preferred to believe that whoever had set the fire had thought she was in Suffolk, but that might just be wishful thinking.

She opened the curtains, made the bed, and went downstairs where the pleasant smell of freshly ground coffee hung in the air. Apostle was sitting at the kitchen table, going through a pile of paperwork.

'Morning,' he said, looking up. 'Did you sleep all right?'

'Out like a light. Thanks for washing my clothes, and for the bed. I'll find somewhere else to stay tonight, book into a hotel or something.'

'What for? You're welcome to stay here as long as you need. No point wasting money on hotels.'

'I don't want to impose on you.'

'You're not. It'll be a while before your flat's ready to move back into, that's if you even want to. Do you?'

'I don't know. It's not exactly full of happy memories. Maybe I'll look for somewhere else. God, sorry, I never meant to cause you all this bother.'

'What bother? It's hardly a massive inconvenience. Help yourself to coffee, and there are some croissants in the oven. They should still be warm.'

'Thanks.'

Julia retrieved the croissants, took a plate off the drainer, poured herself a mug of coffee from the percolator and sat down.

'You had a phone call this morning from our favourite cop,' Apostle said. 'He wanted to come over and see you, but I told him this morning wasn't convenient, that you needed to catch up on some sleep.'

'Vyse?' she said, startled. 'How did he know I was here?'

'He rang the office – that woman DC must have told him where you'd gone – but I have the calls put through to here when the office is empty. I said he could come round about two. Is that okay?'

Julia nodded. 'That's fine.'

'I'll make myself scarce when he gets here.'

'You don't need to do that,' she said quickly. 'I'd rather you stayed if you haven't got anything else you need to be doing.' Then, because she felt the need to provide some kind of explanation, she added, 'Cops make me nervous. I don't like being alone with them.'

'Know the feeling. Sure, I can stay if that's what you want.'

Julia nodded, relieved. There could be no talk of them having slept together while Apostle was around, no awkward conversations, no straying into territory of a more intimate nature. She pulled apart one of her croissants and took a series of small bites, surprised by how hungry she was. 'I wonder if they've found out anything. Did he say? No, I don't suppose he did.'

'No. He did seem a touch surprised at you being here, though.'

Julia shrugged as if she wasn't interested in what surprised the inspector. Then, suddenly, she remembered how the only person who had been in her bedroom apart from herself was Michael Vyse. Could he have taken the key to the bars on the window, slipped it into his pocket before he'd left? The very idea made her blood run cold. He couldn't have, wouldn't have.

'You all right?' Apostle said.

'It's all just catching up with me. My head's a bit frazzled. I don't know. It's a weird feeling, knowing that someone might have tried to kill me.'

'Yeah, it can't do much for your peace of mind. Although, like you said, it could have been someone who thought you were away.'

'I hope so. I mean, that's marginally better, isn't it? At least they wouldn't have been trying to burn me alive.'

'Always a plus. Any idea of your next move?'

'Call my landlord's agent and let him know about the fire, talk to the police, let my mum know where I'm staying, buy some new clothes, and probably all sorts of other things I haven't even thought of yet.'

'Feel free to use the phone. And there's a market at Brick Lane. I don't suppose there'll be much else open today, but you can pick up the essentials there and hit the shops tomorrow. We can drive over when you've finished your breakfast if you feel up to it.'

'Thanks,' she said, hoping she could at least find some underwear in the market and perhaps a few other items. 'If you really don't mind, that'd be great.'

'And don't worry about coming in to work tomorrow. I can cover the roster.'

'You don't need to do that, although having the morning off would be useful. How about I come in for the afternoon? To be honest I'd just as rather be working. It'll give me something else to think about.'

'Whatever's good for you.' Apostle slurped some of his coffee and said, 'What about the rest?'

'The rest?'

'There's a list of suspects from what you were telling me. When it comes to the fire, I mean. And the murders. Who's top of your list?'

'Pick a name, any name,' she said. 'I don't have a clue. Or maybe I have too many clues. Either way, I can't pick one person for sure. Most of them would have been at the Fox last night, but that doesn't mean anything. The fire wasn't started until the early hours.'

'Someone who has a car then. You're hardly likely to jump in a cab with a can of petrol in one hand and a box of matches in the other.'

'I don't know about Mark Grey, whether he's got a car or not. Tom has, and so does Frankie. I don't think Pauline does, but she might have access to her dad's van.' Just thinking about it all made Julia's head spin. 'I suppose whoever did it was either trying to kill me or to destroy whatever evidence they thought I might have in the flat. Someone tried to break in a while ago but didn't get very far. Perhaps they decided to take a more destructive route this time.'

'What kind of evidence?'

'I'm not sure. Something that Angel might have sent me – diaries, perhaps. No one seems to know if she was still keeping one, but if she was, she might have written down things they don't want me to know about. Or what they don't want the police to know about.'

'What sort of things?'

'I've no idea.'

'If you had those diaries, you'd have read them by now.'

'I know. It could even have been letters they were worried about, or something Angel might have told me on the phone. Perhaps they've been trying to figure out if I'll keep my mouth shut.'

'And come down on the side of unlikely.'

Julia ate some more croissant and drank some more coffee. 'It looks that way.' She glanced up with a wry smile. 'I hadn't actually talked to Angel in years, but I gave the impression that I had. Now they all think ... Christ, I don't know what they think.'

'We'll have to work out a way to flush them out.'

'Us?' she said, startled. 'Shouldn't we leave that to the cops?'

'And what kind of a job have they done to date? You're going to be looking over your shoulder every minute of every day until you find out who torched your flat.'

64

Pauline hadn't been surprised when the two uniformed cops turned up on her doorstep before she'd even had breakfast. She'd been expecting them – Carol had dropped by in the early hours of the morning to tell her about the fire at Julia's flat – and she'd guessed it was only a matter of time before Vyse sent his minions round to pick her up. The questioning had been the usual: what she was doing last night, where she was doing it, what time she left, what she did after, whether there were any witnesses.

Vyse had raised his eyebrows in that familiar way when she'd told him she'd been on her own from about eleven fifteen, after she'd walked back from the pub with Frankie. Why had Tom left early? She'd shrugged. Had there been a row? No. Where had her father been last night? Off shagging his lady friend. Vyse had smirked, the way men often do whenever sex is mentioned. Had she gone out again? No. When was the last time she saw Julia Reeve?

It was this that had caused her a moment's hesitation. But

she'd known almost instantly that there was no point lying about it. Julia *said* she could keep her mouth shut, but she might not be inclined to after someone had tried to burn down her flat. So, she'd told the truth, or at least some of it. That they'd bumped into each other in Kellston yesterday afternoon and gone to Connolly's for a cold drink and a chat. A chat about what? This and that. And Mark Grey, she'd added. Yeah, we talked about him too. I know you don't think he's guilty, but I do.

Pauline had said nothing about Carol, nothing about Angel and Frankie. If Julia decided to spill the beans, so be it, but she wasn't giving the law anything she didn't have to. Vyse hadn't been happy, but he'd had to let her go. Her dad wouldn't be happy either, not when he learned she'd been dragged down Cowan Road again. And if she didn't tell him, one of the neighbours would. Or one of his customers. Nothing was private on the Mansfield estate.

She reached out for the phone, lifted the receiver and put it down again. Tom would call when the law let him go. He always called. The day he didn't, she'd know something was seriously wrong.

65

The market was busy, and Julia quickly went from stall to stall searching for enough clothing and other essential items to see her through the next week or so. Apostle didn't crowd her but hung around on the periphery of her vision like an unpaid bodyguard. She was glad of his presence but a little uneasy about it too. Their employer/employee relationship had slipped into something more hazy, and she wasn't sure how to deal with it. They were hardly friends – she hadn't known him long enough for that – but he felt like more than her boss.

Julia noticed how people got out of his way as he walked along the aisles, his sheer size making them wary. Or perhaps it was that scar on his face. Or the expression that he wore, something that suggested he wasn't the type of man to appreciate random jostling. But he'd shown her nothing but kindness since she'd turned up at the office in the early hours of the morning. Had she misjudged him? Perhaps, for the first time, she was seeing him as Una did. He had even lent her one of his jackets, far too big but warm enough to keep the cold out.

Over an hour of hurried shopping saw her buy underwear, socks, tights, two pairs of trousers – one black, one grey – a pair of black ankle boots, two sweaters, a dark grey winter coat and a couple of white shirts. To this she added a few cheap T-shirts, some moisturiser, deodorant, shampoo and conditioner. She was thankful that she had money in the bank but was still careful not to spend too much. There were other things she'd need, and she worried about running out of cash.

It was a godsend that she'd saved her handbag from the fire; she always had some emergency make-up and a comb in it, as well as a small bottle of perfume. None of what she'd bought was high fashion, but it would have to do for now. She could pick up other things, like a smart dress, high heels and a rain-coat, during the week. She didn't need to be dressed up to the nines for work, but there would be occasions when she'd have to look smarter.

To thank Apostle for taking her to the market, and for everything else, Julia insisted on buying lunch. He chose a local burger bar, and she wasn't sure if this was out of concern for her finances or simply because he liked burgers. They both ordered glasses of Coke to eat with their meal.

'We'll make a list when we get back,' he said between mouthfuls. 'All the suspects. You can talk me through it.'

'I had one of those. It's not a long list.'

'Shouldn't be too hard to figure it out then.'

'If it was easy, I'd have done it by now.'

'Perhaps you're too close,' he said. 'Can't see the wood for the trees and all that. Didn't you say Frankie was a mechanic? He'd have easy access to petrol.'

'Everyone's got easy access. It's not hard to get hold of.'

'How's the boyfriend?' he said, suddenly changing the subject. 'Have you let Alex know about the fire?'

'Ex-boyfriend,' she said, too exhausted by everything that had happened to keep up the pretence. 'And before you say I told you so, that long-distance relationships never work, it was on the rocks before I even left Suffolk. He wasn't what you'd call the faithful sort.'

'Ah, a cheater. Why do men do that?'

Julia gave him a scrutinising look, as if his tongue might be firmly in his cheek, but his expression was more enquiring than amused. 'To prove that they can, I suppose. Some kind of ego thing.'

'Sounds like a lot of bother to me, all that stress over being caught out, all the worry and the lies, not to mention the joy of bumping into them or one of their friends when you're wining and dining the fancy piece. Then the confrontation, all the rows and recriminations. No, it's not for me. Makes me tired just talking about it.'

'You've given it some thought then.'

Apostle grinned, but then his expression grew serious. 'I've never cheated on a woman I've been in a steady relationship with. There are girls I see on a casual basis, but they know where they stand, and so do I. I like to keep things simple.' He scoffed another quarter of his burger. 'Women cheat too, of course. It's not an exclusively male pastime.'

Julia heard an unexpected edge to his voice and recalled what Una had said about Alice Irwin, the girl who had died of the drugs overdose. 'I'm just glad it's over. Being single has a lot to recommend it.'

'Does it?' he said pensively. 'I'm not so sure.' He gathered up some fries and shoved them in his mouth. Then he ate the last of his burger, chewed, swallowed and sighed. 'Ah, that's better. I haven't eaten all day.'

'Didn't you have croissants at breakfast?'

'They don't count as real food.' Apostle wiped his hands on a napkin. 'So this ex of yours. Is he the vengeful type?'

'God, no. And he certainly didn't set fire to the flat, if that's what you're thinking.'

'Okay. We can cross him off the list then.'

'He was never on the list.'

'Good. That's one less person to worry about.' Apostle checked his flashy watch. 'We should get going. Vyse is due at two.'

Julia's heart sank at the prospect. Wearily, she got to her feet.

'Perhaps he'll have good news for you.'

'I live in hope.'

'Try telling your face that.'

Julia took a deep breath and exhaled. She wasn't looking forward to seeing Vyse, not one little bit.

66

DI Vyse accepted a cup of coffee as he sat down opposite Julia at the kitchen table. His gaze kept flicking between her and Apostle, his brow crunched into a frown, as if he was trying to understand what she was doing there. She could tell he'd prefer to talk to her alone but she had insisted that Apostle stayed.

'I've told him everything,' she said, before quickly correcting herself. 'I mean, everything to do with Angel and Lindsay. He knows about the murders and the attempted break-in. Do you have any news on the fire?'

'Nothing more than you've already been told. I had all the usual suspects brought in this morning, but they're denying any knowledge of it.'

'Big surprise,' Apostle said.

Vyse threw him a hostile look and made a point of addressing only Julia. 'All in bed allegedly, apart from Tom Finch who claims he "went for a drive" in the early hours but can't remember exactly where to.'

'You don't believe him,' she said.

'I don't believe any of them.'

'Wouldn't Tom have got himself a better alibi if he'd been planning on burning down my flat? He'd know you were bound to talk to him.'

'Sometimes people panic, do stupid things. He admitted that you'd told him you were going to Suffolk, and that he told the others in the Fox last night. How come you changed your mind?'

'I decided to leave it until next weekend, spend a couple of days there instead of just one. I had some calls in the evening, but I didn't answer the phone.'

'Why not?'

'I wasn't in the mood for chatting. It upset me going to the river with Tom, seeing where Angel died.'

'I called about six,' Vyse said, 'to see how you were doing. When did the other calls come in?'

'One around half five, another after eight o'clock. I went to bed early so there could have been later ones that I didn't hear.'

'I'll get the phone records checked, see if we can trace the other calls.'

Julia was aware of Apostle looking at her, as if he sensed there was something more to all this, and deliberately avoided meeting his eyes. 'Do you think someone was ringing to see if I was there?'

'Could have been.'

'Or not there. I mean, that's possible too, isn't it? Someone checking that I *wasn't* in the flat.'

'It's an option.'

'What about Mark Grey? Have you talked to him?' Julia knew that her voice sounded tight and strained and knew too that only part of that was down to the ordeal she'd been through. It was hard sitting there, looking at the man she'd fallen into bed with so recently, the man she'd had feelings for, the man who was married. She was fighting hard to keep the resentment from her tone; this wasn't the time for settling scores.

'Asleep,' he said. 'You've been chatting to Pauline.'

'Yesterday afternoon. She seems convinced he's involved.'

'Despite the lack of any evidence whatsoever.'

Julia shrugged. 'I don't trust him. He's hiding something.'

'That could be said of any of them, all of them.'

Apostle sat forward. 'They could have killed her. She was lucky to get out of that flat alive.'

'I'm well aware of that,' Vyse said curtly. 'Why do you think I'm here?'

'God knows. You don't seem to have anything useful to bring to the table. Wouldn't you be more gainfully employed back in Kellston, trying to find out who the arsonist is?'

'What do you think I have been doing?'

'Without much success by the sound of it.'

The two men glared at each other like a pair of street dogs gearing up for a scrap. It was nothing to do with her, with the fire, with Angel, and everything to do with their own male egos. Vyse was the first to look away, transferring his attention to Julia. 'Believe me, we're giving this our full attention.'

The last thing Julia needed was these two at each other's throats. She had her own reasons for resenting Vyse, and this was just an extra dose of trouble. 'I know. I understand. Do you have any idea what state the flat's in?' she hurriedly asked before things between the two men escalated.

'From what I've heard there won't be anything salvageable. Sorry. The place was pretty much gutted. What are your plans? Will you be staying here or . . .'

'No,' she said.

'Yes,' Apostle said at the same time. He glanced at Julia. 'You may as well. It's better than some grubby B & B.'

Julia didn't contradict him. She had no intention of staying more than a few days but that conversation could wait. Her thoughts had turned back to the missing window key and whether Vyse could have taken it. Sleep with her and then try and kill her? Was that possible? And if so, why? Her mouth had gone dry. No, he had no reason – or at least none that she could think of.

'You all right?' Vyse asked. 'You're looking pale.'

Julia rubbed her face. 'It's just the shock of it all. I can't get my head around it.'

'I know. It's shit. But we'll get whoever did this.'

Apostle rolled his eyes.

'I hope so,' she said.

'Well, we'll keep you informed,' Vyse said, rising to his feet.

Julia showed him out. At the door he turned, placed his hand on her arm and said, 'Are you sure you're all right? Carol should have called me when she heard about the fire. I'd have come over myself.'

'There's nothing you could have done,' she said, moving slightly to the side and extricating herself from his hold.

Vyse's eyebrows shifted up enquiringly. 'Julia?'

'This is all too complicated,' she said, keeping her voice low so Apostle wouldn't hear. 'You and me. Sorry, but I can't deal with it. There's too much going on. I think it might be better if . . . you know . . . we just keep things on a professional footing for now.'

Vyse looked pained, then gave a shrug. 'If that's what you want.'

'I think it's for the best.' Julia could have mentioned Mrs Vyse, but she didn't. She didn't want to hear the story about

398

how his wife didn't understand him, or some such other guff. And she didn't want to antagonise him either. Not while he was working on the case. Once it was over, she could say what she liked.

'Take care of yourself,' he said, although his expression had changed, and she wasn't sure how genuine the sentiment was.

'You too.'

When he'd left, she leaned against the door for a few seconds, listening to the retreat of his footsteps, relieved that he had gone. Then she went back into the kitchen.

'What was all that about?' Apostle said.

'I was about to say the same thing. You two were at each other's throats from the minute he got here. I know you don't like him but . . .'

'I can't stand the man. He's a waste of space. A few years back, if he'd had his way, he'd have locked me up and thrown away the key. Never mind the evidence – or lack of it – he put me well and truly in the frame. He's a lazy bastard, always after an easy collar. It cost me an arm and a leg in solicitor's fees to get off the charge. And I wasn't guilty, in case you're wondering. Anyway, that's my gripe, what's your story?'

'What do you mean?'

'You two whispering at the door. What was all that about?'

'No one was whispering,' she said.

'Sounded like it from here.'

Julia feigned innocence. 'I've got no idea what you mean.'

Apostle stared at her for a while and then shook his head. 'Okay, it's your business not mine. I'll shut up.'

Julia sat down, drank some coffee and watched him over the rim of her mug. The seconds ticked by. She didn't want to tell him, wasn't going to tell him. Some things were private. She absolutely wasn't going to go there.

'I did something stupid,' she said.

'You wouldn't be the first.'

Julia groaned. 'What can I say? I'm a fool. It's no excuse, but I didn't know he was married.'

'Forgot to mention it, did he?'

'It was just the once. Not that that makes it any better. I've just told him that we should leave it now, that's it's too complicated, what with the fire and the other investigations still going on.' Her mouth twisted. 'God, why am I such an idiot? My taste in men is beyond the pale.'

Apostle gave a snort. 'I know the feeling. Not men, obviously, but I've kissed a female frog or two. Come on, it's not the end of the world. We all screw up from time to time and right now you've got more important things to worry about.'

'You're right.' Julia reached out and slipped a sheet of paper from the pile in front of him. On it was the newly written suspect list. She stared at the names, willing one of them to jump out at her. 'Perhaps they're not even on here. Perhaps it's someone I've not thought of.'

'It's one of them,' Apostle said. 'It has to be. So are you up for it?'

'Up for it?' she echoed, frowning.

'Nailing them once and for all. You can't go on like this. We have to flush them out, make them break cover.'

'This isn't your problem.'

'You keep saying that but of course it is. Next time you might not be so lucky. And then what? I'll be left looking for a new PA.'

'You're all heart.'

'Just being practical,' he said, grinning. 'And we can't rely on Vyse. If we want this sorted, we'll have to do it ourselves.'

'And how do you suggest we do that?'

'Call their bluff. Tell them you know everything. Tell them Angel told you.'

Julia shook her head. 'They're not going to fall for that. It's only going to take thirty seconds for that little ploy to unravel.'

'Depends how you play it. It'll be enough to get them worried, enough to ensure they take notice and show up. One of these alibis, maybe more than one, is fake. They have to be. Someone knows a damn sight more than they're saying.'

'Why do I get the feeling this could end badly?'

'It will end badly,' he said, 'if you don't take control now.'

'Of course,' she said. 'But . . .'

'No buts.'

He was right, Julia thought. She could be a victim, waiting for the next bad thing to happen, or she could take the initiative and face it all head on. She stared down at the list of names for a moment and then looked up again. 'Can I use your phone?'

67

Julia had chosen to meet them on the green, close to where they lived but far enough away from prying eyes and ears to grant them some privacy. Although Connolly's wasn't closed on a Sunday it was too big a risk to have the kind of conversation she wanted there. They could have gathered in a flat, Tom's or Pauline's perhaps, but she had no desire to be in a confined space with people that she couldn't trust. Anyway, out in the open they could talk freely.

She and Apostle arrived early. He parked the car down a side street, and they crossed the road and walked together to the scrubby piece of land that lay adjacent to the high street. At the far end was a row of houses and either side was bounded by trees and shrubs. Autumn leaves lay thickly on the ground, a crumpled rustling blanket of russet and gold.

'I'll make myself scarce,' he said, looking round. 'I can see the green from the car.'

'They're just going to deny everything.' Julia sighed into the chill afternoon air. 'It won't take them long to realise I'm bluffing.'

'But you're not bluffing, not entirely. There are things you know about Frankie, about Pauline, that they don't want to be public knowledge.'

'The Frankie and Angel thing is no big secret. Well, not in the group – or what's left of it.'

'Yeah, but the law don't know.'

Julia was starting to wonder if she'd told him too much, but in the aftermath of the fire he'd been the only person she could talk to. 'Blackmail them, you mean?'

'One of them burned your flat down. This isn't the time for scruples.'

And she supposed he was right, although it didn't sit well with her. She had some leverage if she was prepared to use it. 'I guess.'

'Play them off against each other,' he said. 'Something's got to give.'

Julia nodded, even though she wasn't entirely persuaded by the argument. She glanced at her watch. 'You'd better go. They'll be here soon.'

She watched as he walked away, wondering if she could hold her nerve. Think of the fire, she told herself, think of how things might have turned out if her wonderful upstairs neighbour hadn't come to the rescue. She'd have to take him something, a bottle of whisky perhaps, although it seemed small reward for saving her life.

Julia's chest still felt tight, a legacy from the smoke. She put her hand to her mouth and coughed. Her gaze raked the green. It was getting dark, dusk falling, the light shimmering into a dull gunmetal grey. There would be no Mark this afternoon, despite Pauline's insistence of his guilt. None of the other peripheral characters either. The answers lay with the old gang. Was she sure of that? No, she wasn't sure at all, but she had to start somewhere.

Frankie was the first to arrive, parking his white van on double yellow lines near the edge of the green. He was wearing a khaki parka and pulled the hood up against the drizzling rain as he walked towards her. He smiled but his face was tight.

'I heard about the fire. Shit, that was awful. How are you doing?'

'About as well as anyone who's just escaped death by the skin of their teeth.'

'Jesus, why would anyone do that?'

'I wish I knew.'

'What do the law think?'

Julia didn't get the chance to answer. Tom was striding across the green with Pauline at his side. Her expression, just for a change, was thunderous. She stomped up to Julia and glared at her. 'What the hell's going on? Tom said you wanted to see us, *demanded* to see us. We're not at your beck and call, you know. Some of us have got things to do.'

'I didn't say she demanded to see us,' Tom said calmly, 'only that she'd like to see us.'

'That wasn't the impression I got. On the green at three thirty, you said. I don't remember anyone saying please.'

Julia inclined her head and stared back at her old adversary. Somehow Pauline always made everything about her, as if *she'd* been the one fighting for her life last night, sucking in the smoky air, wondering if she'd ever get out of a burning deathtrap flat. 'Don't worry, this won't take long.'

'Well, I could do without standing around here in the rain and the freezing cold. Why don't we go to the caff?'

'I'd rather we stayed here.'

Pauline opened her mouth, thought better of it and closed it again.

'So what's the big mystery?' Frankie said. 'What did you want to see us about?'

Julia cleared her throat and prepared for battle. 'I know what you did,' she said to no one in particular, trying to keep her voice firm. 'And I'm guessing that someone here knows that I know, someone who wants me to keep my mouth shut.'

There was an odd silence, followed by a dull laugh from Pauline. 'What *we* did. I might have guessed you'd be looking to blame us for something, but what exactly? I'd like to know what we're being accused of. I'm sure we all would. Perhaps you'd like to enlighten us.'

Julia, who didn't have an answer to this, resorted to deflection. 'And I'd like to know who tried to kill me last night or burn my flat down at least. I'd like to know who tried to break in a while ago, who's being trying to scare me rigid, who left me a lock of Lindsay's hair after she'd been murdered.'

'What?' Tom said. 'Lindsay's hair? No, shit, are you serious?'

'It's hardly something to joke about.' Julia had promised Vyse that she wouldn't mention the hair, but she needed to shock her old mates out of their smug sense of security and throw them off balance.

'Mark Grey,' Pauline said. 'That bastard must have done it.'

'Mark Grey doesn't even know where I live.'

'So what are you saying – that it was one of us?' Pauline snorted and waved her hands around. 'You see, didn't I tell you? She's been trying to pin something on us ever since she first showed up.'

'You've all been lying to me ever since I first showed up.'

'That's not true,' Tom said. 'What have we lied about?'

'About Angel and Frankie for starters.'

'Oh, not this again,' Pauline said. 'Change the record, can't you?'

'I could go to the police with what I know, with what Lindsay told me, but I thought I'd give you the chance to explain.'

Frankie put his hands in his pockets and kicked at the ground with the heel of his foot. 'Don't blame them; they were just protecting me. But I swear on my kids' lives that I didn't kill Angel. I *didn't*.' Then he paused as if what she'd said had only just registered. 'What do you mean what Lindsay told you?'

'When we met up in Covent Garden.' Julia was whistling in the wind, trying to provoke a reaction, hoping to latch on to a thread of truth. 'About Angel's diaries.'

Pauline shook her head. 'How many times have I told you? Angel stopped keeping a diary years ago.'

'Did she? Are you certain about that?'

'She never lied to me,' Pauline said, although now she didn't sound so sure of herself. 'Did Lindsay tell you something different?'

'Lindsay told me all sorts of things. She was scared, you see, afraid of what would happen to her if the truth came out. And she was right to be afraid, wasn't she?'

'Bullshit,' Pauline said.

'What would she be afraid of?' Tom said.

Julia, who hadn't got a clue, stared right at him. 'You know what.'

Tom instantly glanced away. He had the guilty look of a five-year-old caught with his hand in the biscuit tin.

'I'll just take what I know to the law then, shall I? Let them sort it out. Everything out in the open so they've got the full picture.'

Pauline, probably thinking about Carol Forshaw, didn't seem happy at this prospect and was perhaps beginning to regret her earlier attitude. 'For God's sake, Julia, there's no need for that. Do you want to ruin Frankie's life? The law are going to think he killed Angel to cover up them sleeping together.'

'Which I bloody well didn't,' Frankie said. 'Kill her, I mean. I wouldn't have touched a hair on Angel's head. You believe me, don't you, Julia? You said you did. I'll end up in jail even though I didn't do it. Clare's going to leave me if this comes out. She'll take the kids and go.'

'Is that what you want?' Pauline said. 'To ruin his life, to ruin all our lives?'

'How would I be ruining all your lives?'

Pauline made a huffy noise in the back of her throat. 'Don't you think we've been through enough?'

'Don't you think *I've* been through enough?' Julia said, throwing it straight back at her. 'I could be lying in the morgue right now. And I'm not going to wait for someone to have another go. So, to get back to the diaries – we have the last five years missing. You see, I thought at first that it was all to do with covering up for Frankie, but it's more than that, isn't it?' She'd rehearsed this bit with Apostle in the warm kitchen at the Barbican, a shot in the dark but worth trying. 'Lindsay was worried about something else coming out.'

Pauline rolled her eyes. 'Lindsay didn't get much attention. I dare say she was just trying to make herself sound interesting.'

'No, it was more than that.'

Tom was keeping quiet now, gazing off into the middle distance as if he'd disconnected from the conversation.

'Tom?' Julia said.

'Huh?'

'What do you have to say?'

Tom shook his head. 'I know you think we're hiding things but we're not.'

'You can say that as often as you like, but I still don't believe you.'

'Lindsay could be a bit . . .'

'A bit what?'

'Over-excitable, I suppose,' Tom said. 'Nervy. Angel's death knocked her for six. Well, it knocked all of us for six. I don't know what she suggested to you, but we're not responsible for Angel's death. None of us are.'

'So what are you responsible for?'

Tom shrugged, looked away. 'Nothing.'

'Angel didn't stop keeping a diary,' Julia said, trying to sound confident. 'Well, perhaps for a while, but then she started up again. She didn't tell any of you because she knew you wouldn't approve. No, it would have been more than disapproval. Dangerous, perhaps, if those diaries fell into the wrong hands.'

'Dangerous,' Pauline scoffed. 'What the hell could Angel write that could be dangerous?'

'Something from the past,' Julia said.

'What kind of something?' Frankie said sharply.

Pauline threw him a warning glance. 'Don't listen to her. She's just making it up as she goes along.'

'You want to take that chance?' Julia said. 'I might not have all the details, but I've got enough to shake things up.'

'You've got nothing,' Pauline said.

'So there is something?'

'I didn't say that.'

Frankie started to walk away. 'Come on, let's get under the trees. It's going to pour down.'

As they all shifted to the edge of the green, between the tall sycamores and the bushes, Julia glanced towards the side street where Apostle was waiting in the Jag. She would be passing out of sight of him – and him of her – and had to suppress a sudden jolt of fear. Three against one if they decided to silence her for ever. But why would they? She sensed that she was rapidly losing the advantage, if she'd had any to begin with, and that they knew her threats were empty ones.

'We're going round in circles here,' Pauline said, the exasperation clear in her voice. 'There weren't any diaries, none of us killed Angel, none of us set fire to your flat. Why can't you understand that? It's like you *want* us to be guilty.'

'I just want you to tell me what's going on.'

'What's going on,' Pauline said, 'is that we're being dragged down the nick every five minutes because DI Vyse wants to blame us for every crime in London. And to be honest, Julia, you're not helping. I'm sorry about your flat and everything, but none of us had anything to do with it.'

'Okay, have it your own way,' Julia said.

'What's that supposed to mean?'

'If none of you are prepared to be honest with me, I'll have to go and see Vyse.'

'Go ahead,' Pauline said. 'You're only going to make yourself look stupid.'

'For fuck's sake, Pauline, do you want to see me in jail?' Frankie said.

'You don't go to jail for sleeping with someone.'

'He'll tell Clare. You know what the bastard's like.' Frankie turned pleading eyes on Julia. 'Please don't. She won't forgive me; I know she won't. And once Vyse hears that I lied about Angel, he'll find a way to stitch me up.'

Julia suspected that he was right. From what she'd learned about Vyse, he wasn't much concerned with the niceties of the law. 'So tell me what's going on.'

'I've had enough of this,' Pauline said. 'I'm going home. Are you coming, Tom?'

Tom nodded, then looked at Julia and said, 'I'm sorry. I mean about everything that's happened to you. I really am.'

But Tom's sympathy wasn't what Julia wanted or needed. Frustration rippled through her. She was no better off now than when she'd arrived, Angel's killer still on the loose, her arsonist still unknown. She'd played her cards and lost. They were all sticking to their story, sticking together, and that's how it was going to stay.

Julia folded her arms across her chest as the two of them left. Rain was dripping down from the canopy above and sliding down her neck. She felt cold, beaten and demoralised, no better off now than when she'd arrived.

'Do you need a lift?' Frankie said.

'No, thanks, I'm . . .' She was about to say that she'd come with someone but then changed her mind. The less anyone knew about her business the better. 'I'm fine. I'll get the bus.'

Frankie shifted from foot to foot, glanced at her and glanced away. As if he was trying to decide whether to say something else or not. She kept quiet. He waited until Tom and Pauline were out of earshot, and then said, 'There's something I need to show you.'

'What's that?'

'It's in the van. You can't tell the others though.'

'God, Frankie, haven't there been enough secrets?'

'Do you want to see it or not?'

Julia nodded, and then followed him as he wound through the back of the trees, faintly excited by this new development. Something and nothing? Probably. Or, with the most to lose, was he about to break ranks with the other two? They emerged onto the high street a few yards behind the van. From here her view of the Jag was still obscured – the van was in the way – and she wondered if Apostle was getting tired of waiting. He'd be disappointed if she came back empty-handed, but not as disappointed as her.

Frankie slid open the side door to the van and jumped inside. 'It's here,' he said, pushing aside a heap of old coveralls and tools. 'Get in the van. I don't want it to get wet.'

Julia should have thought twice but she didn't. The lure of some new evidence was too much for her. She joined him in the back, hunching down and peering through the murky light. 'What is it?'

Frankie retrieved a dark-coloured book, about six by four inches, and held it up. The front was embossed in gold with the date 1989. 'Is this what you've been looking for?'

'Is it Angel's diary?'

Frankie passed it to her.

No sooner was it in her hand, no sooner had she opened it to the first page, when the blow came to the side of her head. She felt a sharp pain, then felt herself keel to the side as darkness descended.

68

Julia wasn't sure how long she'd been unconscious. Not *that* long, she figured, as her eyes flickered open, but long enough for Frankie to tie her hands behind her back. She was lying on her side with her knees pulled up. It was dark. The floor smelled of old dust, grease and petrol. There was a throbbing from the side of her head. The van was moving and every jolt in the road made the pain a little bit worse.

Why had she been so stupid as to get into the van? Hardly a question she need linger on right now. More importantly: what was Frankie planning on doing with her? And the answer to that was so blatantly obvious that a shudder ran through her body. He had fooled her completely, made her believe in his innocence, when all the time he was a murderer. He had killed Angel and taken her diary so the police wouldn't find out about the affair. Did the others know? Or had he relied on them to believe in his innocence?

Julia tried to twist her wrists, to free herself, but only succeeded in chafing the skin. She swore. God, she had only just escaped death by the skin of her teeth and now she was staring it straight in the face again. A groan escaped from her lips. Her pulse was racing, her heart thumping in her chest. It was cold and her teeth had begun to chatter. What had possessed her to get in the damn van?

But she didn't need to worry, surely, because Apostle must be hot on their heels, right behind them. However, the comfort this brought was only temporary. Perhaps he wasn't. Apostle would have seen Tom and Pauline leaving and waited patiently (or impatiently) for her to appear. Then, because he wouldn't have been able to see behind the van, the next thing he'd have noticed was Frankie driving off alone. What would his first thought have been? Not that she was in the back of the van but that something had happened to her on the green. He would have got out of the Jag, run across, searched among the trees and by the time he realised she wasn't there, the van would be long gone.

Julia felt her stomach plummet. She was on her own. There would be no one to come riding to the rescue. She felt the van begin to slow, to turn a corner, then continue for a few hundred yards until it came to a halt. By now she was trembling, trying to think straight and failing. What to do? She didn't know. This was Frankie, she reminded herself, the boy she'd grown up with. Could he really kill her in cold blood? But if he'd killed Angel then familiarity was clearly no obstacle.

She heard the van door shut and then Frankie slid open the side, allowing a grey oblong of light to filter through the space.

'Don't make a sound,' he said, leaning in. There was a flash of silver: a knife in his hand.

'What are you doing? This is crazy.'

'What did I just say? Keep your fuckin' mouth shut, Julia, or I'll finish it right here.'

Julia nodded, blind obedience being the most obvious course of action. Until she could work out a way to escape. What were the chances? Slim but not impossible.

Frankie grabbed her arm and half yanked, half dragged her out of the van. Her left hip and knee scraped against the hard metal of the floor. Her right elbow felt in danger of dislocation. She winced, sucked in a breath, landed shakily on her feet and looked around. Instantly she knew where they were: a deserted part of Kellston, an out-of-the-way lane with a few dilapidated sheds but not a house in sight. It was a route they'd often used as kids, their own secret path into the old part of the cemetery.

'You know the way,' Frankie said, closing the van door and lightly shoving her in the back.

Julia realised there was no point in screaming because there was no one to hear. It was almost dark now and the cemetery would be locked up for the night. Where better to dispose of a body? She tramped ahead of him along the narrow muddy path. Making a run for it didn't seem on the cards; it was hard to sprint with your hands tied behind your back. The rain was coming down hard now, soaking them both.

The path wound round until they reached a slatted wooden gate to their left, its presence almost obscured by undergrowth, its hinges close to being rusted away. Frankie leaned around her, forced it open and pushed her forward. Now they were inside the cemetery, it was tougher going, the ground uneven, the long grass brushing against her legs. This part had always been neglected, the ancient headstones leaning, their epitaphs worn thin by the years. An occasional stone angel loomed into view, tall and imposing, hands clasped in prayer.

'They'll know it was you,' she said.

'I left you at the green,' he said. 'I offered you a lift, but you said you'd rather get the bus.'

'They won't believe you.'

'We'll see.'

Keep him talking, she thought. They were approaching the old mausoleums now, a cluster of small stone buildings like tiny houses for the dead. As a kid these resting places had both fascinated and appalled her with their heavy iron doors and their locks and the awful horrors that lay within. 'You could at least tell me why.'

'This is as far as we go,' he said.

Julia stopped and looked over her shoulder at him. 'Here?'

'Why not?' he said. 'It's as good a place as any.'

She strained her ears, hoping for some slight sound, for an indication they were not alone. Even now, when the possibility seemed remote, she was still hoping for salvation. But there was nothing, only the heavy beat of the rain and the wind shifting busily through the trees. She would not be found, she thought, for a long time. No one visited this old part anymore. Although maybe the smell would eventually alert someone, a sickening aroma floating on the air.

She leaned back against the edge of a crumbling tombstone, still attempting to free her wrists from the rope that bound them, frantically wriggling her hands even though it made no difference. Keep him talking. 'Why did you kill Angel? I don't understand. I thought you loved her, cared about her at least.'

'How many times?' Frankie said. 'I didn't kill her. Why would I kill her?'

'So what am I doing here?'

'Christ, Julia, why do you think? You said you were going to the law.'

'And that's a good reason to tie me up and bring me here, to threaten me with a knife, to . . .?' Julia couldn't quite bring herself to finish the sentence. To say it out loud might remind him of what he intended to do, even propel him into action. 'You're just making everything worse.'

'It couldn't get any worse.'

Julia was at a loss. If he hadn't killed Angel, then what were they doing here? This couldn't just be about Clare finding out about the affair. 'I won't go to the law. You know I won't. It was just something to say. I didn't mean it. So it was Mark Grey who murdered Angel? Or do you still think she killed herself?'

Frankie was looking round, probably keeping his eyes peeled for any unwelcome company. The two main gates might be locked to the public but there could still be cemetery staff roaming through the grounds. She had the feeling he wasn't really listening to her. 'Mark Grey,' she repeated. 'Was Pauline right all along?'

Frankie focused his eyes on her again. 'Mark Grey,' he echoed sneeringly. 'As if he'd ever have the nerve. For a bright girl, you can be incredibly stupid at times.'

'I don't get it,' she said.

He gave a thin laugh as if she'd just proved his point. He waved the knife, long and sharp, towards the mausoleums. 'Do you remember this place?'

'Of course I do. We used to come here when we were kids, dare each other to run up and knock on the doors. It always creeped the hell out of me.'

'Yeah, Angel would never do it. She was scared that someone inside might actually open up.'

A silence fell between them, and Julia was transported back to the time of their adolescence. In the hot summer months, the five of them, pre-Pauline, would come here, hunker down between the graves and talk of . . . She tried to remember what it was they *had* talked about. Not that it mattered. She had to keep her wits about her, not get distracted by the past.

Frankie walked a short way towards the mausoleums, turned and retraced his steps. He seemed unsteady on his feet, and she wondered if he was drunk. She hadn't noticed it on the green and when he'd pulled her from the van, she'd been too terrified to notice anything. But now she took note of his weaving gait and of the glaze in his eyes. Was this a good or a bad thing? Good in that he might make a mistake, give her an opportunity to escape somehow; bad in that the booze might give him the courage to do the unthinkable.

'So Angel *did* kill herself,' Julia said, trying to engage him again. All she could do was play for time until she came up with a better idea. 'It was suicide.'

Frankie's lips twisted into a bitter smile. 'No, it wasn't suicide.'

Julia mentally ran through her original list of suspects: Tom, Pauline, Clare, George? 'Come on, Frankie. What difference does it make? You may as well tell me.'

Frankie was looking round again, head cocked, ears alert to any sound, like some small jittery animal used to being preyed on. Night was descending, the twilight throwing a grey wash over everything, blurring the edges. Soon it would be dark. Was that what he was waiting for? He was quiet for a while. She thought he wasn't going to answer, but then slowly he began to speak.

'I did think she'd killed herself at first. It wasn't beyond her. She liked grand gestures.' He frowned. 'Is that what I mean? I dunno. Just that things got her down. She couldn't always see the bigger picture. She lived in the moment and if that moment was bad then ... I'm just saying that she could have done it. A spur-of-the-moment thing. But then Pauline started up with all her Mark Grey suspicions and I began to think that maybe she was right.'

'But it wasn't Mark, was it?'

417

'Just listen,' he said sharply. 'Shut up, right? I got to thinking, that's all. Late one night when Clare and the kids were in bed, I went round to see Lindsay. I figured if Mark had done it, then she'd know. Maybe she was covering up for him. I wanted some answers. That's not too much to ask, is it? Just some bloody answers.'

Julia nodded, too wary at this point to open her mouth again.

'Anyway, she got the hump when she realised where I was going with it all. Her Mark a murderer? I was crazy, I was being fuckin' ridiculous and all the rest of it. Like I was insulting her by even suggesting it. He'd never do anything like that. Why would he? What was the matter with me? Then she got all upset and started crying and I felt shitty because I hadn't gone there to make her feel bad. So I apologised, said I wasn't thinking straight, that I wasn't coping and hadn't meant any of it. She went to make me a coffee, and that's when I saw it lying on the table. You know what I mean, right?'

'The diary,' Julia muttered.

'Yeah, the diary. She was in the kitchen, so I flipped it open and that's when I realised that it was Angel's. Weird, right? I mean, what was Angel's diary doing at Lindsay's? That didn't make any sense. Not unless ...' Frankie stopped, frowned, glared at her. 'Do you see where I'm going with this?'

Julia did see and was wishing now that she hadn't asked him to explain. Once the words were out of his mouth, there was no going back. By then she would know too much, and the outcome was inevitable. Not that it was exactly in the balance now. 'But Lindsay was with Pauline all afternoon. She couldn't have killed Angel.'

'Alibis,' he scoffed. 'The two of them cooked that up between them. They must have done.'

'Why would they?' Julia said, although she was already

beginning to suspect. Pauline had gone to see Carol perhaps, a fact she wouldn't want anyone else to know about. And Lindsay, if she'd done what Frankie was suggesting, would have been more than happy to oblige her with a rock-solid alibi for the missing hours.

Frankie didn't answer. He had begun to wind between the gravestones, stopping and starting, muttering to himself. Occasionally he paused to stare at one of the mausoleums as if weighing it up for an additional occupant. Then he turned back to Julia and narrowed his eyes.

'She told me Angel had asked her to fetch a mug from her bedroom and she'd spotted the diary lying under the bed. The key was in the lock and so she'd opened it. Curiosity, that's all. And there was Mark's name, and her name, and so she'd shoved it in her bag and taken it home with her.'

'What else was in the diary?' Julia said.

Frankie looked at her, gave a low laugh. 'Everything Lindsay didn't want to read. That Angel was going to meet Mark that afternoon to get her birthday present. And a load of stuff about him chasing her, the gifts, the promises, how he'd leave Lindsay for her – all she had to do was say the word. All laid out in black and white like a stab to the heart. It was Mark she should have hated, Mark she should have taken to the river, but instead she focused all her rage on Angel.'

'And she just told you all this, confessed to killing her?'

'Bang to rights, wasn't she? Caught red-handed. She didn't even try to deny it. She said Angel had led him on, that she'd got what she deserved. Bare-faced the bitch was. Cold as ice. And then she laughed, she laughed, for fuck's sake. Like she'd done something clever and got away with it. She said Angel hadn't suspected a thing when she'd called half an hour after leaving the flat, that she'd thought going to the river was all part of her birthday celebrations, something I'd planned to surprise her. Well, I saw red, didn't I? She'd killed Angel, left her to drown, and now she was laughing about it.'

While Julia was coming to terms with all this, she was also trying to work out if she could get close enough to Frankie to give him one debilitating kick to the balls. But how far could she run before he recovered sufficiently to chase after her? If her wrists hadn't been bound, she might have stood a chance of reaching the newer part of the cemetery where there were houses backing on, where there were people who might hear her screams. As it was, she'd be hard pressed to make a few hundred yards. Her head still throbbed from where he'd hit her. The knife was gripped tightly in his hand. If she misaimed, if he dodged out of the way, she'd be dead for sure.

'I'd gone there in the van,' Frankie said, as if now he'd started, he had to give her every detail. 'When I got to the estate, I realised I still had my tools in the back. That place is full of thieving toerags, so I took the bag up with me. Better to be safe than sorry, right? Anyway, I couldn't stand it, Julia, listening to her come out with all her garbage. You understand, don't you?' He didn't wait for a reply. 'I just lost it, opened the bag, took out the hammer and . . .'

'Yeah, I understand,' Julia said softly, moving away from the grave she'd been leaning against.

Instantly Frankie was on the alert. 'What are you doing?'

'I'm cold. I need to move around a bit. Why did you set fire to my flat?'

'I didn't know you were there, I swear. Tom said you'd gone away, gone home for the weekend. I rang from a phone box in Camden and there was no reply. There was no light on either, so I thought . . .

'Yeah, but *why* set fire to it?'

420

'I thought you might have the other diaries. I thought Angel might have given them to you.'

'But you already had the important one, the most recent, the one you wouldn't have wanted Clare to see. What did it matter if I had the others?'

Frankie's eyes grew sly. 'Did you?'

Julia shook her head and moved a step closer. 'No. What was so important about them?'

'Nothing,' he said, but she knew he was lying. 'Stay where you are.' He brandished the knife as she shifted forward a little more.

'You sent me the hair too, didn't you? Lindsay's hair.'

'I meant to plant it on Grey – it was the least he deserved – but I couldn't get into his flat. It was too risky to hold on to it, and you were asking all those questions and I thought it might make you back off. I just wanted to keep you safe, Julia. None of this had anything to do with you. You should have kept out of it.'

'I had to find out what happened to Angel.'

'You should have let things be.'

Julia was starting to wish that she had. She knew that confession wasn't good, at least not for the person being confessed to. He couldn't let her go now. She knew too much. A distraction was what she needed, something to make him take his eyes off her. Just for a second, just long enough for her to get within kicking distance. While she waited for some inspiration, she tried a spot of wheedling.

'It doesn't need to be like this. We've always been mates, haven't we? Did I tell Clare about you and Angel? No. I kept my mouth shut. And I won't tell anyone about Lindsay either. I mean, she killed Angel, didn't she? She only got what she deserved.'

'It's been a long time since we were mates, Julia.'

'I'm not going to go running to the law.'

Frankie sighed into the gloom of the evening. 'I wish I could believe you, but I don't.' He looked at the knife, looked at her. She could almost see the decision landing on his face. It was now or never.

'Over here!' she yelled, staring over his shoulder.

Frankie automatically turned his head, and she seized the opportunity to lurch forward, pull back her right leg, bend her knee and aim her foot straight for the sweet spot. The toe of her boot made contact, and she heard a heavy grunt and a reassuring intake of pained breath. He yelped, doubled over, and she didn't hang about.

Julia set off at more of a stumbling jog than a run, zigzagging between the gravestones, cursing the rope around her wrists that stopped her from using her arms and achieving any speed. It was only sheer determination that propelled her forward in this ungainly despairing manner. She hadn't gone more than twenty yards before she heard him behind her, his breath ragged with rage, the distance between them rapidly closing. He was angry because she'd tricked him, was trying to escape from him, but most of all because she'd committed the ultimate violation. A man and his balls were not to be messed with.

She ducked and dodged, but the outcome was never in question. He was hot on her heels, swift-footed, purposeful, almost within reach, and then his arm was round her neck and he was hissing in her ear. 'Bitch! I knew I couldn't trust you.' His hold tightened on her windpipe making her gasp for air. All for nothing, she thought. Her head was beginning to swim. This was it. Now he wouldn't hesitate to kill her.

69

Julia was almost resigned to her fate. She tried to kick out at his ankles, a last-gasp gesture in a vain attempt to get him to loosen his grip, but most of her strength was gone. It was like she was back in the flat again, being starved of oxygen, knowing that the end was coming and there was nothing she could do about it. Like Angel, like Lindsay, she was about to be wiped from the earth. She wanted to plead with him, but the words were trapped in her throat.

Julia thought of her mum, of all the petty rows, of all the times she had not appreciated her. A different sort of mother, but a still a loving one. And now she would never see her again, never get to hear her rattle on about her yoga or the ozone layer or the latest demo she'd been on. She would never go back to the falling-down house in Suffolk, never eat lentils again or meet Darcy, the cat with attitude. She was going to die here in this place where she'd hung out as a kid, back when the five of them had everything to look forward to.

Then, suddenly, Frankie's whole body tensed, and she

prepared for the worst. But instead of tightening his grip he abruptly loosened it, allowing her to breathe again. She spluttered and gulped in air. A change of mind? He couldn't go through with it? No, it was something else. He was shifting back, dragging her with him. Then he moved the knife into his right hand and held it to her throat. She felt the sharp blade against her skin.

'Stay there! Don't come any closer!'

Someone else was here. Two people. They weren't alone. Frankie was starting to panic. She could just about see them approaching, two dark silhouettes almost blending into the twilight. And then a voice that she recognised. Tom's.

'Jesus, Frankie, what the fuck are you doing?'

'Stay back!' Frankie repeated loudly.

Julia could smell the booze on his breath now, and the hot stink of sweat and fear. She could almost hear the cogs turning in his brain. He didn't know what to do, where to go, and anything might happen if his hands began to shake.

Apostle and Tom stopped, and for a moment there was a weird kind of stand-off before Frankie began to drag her towards the mausoleums. 'One move,' he yelled, 'and I'll slit her throat. You understand?'

Julia hoped they did understand. This wasn't the time for any kind of heroics. She was the one with her carotid artery on the line. Frankie walked backwards, glancing over his shoulder while he also tried to keep his eyes on the two men. They made stumbling progress through the long grass and weeds, until they reached the overground tomb of the Laithwaites, four long-dead generations gathered together under the same roof: mothers, fathers, children. The stained grey stone was overrun with moss and ivy as if Nature had claimed it for her own. Saints guarded the heavy metal door with watchful eyes.

'You remember this place, Tom?'

Tom didn't answer.

'Hey, I'm talking to you.'

'I remember,' Tom said.

'You tell anyone about this, and I'll tell the law what we did that day. You get what I'm saying, mate? It doesn't make any difference to me now.'

'Just let her go, Frankie.'

'Do we have a deal?'

'Yeah. Sure. It's a deal.'

'If I let her go, you don't come after me, right?'

Apostle was keeping quiet for once. Watching. Listening. Taking it all in. *Please don't do anything stupid*, Julia was thinking. She needn't need any white-horse heroics.

'No, we won't come after you,' Tom said.

'Swear you won't.'

'I promise,' Tom said. 'I swear we won't.'

But still Frankie didn't release her. He was breathing heavily, and she thought he might be crying. His voice was starting to waver and his body, pressed hard against hers, had a juddering feel to it. Slowly he began to move again, taking her with him, keeping the knife against her throat. They skirted around the mausoleum, heading back towards the path. What if he was going to push her into the van again? Take her hostage? Or take her somewhere else to finish the job? This wasn't the deal. He was supposed to let her go.

Then, abruptly, Frankie did release her, shoving her hard in the back so she stumbled forward and, unable to get her balance, fell onto the ground. Her knees took the worst of the impact, but fortunately the earth was soft. Relief flooded through her. By now Frankie was running, sprinting, and no one was following him.

It felt like an age before Tom and Apostle reached her, although it couldn't have been more than a few seconds. She heard the roar of the van's engine as Frankie reversed down the path. Tom tried to undo her hands, but his own were shaking, and Apostle had to step in to finish the job. Tom kept asking over and over again if she was all right, and she felt a weariness roll over her, knowing she would have to explain everything, and that the explanation would shatter him.

'Can you stand up?' Apostle said.

Julia rubbed at her wrists where the rope had left red marks, then tentatively touched the spot on her head where Frankie had hit her. 'I think so.'

Apostle peered at the head wound. 'I don't think you'll need stitches. It's hard to see properly in this light. It's stopped bleeding at least.' He put out his hand and gently hauled her to her feet. Her legs felt shaky, and she had to hold on to him for a moment until she felt steady enough to stand alone.

'How did you find me?' she asked.

'That was down to Tom. When I realised you'd disappeared, that you must be in the van, I drove on down towards the Mansfield and caught up with him and Pauline. She didn't seem too keen on joining the hunt, so it was just the two of us. We went to all the obvious places – Frankie's house, the garage – but there was no sign. That's when Tom thought of here, somewhere you used to come when you were kids.'

'Good work, Tom,' she said, trying to sound like she wasn't completely traumatised by what had just happened. 'Thank you. Thank you both.'

Tom raked his fingers through his hair, nodded, frowned, laid his hand on her arm as if to reassure himself that she was still breathing, still alive. 'I don't know why I thought of it. It just came into my head. Somewhere quiet with no houses around.'

'I won't pass comment on how bloody weird you kids must have been,' Apostle said.

Julia raised her eyebrows. 'I think you just did.'

'I never guessed,' Tom said, 'not for a minute. Not Frankie. Why did he do it? Why did he murder Angel? I thought she killed herself. I really did.'

'He didn't,' Julia said. 'Lindsay killed her because she discovered Mark was still chasing after her. Frankie killed Lindsay when he found out.'

Tom's eyes widened. 'What?'

'I know,' she said. 'It's hard to take in. It's a nightmare.'

'But how could she? She was with Pauline. Do you mean the two of them . . .'

'No, Pauline didn't know anything about it.'

'I never thought I'd say this, but you've got to tell Vyse,' Apostle said. 'Frankie's a loose cannon. He needs to be taken off the streets before he kills someone else.'

'Not yet,' Julia said. She looked at Tom. 'First, I need to know what he meant about this place. Why was he asking if you remembered it?'

'We can do this later,' Apostle said. 'It's almost dark. Let's get out of here.'

'Tom?' she said.

But Tom wouldn't look at her. 'I don't know. Just from when we were kids, I suppose.'

'No, he meant something else.' Julia walked back to the old Laithwaite mausoleum and stared at it. 'He was talking about here.'

Apostle was getting antsy, his gaze flicking anxiously between the graves as if one of them might suddenly creak open and the occupant try to drag him inside. 'We can do this in the car.'

Julia shook her head. 'In a minute. Tom? It was something about telling the law what you did that day. What did he mean?'

'You don't want to know,' Tom said.

'I've had a knife held to my throat, I've had my flat set on fire, I've almost burned to death so there's nothing you can tell me that will make this any worse.'

'Just tell her for God's sake,' Apostle said. 'Then we can get out of this goddam place.'

70

It felt like Tom wanted to speak and he didn't, two conflicting urges that battled inside him. He shifted from one foot to the other, glanced around, looked at Julia, and sighed. She glared briefly at Apostle, willing him not to try and persuade them to leave again. This was the time for truth. Now. She knew it. The minute Tom passed through the gate, he would close up like a clam, shut his mouth and refuse to speak.

'Please, Tom,' she implored. 'Tell me. Tell me what happened.'

Tom jigged around, trying to keep warm, or just wanting something to do with his body. His gaze flicked between her and the mausoleum. For a moment she was drawn back into the past and imagined Angel being here, fair hair streaming down her back as she ran halfway to the iron door before stopping suddenly, her courage failing. And the boys shouting out to her. 'Go on, Angel! Go on!' How old? Eleven, twelve. On the cusp of change, of being teenagers, of seeing each other differently. Not innocent exactly, but without the burden of raging hormones.

'It was five years ago,' Tom eventually said. 'He was back on the scene. Liam Crosby.'

'Liam?' Julia said, startled. She had not expected that name to come flying back from history.

'Yeah. They were seeing each other, him and Angel. Well, you know, hooking up occasionally after a night down the Fox. Nothing serious. I think she wanted more but he wasn't interested. Anyway, he showed up at her flat late one Saturday afternoon. Renee was at work, and she was on her own. He was pissed and demanding, aggressive, not taking no for an answer. She tried to fight him off, but he wasn't having any of it. Called her all the names under the sun and gave her a beating too.' Tom paused, shoved his hands in his pockets and took them out again. 'She was only defending herself. She picked up what was nearest to hand, a vase of flowers, and threw it at him. That didn't do much damage – he dodged out of the way – but he was too wasted to keep his balance. He fell backwards and hit his head on the edge of the sideboard. It was a freak accident – or maybe he had some kind of weakness in his skull. Either way, he was stone dead.'

Julia sucked in a breath.

'I take it she didn't call the law,' Apostle said.

'She called Pauline, and Pauline called me, Frankie and Lindsay. We all went round there and tried to decide what to do. It wasn't so much the law we were worried about as Liam's family. He had two violent brothers and a father who'd spent half his life in jail. Even if the police believed her story, *they* weren't going to accept it. An eye for an eye is how the Crosby family operates.'

Julia was standing very still, afraid to move in case Tom stopped talking. She had pleaded with him to tell her and now the truth was tumbling out, one terrible fact after another, a stream of revelations that made her blood run cold. She felt no

430

pity for Liam – why should she? – but she could imagine the panic, the desperation, the fear that Angel had felt.

'We decided that she'd never be safe if they found out she'd killed him, even it was by accident. Self-defence against a rapist shithead. But what would they care about that? So we cleaned the room, waited until it was dark and then Pauline went to the ground floor and worked her way up, putting "out of order" signs on one of the lifts. We took him down to the basement, carrying him between us like he was too drunk to stand, in case there was anyone around. We were lucky; the basement was empty. We put him in the back of Frankie's van, wrapped him in a blanket and brought him here.'

Julia's gaze shifted to the Laithwaite mausoleum. 'Oh God. You put his body in . . .'

'Fuck,' Apostle said. 'He's still there?'

'Frankie had to force the door open, but he managed it eventually without too much damage. We figured it was the safest place. It's been closed for years, over a century. The cemetery staff might do a cursory check every now and again, but no one was going to go inside without good reason. We laid his body at the back and got out of there as quickly as we could.'

Apostle, forever practical, said, 'You wipe all your prints off the door?'

Tom nodded. 'We wedged it closed again, but it wouldn't be too hard to open if you put your shoulder to it.'

'That's why Frankie thought of here,' Julia said with a shiver. 'What difference would one more body make?'

'I don't know.' Tom said. 'Maybe.'

'What about Pauline and Lindsay? Did they know where you put Liam?'

'They stayed behind to take care of Angel. We never told them. We thought it was better that way.'

431

'But Lindsay reckoned she was safe confessing to Angel's murder because Frankie had disposed of a body, and he wasn't going to want that coming out.'

'I don't know,' Tom said again.

'What about Liam's family? Didn't they come looking?'

'We had a story in place in case they did, that he'd dropped by but only for five minutes. Just in case someone had seen him go into Angel's. But no one ever made the connection, or if they did, they didn't bother telling the law. He was due in court the following week, and everyone just presumed he'd done a runner.'

'Five years,' Julia murmured. She didn't want to think of the rotten remains inside the tomb but could think of little else. Perhaps, after all these years, there wouldn't be much more than a skeleton. Or was it different when bodies were kept in mausoleums rather than buried? She swallowed hard, trying to blank out the images that were filling her mind.

Tom hung his head. 'I've always felt shit about it. The bad stuff always catches up with you eventually. We panicked and did the wrong thing even if was for the right reasons.'

'Let's get out of here,' Apostle said impatiently.

They walked back to the Jag, stepping carefully through the almost dark. There were rustlings in the long grass, indications of nocturnal life, but otherwise the silence was profound. They got into the car and put on their seatbelts. It was only as Apostle was reversing along the lane that Tom asked, 'Are we going to Cowan Road?' He sounded more resigned than anxious.

Apostle looked at Julia. 'It's up to you.'

Julia rubbed again at the raw red marks on her wrists. She thought about Frankie, about Tom, about Liam Crosby, weighed things up, but couldn't come to any firm conclusion. She wondered what she'd have done back then in Tom's position. How far would *she* have gone to protect Angel? She didn't want to be responsible for sending anyone to prison.

'Not yet. No. I just want to go home.'

'Home it is,' Apostle said. 'Or the nearest thing to it.'

71

They had dropped Tom off at the Mansfield and watched him walk onto the estate with hunched shoulders and downcast eyes. She hoped he wouldn't go to Cowan Road and hand himself in but thought on balance that he wouldn't. And not because he feared his own exposure but because he wouldn't want to incriminate Pauline or make anything worse for Frankie. Could things get any worse for Frankie? Well, murder, attempted murder and disposal of a body wouldn't exactly help his cause.

Now back at the Barbican, she sat at the kitchen table and sipped the brandy that Apostle had poured her. 'I don't know what to do.'

Apostle was looming over her, dabbing ineffectively at the cut on her head with a wad of cotton wool and some antiseptic. 'What do you *want* to do?'

'Ouch,' she said, flinching as the TCP stung her scalp again. 'Be careful with that.'

'Don't be such a baby. Do you want to die of blood poisoning?'

Julia was glad he wasn't treating her with kid gloves. Too

much sympathy and she'd have started crying and never stopped. 'What I want,' she said, replying to his earlier question, 'is to make all this go away. But there's no chance of that. I know I should tell Vyse – about Frankie at the very least – but that means all the other stuff will come out too.'

Apostle snorted. 'That guy could have slit your throat.'

Although it was warm in the flat, she shivered. She'd had another close shave with death and the cold of the graveyard was still in her bones. The expensive brandy was helping though. She took another sip, resisting the urge to gulp it down. 'I'm not sure he'd have gone through with it.'

'You certain about that?'

Julia wasn't certain, far from it, but she wanted to believe that at the last minute Frankie would have spared her. It was easier than believing the horror of the alternative. 'I'm just glad I didn't have to find out. If it hadn't been for you and Tom . . .'

But Apostle wasn't a great one for gratitude. He shrugged off her attempt to thank him again, dropped the cotton wool in the bin, refilled her glass and sat down opposite her. 'You know what I don't get? It's just a loose end but I thought Pauline and Lindsay were together until they went down the Fox on Angel's birthday. And if they weren't then why didn't Pauline ever suspect her?'

'I'm only guessing, but I think Pauline might have gone off to see a friend for a few hours, someone she didn't want anyone else knowing about.'

'Why not?'

'Pauline was the girl I saw in Gigi's.'

'Ah,' Apostle said. 'A *girl* friend.'

'And a cop. It was Carol Forshaw.'

Apostle's eyebrows shifted up. 'If Pauline was seeing Carol on the afternoon that Angel died, then surely she knew, they *both* knew, that Lindsay didn't have an alibi. Shouldn't that have put her in the frame?'

'Yeah, I've been wondering about that. After Angel went missing Pauline must have suggested to Lindsay that they alibi each other to account for the missing hours. She always had a low opinion of her, but I don't think, even for a second, that she'd have imagined her capable of murder. And Carol would have gone along with it because she wanted to protect Pauline – and didn't want to be thrown off the case.' Julia shrugged. 'It's just a theory. I can't prove it, and I don't want to. It explains things though.'

'The danger of underestimating people.'

'Pauline was so convinced that Mark had killed Angel, she wasn't looking anywhere else. She couldn't see that the killer was right in front of her.'

'Carol Forshaw must be a bloody idiot.'

'I doubt Pauline gave her all the facts. No one ever suspected Lindsay, not really. Even without the alibi, she'd have been way down the list of suspects. A nice girl with nothing to gain. Well, not on the surface. Who could have guessed?'

'Pauline could have guessed. She knew that Angel was messing about with Mark.'

'Easy with hindsight. When you've known someone a long time you think you know what they are, and what they're not, capable of.'

Apostle's fingers danced on the tabletop, drumming out a beat. 'Maybe you should go home for a few days, go back to Suffolk. I can take care of things at work.'

'What's that going to solve? The problem will still be here when I come back.'

'It'll give you a chance to clear your head, sort out what you want to do. And it gets you out of London for a while. This doesn't seem a very safe place for you right now. I don't mean *here*, just the city in general. At least you might be able to relax in Suffolk.'

The idea was tempting but she wasn't sure if it was the right thing to do. 'Wouldn't that be like running away?'

'Nothing wrong with running every now and again. If you're not going to tell the law about what happened today, you can at least put some distance between you and Frankie. I mean, personally I'd like to see him behind bars; the guy's clearly got a screw loose and he's already killed once.'

'You think I *should* tell the police?'

'It's your call. I can't decide for you.'

'But if you were in my shoes . . .?'

Apostle pulled a face. 'I know it's complicated. There are people you want to protect, only you've got to protect yourself too. He *did* murder Lindsay.'

'And Lindsay killed Angel.'

'That doesn't make it okay.'

'No, I know that. Of course not. And Liam Crosby, or what's left of him, is still lying in a mausoleum. That's not right either, is it? And what about Renee? She deserves to know how her daughter died, but if I tell her then . . .'

The phone rang, interrupting her deliberations, and Apostle went to answer it. 'Ah, Inspector Vyse,' he said. 'What can I do for you?' There was a short pause. 'Julia? Let me check. I've only just got in. I'll give her a shout.'

Julia frantically shook her head and waved her hands around. She really didn't want to talk to Vyse right now. She needed more time to get her thoughts in order.

Apostle grinned, put the phone down, went to the kitchen door and shouted up the stairs. 'Julia? Julia?' He waited a few

437

seconds before returning to the phone. 'She's not here. You want to leave a message?'

Julia watched as he nodded into the phone, his expression suddenly serious. She felt her heart sink, sure that there was more bad news coming. What now? She couldn't face a grilling down Cowan Road. Apostle wasn't speaking much, just saying things like 'Right, I see' and 'When was this?' before eventually asking 'Are you going to need to talk to her? Only I think she was planning on heading to Suffolk this evening.' A pause. Then there were a few final words before he said goodbye and hung up.

'What is it?' Julia said. 'Tell me quickly before I put my hands over my ears and refuse to listen.'

'It's Frankie,' he said. 'He crashed his van about half an hour ago, drove straight into a brick wall.'

'Oh God, is he . . .?'

Apostle nodded. 'Yeah, he's dead.'

Julia felt relief, and then guilt at the relief. Frankie was gone and she never had to be afraid of him again, but he left behind a wife and two kids who would mourn him. And he had been a friend once, even if that did feel like a long time ago. 'What else did Vyse say?'

'That he'd been drinking. That it looked like an accident.'

'Looked like?'

'He didn't elaborate.'

'I wonder if he knows about us meeting up on the green this afternoon. Does he want me to call him back?'

'He didn't say so. I think he just wanted to pass on the news.'

The news was still slowly sinking in. Julia knocked back the last of her brandy, trying to fit everything into place, what had happened, what would happen now, how to avoid the truth coming out. There was no need for Clare to know about Frankie killing Lindsay, or the reason for it. What good would come of that? It would only be another pile of heartache. But the decision wasn't entirely hers. Tom might have other ideas.

'What are you thinking?' Apostle said.

She looked up at him. 'I'm thinking I might take you up on that offer and go home for a few days.'

'Good. I'll drive you.'

'You don't need to do that. I can get a train.'

'I'd rather make sure you stay in one piece. You've not got a good record on that score.'

'I'm a liability,' she said.

'Your words, not mine. Anyway, I like to give the Jag a good run every now and again. She gets antsy when she's stuck in the city for too long.'

'She?'

'Everyone knows that cars are called she. Like ships or nations or nature.'

Julia was rummaging in her bag for her address book. She took out tissues, a notepad, a paperback, her keys, and laid them all on the table. It was then that she noticed it, the tiny silver-grey key nestling between the bigger ones. And the memory suddenly flooded back of when she'd moved into the Camden flat, of how the key to the window bars in her bedroom had been lying on the sill and how she'd decided, so it wouldn't get lost, to add it to her key ring.

'Oh my God,' she said, holding it up.

'Huh?'

'The key to the window bars. I could have burned to death and the damn thing was on my key ring all the time. I remember now. I thought it might slip off the sill and so I put it on here for safekeeping.'

'The dangers of being organised,' he said. 'Sometimes it pays to just let things be.'

'A bit late for that,' she said.

Apostle pulled out a chair and sat down. 'Do you think Frankie got rid of the diary?'

'It depends whether it *was* an accident or not. I'm presuming it wasn't so let's hope he dumped it somewhere it will never be found.'

'Do you reckon there were others?'

Julia shook her head. 'I could be wrong, but I suspect Angel didn't start keeping one again until this year. Perhaps she wanted to write about Frankie. The whole Liam thing would have put her off diaries for a while. That's the last thing you'd want to put down on paper.'

'I've had a thought about that, about Liam Crosby I mean.'

'Go on.'

'Well, if we wait a few weeks, give the dust time to settle, I could make a 999 call from an out-of-town phone box, an anonymous tip-off about where they can find his body. There's an element of risk, of course – fingerprints, the blanket they wrapped him in, but I don't imagine there's much evidence left after all these years. You'd have to discuss it with Tom.'

Julia thought about this. It sat uneasily with her that Liam's family – no matter how awful they were – had no knowledge of what had happened to him. And she suspected it didn't sit any better with Tom. 'What if someone recognises your voice?'

'They won't. I'll put on an accent, keep it muffled and keep it short. There's no reason why the law should connect his death to anything that's been going on recently.'

'I suppose that could work. But what about Renee? What do I tell her?'

'That's up to you. Some of the truth? All of it? I don't suppose she'll go running to the law. Not much to be achieved, is there? Lindsay's dead, Frankie's dead. Everyone's paid the price in one way or another.'

'I guess that's true. But I won't tell her about Liam. She doesn't need to know about that.'

'Your choice,' he said.

Julia made a couple of phone calls, one to her mum and the other to Tom, before she went upstairs to pack.

She sold him out. Now he's out for revenge . . .

After her murderous ex-boyfriend who she turned in to the police was released from prison, Jem Byrne fled to London, desperate to hide herself in the hustle of the big city. Now she spends every day watching her back, waiting for him to catch up with her. But the Mansfield estate is far from a safe place to hide, and Jem soon learns she's only ever one wrong move away from being found out – and *sold* out.

Private Investigator Harry Lind makes a living out of other people's secrets. When he meets Jem, he can tell she's hiding something big and he's desperate to find out what. But his talents have already been enlisted by another: an aging mother hoping to discover the truth about her daughter's disappearance fifty years earlier. There's also the two kids from the Mansfield pestering him to find their missing dad. Could Jem be the key to cracking both cases?

And then there's Philip, the Mansfield estate's newest resident. He's lurking in the shadows, watching it all unfold. Or is he doing more than just watching?

Available now . . .